A SACRIFICE OF FLESH AND FURY

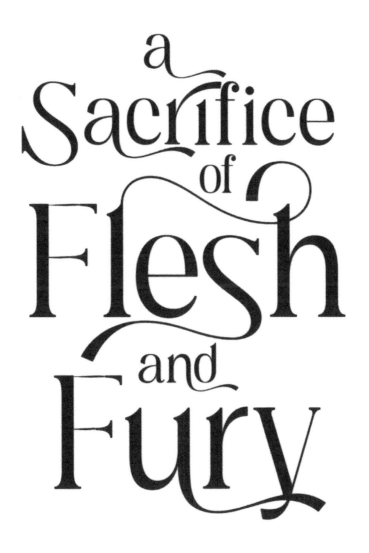

A Sacrifice of Flesh and Fury

JENNIFER BRODY

Podium

All rights reserved. No part of this publication may be reproduced, stored in a retrieval system, or transmitted in any form or by any means electronic, mechanical, photocopying, recording, or otherwise without prior written permission from Podium Publishing.

This is a work of fiction. Names, characters, places, and incidents are either products of the author's imagination or used fictitiously. Any resemblance to actual events, locales, or persons, living, dead, or undead, is entirely coincidental.

Copyright © 2025 by Jennifer Brody

Cover design by Damonza

ISBN: 978-1-0394-5367-8

Published in 2025 by Podium Publishing
www.podiumentertainment.com

To all those who have loved and lost—and lived to love another day. This book is for you.

A SACRIFICE OF FLESH AND FURY

PROLOGUE

We saved the world from the Astrals.
The Earth Federations united after we discovered their plan.
We stopped them from invading Earth.
Or so we thought.
But that wasn't the end . . .
It was only the beginning.

I scream into the void—
It's been a week. How has it been a week?
I'm breaking down.
I miss you more than all the stars in the skies.
Do you miss me?
Do you even think of me?
—Kari

Do you dream of me?
Have you touched the stars?
Kissed the sun?
How close can you fly . . .
And not catch fire?
Do you remember the Earth?
—Drae

Yesterday—
I named a star for you.
Can we defy gravity?
We are made of stardust.
The universe is always expanding.
So is our love. Do you promise?
—Kari

I promise.
Will
You
Wait
For
Me?
It's hell on earth to be away from your heavens . . . I don't wait gently.

I burn for you.
—Drae

Our LOVE is like a new star.
Dazzling. Fiery. Expansive.
But will we burn out?
Will the cold expanse snuff us out?
I am afraid. And I am so far away.
Tomorrow, I leave for deployment.
I will be even farther away.
Will you wait for me?
Will you . . . wait?
—Kari

PART 1

RECONNAISANCE

Know thy enemy and know yourself; in a hundred battles, you will never be defeated.

—Sun Tzu, *The Art of War*

CHAPTER 1

KARI

You save the world from aliens one day, and the next day everything is supposed to go back to normal.

And for everyone else, it seems like it does.

Well, *normal* for us . . .

Which means serving as guardians in Space Force.

My platoon celebrated, then deployed for their chosen specialties. Percy got engineering, Genesis is going into medical, Nadia got front lines, while her twin brother, Anton, landed his top choice—postal. It sounds a bit silly, but the Space Force Postal Service is the backbone of our interstellar communications, and he played a key role in thwarting the Astrals.

Everyone else slid right back into their routines. But not me.

No matter how hard I try, I can't forget what happened.

I still wake sweaty in the night from flashbacks to blaster fire and my battle buddy crumpling to the ground, while enemies descend on us like a swarm of black flies; or sometimes, it's the Siberian warships gunning for us, with white-hot flashes exploding our engines.

I thrash and scream for *Bea! Nadia! Dad!* and everyone else I love.

This remembering has the power to drag me back and ruin everything.

Death can happen in the blink of an eye. I learned that the hard way when aliens called Astrals tried to invade Earth and destroy humanity by tricking us into another Great War in space.

We barely stopped them . . . *barely*.

Now, I'm supposed to return to my duties and follow orders like nothing happened, but I can't help it. Everything looks different now. Everything feels different now.

And a lot of it is because of . . .

Drae.

His name shoots through my head like the twin flames trailing our ship.

I can't explain it, but he changed me. When our minds linked, and then our bodies followed hungrily, it made something inside me break open. This impenetrable wall that I'd had up since my father deserted, maybe even my whole life, crumbled and broke wide open. Some dark alchemy must have occurred for the impossible to happen—

For me to fall in love.

We're talking *head over heels, can't-stop-thinking-about-him, lusting and yearning and dreaming of him* love. The sort of love that I used to think wasn't real—or, if it was like my best friend Rho claimed, that it would never, ever in a million light-years happen to me.

What started as a curse when Drae tried to kiss me in high school and we got paired together in the Sympathetic Program, transformed into something different once we started exchanging our neural communications. It became something hot and searing and all-consuming, like the fiery birth of a new star that explodes every bit of space junk out of its blazing path.

That's what our love is—

A new star.

But new stars are dangerous. They're unstable and unpredictable. They fling planets out of orbit on a whim. They can burn too hot, voraciously consuming all their fuel and quickly exsanguinating, or worse, they can go supernova and collapse into a black hole, crushing everything like in my worst nightmares.

Please, Drae . . . don't hurt me . . . don't crush my heart . . .

That fear is enough to rouse me from the depths of drugged slumber.

Where in the blazing stars am I?

My neural implant pipes up on cue, triggered by my errant question. *I'm sorry, Kari. Your location is classified.*

Still hazy, I gaze out at the dark expanse enveloping our transport like a thin membrane poked through with stars and reflective space dust that shines like diamonds. My reflection stares back at me—dark eyes and hair like my mother, cat eyes like my father and sister, high cheekbones. My hair is buzzed short per Space Force rules. My body still feels remade by basic training, strong and rippling with lean muscle.

It all comes rushing back in a torrent. I'm being deployed to interstellar space. I'm still in transit, almost at my new outpost. That's why I'm awake. The drugs are wearing off at long last.

Suddenly, the transport tilts and I see it—the planet looms below us, swathed in cottony clouds. I spot not one, but two suns simmering in the distance. This planet has rings, kind of like Saturn. We don't head for the surface, which is probably liquid gas and uninhabitable, but for one of the moons orbiting it in that shimmering belt that glitters with space debris instead.

But where is this moon? I miss Anton with a sharp pang. He'd be talking my ear off about that moon; he might even know where this star system lies. But he's back on Ceres at the post office, assigned to Postmaster Haven, one of my only true confidants in Space Force.

I summon my neural implant.

Harold, you said the location is classified. But can't you give me a hint? How far from Earthside is it?

The stilted male voice echoes through my head again.

I'm sorry, that's classified.

Nobody else can hear it; the annoying responses are reserved only for me.

I guess I'm lucky that way.

Okay, then what's the name of the base? It's a base, right? Just tell me something.

I'm sorry, that's—

Classified, I repeat, injecting annoyance into my words.

I'm not going to get anywhere with Harold. I give up and focus on my surroundings as we hum steadily through deep space toward our *classified* destination. My orders were switched at the last minute from front lines, which I'd requested for double pay. Luckily, Ma and Bea escaped from Earthside to be with my father on his Raider ship, so I don't have to worry about them anymore. Instead, they gave me a fancy ranking and shiny new assignment—

Special ops.

That means . . . intel. But intel about what . . . or who . . . exactly?

I have a hunch it involves . . .

Them.

Even thinking that sends a chill shuddering up my spine and threatens to spike my anxiety. I mean the Astrals, of course. The aliens who tried to destroy us. But it's only that . . . a hunch. I wish I weren't so in the dark. I wish that they'd tell me something, anything, to keep me from going crazy speculating and worrying like this.

Just a hint! I want to scream.

Sorry, that's classified echoes through my head again for good measure.

Thanks a lot, Harold. Mute, please.

He falls blessedly silent, but maybe silence is worse. Everyone seems to still be sleeping in the cabin. Dimly, I wonder if that means my nightmares are worse than theirs, that my sleep is more troubled. I'm glad Harold doesn't chime in. I don't want to know the answer.

My thoughts turn darker.

It's been a week since we stopped the Astrals. Or maybe a month. Or maybe only a single day; I can't be sure.

Interstellar travel does that; it bends reality, warps us through the fabric of time itself, and spits us out millions of light-years away. If not for the warp shields protecting us from time dilation, we wouldn't age, while everyone else back on Earth would turn old and gray and eventually pass into oblivion, all while we hurled around from galaxy to galaxy, nebula to nebula, stuck in perpetual youth like bugs preserved in amber, only the amber is our spacecraft, and likewise also our eventual tomb.

I gaze through the window at the darkness beyond our little light of a ship. I wonder if they're out there right now even, watching us, lurking in the void, planning their next attack. It's coming; we know we only set them back. We didn't defeat them. And worse, we know almost nothing about them.

"Harold, come on," I say, speaking aloud this time. "Please tell me something. How long was I asleep?"

Sorry, that's classified.

Yup, they knock us out for a reason. There's a purpose behind everything.

"Ugh, don't you care about me?"

But another voice replies.

"You really think guilt trips work on AI programming?" Luna says, cracking her eyes open beside me.

At least I'm not alone . . . going to wherever the hell we're being deployed. Space isn't like back on Earth; out here, there aren't any recognizable clues or road maps that tell us where we are. Because essentially, we're nowhere.

Luna runs one hand through her buzzed blonde hair and yawns, struggling to come out of her slumber. The sling chair grips her body and adjusts. She's tall and lean like me, but where I'm darker, she's lighter. We may contrast, but our personalities don't.

"Guilt trips, no," I say. "But maybe passive-aggressive questions will break him, so he answers my question."

No, that won't work either, Harold replies with his usual zero sense of humor. *Sorry, that's classified.*

"What did you ask him?" Luna asks, recognizing the glazed look in my eyes when I communicate with my implant.

"Where the hell they're sending us." I point to the moon growing larger as we approach. "Then how far from Earthside. Finally, the name of the base."

"And what did he say?"

I deadpan, "*Sorry, that's classified.*"

"At least Harold didn't say *that's above your pay grade* like Nadia. Or *keep your mouth shut, recruit!*" she barks to impersonate the drill sergeant.

"You're a lowly grunt greener than the turf back Earthside!" I chime in.

"Now drop and give me twenty!"

I arch my eyebrow. "Is it weird that I actually miss the drill sergeant?"

"Yeah, they call that Stockholm Syndrome," she says with a snort. "It's when you fall in love with your captor. You should get your head checked out."

That makes us both laugh, despite the fogginess still obscuring our brains.

But worry does stir in my heart. Is that why I fell in love with Drae? The forced proximity of the program? Or are my feelings real and genuine—and most importantly, entirely my own?

The problem is, I don't know, or maybe I don't want to know.

So, I shove it back down. That's something I'm good at . . . locking my feelings away. Or at least, I used to be good at it before this dumb love stuff hijacked my brain. Maybe Luna is right, and Draeden Rache kidnapped me.

Luna gives me a look.

"Still thinking about . . . *him*?"

"Was it that obvious?" I say with a groan. I can't hide anything from her; we were rack mates back at basic training. "I hate being like . . . *this*."

"By this do you mean, caring for someone else? That's not related to you? And risking the possibility of them . . ."

She trails off.

But I know what she means—

Breaking your heart.

"Not true! I care about you," I say, trying to change the subject and avoid her pointed interrogation. "And Nadia, Anton, Percy, Genesis," I say, naming off our crew of besties from our platoon.

She doesn't fall for it. There's a reason she got special ops, too.

"Yup, we're friends—and that's important," she replies. "But he's different. And you damn well know it."

Her words hang in the stale, recirculated air of the cabin, chilling me and spiking my anxiety again.

But it's true—and I can't run away from it this time. It's an open secret among my close friends that I fell hard for my Sympathetic. They found out when he showed up in space on a Raider ship with resistance intel that the Golden Gate terrorist attack on Earth was alien in origin. They were trying to provoke a war by blaming our enemy, the Siberian Federation, so they could sweep in and take Earth without fighting.

With that evidence disseminated by the postal service, we were able to stop the Proxies from obliterating each other, and instead, they united and stopped the invasion. Now, we're the Earth Federation Space Force sworn to the common cause of defending Earth.

Luna lowers her voice. "Are you worried . . . that they'll find out? About you and Drae?"

"Not just worried," I reply softly. "Petrified, terrified, plus a healthy dose of embarrassment and mortification."

Falling in love with your Sympathetic is strongly advised against by the secretive powers-that-be who run the program. Nobody knows who they are. For all we know, the whole thing could be AI like Harold.

The worst part is that they don't tell you why it's bad exactly. They just make a big deal about cautioning you against crossing any boundaries beyond mere friendship.

And, well, once Drae and I overcame our differences, we blasted right through those boundaries and flung ourselves headfirst into each other's minds and bodies the first chance we got. I tend to be impulsive, plus the exhilaration of adrenaline after saving the world simply overtook us.

Yeah, we had sex.

A lot of it. Or made love.

I'm still not even sure what to call *what* we did. My cheeks flame hot even remembering his strong arms, soft, full lips, and the way he explored my body, every inch of it.

And then, after we were spent, we had some lazy, deep conversations while lounging on a bunk hurtling through space on my father's pirated ship, far away from our real obligations with him at college and me in Space Force. We talked about our hopes and dreams and innermost desires, all while cocooned in the safety of our own little world and connected by our neural implants.

And making love while connected like that—him seeing through my eyes and feeling through my flesh, while I'm inside his head too, and we're both like one being in mind and body and soul—is mind-blowing stuff. (I still need to debrief Rho about this next level.)

But then, reality hit.

Like blaster fire. And now we're millions of light-years apart, farther away than we've ever been. I sent my last message before I deployed. I don't know when I'll receive his response, or how long the lag time out here will be.

Can a new relationship survive that?

Again, I don't want to know the answer. The idea terrifies me.

Luna's voice snaps me back.

"Well, let's hope what we did bought you some leeway," she says, referring to the top-secret nature of our role in stopping the Astrals. "And him, too."

"Let's hope," I agree. "It has so far."

But hope feels fragile on my lips. Our connection *is* the reason I trusted him when he brought me that intel. If we'd still been enemies like back in high school, it's possible I'd have sent him back to Earth without giving him a chance to explain or, worst case, blasted him.

In a way, our love saved humanity. A part of me thinks they understand that, and it's why we've been allowed to continue our pairing. That's why they haven't severed it and assigned me a new Sympathetic, an idea that rattles me to my core. I can't imagine deploying and facing everything that lies ahead without him on the other end of those warp mail exchanges each week.

But worry seeps in anyway. How long will the grace from that secret protect us? How long will those in charge remember what we did?

If I know anything, humans tend to fall back into their old ways.

That's my last thought before they announce that we're docking, and the whole world decelerates and spins in a sickening way, and all I can do is try not to hurl my guts out as we torpedo toward our destination—and my future.

"Captain Hikari Skye . . . and Private Luna Starfire," a stern voice announces after we land inside the base on that moon. "Welcome to your destination."

I'm still dizzy from the spinning and descent, not to mention a bit nauseous from the sleep meds. I peer through the window into the docking bay. It doesn't look like much.

The voice pipes up again.

"Please disembark from the ship."

No other names are called, and no other information is given. We're the only two getting off here. Most of the other guardians on the transport are still knocked out by heavy meds and bound for other outposts.

Why are we the only ones? What is this place?

Before I can worry more, arrows light up on the floor directing us toward the exit. We both rise from our sling chairs, feeling them wobble and snap back into place.

"*Captain* . . . Skye?" Luna says. "So, does that mean you outrank me now?"

I feel my cheeks burn. I may have the title, but I don't feel worthy of it.

"Uh, right. When they changed my orders, they sort of promoted me, too."

"Well, don't let it go to your head," she says with a teasing smile as we head toward the exit. It automatically swishes open, releasing the pressurized oxygen with a sharp gust that clouds the air.

As we clamber down the ramp, I whisper into her ear.

"Don't you think it's weird they're not telling us anything? Not even the name of the base?"

She shoots me a knowing look.

"Welcome to intel," she whispers back. "Where even secrets have secrets."

More questions bubble up in my head, but I push them back down. I may have a higher ranking, but I'm still very much in the dark about, well . . .

Everything.

With Luna's ominous words replaying in my mind—*even secrets have secrets*—our boots touch down on the metal floors. The gravity feels about the same as Earth and Ceres Base for one reason—because they generate artificial G to match. But my legs buckle slightly and wobble as we proceed into the docking bay, still following the green arrows.

They have great meds to knock you out, but they haven't fixed the muscle atrophying part. Thankfully, my hard training in PT will help my body adjust and rebuild quickly. I scan the area.

This base looks smaller than back on Ceres. It's clearly not a big hub, judging by the fleet of smaller vessels parked in the docking bay. There are no larger transports of warships. But something else bothers me. It looks deserted, aside from our transport now rebooting so it can depart. It's also eerily quiet.

Nobody appears to welcome us. Only those eerie green arrows beckon.

"Where is everybody?" I hiss to Luna. "This place is . . . deserted."

"Yeah, it's weird," she agrees. "But intel is like that. We have to go places nobody else goes, find out things nobody else knows . . . and keep our mouths shut when it's not our job."

Her message is clear—I'm already failing miserably at that part. I'm asking too many questions. And that can get us both into major trouble. But still, I have an uneasy feeling about it. I glance up at the skylights, but only darkness rains down. It's this moon's night here.

Suddenly, I wish I'd gotten my request for front lines like Nadia. At least it's more straightforward. We're trained for one thing and one thing only—*fighting*. But special ops?

I know it involves information and, yes, secrets. School wasn't my strength. I barely graduated from high school. Even if I'd had a ticket to university like Drae, I doubt I'd have taken it. Intel feels like the college version of Space Force. Fighting is all I've ever been good at. But there's nothing I can do about it.

Plus, the drill sergeant told me they needed me when she handed down my new orders. I have to trust them. Besides, it's not like I have a choice.

Space Force owns me.

Suddenly, a deep voice echoes out, making me jump. "Captain Skye?"

A long shadow falls over us.

I pivot to see an officer standing behind us. He's clutching a tablet.

The first thing I notice is that he's dressed in the typical Space Force uniform with lots of decorations indicating he's important. Not some lowly grunt. The second thing is that he's . . . well . . . insanely attractive.

I can't help taking in his dirty-blond hair sheared into a military cut; full, heart-shaped lips; square jaw with a cleft; high cheekbones; and aquamarine eyes as clear as the sky after a hard rain.

They ripple, seeming to shift in color. They're also sharp and lock onto me.

Under that intensity, I feel myself wilting and avert my gaze.

Luna has to nudge me to remind me to speak.

"Uh . . . yes, sir," I blurt out. My awkwardness makes me blush harder.

Luna nudges me again. *Oh, right*, I think in mortification. I salute him.

He snaps a salute back and introduces himself.

"I'm Major Apollo, your new commanding officer." But nothing about his face is friendly. He's all business, and I'm acting like a complete and total fool. *Please murder me now.*

"And then you must be Private Starfire?" he says to Luna, double-checking that against his tablet.

She snaps a salute. "Yes, sir."

He returns the gesture.

"Private Starfire, please grab your duffel and follow the green arrows. They will lead you to your barracks."

"Yes, sir!"

He waves her away with a practiced motion. "Private dismissed."

She shoots me one last look—quick, with a flicker of concern—before she hops to and follows orders. But that look tells me everything I need to know.

Despite her bravado, she's worried about what we're doing here, too.

Once she heads off, following the arrows, Major Apollo turns back and settles the full weight of his attention onto me. I feel heat rush through my body like a solar storm.

I'm completely mortified. This isn't like me at all.

Sure, he's incredibly . . . well . . . *hot*. And not just any kind of hot, but commanding, military hot. Something about the casual air of authority that wafts off him, combined with those deep eyes that hint at more beneath his composed veneer.

Usually, I wouldn't care. I've never particularly paid attention to men. But suddenly, I can't ignore it. What is going on with my emotions lately? They've felt uncharacteristically powerful and erratic. It's as if being with Drae awoke something inside me. Something fiery and dangerous and unpredictable. Something that I don't know if I can fully control anymore, especially based on my inappropriate reaction to my commanding officer.

Is it my imagination—

Or do his eyes linger on me a little longer than normal?

"Captain Skye," he says. "I need you to follow me."

We proceed in lockstep at a fast clip, heading in the opposite direction from Luna. I wish he hadn't dismissed her. That I wasn't facing . . . well, whatever this is alone.

I have to struggle on my wobbly legs to keep up with him. That's when he speaks again, lowering his voice. Even that sends fire racing through my body.

"Captain Skye, welcome to here . . . wherever in the stars *here* is. Let's just say, you're not in Kansas anymore." He swipes at his tablet, then frowns. "Please follow me for your intel briefing."

"Sir, is it about . . . *them*? The Astrals, I mean." I know I'm speaking out of turn, but I can't help it. Something about his reaction worries me. He gets my drift.

"Just hurry," he says in an urgent voice. "You'll find out soon enough."

Again, I have no idea. It's another minute before my stupor breaks and gives way to the familiar tension and worries that usually grip my spine. Quick flashes rush through my neural synapses. MOS orders switched to special ops at the last minute. Yanked off the front lines. My destination is still secret, as is my mission. In short, I'm in the dark . . . about, well . . . everything.

Harold, where am I? I think, my gaze fixed on the window. The cabin expands around us, our own little pressurized, oxygenated bubble in the void of space.

I shudder, realizing how alone we are out here, how even sound can't exist out here, how it's snuffed out like smoke.

CHAPTER 2

DRAE

I never realized you would prove me wrong. I never knew I'd . . . fall in love.
Until you.

Kari's words echo out of her lips, chased by the fog of her frozen breath. She's standing on the surface of Ceres, the icy dwarf planet in the asteroid belt. Her dark eyes search mine. I feel her emotions emanate out with those words, hitting me full force—yearning, desire, fear, sadness, and most of all . . . her love, boundless and enduring.

No, don't go! Please, I need you like I need oxygen to breathe! Kari, please!

I want to scream to her, beg and plead for her to delay her deployment or, worst case, desert and find me. We can run away together on her father's Raider ship, fugitives to our dying breaths, protected by our love.

But my lips won't move; I can't speak to her. I want to hug her and kiss her deeply, but I can't do that either. This communication was recorded and beamed down to me on Earth. It's the past that I'm witnessing. I know one thing with certainty, and it feels like a punch to the gut that steals my breath.

She's already gone.

Drae . . . I'm going dark for my deployment . . . I'll reach out when I can.

That's the last thing I hear and feel before that brain-sucking feeling envelops me and spits me back out.

Exchange complete, Estrella communicates. *Disconnecting neural implant.*

I'm breathing heavily with tears streaming down my cheeks. I didn't even realize I was crying. That's the power of the warp mail exchanges. We jack into the pods with our neural implants; we experience each other's thoughts, feelings, fears, secrets, and dreams.

I feel what she feels, and it's like a torrent after what happened.

That one day—or was it a night?

In space, things like day and night don't happen that way. It's more like one endless night filled with starlight, and no gravity, just floating through the void that we filled with our bodies and our minds, with fervent gasps, entwined in each other's arms, feeling each other through our linked minds.

I blink my eyes to clear the tears and try to orient myself as it feels like my brain is being sucked out through the back of my skull. It's not pleasant, but it does jerk me back to reality.

No exchange to record today, Estrella reminds me. *Your Sympathetic is being deployed. Waiting to receive her location before the next exchange.*

I already know that. The postal worker briefed me before she took me to my pod. But it still breaks me a little. The idea of Kari barreling through space, warping through rips in time itself, with no idea where they're sending her, is enough to petrify me.

But there's nothing I can do. This is what we both signed up for. Her tour of duty is eight *long* years. My job is simple—I have to be there for her.

No matter what.

I can't let it break me, not when she depends on me. Not when we've both fallen in love—something that was never supposed to happen. Not to us.

The lights in the warp mail pod fade up slowly to let me adjust, while the aromatherapy stench surrounds me, meant to calm my fractured nerves. It doesn't work, not even close.

I'm a hot mess.

And worse—I'm late for class. The pod cracks open, and I bolt out.

The Berkeley campus spreads out before me—manicured courtyards cut through with paths weaving between stately buildings. It looks just as idyllic as when I left last week. Autumn looms but never falls hard in California. Still, the trees are starting to change color, as if stuck in some primal, ancient rhythm.

Drae, you're late for class.

Estrella pings me as soon as I leave my exchange. *I know . . . I'm going.*

My schedule flashes in my retinas, along with the route. Great Books is next. It used to be my favorite class.

Not anymore.

My *before* life. *Before* the Resistance. *Before* getting paired with Kari and the Sympathetic Program. *Before* we discovered the Astrals' plan to invade.

But I can't live in before. Now, I'm in my *after* life, though sometimes it feels more like the aftermath, where everything I knew and trusted got blown up like that bus with the kids.

Estrella pings me again.

Great Books start in fifteen minutes—

Ugh, I know, I think back. *I'm going.*

I rush from the campus post office, passing a few students on their way in to receive their exchanges and record their replies . . . if their Sympathetic isn't currently being deployed like Kari. We all keep our heads down; details of the program and our pairings are secret.

I cut through students, weaving to pick up speed. I'm not sure if I'm rushing to class or running away from . . . well . . . from what happened back there. Tears still stain my cheeks.

I lick my lips, tasting the salt already crusting up. I run one hand through my wiry curls. I let my hair grow out, and Kari liked the change. It complements my lighter eyes and darker skin.

I've only been back a week.

One *short* week.

Though it feels like much longer since I journeyed to space. Images rush through my head, already dissipating like the effervescent and impermanent tendrils of dreams.

Getting recruited into the Resistance. Discovering the Golden Gate Attack was alien in origin. Boarding a Raider ship and going to space. Stopping the war. Kari and my . . . well . . . bonding.

I feel a flush of heat remembering that part. The softness of her skin. The way her lips bent to my own. Our thoughts melding through our implants as my body responded to her, and we opened to each other fully and deeply.

But it's like I blinked, and I was back to normal life. One second I was in space, wrapped in her arms, where I wanted to stay forever, our bodies intertwined like one being while our minds locked together through our neural implants—and the next, I was getting dropped off back Earthside to resume my freshman year like nothing happened. And I have to pretend I didn't do any of that because half of it is top secret and highly classified, and the other half they still don't know about.

And all of it could get me expelled, and Kari dishonorably discharged.

Or worse.

So, I'm supposed to study and go to class, do my reading and homework, and even hit some parties for fun.

Only nothing feels *normal* anymore.

The one noticeable change is that Jude and Loki, my best friends from high school . . . actually . . . *former* best friends, got kicked out. I caught Jude sexually assaulting a girl in our dorm room. I wish I'd reacted better, but the truth is that I beat the living shit out of him, despite Loki trying to stop me.

I shudder at the memory of his blood splattering my fists. Of that poor girl running off, crying, with her clothes askew. Of the damage to his broken face. I don't miss either of them.

That's for sure.

My new roommates are great. I can finally have a fresh start away from their toxic influence. But I do miss one person. *Rho.* She's Kari's best friend. And after everything we went through together this year, my best friend, too.

But she couldn't stick around Earthside, not after she caught feelings for that Raider pilot. She's like that, driven by her emotions, prone to fall in love. Her nano hair and eye implants reveal her ever-shifting emotions.

I look up at the cornflower-blue sky. The barest sliver of moon—a ghost moon, really—peeks through in broad daylight. *They're both up there*, I think.

Kari and Rho.

And I'm stuck down here on Earth. How fates can change in the blink of an eye. I'm mesmerized for a second, drawn toward the stars like they have their own special gravity.

Estrella pipes up again.

Drae, are you lost?

I didn't realize I'd stopped moving, so lost in my memories and thoughts.

But that gets me moving again. Shouldering my heavy backpack stuffed full of books, I join the throngs of students crowding the walking paths, all heading for class. *Real* books, checked out of the library before I left campus. That means they're overdue.

I'm late for Great Books, but I have to stop by the library first. I turn left, cutting across Memorial Glade and heading for the main library. The front is studded with columns, giving it a stately air. Just seeing it makes my heart beat faster. After this, I have a full day of classes, just like any other freshman.

But there's more.

I'm a spy now, secretly working for my old professor, Trebond, who heads the Resistance. Their mission is to "Disarm the Stars." They're pacifists allied with the Raiders, glorified space pirates who deserted from Space Force and remained up there, raiding the supply lines and fighting for peace.

They're also officially enemies of the Earth Federation, now headed by Secretary-General Andromeda. My mother is a war hero, and my father works for the government. But with the new Astral threat, they have something in common now—the same adversary.

The Astrals.

Some graffiti on campus catches my eye, spray-painted on the walls. Cartoonish, elongated alien faces. I see both pro-Astral and anti-Astral slogans. While it's dangerous to talk about it—and it could get you arrested—some see the aliens as our potential saviors. They believe that humans haven't been good stewards of this planet. All the wars and environmental destruction. They believe a higher being—a more advanced alien species—can save us from ourselves.

But I know the truth. They killed those poor kids. They staged flyovers designed to look like the Siberian Federation over Kari's base, hoping to bate the Proxies into another war. They were planning to invade and destroy us.

I see colorful flyers pinned to bulletin boards for meetings to discuss the impact of the Astrals. What it means for humanity. For our future existence.

The truth is . . . we don't know.

The *not knowing* is the scariest part. Who are they? Why did they target us? Why would they want to invade Earth? We have more questions than answers.

The worst part—

When will they strike again?

We know they're out there, lurking in the darkness of space, that endless, ever-expanding void. We deterred them . . . we didn't stop them. More worrisome, Kari is up there and closer to the threat. That makes me feel afraid.

But she's brave and strong. I just hope she sends me a message soon. I don't know where she's being deployed, only that it's an interstellar outpost, and therefore the lag time will be greater.

I should be heading for Wheeler Auditorium for my Great Books class, but I veer left and finish crossing Memorial Glade.

Drae, you're going the wrong way. Do you need directions?

Estrella protests my change in direction, but she doesn't shock me . . . yet. Maybe I've bought myself some leeway with the whole *averting an alien invasion situation*. I tell her to mute.

Finally, I reach the library steps. They span before me, leading through the stately columns to my favorite place on campus. These books were checked out right before my secret jaunt to space.

That means they're overdue.

But it's more than that. I'm desperate to return them, so I can check out more. I guess Rho and Trebond rubbed off on me; I'm a certified book addict now.

I sprint up the steps and into the library—one of the largest left in the world, with real books, not digitized relics uploaded. I inhale the scent of books. It's like perfume to me now.

These books are printed on real paper, even if it's aged and yellowing, and bound in worn leather. Many of them are older than our federation. I think of Rho. If she misses anything about dropping out of college and sailing around the star-seas with her Raider girlfriend, it's this—*The library.*

Knowing Estrella could shock me at any second for being late *and* in the wrong building, I rush to the front desk.

The first thing I notice is the new librarian, only she's much younger than the others I've become acquainted with. Yes, it's true . . . I'm a regular here.

Her purple eyes graze over my face, taking it in. *Purple* means nano retinal implants, but they're not like Rho's, where they change color constantly with her emotional state. They remain deeply pigmented and unblinking.

Strangely, I wonder if I detect a hint of recognition. The way they lock onto me and sharpen, swirling with various deep purple hues. Her hair is choppy, cut into a pixie style, also shifting purple shades that match her eyes. Her face is round with a button nose and smallish ears, giving her a slightly elvish appearance, judging from what I've read in *The Lord of the Rings.*

She looks about my age, too. She's dressed in a flannel shirt and has an array of tattoos and piercings—eyelid, septum, ear lobes, too many to count.

This contrasts sharply with my preppy appearance. Suddenly, I feel inadequate and terribly uncool. Despite that, I feel a shudder of attraction push through my body, melting me in some places and hardening me in others.

Also terribly uncool.

But I have no choice. I approach and hand over my books. She accepts them and starts scanning the codes. *Beep. Beep. Beep.* Awkward silence fills in the gaps, stretching out and elongating.

"Uh, are you a transfer student?" I ask in a stilted voice, trying to fill it. I haven't seen her around campus and know some students work part-time in the library in exchange for tuition.

She smirks and keeps scanning with her head turned down. *Beep. Beep. Beep.* "No, I'm a real student."

I cringe, but then she grins.

"Just messing with you. Yeah, I transferred from Santa Cruz." She holds one of my books up and sniffs it like a drug. "Their library is okay, but nothing like this. Don't you think?"

I feel something that I haven't felt in ages. A glimmer of the old me. The one who flirted ceaselessly and had many girls dying to date me. But I tamp it down right away. I *love* Kari. However, my body has its own mind seemingly.

I feel my face flush. I lean in closer, and catch her scent, as alluring as the library itself. Earthy, like essential oils, but also sweet and fresh at the same time. She seems so very alive. Even her eyes twinkle at me. But then her lips move.

They whisper—

"Act like you're just returning books. And asking for help. But listen closely."

I jerk to alertness. Our eyes lock together. Hers have gone steely.

"Nod if you heard me."

I nod, once, quickly.

"Good. Nice to meet you, Drae."

"Wait, how do you know my name?" I say before I can stop myself.

"Well, I do have your library card in front of me." She points to the monitor inputting the book returns. "But yes, I've been waiting for you. Trebond sent me."

"You're Resistance?" I whisper, glancing around and feeling paranoid.

She nods, not breaking eye contact. "Trebond said you frequent the library, thanks to her influence. So this cover would be perfect for me. Officially, I'm a work-study transfer student."

"And unofficially?"

"I'm your new agent handler—and this is my cover. You report to me now."

Shock hits, chased by a stab of fear. Suddenly, everything feels *very* real.

CHAPTER 3

KARI

Major Apollo ushers me to his office. We traverse through corridors in the underground outpost, which is smaller than Ceres Base, where I did basic training. I'm guessing there are deeper levels, but we don't go there. He leads me into a typical Space Force office—overhead lights, desk, plastic chairs, and monitors on the back wall. It's utilitarian, without any hint of color or design.

Skylights line all of the ceilings on this upper level, even in this office. That's the real draw. Through them I see one of the suns piercing the horizon. Light spills over the surface.

I'm shocked to see . . . *things* . . . growing. I don't know if you can call them plants exactly. They don't look like anything on Earth. More crystalline with jagged branches stretching toward the sky, letting the sunlight filter through them and casting prisms on the ground. But the way they grow feels organic.

"Ah, yes." He notes my surprise. "Haven't seen that before, have you?"

"There's . . . life out here?"

"Indeed, but it's very different than back home. They call it *alien* for a reason. Part of this base is a research installation to study it. Those are astrobiologists. We're still not sure what it feeds on, but it may be a different sort of photosynthesis involving crystals."

I notice some guardians in deployment suits bouncing over the surface since it has less gravity, and collecting samples from the crystals. It looks like something out of an *Estrella Luna* comic. I always figured we'd eventually find life outside our system. The Astrals proved that.

But almost everything about our interstellar positions and scientific discoveries remains a military secret. Now, I'm starting to realize just how much they're keeping from civilians.

"Where are we?" I can't help but ask, even though I'm speaking out of turn.

"In a galaxy far, far away," he quips. Then turns more serious. "NTK basis. You may have gotten a promotion, but don't speak out of turn, Captain Skye."

His words are sharp and unbending.

I blink hard. It's official; I hate him already. I can't believe I thought he was . . . *hot*. But what's new? I spent most of basic training hating my drill sergeant, too.

And now, we're not friends exactly. But we do share a mutual respect. She came through and helped me when it counted. I didn't understand it then. The hazing, the psychological abuse, tormenting me over my deserter father.

But now, I understand they were testing me that whole time. To make sure I could handle this. Deployment.

I let the silence fill in. I need to wait for him to speak. He taps his tablet.

"I'm sure you're wondering why you're here," he says. "Why your MOS orders were switched at the last minute. And why they sent you here . . . to me."

"Yes, sir," I reply as expected.

I've learned to just shut up and agree with commanding officers. Arguing or, worse, offering your opinion just gets you punishment in the form of extra PT.

"I was wondering the same damn thing," he continues, flipping through my file. "A grunt barely out of basic? Then I got your file. There are a lot of *blanks* in it. Officially speaking."

I swallow hard. "Yes, sir."

"And a promotion to captain?"

"Yes, sir."

"You don't deserve that. Not based on what's down here. Yeah, yeah . . . first in your platoon on your graduation test. But that's virtual reality—it's not real."

That hits me and resonates.

"You're correct, sir. I agree. I don't deserve it. I was as surprised as you."

He shuts his tablet, clicking it off. Then pulls on a different file, a manila envelope with actual paper clipped inside it. Because electronic communications are inherently unsafe and easy to hack, combined with reverting to a hard mail system due to the interstellar distances and warp drives, I realize that they must have gone back to hard files. At least for intel. You can't hack paper, not like that.

You'd have to come all the way out here and steal the physical copy like some kind of crazy space heist. That's pretty genius. The rush to advance technology without thinking through the consequences has sent us fleeing back to paper. I wonder if the Astrals are part of the reason for this; I'd bet anything they've hacked into our electronics.

He starts flipping through the file. I spot my name at the top. I also see my father's name below that . . .

My deserter father.

Here we go again, I think, bracing myself for the usual shit-talking diatribe about his sullied past, even though I know the truth—that he's actually a war hero and Raider captain fighting to bring peace to the stars. It was Drae's mother who shot up that platoon—and my father was the guardian who stopped her, but she blasted him, leaving him to die. A nearby Raider encampment picked him up and saved his life. And the rest is history.

But I can't say any of that out loud. They would send me packing on the first transport back Earthside.

"But this file tells a different story," he says, tapping it. "Do you know what's in this? Permission to speak."

I'm taken aback by that. "Uh, something about the Astrals? And my Sympathetic? And illegal stuff?"

"Captain Skye, you and your Sympathetic are the only reason we prevented that invasion. You're needed in intelligence." He leans forward, scrutinizing me. I wilt a little bit.

He waits a long minute, before continuing. "Look, I'll be frank. It wasn't my idea. I have my own team that I personally assembled. They're smarter and much more experienced than you."

"Yes, sir. I'm sure they are. I didn't ask for this . . . I wanted front lines."

That makes him reconsider me, but only for a second. Maybe he respects my bravery—or stupidity—for that choice.

"Skye, let me make something clear," he says. "Your rank means nothing. Even with what you supposedly did to stop those bastard Astrals, you don't deserve it. You're still greener than the stars."

"Yes, sir."

"Is that all you want to say?"

Now I get it—he's trying to provoke me. To make me angry, get me to lash out, speak out of turn, do something rash . . . or worse. This is a test. I learned the hard way that everything at Space Force is designed to mind-fuck you.

I wrestle my emotions and compose my face into a blank mask.

"Yes, sir."

He leans back. "Well, maybe your drill sergeant did teach you something after all. She's one of our best."

"Yes, sir . . . I hope so. And for the record, I agree with you," I say, feeling deeply unworthy. "You're right. I'm just a lowly grunt. I don't deserve that rank, and I don't deserve to be here."

He gives me a nod of approval.

"That's good news. We agree on something. Thought I was gonna have to put the fear of the stars in you."

"Respectfully, my drill sergeant already did that, sir." I decide to push it. "Only she didn't put it as nicely."

He doesn't smile, but I can tell something shifts inside him. He warms up to me. It's subtle, a slight change in the immediate atmosphere. But I can sense it, nonetheless. Is it possible that he likes me? I study his face. But it's a mask that gives nothing else away.

His words do though.

"Maybe deploying you to my outpost wasn't such a mistake. You asked earlier, but our location is above your clearance. For now. You're here for one reason—and one reason only."

He lets that hang in the air. I can't help it; I fill the silence with two words.

"*The Astrals.*"

He nods sharply. "We have to prepare. That first invasion attempt? That's all it was—a *first* attempt. Believe me, they're already regrouping and plotting for their next invasion."

"Yes, sir. I agree."

"And what's coming?" He flips to images from the attack and the burning school bus. "Won't be nearly as nice." He turns my words back to me.

"Yes, sir."

I take that in as outside, the sun rises higher and the second sun eclipses the other horizon, igniting the crystalline life formations with fiery light. Prisms explode over the surface, transforming it into a kaleidoscopic light show.

But all I can see is burning. All I can feel is flame. And all I can hear are screaming children from that terrorist attack. What the Astrals did . . . it's horrific . . . beyond comprehension. Killing innocent kids to spark a war.

I think of Drae. He's back Earthside, vulnerable to the next attack. And every other civilian trying to live out their lives. Major Apollo is right. We deterred them and uncovered their secret plant, but we didn't destroy them.

His next words are chilling, dousing all the flames burning wildly through my mind. Everything in me freezes.

"Mark my words," he goes on. "The Golden Gate Attack will look like *nothing* compared to what happens next . . . if we don't act quickly."

He pulls up a map on the monitor behind him. It's of this far-flung moon.

"Excuse my language," he says with a frown. "But they caught us with our pants down. They'll try again. And again. And if we don't find a way to counter them, then they will succeed. They're far more advanced than us."

I feel a shiver of fear. The only reason we survived was because we caught them by surprise. They didn't expect us to avert the war. They'd studied us. Realized how warlike and barbaric humanity was. They didn't think we had it in us to unite and defend Earth.

But we proved them wrong.

For now.

But how long will the fragile peace between the Proxies last? Already, I hear whisperings of fractures within the Earth Federation. Our old enemies, the Siberian and Arctic Feds, are upset that California is in charge and vying for power, maybe even for a coup.

How long can our tentative alliances hold? Before old grievances and greed tear us apart? I know our sullied history. I read about the failed attempts to unite the world in the aftermath of World War I, and the UN that came later but also failed to prevent the Great War.

It was so destructive that it led to Earth Disarmament and the creation of Space Force, exporting all our militaries up here. If history is any judge, then humanity is already condemned.

But another voice speaks up inside me. It pleads with me—*We can be better. We can do better. We can evolve. We can grow. We can change. Humanity isn't a monolith. We aren't all hateful warmongers.*

I don't say any of this out loud, of course. That would be like branding yourself a pacifist inside Space Force. Not good for building a military career.

But Major Apollo shoots me a surprised look. Almost like . . . he could hear me. However, that's impossible.

I rub my tired eyes. I'm just tired from the interstellar trip. I still haven't readjusted to the artificial G. My bones ache, and my muscles feel weak and shaky. Plus, I just realized I'm starving. My stomach lets out a pitiful growl.

Major Apollo's voice jerks me out of my thoughts. "Here's everything we know about the Astrals," he says, hitting his tablet to project the intel onto the monitor. A blank page pops up.

I stare at it in confusion. There's nothing on there. I look back at him.

"I . . . don't understand. It's blank."

"Exactly, Captain. We don't know a stars-forsaken thing about those alien bastards. Other than that they're strategic. They're smart. They're ruthless and hellbent on exterminating us."

"But what . . . can I do?" I say, feeling another stab of unworthiness.

I'm an imposter; I didn't do anything really. Drae and the Resistance got the evidence and smuggled it up to space. I just helped disseminate it, that's all. And even with that, I had help. My friends from my platoon played a critical role. We'd be dead if they hadn't trusted me.

He gives me a serious look that bores into me. Again, it feels like he can read my face, even see inside my mind, though I know that's impossible. The neural implants don't work that way.

"Look, I've reviewed your file and psychological profile. You were open-minded enough to understand the truth," Major Apollo says. "And act on it. I can't say that about most of Space Force, or our federation government."

"But it's better now," I say, quoting the newsfeeds. "Once they got our intel, the Proxies united to stop the invasion. We have a new government . . . even Space Force is united now."

Finally, he cracks a smile. "Don't bullshit me, Captain. I know you've heard the rumors. Andromeda puts on a good face. But things aren't as . . . *peaceful* . . . as they appear on the newsfeeds. That's all glorified propaganda—and you know it."

Confide in him, or keep my true feelings closely guarded?

I make a split-second decision. I take a chance.

"The Siberian and Arctic factions. They hate California. They resent that our representative became the secretary-general of the new Earth Federation government. They want to be the ones in charge."

He nods. "But it's not just them. Many federations practiced extreme isolationist policies for years. Vowing not to intervene in intergalactic conflicts."

"Like the Florida and Indiana Federations. They succumbed to religious fundamentalists preaching about the end of the world. Many citizens still believe that the Astrals were sent by God himself to destroy the sinners. That we should welcome the invaders."

"That would be suicide, of course," he agrees. "For obvious reasons, they're uncomfortable with the new government. And then there's . . . Mars."

"They're a neutral territory," I say right away. "The planet used to be divided between two colonies—one controlled by the California Fed, the other by the Siberian Fed. It was a constant Proxy battlefield. But they fought back in a revolution and liberated themselves."

"Yes, and now? They wonder if they shouldn't control everything Earthside, too." He lets that sink in. "And then there's the Raiders. They grow more powerful every day as more deserters join their ranks. The Astral invasion didn't help; in fact, it made it worse."

"Space trauma," I say, worrying that I might have a touch of it. My dreams have been darker of late. "I heard there's been a sharp spike, though the newsfeeds aren't reporting on it."

"And why do you think that is?" he says, looking disturbed. "Why are more guardians deserting our ranks?"

"Sir, many of us signed up to fight the Proxies—but not aliens. I guess the shift was too much. It . . . broke them."

I look down at my hands. I don't mention my father. How he's told me about what happens when guardians with space trauma show up broken. How their hands shake, and their eyes go wild, and it takes months for them to calm down enough to begin the healing process. How he was one of them.

How many who don't get help choose suicide instead. That makes me shudder, though I try to hide it. Luckily, Major Apollo doesn't seem to notice.

"So, the Raiders grow more powerful every day," he goes on. "More guardians join their ranks, and more of our ships and supplies go missing. But can we count on them for support? Or will they turn on us again?"

The weighted question hangs in the air. I need to remember my role here—I'm fresh out of Basic. I can't admit that I know more about the Raiders than anyone at Space Force because secretly, my father is their leader. I know that part isn't in my file. It's been withheld.

They helped us stop the Astrals, and as part of a tentative alliance, the terms of which are known only to my dad and Secretary-General Andromeda, they remain independent but sworn to help Earthside fight the new Astral threat.

But I feel that Major Apollo is testing me, pushing at my defenses, and trying to get me to spill my guts to him and divulge all my secrets. I glance at my file. He's smart; a lot of that is redacted. I see the thick black ink marring the pages. Whole sections are blocked.

That means he knows they're not telling him everything about me, even with his high security clearance. I remember how the drill sergeant was always mind-screwing us in Basic.

So, I keep my mouth shut, even though the truth is that my father will support whatever I support. He would never betray me. But I don't want anybody figuring that out, especially my new commanding officer. That kind of power is too dangerous.

It can get you killed.

I know because my father told me. It was one of the last things he said before I returned to base and my service.

"The Raiders are unpredictable and prone to violence," I say instead, summoning my most diplomatic voice. "The truth is that nobody knows what *in the stars* they'll do. At least that's what the newsfeeds are reporting."

"Correct, Captain." He's forced to agree with me. "They're a wildcard."

Luckily, the tension abates. I breathe a sigh of relief. But it's temporary before worries resurface in my head. He seems to share my uneasiness.

"Frankly, I don't like it," he says, running one hand over his buzzed hair. "I don't like any of it."

"What do you mean, sir?"

"Well, we've got Raiders stirring things up over here. We've got growing Proxy tensions inside our government. Not to mention, the Astrals likely planning a second invasion. It's a dangerous combination, like a nuclear warhead waiting to detonate at the slightest provocation."

"You're right. That sounds dangerous. And unpredictable, too."

Silence rushes into his office. Only the soft *hiss* of the air vents is audible. In the void, I shift in my chair uncomfortably. My legs ache after the long interstellar trip, and my muscles are complaining about the increased gravity.

He doesn't speak, but worry animates his impossibly handsome face, making him look older suddenly. He's letting his guard down a little. I can feel it like a slight shift in the atmosphere.

But there's more under the surface. He's too cunning and smart to simply let me in. He's waiting to see what I'll do when left in uncomfortable silence.

I glance at the blank monitor behind him. Overhead, through the skylight, the second sun rises higher, covering the alien surface with purplish light. I shiver at the strange landscape. A million questions run through my head. But I settle on the most pressing one.

"Sir, pardon my speaking out of turn," I venture cautiously. "But what does all of this have to do with me?"

I can tell he wants to tell me off for breaking protocol. But then, he gives me a measured look of respect. Sometimes taking a risk can pay off, I realize.

"Captain, I'll be candid," he says with a frown. "My operation is under a major ticking clock. We started fighting this war from *behind*. Based on the new analysis of the Golden Gate Attack, we know that the Astrals have more advanced tech and weaponry than us."

I nod. "They were also able to infiltrate Earth without being detected by our advanced security systems."

"Right, we're still trying to determine how they accomplished that." He lets out a deep sigh, sounding frustrated. "So much about them remains a complete mystery. That brings me to our core mission on this base."

"Yes, sir . . . and what's that?"

"Our job is to produce actionable intel on them. Something, anything that she can use to win this *blasted* war."

"Sir, who is . . . *she?*"

"Secretary-General Andromeda oversees our operation personally."

I have to shut my mouth to keep from gasping out loud. He lets me absorb that fully. It sinks in, making me feel more anxious before he continues.

"She needs to show progress to the Earth Federations—and fast. Each day that we don't deliver fresh intel, her tenure grows ever more perilous. Everything depends on us now . . ."

The unsaid rest of that statement couldn't be clearer—*or we're all dead.*

Worries run through my head as I struggle to wrap my head around everything. I've been deployed to a secret outpost in deep space to work on a classified military intel operation dedicated to learning about our enemies.

The Astrals.

Before it's too late, and they invade Earthside again.

Only next time, we won't have the element of surprise to fend them off. They thought they could divide us and provoke a war where we destroyed ourselves. Now, they know that we are united and won't be fooled like that again. They underestimated us. They won't make that mistake a second time. That terrifies me.

"*Actionable* . . . intel," I repeat. "Our job is to find something we can use against them. That's why I'm here?"

He fixes those eyes on me again. That sends another shiver up my spine. "Not just against them—but something that Andromeda can use to destroy them . . . once and for all."

CHAPTER 4

DRAE

"Wait, you're my new contact?" I whisper, unable to conceal my surprise. Students continue to rush into the library. I glance around nervously. I feel like we're being watched. She winks at me from behind the desk. Her purple eyes shine brighter (another trick of the nano implants). Her eyes don't change colors with her moods, but they do darken and brighten for emphasis. She glances around, then keeps her voice low.

"Full-time student, part-time librarian . . . and Resistance fighter, at your service."

She looks too young . . . and, well . . . too cute. I feel another rush of heat. I don't say it, but she reads my face. Making it worse, Estrella chimes in to tell me I'm *late* again.

But I quickly *mute* her.

"High level, if you must know," she says. "Since birth, practically. My parents were founders. They're both vets who deserted. I grew up in the Resistance bunkers and secret bases."

"So, you're deserter spawn?" I say before I can stop myself. Even though I know the truth now, the bias runs deep.

She winces at the derogatory term.

"Sorry," I backpedal quickly. "That's been drummed into my head since birth by my parents. I don't mean it . . ."

I trail off in shame.

My cheeks flush.

"It's okay . . . I've read your file. We know change takes time. It's not easy to reprogram targets after they get brainwashed. It's not just your parents, but the newsfeeds, your friends, teachers, school curriculum . . . well . . . basically *everything*," she says while piling my book returns onto a rickety wooden cart. The library feels like a relic of the past, something preserved in this time capsule for one simple reason. It wasn't destroyed in the Great War.

"Wait, I have a file? Didn't realize I was that important. Trebond sent you?"

"That's right," she whispers back. "It's too dangerous for her to come to campus. I'm sure you understand. From now on, I'm your go-between to deliver communications."

I flash back to what happened. My favorite professor had to flee in the middle of the night to avoid being arrested. She's the one who recruited me and Rho to fight to "Disarm the Stars."

"Well, you already know my name," I say in a clandestine voice.

Or at least I think it's sneaky and subtle. And maybe a little sexy, too. Like the spy characters in the books I've read.

"That's right—I have your library card." She smirks, sliding it back to me.

A moment passes between us. I can feel her studying me, sizing me up, trying to figure me out. Do I measure up to what she's been told? Or heard?

Finally, she says, "My code name for this operation is . . . Willow."

"Nice to meet you—" I start, but she glances at the time and cuts me off.

"You're late for class," she says quickly. "I have your schedule, too. Spy 101—don't be late for class, or do anything to draw attention to yourself. You need to act like a model student. Starting right now. Is that clear?"

"Yes," I say, feeling lame.

"Good," she replies, glancing around on high alert. "We've already been talking for too long. Now, get out of here . . . fast. Much is at stake. More than you know. I'll be in touch."

With that, I'm dismissed. I feel foolish—and crazy paranoid at the same time.

I rush out and head to class across campus, feeling like I'm being watched.

Probably because I am.

My head still spinning from meeting my new contact, I make it to class. Despite my detour, I'm not late. Estrella informs me of this as I slide into a chair near the back of the sprawling auditorium. She sounds annoyed, too. I guess I got here faster than she projected.

Is my neural implant developing a personality? It is an AI learning model. So, I suppose it's possible. I named her after my favorite comic book character, Estrella Luna. It's an old story from the early days of Earth Disarmament and Space Force.

In her defense, I did sprint across Memorial Glade and took a shortcut through the back alleys. Fed Patrols still roam campus . . . *for our protection.*

That started after the Proxy tensions heated up, secretly spurred on by the Astrals and their subterfuge. The patrols—AI robots on wheels, basically—randomly stop students to scan them. Luckily, I didn't get stopped. My back routes help reduce the odds. But I'm still a bit breathless and sweaty.

Regardless, I'm relieved to be on time. I can't afford to draw unwanted attention. I glance around as the lecture hall fills up with students. The room is wood paneled in a blond shade with insulated ceilings to dampen ambient sound. It doesn't work, not fully. The rustling of feet and backpacks, the slapping of seats jerking back, and the low mumbling of voices fill the room. The seats are wooden and tiered down toward the stage, where a podium waits for our instructor.

This is Great Books, or what used to be Great Books before Professor Trebond fled, and they replaced her with a federation stooge who only teaches glorified propaganda. Today's reading was *The Space Force Diaries: War Heroes Speak*. These are compiled testimonies from our most awarded officers. I was shocked to see my mother included in the dense book. I know it's a lie and what she really did up there.

But I wouldn't dare say that.

Professor Goode enters from a side door by the stage and ambles to the podium. This is a required class for all freshmen, so it's a sizable class. She scans her notes on a tablet. Her bland expression matches her bland beige suit and stiff bun, her usual uniform. Her eyes are what really freak me out. They have this unblinking, frozen quality.

I'm sure this is going to be another boring lecture. I just hope she doesn't decide to call on me and single me out because of my mother. She's what you'd call . . . *famous*. I grew up with everyone knowing what she'd done to save our federation from the barbaric Raiders.

While I wait, students around me pull out their tablets to take notes, even though the professor will pass all of us no matter how we actually do. We're Ringers—the privileged children of Space Force guardians—and we're supposed to run everything one day.

Can't have us flunking out of Berkeley.

My mind drifts to Kari like it always does. I want to tell her everything that happened with Willow this morning right away. Only, I can't anymore. Not that I ever could. We always had lag time. When she was at basic training, it was about twenty minutes. But now, she's gone interstellar. Who knows when I'll hear from her again?

The *not knowing* is the worst part. I think back to her last message, sent right before she deployed. Her words make my heart thump faster and keep me going, giving me a reason to exist. There was so much she didn't say—or couldn't say—in that exchange. But I could feel it in her emotions. She was afraid . . . of what? Take your pick.

Deployment. Interstellar space travel. The Astrals. Another alien invasion.

They brief us on the logistics of the Sympathetic Program, of course. It's covered in our orientation. But hearing it and living it are two different things.

Put simply—

I miss her like a hole in my heart.

Finally, everyone settles down. The professor launches into her lecture. "*The Space Force Diaries* teaches about the sacrifices made by guardians to protect Earth and keep us safe—"

But then the doors to the lecture hall swing open again with a sharp . . .

Bang!

Everyone turns to see the late student. He saunters in with a smug expression, not even caring that he's disrupting class. He strides down the aisle like he owns the school.

I'm in shock; I can't believe my eyes.

It's Jude.

My former best friend turned enemy. I take in his blond hair cut short and icy blue eyes. He spots me and sneers.

Anxiety explodes in my chest, making my heart thump like crazy. Last I heard, he was kicked out and transferred to another college. The same thing goes for Loki, our other friend.

What in the stars is he doing here?

CHAPTER 5

KARI

I hear Major Apollo's words: *Destroy them.* His face tells me just how serious this mission is. He leans forward at his desk and meets my shocked gaze.

"In order to find their weaknesses—and exploit them—we need to better understand the Astrals. Right now, to put it bluntly . . . we know fuck all."

I sputter a laugh despite myself.

"Sorry, sir . . . it's just that . . . you're right. Even the newsfeeds say that."

"Yes, Captain. Not our technological gaps, but our near-total lack of intel about our enemy is by far our greatest weakness. Andromeda agrees with me."

That makes me wonder just how often Andromeda speaks to him. The emphasis on *agrees with me* makes it clear how high up Apollo is . . . and how much he has her ear. I also wonder why he's not a general or higher. But then I remember he's special ops and needs to keep a lower profile, especially with all the tensions within the fed.

"You can't fight an enemy you don't know," I say, thinking back to my battle strategy classes in basic. "Sun Tzu writes about it in *The Art of War*."

"So you did pay attention."

"Uh, right, I tried. I know my grades . . . weren't always the best. But I promise, I make up for it with a blaster."

"I'm sorry to report, but blasters won't win this war. I wish it were that simple. However, Sun Tzu just might. *Know thy enemy and know yourself,*" he quotes. "*In a hundred battles, you will never be defeated.*"

I nod in recognition. "One of my favorite passages. Some have theorized that the Astrals studied us, including our philosophy. That they're using our own knowledge and history against us."

"That's precisely what they're doing. They know everything about us, while we know . . . *nothing*. We have to find a way to reverse that. That brings me to the purpose of our base's location."

He swipes at his tablet, making the monitor on the wall behind him come to life and resolve into a map. I'm guessing it's this moon. An area is highlighted in red. I zero in on it, trying to decipher the significance. I also notice that even this map lacks any proper name or stellar coordinates. Unnamed base, indeed.

"We got lucky," he goes on, pointing to the map. "Using trace elements from the explosive device used in the Golden Gate Attack, we located an abandoned Astral settlement located on this moon. That's why we're all the way the fuck out here in the middle of nowhere."

"An Astral settlement?" I glance at the skylight, half expecting one to jump out. But then I remember . . . we don't even know what they look like. "On this moon? You're certain?"

"Yes, we call it . . . Area Alpha," he says, indicating the highlighted area. He flicks at his tablet, making it zoom in.

I can't believe my eyes as images of the settlement flash across the screen. It's strange and crystalline, constructed deep into the moon's underground cave systems, and obviously abandoned. Probably for some time. This intel takes me totally by surprise.

It's definitely not being broadcast on any of the newsfeeds.

"But . . . sir," I stammer through my shock. "I didn't know we had any idea about them . . . or where they lived."

"Almost nobody does. You can understand why the intel is so sensitive. We can't have the Astrals finding out that we're out here, now can we?"

The ramifications hit me. If they knew, they could destroy our base.

"Have you uncovered anything?" I ask, riveted by the alien images.

The tunnels look like they've been excavated following veins of crystal into the earth. The tunnels look crated, but also natural at the same time. Everything shimmers with pale, purple light as if lit by some internal power source that feeds the crystals, which seem alive too.

Suddenly, the screen glitches into static. **WE SEE YOU!** flashes at me.

Bold letters. Filling the screen.

Blotting out the images.

I gasp and start to speak, but just as fast as it appeared, the monitor returns to normal. No words anymore. Only a soft gasp escapes my lips. But my heart is hammering, while sweat percolates on my clammy skin. Another flashback? I've been having nightmares again, too.

Secretly, I'm worried it's the early stages of space trauma after everything we went through in averting the invasion. But I'm not sure, and I certainly don't want my superior officer to find out. The last thing I need is to be declared a head case, or worse, shipped back Earthside on medical leave.

If it gets any worse, there's no way I'm going to the Space Force shrinks. They just pump you full of drugs. I plan to talk to my father about it. The Raiders have more experience with treating space trauma—and healing it—than anyone else in the known universe.

Luckily, Major Apollo is busy flipping through the intel on his tablet.

But suddenly, he looks up.

His eyes lock onto me. It's almost like he heard me thinking about him, even though that's impossible. I try to steady my heart, so he doesn't notice.

"Everything okay, Captain?"

"Uh, yes . . . sir," I say quickly. "Just, I'm shocked . . . by the settlement . . ."

"Of course. Takes some getting used to, doesn't it? The idea that we're not alone out there? When it's theoretical, that's one thing. But to see it with your own eyes . . ."

I shake my head, marveling at the screen. "It's shocking, to say the least."

With that, he flips to crystalline structures buried deep inside the caves. They form what looks like a more complex matrix with some purpose. But what they could be completely eludes me. And apparently, them too.

"Their technology is unlike anything we've encountered," Apollo continues, pointing to the monitor. "Our military scientists speculate that these might be computer systems . . . if you can even call them that. It's almost like . . ."

I watch the purple light undulating through them. It's like I can almost *feel* the pulsating matching my heart rate.

"They're alive?" I say, leaning closer to the monitor, feeling unsettled.

He looks surprised—but also wary.

"Yes, but how did you know that?"

I shrug. "A good guess?"

When that doesn't satisfy him, I add, "Sir, you said it yourself when you read my file. I'm more open-minded, right?"

He nods. "That's true, Captain. Well, your *lucky* guess was accurate."

He zooms in on the crystals that look like they're channeling the lightest.

"Our scientists theorize that there's some sort of biological interface. And these crystals right here? We tried to measure their energy source. They seem like they carry signals. And they seem capable of broadcasting them, too."

"Sir, are they operational?"

"Right, we're still trying to determine that. Which points to the danger of this mission. What if they are still operational? And the Astrals find out we're here? Lurking in their settlement? Messing with their tech . . . trying to hack into it, even . . ." He trails off. I remember the explosion and smoke from the school bus on that bridge. The screams of the children.

That would be . . . bad.

Neither of us says it out loud, but the heavy moment lingers before he flicks his tablet off and sets it aside. The monitor falls dark. It's just us now. Me and him in this office on this abandoned moon with two suns hovering in the magenta sky. Well, it was abandoned . . .

Until we got here.

"To summarize . . . this operation is a major SNAFU," he says, using the military slang. "We're completely stumped. We're running out of ideas and time. Are your orders clear?"

I set my lips. "Yes, sir! Learn about the Astrals—so we can destroy them."

"Very good," he says and hands me a briefing package. "Your homework."

It's just a tiny drive, but I can scan it later. I slip it into my front pocket.

"Oh, and Captain Skye?" he stops me. "One more thing. I take it you're already acquainted with Private Starfire?"

"Yes, sir. She was in my platoon in basic. She was deployed here, too. If I may say, she's a very capable guardian. She was the best recruit in our platoon."

"Nice try being humble," he says. "But there was someone better . . . you."

I blush at that. "Right. But it was close. Trust me . . ." I almost mention Nadia, too. But the words dry up.

She's fighting on the front lines. Plus, she would hate intel. It's too much reading and thinking . . . not enough action. She likes to be in the thick of it. Even if it might get her blasted to pieces. I remember carrying her broken body after the Siberian Fed attacked us.

Major Apollo's voice snaps me out of the flashback. "Private Starfire is stationed here for one reason and one reason only—to help you. She's assigned to your intel team. As we speak, she's being briefed. She'll meet you at your barracks. You're bunking together on base."

Relief surges through me.

I'm not alone.

Before the weight of the world collapses back on my shoulders. I'm starting to feel overwhelmed and dizzy, too. The memory of the battlefield haunts me like a bad dream. Thankfully, he dismisses me with a sharp salute.

I scramble up from the hard plastic chair, feeling wobbly. I still haven't recovered from the trip, warping through space, bending the fabric of time. Put bluntly, it feels like my body was wrenched out and hung up to dry.

I hurry from the office, clutching the packet in my hand. Is it my imagination, or do his eyes linger on me . . . longer than necessary? I get that strange feeling again like he's prying into my mind.

But I shake it off. That's impossible. I'm just delirious and overtired. And clearly, he's trying to size me up.

I stagger into the corridor with worries circling through my head. Major Apollo said they were stuck and counting on me. But I fear that his faith is misplaced. I don't know anything about collecting intel—let alone intel on aliens hellbent on destroying us.

The truth is that I got lucky when we prevented that invasion. The Resistance and my father did all the hard work—and Drae, who smuggled the intel to space. I just helped disseminate it.

My heart drops like a stone under gravity. I'm lost and out of my depth. I hear my old battle buddy Nadia's voice in my head—*This is above your pay grade.*

Or put another way, I'm fucked.

Still unsettled, I leave Major Apollo's office to the green arrows lighting up and showing the way. It's a guidance system installed to decrease the need for actual workers on this base.

The reason is clear. Fewer people means less chance that intel leaks out.

Where are they taking me?

Harold responds, *Kari, follow the arrows to your barracks.*

They lead me down back toward the docking bay. I glance up at the skylights tracking the corridor. Soft amethyst light shines down from the two suns. They're about to eclipse each other in the pinnacle of the sky. Veins of crystal grow into the skylight, sprouting out in starbursts that look like frost cutting across the frozen glass.

I still can't wrap my head around what I just learned in my briefing. There's an abandoned Astral settlement on this moon. The images of the cave systems flash through my head, spiking my curiosity. They think those crystal networks might be computer systems. Their tech seems both mechanical and also organic and deeply alive.

Beep! Beep!

The piercing noise jerks me out of my thoughts. Several bots swerve and scurry by me, annoyed that I'm blocking their path . . . but no guardians. I glance around. The whole base seems deserted. I haven't seen anyone since I left Major Apollo's office. The emptiness gives it an eerie vibe. I shudder and keep following the arrows, trying to resist the urge to deviate from them.

It's the opposite of Ceres Base, which was always bustling with platoons of new recruits getting their asses kicked by drill sergeants. It was also a major communications hub with postal ships constantly blasting off, along with guardians to defend the critical position in our system.

Where is everybody?

I don't mean to ask my neural implant, but Harold starts to reply. *Sorry, guardian locations are classified—*

Mute, please, I think back. I don't need the reminder that he can't help me.

I keep going, passing the docking bay. It's also empty. The transport that brought us here has already departed. Not even one postal ship idles, waiting to deliver mail and take packages.

Strange, I think as I continue across the docking bay and into the corridor that branches off the other side. Maybe it's being so deep in interstellar space, the emptiness of this moon base, or the existence of actual alien lifeforms . . .

But I get a bad feeling.

That's when I spot an actual person, marching down the corridor at a fast clip. Only, she's not in uniform. Instead, she's wearing a crisp, white lab coat.

"Captain," she says and passes me with a stiff nod. Her blonde hair isn't buzzed off like mine, but tucked into a tight bun. That means . . . she's not a guardian. Probably a civilian scientist.

Major Apollo mentioned military scientists. Space Force recruits them. This is a research base, after all.

She clutches a tablet and doesn't meet my eyes. Something about how she keeps her head down tells me she doesn't want to engage with me . . . and more than that . . . she's wary, too.

I continue after the green arrows, not wanting to draw attention for *snooping* (even though it's sort of in my job description now). But I flick my eyes back in her direction. This part of the base doesn't have skylights and feels more enclosed and claustrophobic.

She walks up to what looks like a complete dead end and stops in front of the concrete wall. That's pretty weird.

She continues staring at the wall, then suddenly—

Beep!

The wall starts to . . . *unfold*. That's the best way I can describe it. The solid barrier comes alive, breaking apart and retracting away, revealing a secret door.

Beyond it—*for a split second*—I glimpse lots of people. They're all in white lab coats with tablets like the woman, hurrying around like it's an emergency drill and tending to advanced-looking lab technology. All sorts of machines crowd the space.

What are they all doing back there?

Luckily, Harold is still muted.

Before I can ascertain anything else, she marches through the opening. The wall refolds itself. Now, it looks like ordinary concrete again. A dead end.

I skid to a halt. The green arrows under my boots start flashing faster, expectantly, urging me to keep going.

But I hesitate.

My heart *thumps* faster. Curiosity grips me. I know I shouldn't, but my impulsive spirit rises up like back when I used to ditch high school. I double-check to make sure the corridor remains deserted, then approach that wall.

My breath catches in my throat. I inspect it closer but don't see any cracks or indications of how it opens. I try touching it, running my hand over the cold-feeling surface. Suddenly—

The whole wall flashes with a red X, an alarm buzzes loudly, and two words blaze through my retinas:

ACCESS DENIED

I startle back. Harold pipes up too.

Kari, you're going the wrong way. Please proceed after the green arrows.

Even his voice speaks in an urgent tone, not his typical relaxed cadence.

Arrows flash under my boots insistently, pointing me away from that wall. The message couldn't be clearer.

"Sorry, Harold," I mumble and back away. "I just got turned around."

I don't need to speak out loud, but I do just in case someone is listening . . .

Spying on me even.

That freaks me out even more. I quicken my pace the other way.

This time, I stay on course and follow the arrows. The back of my neck prickles like I'm being watched.

But when I jerk my head around, nobody is there. The corridor is empty.

Still, I can't shake the feeling that there are things going on at this base that they're not telling me . . . big things . . . secret things . . . dangerous things . . . but that's above my pay grade.

I've been briefed. I'm strictly NTKB . . . *need to know basis*.

I have to stop asking questions and sticking my nose where it doesn't belong. And fast. Even if it's technically my job now. But something else worries me.

Now, there's a record of me trying to enter that restricted area with the secret door where the woman in the lab coat went. I remember the *flash*—and glimpsing the workers in lab coats busting around—before the wall contracted again.

What were they doing back there? And why is it so restricted? I remember how the alert flashed in my retinas, along with that horrible noise in my ears, thanks to my neural implant.

I hope I don't get in trouble. Obviously, I'm a terrible secret agent since I got caught spying on my first day. I especially hope this doesn't get back to Major Apollo.

That makes me wince. He seemed so skeptical at first. But by the end of our briefing, it felt like he was warming up a little. Not being friendly exactly . . .

But not about to ship me back home either. However, this could ruin that.

My stomach twists with anxiety. I don't have to worry about Ma and Bea now that they left Earthside behind to sail the star-seas, reunited with my long-lost father, but I do worry about Drae and everyone else back home.

Even if Major Apollo gets notified of my mistake, I'm hoping that my newbie status will buy me a pass this time.

They'll just think I got lost, I reassure myself, though my heart races anyway. But I need to be more careful next time.

That excuse will wear off fast. My head spins with worries about the abandoned Astral settlement, my new orders, and the secret underground lab. I feel like I might puke. Suddenly, going back to the barracks and facing Luna and this briefing package feels like too much.

Suddenly, I miss Drae like a knife to the heart. I've become so used to sharing *everything* with him that the absence of our communications tears that gaping hole in my heart wider. I also don't know what he's doing either. This has to be the longest we've gone without any sort of communication.

Even in high school, when he was my archenemy, I still saw him with his Ringer friends in the halls most days. Back then, he drove me crazy. Let's just say, I hated his stars-forsaken guts more than there are stars in the universe.

How long has it been? Though I can't be sure . . . I'm guessing over a week has passed since I sent my last Sympathetic exchange, right before I deployed here.

One *unbearable* week.

Seven long days.

My heart skips a beat. I've never felt more in the dark or lost without somebody else. Being together in person was like melding into my other half. There was the intensity of our physical connection, and then when our neural implants locked in, they made us feel each other's emotions and more . . .

I shiver as the memory of that day sweeps through me again. It was intense. Beyond intense. Mind-shattering, body-shaking. It altered my brain chemistry . . . and now . . .

I feel an echo of that connection, but it's only a pale shadow of what we shared, for it's just the remembrance, imprinted on my neural synapses. But even that makes my knees buckle. And I know it's not the artificial G. This is . . . *love*. And it has the power to level me.

I need to go to the barracks and rendezvous with Luna. I also have homework. The tiny package feels suddenly heavy in my front pocket. Plus, I'm exhausted and need to lie down on my bunk and rest.

But my heart beats emphatically, telling me that don't have a choice about where I go next. *Thump, thump, thump* goes my heart. *Go, go, go . . .*

To him.

I don't even know where the post office is located on my new base, or if I'm allowed to send my Sympathetic an exchange yet. My heart sinks at that thought. *Oh, Draeden.* I picture him at Berkeley, slumped over in class tapping out notes on his tablet, or sprawled out on his dorm bed, free of his old roommates . . . his former best friends.

He's changed so much since we first got paired together, shedding his cocky Ringer status for . . . humility, the pursuit of knowledge . . . and for love . . . for me.

He's not the same person anymore, and neither am I. The Sympathetic Program has invaded our brains, rewired their chemistry and connections, and reforged us into new beings, once that can never be parted.

I feel a lurching in my soul. He's probably worried about me. He has no idea where I am—or when he'll hear from me again. I can't leave him flailing around in the dark like that. It's not fair. The torment within me only amplifies the more I think about him, and the more I remember him. I need to send him a communication right away. But then, fear rushes through me. What if something has changed about how he feels about me? Or how I feel about him?

That kicks me into action.

I summon my neural implant—

Harold, I need to send a Sympathetic Exchange. Which way to the post office?

There's a long pause—and no response comes through yet. The green arrows keep flashing under my feet, leading me toward the barracks . . . the wrong way.

Harold must be seeking out approval above my status. With a grimace, I wonder if Major Apollo is being personally notified of my request. It's likely . . . he is my commanding officer . . . which means he basically runs my life now. Something else makes me worry. The way he looked at me when I left his office. And how I felt when I first saw him. The obvious attraction that erupted in my body despite my strong mental protests that *I love Drae* and *he's my boss and would never cross that line.*

Ugh, not now . . . I think, then direct my attention to Harold to cancel my request. Clearly, I'm about to get denied just like every other request I've levied since I arrived.

But then, Harold speaks up.

Request approved for Sympathetic exchange. Rerouting now. Stand by . . .

Elation surges through me. The green arrows divert, leading me down another corridor. I follow them, filled with anticipation. I'm both thrilled and nervous at the same time. The jittery mix of emotions makes me feel dizzy.

The closer I get, the worse it becomes. I guess this is love. The kind Rho used to rhapsodize poetically about while I nodded along, clueless. I never understood her impulsive actions when it came to her lovers, not until now.

After you fall for someone, it's like nothing else matters but them, and everything else falls away into the void, as if your very existence, your soul even, has been divided into two parts. What I should've asked Harold is—

Which way to the other half of my heart?

CHAPTER 6

DRAE

I stare at Jude in shock. My old friend and roommate is back?
But that's impossible.
He got expelled.
I blink hard at the blond figure striding through the doors into the lecture hall, hoping I'm just mistaking him for another lookalike freshman.

But he locks right onto me—and his eyes narrow. Meanwhile, the whole lecture has fallen silent at his appearance. Guess news of what happened did circulate campus, while I was on the run and off in outer space.

Loudly, as if trying to draw as much attention to himself as possible, he makes his way down the row toward me, sliding past other students and stepping on their bags. He doesn't care.

I wait for the professor to rebuke him and order him to take a seat—and to save me from what's heading my way, in slow motion almost. But she doesn't.

Instead, she smiles broadly.

"Mr. Luther, welcome back," Professor Goode says warmly. "Please take a seat, so we can get started."

She waits with a plastered-on smile, holding up her lecture just for him.

No surprise there. She's bought and paid for. I know she was planted here to spy for the federation. We may have saved the world and ended the Proxy Wars, even united the Proxies, but I realize something sickening. The more things change, the more they stay the same. Systems resist true change.

Jude has almost reached me. He tramples another backpack, but the poor freshman doesn't object. Instead, the kid whispers, "Sorry . . . about that . . ."

My stomach churns, making me want to puke. I feel like a missile has targeted me with its tracking. Now that he's closer, I notice the freshly healed scars on his cheeks. Raised flesh where I hit him. And kept hitting him. His nose is also swollen and slightly askew, clearly reset by doctors, though it didn't heal right. Despite advanced nano helping, some damage can't be undone.

Not fully.

His new visage imbues him with a sinister aura. That part suits him. I swallow against the acid in my stomach. That moment when I snapped, when I saw who he really was at the core, can't be reversed either. I hate him more than all the stars in the universe.

I flash to the librarian—Willow—my new agent handler. Maybe she knows something about what he's doing here.

After what feels like an agonizingly long parade, Jude slides into the seat next to me. He leers at me with his sickening smile. The edges curve into sharp lines that bisect his face, emphasizing his fresh scars. The ones that I put there with my bare fists.

"Hey there, Drae," he says in a darkly sinister voice. "You miss me?"

The torturously boring lecture barrels forward, but I barely retain a word that Professor Goode says in her boring monotone voice. There's one big reason.

I can't believe Jude is sitting next to me—that he's back at Berkeley.

I'm rigid at my desk, frozen with tension, and unable to take notes.

"One second while I pull up next week's reading assignment," Professor Goode says, shuffling around the podium. The monitor behind her boots up. Finally, a break in class. I can't take it; I've kept my mouth shut too long.

"What are you doing here?" I hiss at Jude, trying to keep my voice down.

He sits there like a model student with his tablet out to take notes. But I know it's all an act. He's good at that.

He whispers in my ear, so close I can feel his breath on my neck. "Thought you could get rid of me that easily?"

My blank expression says it all: I'm still in complete shock, denial even.

This is the first time we've spoken since the incident that got him kicked out . . . *temporarily*, as it turns out.

"Well, I've got some bad news for you," he continues. "There was a part of me that hoped you'd be excited to see me . . . and realize your mistake over that *unfortunate* misunderstanding."

Everyone is staring at us. There's a deathly silence that's fallen over the auditorium. Even the professor looks up from the podium. Jude relishes all the attention; he soaks it up.

"Misunderstanding?" I say, finding my voice. It comes out in a hiss. "But . . . you *sexually assaulted* a student."

"So she says," he says smoothly. He has all his father's politesse and charm. "You see, it's her word against mine."

"And mine," I say, biting off the words. "I witnessed what you did, too."

"Well, that's too bad since Loki backed my version of events. And unfortunately for you . . . she vanished. Nobody can find her. No victim statement. Plus, you know my father."

I swallow hard. I do know. And that's the problem. I also know the Resistance helped her escape and go into hiding. Making enemies with Jude and his family was dangerous for her.

Of course, I can't reveal any of that. But I can see how his dad twisted that and used it against her to protect his abusive son. Her disappearance made her look shady. But it's better than being dead in a ditch, because that could've been her fate had she stuck around campus and tried to testify against Jude.

As for me, my father is also connected. My mother is a war hero. She's interviewed in this book even, which is basically fed propaganda.

"That's right," Jude goes on, watching as I put all the pieces together. "Dad pulled some strings. At first, the dean said I had to transfer . . . Loki, too."

"That's what I heard."

He shrugs. "Yeah, that sucked. But Dad got them to change their minds and see my side of the story. I just had to complete a week of anger management classes, and then the dean agreed to readmit me to the freshman class. Loki decided to transfer to Santa Cruz anyway. Guess he'd had enough of studying . . ."

He trails off as ambient noise fills in and the lecture continues, but Jude leans in and whispers to me while tapping at his tablet to fake paying attention.

I hiss back, "A week, that's all?"

He grins. "Yeah, I even met a hottie at the classes. Turns out she had some squabble with her dumb roommates."

"You picked up a girl . . . in your anger management class?"

"Punishments can be opportunities," he says with a wolfish grin. "Like I said, that was a misunderstanding."

He pauses, then says—

"As in . . . that girl made a mistake."

Horror rushes through me, but he continues, "Don't worry. We'll find her. Slandering my name like that. Dad is on it . . . your father, too. It won't be long."

"And then what?"

"You don't want to know," he says and clams up. But darkness brews in his eyes, and I know what that means.

Horrible thoughts rush through my head. I can't believe my former best friend *turned* archenemy is here. He taps at his tablet. I thought that I'd finally escaped him, something I'd been unable to do since high school, when I started to realize that I wanted to change. That I didn't want to be a privileged jerk anymore. Kari called me out on that. Our relationship is what really transformed me. I also learned that I'm not a coward. However, I feel ashamed to be sitting here with my mouth clamped shut, not speaking out.

But it wouldn't change anything. Jude's father runs this federation, and his son is the face of the future. Trying to change that, trying to tarnish his name again would just get me kicked out of college, if I'm lucky. It could be worse.

But something darker stirs in my mind. Am I staying silent because I have the privilege to do so? Because deep down, I know my parents protect me, too. That they won't punish me the same way they would someone like his victim or Kari, who grew up a Park kid.

Jude glances at me, surreptitiously looking at my tablet, which is open to an *Estrella Luna* digital comic. Nothing dangerous or contraband; nothing about Kari or the Astrals or the Sympathetic Program. But then it dawns on me.

Suddenly, I wonder if the reason he's here—that the dean allowed him back—is more dangerous . . . if he's here to keep an eye on me . . . spy on me even.

That makes me shudder. All the hairs rise on the back of my neck. Before I went missing and fled to space on a Raider ship, Jude's father already harbored suspicions about me being involved with the Resistance, especially after my old professor vanished.

I overheard him telling my father that my reading habits—and frequent trips to the library—were also suspicious, along with my top grades in Great Books, when I spied on them searching Trebond's faculty room.

But I thought the role we played in thwarting the Astral invasion would buy us some leeway since the Resistance was technically the reason we averted the Proxy War. The new Earth Federation Government is supposed to signal a shift in our policy.

But what if the older hardline factions see us not as the saviors of Earth, but as something else—

Threats to their power.

People like Jude's father. Like my father even. That chills me even more.

All I know is—

I need to get a message to Trebond, and fast. That means I have to find Willow. I also need to get in touch with Kari and report on Jude's reappearance, only I have no idea where she is—or when she'll resurface and send me an exchange via the Sympathetic Program.

The professor launches into the heart of her lecture, but I'm stiff and on edge the whole time. Jude puts on a show of paying attention, typing into his tablet, and murmuring along in agreement. But it's an act. I glimpse the so-called notes on his tablet.

Actually, I realize, it's more like he tilts it my way . . . wanting me to see what he's been typing this whole time. I swallow hard when I see the words.

It's the same thing, typed over and over, almost psychotically.

Drae is a dead man walking. Drae is a dead man walking. Over and over.

When he catches me watching, he types out something else. Slowly, deliberately. The words leech out.

Better watch your back. I don't care what they said you did . . . it's all lies . . . You're dead.

CHAPTER 7

KARI

The green arrows lead me toward the post office, but really they lead me . . .

To him.

As I wind through the underground corridors of this secret moon base, Draeden's name echoes through my head with each heartbeat. The closer I get, the more flushed and dizzy I feel.

Harold's voice pipes up.

Your heart rate and vital signs indicate increased arousal. Are you okay?

That makes me cringe.

"Mind your business," I snap back. "He's my Sympathetic, that's all."

I accidentally speak out loud. My face colors more. I hope nobody heard my childish outburst. But still, the underlying meaning isn't lost on me.

Harold monitors me and sends data to the master system, where it's all compiled into a file like the one Major Apollo had on his desk. I remember how thick it looked. I'm still new to service, but they've compiled so much.

Ugh, I think at the idea of him reading this report. But that's what I signed up for. Once you enlist and sign your contract, they own you. You're always being watched and monitored.

I'm almost used to it. Heavy emphasis on the . . . *almost*.

I still have secrets. But they're the ones that Space Force wants me to keep. Like my father being the head of the Raiders. Or Drae working secretly with the Resistance on Earth. They know the role they played in stopping the Astrals.

I remember reciting my Oath of Enlistment back in my hometown at the Space Force recruiting headquarters, a drab office in a drab building without any decorations aside from a drooping, sad-looking California Federation flag. Even the grizzly bear on it looked depressed, as if it knew it had become extinct more than a century ago.

But that feels like a different lifetime. Eight weeks loom in my memory like an eternity. My *before* life . . . *before* I enlisted and shipped out . . . *before* basic training reshaped and remade me . . . *before* he kissed me and unbroke my heart . . . it all feels like a distant memory, as if it actually belongs to somebody else.

The *Before Kari.*

And the *After Kari.*

Harold breaks into my thoughts. *Destination ahead on the right.*

The automatic sliding glass doors beckon me. The lettering reads: "Space Force Post Office." That makes my heart race faster. I can't wait to send my exchange, but more to receive Drae's reply. I can't wait to hear his voice, low and rumbling. But it's more than that. I want to feel him, mind, body, and soul. Simply put, to be inside his head again.

I try to keep my emotions in check, but they run wild anyway. And turn hotter when I remember the things he did to me—that I did to him—that we did to each other. My breath comes faster, while my cheeks burn with fire.

Lag time though. We've never dealt with this much. Could it take a week? Maybe longer? I burst into the post office, lost in memories and burning with anticipation.

Then I startle back.

My eyes fall on a familiar face.

How is this possible?

Dreamy, blue eyes stare back at me. He has that same wistful expression. His frame is diminutive and on the smaller side, but he looks stronger compared to when he shipped out.

"Kari . . . Skye . . . is it really you?"

He breaks into a warm smile from behind the mail counter. The post office looks similar to the other ones—beige paint, utilitarian furniture, and hard plastic chairs in the waiting area. Only, it's much smaller than the one back on Ceres Base.

I can't believe it. I rush inside and approach the counter. I grin at him.

"Anton . . . *Ksusha.*" I shift into a mock stern voice to tease him, "And that's *Captain* to you. Is that clear?"

"Yes, Captain Skye," he says, snapping off a tight salute.

Then we both break into silly laughter. Tears leak from my eyes. I remember joking around in the barracks, wrung out from PT, and punch-drunk at the same time.

"What in the *blazing* stars are you doing out here?" I'm unable to disguise my surprise to see my platoonmate.

"Asteroid fires, I should be asking you the same thing. Can you believe we've both gone . . . interstellar?"

That dreamy expression is back, the one I remember from the transport off Earthside when we first met. He's a certified space nerd. It's the main reason he enlisted. Being stationed all the way out here must be his dream come true.

"Wild, right?" I marvel at how far we've both come from our first days at basic. "But how is this possible? I thought you were assigned to Haven?"

"I *was* . . . past tense. But a lot has changed since we . . ." He trails off.

What lies unsaid. *Since we thwarted that alien invasion.*

He lets that slide between us like the recirculated air.

"Anyway, Postmaster Haven had me transferred from Ceres Base," he goes on. "He wanted me stationed here."

I take that in, absorbing the impact.

"So, they changed your orders, too?"

"Guess so. Like I said, a lot has changed. But that is the state of the universe, isn't it?" He turns dreamy again. "It's always changing . . . expanding . . . sometimes imploding. I arrived yesterday on a postal ship."

"That explains why you weren't on our transport," I say, piecing it together. "And how you beat us out here."

Postal ships are smaller and faster, designed quickly to carry our communications packages by warping through interstellar space. We're only as strong as our ability to communicate.

"Us?" he repeats. "You're saying, someone else got their orders changed?"

"Indeed. Luna is stationed here, too. She got deployed with me."

"Well, that is good news." He grins unabashedly. They were battle buddies back at Basic. In fact, she's the only reason he made it through. She practically had to drag his ass along.

But then his face falls.

There's a tense pause. He leans in.

"Don't you think it's *random* that we're all stationed out here?" he says while nonchalantly sorting the mail.

But his word choice is intentional. It triggers something inside me.

I remember what the drill sergeant told me once. *Nothing at Space Force is random.* He knows about that.

I decode what he's not saying out loud. Haven wanted him posted near me . . . just in case. But in case of what?

The terrifying possibilities rush through my head—another Astral invasion? A coup inside the Earth Federation? Or something . . . else?

Something worse?

Postmaster Haven has been like my protector since I first enlisted. The postmasters know more than regular guardians for one reason—they handle the communications for every base. All that information gives them power.

So, what does Haven know? Why is he so worried that he'd transfer Anton here to watch out for me?

I don't have the answer. From Anton's questioning expression, I don't think he does either. It's rare for him to be stumped like that. Regardless, I feel a surge of gratitude for Haven. I have Luna and now Anton stationed with me. They've become like my found family. We may be lowly guardians in a big war. But at least we've got each other, and that's what matters.

"Well, random or not, I'm thankful I'm not alone," I say, and I mean it.

He smiles. "Randomness can be a good thing. Lots of evolutionary leaps were the result of random mutations."

"Still nerding out?"

"On a daily basis."

I scan the post office. Like the rest of the base, it's completely deserted.

"Where is everybody?" I ask as a bot beeps and scurries past, pushing a mail bin. Even the bin is mostly empty. "Where are the other postal workers?"

Anton flashes that lopsided smile. He jerks his thumb to his chest.

"I'm the only one. Before me, it was all automated." He nods at the bot. "You're looking at the new postmaster."

That takes me back. A postmaster has a lot of power, and he's so green.

But then I remember, the postmasters operate autonomously from the rest of Space Force and govern themselves. What he may lack in years, he makes up for with his sharp intelligence. He's the smartest person I've ever met.

I give him an impressed nod.

"Postmaster Ksusha?"

He blushes. "Stop it . . . just call me Anton. No need to be so formal."

"But isn't that against the Space Force rules?"

"It's only against the rules if there's someone around to realize it's against the rules," he says with a sly grin.

"Point taken. And would you look at us? Guess we're in charge out here."

We share a moment. He sorts through the mail, reminiscing more. "Asteroid fires, we've come a long way from getting our butts kicked in PT."

I snort. "Ha! You most of all."

"Luna dragged my sorry ass for eight long weeks. I owe her one."

"A *big* one. And I owe your sister."

"Knowing Nadia, she'll never let you live that down. Trust me on that. Even if you do *technically* outrank her now."

"I hope I get to see her face again soon, so she can rub it in deeper."

We both chuckle, but then he turns more serious and gets back to business.

"Captain Skye, what brings you to the post office today? Your Sympathetic Exchange? I've been expecting you."

"Uh, yes!" I blurt out a little too eagerly. "I'd like to message . . . Drae . . . uh . . . I mean . . . my Sympathetic . . ."

He gives me an amused look. Heat blazes my cheeks. I can't believe I'm being so . . . obvious . . . kind of like a schoolgirl with a secret crush . . .

Anton knows how my relationship turned romantic. He even met Drae when he came to space, which is highly unusual since Sympathetic pairings are protected and kept secret.

"Right this way, Captain Skye," he says smoothly, glossing over my embarrassment. "I've got a mail pod booted up and waiting for you."

He leads me back into the bowels of the post office, opening the security door with a retinal scan. We continue into a corridor that looks utilitarian. A few bots scurry by pushing mail carts.

The post offices all have tunnels that connect directly to the docking bay, along with their own fleet of ships. They're like secret passageways that only the postal workers can access.

The corridor is hushed and feels more private. I decide to risk it.

I lower my voice. "Do you know where in the *blazing* stars we are?"

Curiosity bristles in the air between us. But he shakes his head and whispers.

"Even the coordinates for the packages are encrypted. Their destinations are scanned and loaded into the postal ship navigation systems, so they can operate on autopilot."

I'm shocked the postmaster doesn't know either.

"What about the name of the base? You've got to know that at least."

"It doesn't have a name."

"But . . . that's impossible. All the bases have names. They have to . . ."

I trail off. Silence rushes in, amplified by the soft hiss of the recirculated air.

"Not if they *technically* don't exist."

"What do you mean?"

He glances around, but the corridor remains deserted. He leans in closer.

"When Postmaster Haven handed me my new orders, even he seemed worried," he whispers. "He had to pull some major strings to get me stationed out here . . . wherever here is."

"That's creepy. Why so secretive? Why not even give the base a name?"

"I don't know, and that's what worries me. My guess is this is a hub . . . for what, I don't know. But something important. Probably dangerous, too."

"Right . . ." I say, feeling uneasy.

"Look, we all played key roles in stopping the Astrals. And now we're all deployed to the same base. They wouldn't ship us off to nowhere land—unless there was a good reason."

"You're right. That can't be random . . ." I start, but then clam up.

"And I'm guessing that it's probably got something to do with . . . *them*."

My briefing with Major Apollo replays in my head. Anton studies my face. He can tell that his hunch is right. However, as much as it pains me, I can't tell him about any of that. It's classified. I'm not used to keeping secrets from my closest friends. In Basic, we talked about everything. Already special ops feels like a burden, one that could alter who I am as a person.

I swallow hard against the bile that rises up in my throat. But I have to keep my mouth shut . . . for now . . .

Even if it kills me.

"I'm sorry . . . but I can't . . ." The words dry up in my throat, choked off.

But he nods and gives me a wink. "Don't worry. We'll talk more later."

With that, he unlocks the door and leads me into a smallish room filled with only a few mail pods. They're egg-shaped and freestanding. The ceiling and walls are padded to absorb noise. One is clearly waiting for me. He hits the button, and the door opens.

I take my seat in the ergonomic chair. It's kind of like a sling chair, but not designed to withstand G-force, but rather to absorb my emotional fallout. I'm not sure which is stronger—but I do know which is more likely to destroy me, and it's not the gravitational forces.

It's Drae.

Love and heartbreak.

Flip sides of the same coin.

I've seen Rho go through so many wild lovefests that inevitably implode into epic breakups and obliterate everything in their paths, leaving a gaping hole in space and time. I also worry about this possibility. We just fell in love . . . and already I'm thinking about the end of us. It's like I'm skipping through the story and fast-forwarding to the . . .

Unhappily ever after.

I know the reason—it's to protect my heart. I'm so used to bad things happening, terrible things, traumatic things that threaten to break me apart—that the idea of something *good* only makes me worry when it will go *bad*.

Even my parents—who are still madly in love and finally reunited—went through years of challenges being separated due to my father's service and then torn apart after he deserted.

I shudder at the memory. Can we endure my long tours of service and the increased lag time? I don't know.

And that worries me.

"How great is the lag time?" I ask Anton, peering through the pod door.

"Usually a week," he says, making my heart plummet. That means one week for Drae to get my message, and another week before I receive his reply.

"That long?" I say, feeling hopeless. That sounds like a lifetime when I'm already missing him this much.

"But in your case, I've put in a special expedited request. With the rush, we can shorten it to three days."

I breathe a sigh of relief. "Three days. So about a week total? I can do that."

I say that more for myself than him. I have to do it; I don't have a choice.

"You'll have ten minutes today. That's the standard protocol for first exchanges after deployment. Our studies show that anything longer can overwhelm both Sympathetics."

"Overwhelm them . . . how?"

"Their neural synapses. It's powerful technology, as you know."

"You mean, it can fry their brains?"

"Basically."

"Right, we don't want that."

"Exactly. And the stronger the connection with your Sympathetic grows, the greater the danger."

"And our connection?"

"I'm not supposed to say. But I've seen both of your brain scans and neural readouts. They're off the charts. It's the strongest connection the postmasters have ever seen."

"Ever?"

He nods. "According to Haven, in the entire history of the program."

That shocks me. I'm guessing at first it was the *hatred* that was off the charts.

Trust me, Draeden was my enemy.

And now, it's our . . . love. Talk about a mind screw.

"We'll evaluate your scans after your first exchanges and see if we can safely grant you more time. Okay?"

"Yes, I'd like to avoid getting my brain fried. Doesn't sound pleasant."

He smirks. "Duly noted."

The ambient music fades up louder, and I expect Anton to shut the pod, but he hesitates. Then he leans his head in.

"Tell Drae," he whispers. "Tell him . . . *everything*. Don't hold back."

Fear pricks the back of my neck. Sympathetics have security clearance, but they still censor our messages.

"What do you mean?"

He lowers his voice even more. "The postmasters convened. It's rare for them to do that. They only meet in person every few decades. Your exchanges won't be censored. The two of you are too important . . . your connection . . ."

"They convened to talk about us?"

He nods. "Right. They concluded that your connection is the only reason we survived. Censoring what you say in there . . . well . . . it's too dangerous."

"Won't Space Force intervene?"

He shrugs. "If they find out . . . maybe. But the postmasters have a lot of power. They'll protect you both."

I take that in, feeling more on edge. My mind jumps to the briefing with Apollo and the secrets he revealed. That's what Anton means. He wants me to tell Drae about the Astral settlement.

And there's more. This directive is coming from Haven directly. Not just Haven—but all the postmasters.

Before I can ask more questions, and there were like a million fighting to leap out of my mouth, Anton hits the pod door button.

"Enjoy your exchange, Captain Skye. I made sure to get Postmaster Haven's special aromatherapy recipe for you."

Lavender hits my nostrils, meant to relax me, but I feel a rush of adrenaline as the pod door seals with a soft *hiss*.

The lights dim and extinguish.

Harold's voice breaks through the darkness.

Initiating Sympathetic Exchange echoes through my head.

The timer in my retinas cues up:

10:00 Minutes

That's all the time we have today. But it's better than nothing. I remember Anton's warning. And let's just say, I'd rather avoid that nasty side effect.

Before I have time to gather my thoughts, I get the strangest brain-sucking feeling, like my neurons are being yanked out through the base of my skull. It's not pleasant. Everything blacks out, and then suddenly—

I'm somewhere else.

CHAPTER 8

DRAE

With my heart pounding, I rush out of class as soon as Professor Goode utters her final words. I can still see the message he tapped out on his tablet.

Better watch your back . . .

You're dead.

I need to get out of here—and fast. I charge through the doors and hurry into the hall with my head tucked down.

But the classes all let out at the same time, and the halls are suddenly packed with bodies. I get stuck in a logjam.

I fight to get through, feeling like I'm hyperventilating and have to get out of here. His face with the fresh scars and crooked nose keeps flashing in my mind like a warning, saying . . . *You did that. You did that. You did that. You're violent.*

But the swarm just pushes me back. The doors in front of me swing open.

That's when I see Jude.

He saunters out, having exited from the far side of the lecture hall. He looks completely unruffled and unflappable. He's got that Teflon politician smile. His backpack is casually slung over his shoulder. He spots me and grins. But it looks wolfish and predatory on him.

I skid to a halt, feeling the crowd push up behind me and force me toward him.

Then something else happens. Students who I don't recognize filter out of the crowd and form a loose shield around Jude. They stand between us.

Loki may have transferred, but they're clearly here to protect him.

But protect him from what?

Then I realize—

From me.

That sinks my stomach, making me feel sick. I examine them closer.

They're all preppy with short haircuts bordering on a military style and a haughty demeanor. They're the complete opposite of Rho or Willow.

Who are they?

But then it hits me. They've probably been planted on campus, too. I'm guessing they're transfer students.

But all of this for me?

I realize that my role in stopping the Astrals isn't so secret after all. His father works for the federation government. He's high-level. This could be his doing. My father also works with him. But since we stopped the aliens, my parents have shifted their opinion of me. They're both united in thinking the Astrals are our true enemy now.

But my dad warned me when I went back to Berkeley. He said that not everyone at the fed is happy about the shift from fighting the Proxy Wars to the Astrals. They don't support the United Earth Alliance; they don't trust our old enemies the Siberian and Arctic Feds.

Now, I wonder if his father, Mr. Luther, is one of the unhappy agents. The ones my father warned me about. It sounds like the divisions within our government are greater than I feared.

Jude glares at me. "So, you did miss me? Want to go another round, Rache?"

He raises his fists. Just like back in high school. Just like that time Kari embarrassed him and kicked his ass.

"You afraid of me?" he sneers.

The students surrounding him all laugh. That only encourages him. He loves being the center of attention.

He lowers his voice. "I heard about what you did with that *Park Rat*," he spits out, using the slur to mean Kari.

So, his dad did leak that much.

"Don't you dare call her that . . . ever," I spit through gritted teeth. "She's a guardian. She deserves respect—"

"She's deserter spawn and she always will be!"

Anger flares inside me. I want to punch him again. Like I did last time.

Like I did for that girl.

He wants me to take the bait and fight. And surely, I'll get pummeled. I'm badly outnumbered by his ring of protectors. He's hoping I'll swing at him—and this time, I would be the one getting expelled. He has witnesses. They'll say I attacked him unprovoked.

But it's so tempting. I dig my fingernails into my fists. He sees that.

"Come on, Drae! What are you afraid of? Don't tell me you're a coward."

He takes a step toward me, still careful to stay close to his bodyguards.

"Don't you want to finish what you started?" he hisses at me.

But I can't do that. I can't afford to get expelled. Trebond is depending on me, I remind myself. My role working for the Resistance is too important.

But something else holds me back. Something far worse. Getting expelled could damage my participation in the Sympathetic program. I can't risk it.

Losing Kari would destroy me.

Like a supernova.

That stays my fists that I didn't even realize I was clenching so tight.

He takes another step toward me. But instead, I spot an escape route. I turn and bolt through the winnowing crowd, chased by jeering laughter.

I cut across campus. I have one destination—I have to go to the library and tell Willow about what happened. As I traverse Memorial Glade, heading for Doe Library, something stops me.

Campus is crawling with security bots, more than before we averted the Astrals. In fact, the whole campus has a dangerous feeling. Like something is simmering, waiting to boil over.

Waiting to melt down.

The bots swarm around campus, pulling down the illegal, pastel-colored flyers that all proclaim "Disarm the Stars!"—the antiwar Resistance slogan.

Suddenly, I hear a robotic voice.

"Halt, right there!"

I freeze, my heart hammering in my chest. *That's it*, I think. I'm being arrested and detained. The bot focuses on me as its sirens and lights turn on. They resemble small, robotic tanks.

"Don't move!" the voice barks again as it speeds over to me.

I shut my eyes and wait for the worst. But then, it passes by me.

I crack my eyes back open. The bot targets a student behind me, cowering down. The lights hit her and scan her.

"Please . . . I'm sorry . . ." she says in a trembling voice, as she kneels down and puts her hands up behind her head.

The bot searches her. A robotic arm reaches out and snags her backpack.

It rips open.

A stack of flyers falls out of her backpack. The wind picks them up, scattering them across the lawn.

"You're under arrest," the bot barks. "For encouraging student dissidence."

She struggles, but the bot snaps electronic restraints around her wrists. She screams in pain and falls to the ground. The restraints shock you if you try to resist. She learned the hard way.

I watch, feeling my mouth go dry. I wish I could intervene, but I'm helpless.

And there's more—

That could be me . . . if I'm not careful . . .

I can't let that happen. I feel like a coward as I watch the bot drag the student away. They'll expel her.

Between Jude's reappearance and the arrest I just witnessed, I feel even more freaked out. But I force my legs to move. They carry me in a daze to the library. I traverse the steps and burst into the library, breathless and upset.

I lock onto Willow. She's working behind the front desk, scanning books.

I hurry over, feeling super paranoid. Anyone could be watching us. Anyone could be spying on us. I glance around nervously, wondering if any of the library patrons are planted here to spy on me. I can't forget seeing that student activist get arrested in front of me.

I halt at the front desk. When Willow sees me, she immediately knows something's wrong . . . very, very wrong.

"What in the blazing stars happened to you?" Willow whispers. "You look like you've just seen a ghost."

I lean in and lower my voice.

"That's because I did. And his name is Jude Luther. He's back on campus."

CHAPTER 9

KARI

Drae. I breathe out his name like a prayer as the alien landscape unfolds around me. This time, my breath doesn't freeze and cloud the air.

I look down at my boots. They sink into the loamy soil. I'm standing on the surface of this moon, surrounded by a crystalline forest of those organisms that I saw through the skylights on base.

One thing becomes quickly clear. Unlike Ceres, which was a glorified ice rock only suited to house our base because it had plenty of water in the form of ice frozen below the surface, this moon is bountiful and full of life.

Alien life, I remind myself.

That should make me feel afraid, but instead, I feel strangely exhilarated. After all, this is only a simulation of my approximate location. I'm not actually standing on the moon's surface.

Purplish light filters down through the swirl of clouds, refracting through the crystal branches into a kaleidoscopic light show. I take a step and bounce up in the lighter gravity, and then float down to land. My boots sink into the thick soil.

What looks like a trickle of water cuts through the earth ahead, flowing between the trees like a stream back Earthside. But it could be any liquid, I remind myself. Not necessarily potable water—possibly poisonous or worse.

But I'm not here right now to learn about the alien landscape or find out more about the Astrals. I'm here for one reason and one reason only—

I'm here for you.

The words whisper out of my life and dissolve into the thinner air. I summon Drae's memory into being—his light eyes and darker skin and longer hair since he started college. His lax demeanor that hides his keen intelligence and deep insecurities. The dimples that pop out of his cocky smile.

The ones that made me want to punch him in the face back in high school. Which I actually did once.

And I don't regret it.

He was being a total asshole.

But everything has changed. I've changed; he's changed; and here we are.

Drae, can you hear me? Can you hear the racing of my heart? Can you feel it? Even all these light-years away from Earth? This is science. Anton would tell you that.

But if you ask me—it's more like magic.

How they can translate our thoughts, emotions, feelings, words . . . even the beating of our hearts . . . and transport them millions of light-years away back to Earth and inject them into your neural synapses.

Now that is magic.

If only I could kiss you . . . instead of imagining your lips on mine . . .

Suddenly, a WARNING flashes in my retinas. Harold's voice pipes up.

Elevated heart rate detected. Kari, please try to control your emotions—or I'll have to end the exchange and alert medical.

Humiliation curls my stomach. I know how the exchanges work. This is all being recorded for Drae to experience back Earthside. I cringe inwardly, realizing that now he'll know how badly I want him . . . again.

Ugh, how embarrassing, I think back. *Mind your own business already!*

Harold goes mute. I'm guessing maybe Anton saw the warning and disabled it. He said to let go in here. He said our connection saved the world—and might be needed to save it again.

He said to tell you everything.

I see the timer—it's almost halfway gone. I have to get talking . . . and fast.

Drae, you're probably wondering where I am. Just like I'm wondering what you're doing back at college.

I guess we're both equally in the dark.

I knew it would be hard being separated from you. But I didn't realize it would be this hard. Like having half my soul ripped away and hidden from me.

This is so crazy to say, since when we first got paired, I would've done anything to avoid talking to you. And sharing my life with you.

Are you feeling the same way as me?

Do you miss me?

Or are you so happy to be back Earthside . . . that you barely think of me?

My heart sinks at the thought, weighted down with insecurity. I can't hide how I feel from him; that doesn't work in these exchanges. He doesn't just hear my words, but he feels me.

I glance at the timer.

Shit, it's almost run down.

I haven't even gotten to my mission or the Astrals yet. I start talking fast.

I'm here . . . which is nowhere, I say, glancing around. *It doesn't even have a name. It's because of our little friends.*

I start talking, and everything spills out. As quickly as I can, I share what I learned from Major Apollo. I tell him about the abandoned Astral settlement. How Secretary-General Andromeda is personally overseeing the operation. How shaky her position is with the Proxy tensions simmering again.

I know Drae is still working for the Resistance. This intel needs to be shared with them. They're the ones who discovered that the GGA was alien.

Now there's less than ten seconds left. I panic and word vomit at him.

Drae, I miss you . . . I need you . . . don't forget about me . . . because . . .

I love you even from these stars.

That's when the timer ticks down to zero. That brain-sucking feeling hits me again. Everything fades away—the crystalline forest, the amethyst skies.

I'm falling into the blackness.

Exchange recorded and transmitted. Disconnecting neural implant.

I'm breathless with my heart racing when the lights fade up in my mail pod. The lavender tickles my nostrils, making my stomach turn nauseous.

I pry myself out of the sling chair, feeling it release my body. I stagger out on weak legs. I'm still exhausted and adjusting after my trip. But more than that, it's the emotional fallout from talking to Drae. I worry I've pushed myself too far by not resting first.

But I didn't have a choice. My heart wouldn't let me do that to him.

I make it back to the lobby, where Anton waits. He gives me an expectant look. "How'd it go back there?"

I know that he monitors the exchange while it's in progress. He's the postmaster here. I also know he probably saw that heart rate warning.

But I definitely don't want to talk about that. Or anything like that.

Instead, I force myself to smile back.

"It was . . . *everything*."

I know he'll get my coded language. Bots race around, collecting the mail that he's sorting and ferreting it away. I never know how much we're being monitored, but better to be careful.

Anton flashes that lopsided smile.

"Very good, Captain. I'll inform you as soon as we receive his response."

"About a week?"

He nods. "Six days . . . if we're lucky and everything warps on schedule."

But as I step into the corridor, following the green arrows to my barracks, I feel more worried and torn than before. It's because I miss him. I thought sending him an exchange would alleviate the ache for him.

But it didn't. Not even close.

If anything, I miss him even more. And now I have to wait close to a week to hear back from him. I try to suppress my emotions like I used to. But I can't. They're wild and free now, unbridled and unbroken, and they trample me.

Again I wonder. Can we survive the lag time? And being this far apart?

There's no answer except the incessant beating of my heart.

Suddenly, somebody cuts into the corridor in front of me.

"Captain Skye?"

I startle back, so lost in my thoughts and the complicated tangle of emotions that the exchange unleashed. I'd also grown used to the corridors being deserted on this base. I look up.

The woman looks about sixty-ish with graying hair tucked back into a tight bun. Some errant strands still cling to their blonde roots, but the white hair is winning, ambushing and taking over. She's wearing one of those white lab coats. That makes my heart jump.

Two guardians flank her, both armed with blasters. That's a bad sign. Suddenly, I jolt back to the restricted door to the lab that I tried to enter.

Is that what this is about?

Before I can say anything, the woman taps at her tablet, confirming my identity, while the guardians stare me down unflinchingly to make sure I don't run for it. Then she speaks again.

Her voice sounds stern and bereft of any kindness, while her eyes sharpen.

"Captain Skye, please come with us. We need to speak to you right away."

CHAPTER 10

DRAE

"Jude . . . *Luther*," Willow says in surprise. "You're sure?"

The worry in her purple eyes matches mine. She knows who he is—and worse—just how dangerous.

Around us, the library buzzes with activity as students stream into the lobby and line up to check out their books. I'm holding up the line. But I don't care. I'm beyond shocked, but also angry now. I lean in and whisper.

"More than sure."

She takes that in, then nods. "Well, he's back earlier than expected."

"Wait . . . you *knew* about this? Why didn't you warn me sooner?"

She keeps shuffling books through the scanner, trying to act normal.

"Our operatives inside the fed were trying to block it. It seems they failed."

"Yes, they sure did," I shoot back.

"That's unfortunate," she agrees.

"But why keep this from me? Why not prepare me for the possibility of my archenemy showing up back at school?"

"Trebond didn't want you getting distracted from our core mission. We hoped it wouldn't come to this . . ."

"Well, newsflash—you're too late. I'm not just distracted. I'm freaked out. He's got some new facial scars. His nose didn't set right. All thanks to me."

"Right. I've been briefed . . . on what happened . . . between you and him."

She sets her lips. Guilt colors her cheeks. That softens my anger.

But only a little.

"Worse, he showed up in class," I continue in a low whisper. "Sat right next to me. Professor Goode even *welcomed* him back. Instead of taking notes, he spent the whole class typing threatening messages on his tablet . . . intended for me to snoop and read."

"That's not good," she says, pausing her work. "What did he write?"

"Here's the cliff notes. *Watch your back . . . you're dead.* That kind of fun stuff. Very on-brand for him. He's vindictive and never forgets a slight."

"Same goes for his father."

"Exactly. He's right under Secretary-General Andromeda. That means he has power. He works with my dad."

She nods. "He will protect you."

"Somewhat," I say, feeling guilty for my privilege. But it's also part of what makes me so valuable to the Resistance. "But how long will my father's influence keep me safe from them?"

Silence engulfs the lobby. That's answer enough. Neither of us knows.

"We need to check on the girl," I add, glancing around to make sure nobody is listening. The line behind me looks impatient, but they keep a respectful distance. It is a library, after all.

Willow flinches. "The girl? You mean . . . his victim?"

"Exactly. We need to make sure she's safe. If his father got him readmitted to Berkeley, then he'll have his operatives out looking for her . . . to *silence* her."

Willow nods. "I'll get a message to Trebond right away. We've got her in a bunker. She joined up . . . to fight back."

That makes me feel a little better. If she's surrounded by Resistance fighters, then that's the safest place for her. But terrible thoughts rush through my head anyway of what it all means.

"Anything else?" Willow says, handing me a book. "This is for you."

I give her a confused look. I didn't pick out a book to check out. But then I get it. This book . . . it's a message.

"Uh, no . . . that's it."

"Enjoy your book," Willow says with a nod, slipping into her librarian role. "I think you'll find it's a real page-turner. You should read it right away."

"Thanks. I will.

"Oh, one more thing. When you're finished, bring it back right away."

My hands feel the cool leather-bound cover. I tuck it under my arms with a polite nod, then leave her to the line. Her words echo through my head.

She said to read it right away. Her meaning is clear. I just wonder what secrets this library book contains.

One thing I know for sure—

They're dangerous.

Instead of heading back to my dorm room across campus, I rush into the reading room and slide behind the desk. Each desk has a leather chair and a personal desk lamp that looks old-fashioned, like it's from pre-war.

My heart thumping, I examine the book that Willow strategically gave me. She said I needed to read it right away.

A Farewell to Arms is embossed in gold, pressed into the leather. The author is Ernest Hemingway. I haven't read him yet, but I know I should.

I flip through the aging pages, looking for something . . . anything. That's when

I find it. A card is shoved into the pages like a bookmark.

Thick, creamy card stock.

I recognize it right away. The looping calligraphy can only be from Trebond.

My breath catches in my throat. I read the message.

Drae, I'm glad you're back safe and sound. I wish I had better news. But this message is a warning. Watch your back. Jude isn't the only spy being planted at U of Berkeley.

That makes my heart drop. Jude is a spy . . . for the feds and his father. She's also saying there's more of them. I remember the unfamiliar students that crowded around him like a shield.

Then I read the next part.

The Astrals aren't our only enemy. The war for our future isn't over. Far from it. The war . . . it's just beginning.

I've heard that the Earth Federation isn't as united as the newsfeeds want us to believe. That the old factions threaten our unity. Not just our former Proxy enemies, but also hard-liners from inside our own federation. My father mentioned it, too. I'm guessing that Jude's father must be one of them.

And that makes Jude more dangerous. He was sent here to spy on me. But he's not the only one. I glance around the reading room. I spot someone leaning against a bookshelf, pretending to flip through a book.

But they look familiar.

Was she with Jude earlier?

I can't be sure. But she looks like one of them . . . preppy and stuck-up . . . like a Ringer. I hunker down over my book and keep reading the secret letter.

I fear we are fighting an enemy without knowing anything about them—except that they have the power to destroy us.

We need to find a diplomatic solution. We need engagement, not more bloodshed. The wars aren't over. The Proxies have only been replaced by another enemy to fight.

War will only lead to more war. Until we Disarm the Stars, we will never be free.

Her words resonate with me. We've moved from one endless war to another without even pausing to consider if there is actually a military solution. More bloodshed only begets more bloodshed. The Astrals already proved they could infiltrate our Earthside defenses and plant a powerful weapon. We still don't know how they did it.

Trebond is right. We know almost nothing about them, except they've demonstrated how easily they can push us to the brink of war and our own self-destruction. Instead of proving that humanity isn't a violent and warlike species, we're doing the exact opposite.

Trebond is right. We need to find out if there is a diplomatic solution.

I read the last part quickly.

Trust Willow. Do what she says. I've known her since she was a baby. She's one of my most trusted field operatives.

Report any new or suspicious activity on campus to her right away. One more thing. Stay in touch with your friends in the stars. Especially your Sympathetic. You're both more important . . . than you know.

—Your old professor

Those last words make my heart lurch. *Kari*. I don't know when I'll hear from her next. Only that she's been deployed to an interstellar outpost.

I just hope that her exchange reaches me soon. The lag time will be greater. But I can't worry about that now. Too many other worries crowd my brain.

Quickly, I scrawl a message on the back of the card for Trebond. My handwriting is messy and unkempt, nothing like Trebond's elegant calligraphy. The same writing that hooked me and got me into the Resistance back when I thought it was a college secret society.

Jude is back at school, as you know. He showed up in class and threatened me. He also has a lot of "new" friends here.

Fed Patrols also increased on campus. Saw a student posting illegal flyers detained and arrested broad daylight.

The campus feels . . . dangerous . . . like a nuclear warhead waiting to detonate.

—Your old student

I sign it that way, then I slip it back inside the book and return to the front desk. I wait in Willow's queue. Evenings are busy times at the library, due to after-class studying and reading.

I wind through the velvet ropes, getting closer. I study her face. She's a good actress. Her eyes dart my way, but she keeps her movements relaxed and natural as she goes through the motions, scanning barcodes, stacking books, and handing them over to the student.

Finally, I reach the front.

"Next," she calls to me.

Her eyes skim over me. I slide the book back. "I'd like to return this."

"So soon?"

I shrug. "It wasn't for me. Lots of other books have their eyes on me."

She meets my gaze. Suddenly, I feel a rush like the first time we met. Like fire blazes through me, hardening me.

Something about the way the heat sparks between us tells me something else. Something also very dangerous.

She feels it, too.

Her cheeks have a light pink flush, while her eyes dance around me. Her nostrils flare like she's breathing me in. So, I'm not the only one feeling this connection. But I wonder if she knows about Kari? And the true nature of our bond? That it had turned romantic?

Trebond said it was important, more than we realized.

Breaking the moment, I reach over and tap the returned book. "There was an important message in the pages. Hemingway had a lot to say in his story. You should read it, too."

She nods. "Of course. I'd love to *read* it."

She slides the book toward her, then she reaches under the desk and pulls out another book. She hands it to me. "Take this book home instead. It's fantasy and a shorter read, but quite impactful. How does that sound?"

"Uh, yes. Thanks."

The book is slimmer and looks like it's for younger readers. *A Wrinkle in Time* by Madeleine L'Engle reads the front cover. Immediately, I wonder what message lies hidden in the pages. My heart beats faster as I shove it into my backpack and turn to leave.

But Willow stops me.

"Wait . . . Drae . . ."

"What is it?" I whisper back. Our eyes lock again, and I feel those flutters. She glances around. The crowded lobby is dying down. She decides to risk it.

"Look, I'm not supposed to tell you this," she says in a low voice. "They want to control the information flow."

I roll my eyes. "Right. So I don't get distracted and all that nonsense."

She smiles, then turns serious.

"Look, I don't like keeping you in the dark. Things are happening fast, and we have to work together. It's not just you that they're watching. It's all of . . . us."

"Wait, you're saying there are more of us?" I say, surprised. "On campus?"

She nods quickly. "More than you know. I'm not just your agent handler. There's another reason I'm here—I'm recruiting for the cause. And I'm not the only one . . ."

I take that in. It makes sense, too. Jude's father is planting his spies on campus to agitate for war, so Trebond is planting hers, too. And they're both recruiting students to join them.

"For the Resistance?" I ask in a low voice. But she shakes her head firmly—*No*—while slipping the book with the message that I wrote for Trebond into her bag.

Her next words shock me.

"For the . . . *revolution*."

CHAPTER 11

KARI

"Captain Skye, I know we haven't officially met yet," the scientist says.

She led me away to her office. It's nondescript in a different wing of the base from Major Apollo. Otherwise, the furnishings are about the same. The whole way here, my heart was racing.

Not just racing—*pounding*.

The way they intercepted the two guardians made me feel like I did something wrong. They're still posted right outside the doors with blasters ready. The scientist studies me.

On closer inspection, her eyes are so pale blue they're almost white; she also has a pointy nose and high cheekbones. Her frame is thin but strong. Now, I notice that her lab coat has pins on the lapel indicating that she's high-ranking.

"I'm General Titan," she says, following my gaze to her lab coat. "I know my uniform is a little unusual," she says, sliding behind her desk. "But I promise, there's a good reason. I'm the lead researcher on base."

A general *and* a scientist. I stand up straighter and salute her right away.

"Yes, ma'am."

But she shakes me off. "At ease, guardian. You can speak freely here. You'll find that my uniform isn't the only thing that's different about me."

She smiles at me. It's supposed to put me at ease, but something about her gives me the creeps. I can't explain it. Maybe it's because it doesn't reach her eyes. She gestures for me to sit in the hard plastic chair facing her desk.

I do as ordered anyway. I don't want to keep her waiting. My mind spirals with worries, making my mouth go dry.

"General, is this about the lab?" I force out, remembering how I tried to enter the restricted area. "Well, I can explain. I'm new here and just got turned around—"

She shakes his head. "No, it's not about that—it's about something else."

That doesn't make me feel better. My stomach sinks. I wait for her to go on.

"As I'm sure you've ascertained by now, we're a small base. A remote interstellar outpost. In fact, even inside Space Force, few have the security clearance to know about our existence."

Those words chill me.

"Yes, sir. I have noticed that."

She nods. "As the lead scientist on base, the Sympathetic Program falls under my purview."

"Is that what this is about?" I ask, feeling even more worried. I flash back to the exchange I just recorded. They intercepted me leaving the post office.

This is about . . . *Drae*.

"Yes, consider it an intervention," she goes on. "For your own good, of course. And for your Sympathetic, too."

I don't like how that sounds.

"Intervention?"

She shrugs. "Maybe more of a warning." She leans forward, and her eyes narrow sharply. "You are aware that we caution against romantic entanglements with your Sympathetic."

My cheeks start to burn. I look down in shame. "Yes, it was in the orientation. But it wasn't explicitly forbidden . . ."

I feel it's better not to go into any more details. *She knows*, I realize.

"That's because forbidding it would be counter to the intention of the program. We can't have you entering into these pairings with your guard up and trying to shield your emotions."

"Of course not. That would defeat the entire purpose of the program. We have to share everything for it to work."

"Exactly. Well said."

She slides out a file. Suddenly, I feel like everyone on base has files on me.

"We find it best to let your Sympathetic relationships evolve naturally. And then intervene if we have to, rather than have you closed off."

"That makes sense," I say, trying desperately to keep my voice even.

But failing miserably.

"Let me reiterate that you're not in trouble, Captain. I'm not the principal. You're not getting detention."

"More like extra PT," I say with a wince, taking a stab at dark humor.

She cracks a small smile.

"Yes, I can see your drill sergeant taught you well." She taps the file, where a chart is displayed. "Your exchange generated an alert that I received as the officer in charge. So, I pulled your neural readouts. The data shows that your attachment to your sympathetic has grown deeper. And much stronger."

I can see the big spike in the chart. There are dates below it.

The spike is . . . well . . . from right after . . . we . . .

Yeah, that. I want to die of mortification right here and now.

General Titan seems to know what happened, too.

"We only see this level of connection if there are romantic entanglements."

"Uh, right, I'm sorry about that," I stammer, wondering just how much she really knows about what we did. "I'll control my emotions better next time . . ."

I trail off. The tension ripples in the air like electricity. She smiles again.

"You're not in trouble, Captain Skye. Consider this an informal warning, really. Neural connections are powerful. The tech is unlike anything in the history of humanity. In terms of our species, sharing this kind of brain connectivity is a very recent evolution."

I nod quickly. "It's so unlike . . . anything I've ever experienced."

"I know . . . I have one, too," she says, tapping her implant at the base of her skull. "You're also aware of the benefit. I was briefed on your involvement in stopping the Astrals. Even from this data, I can see that the connection to your Sympathetic is rare and so critical, and why you were assigned here."

"That makes it sound like our relationship is a good thing. Strategically speaking, of course. So, I'm guessing there's a catch. What is it?"

That makes her frown. "Yes, there are downsides. When the connection is this strong. If it goes south. If your feelings change . . . or if his change . . ."

"What do you mean . . . change?" I ask, feeling my anxiety spike.

My old fears of abandonment from when my father deserted resurface with a vengeance. Classic daddy issues, even though I know it was my father's fault.

"If you stop . . . feeling so much connection," she says delicately. "Or worse, if he's unfaithful. If you are—"

"Unfaithful? Drae?"

My heart plummets. What does she know? That I don't know about him?

"Don't worry. We're speaking in hypotheticals. Nothing has happened . . . yet. And I don't wish this for you. But you have to understand, it happens."

I nod. "Of course . . . my best friend in high school had a lot of breakups. Uh, she's a bit on the dramatic side."

General Titan gives me an understanding smile, making every bit of my young eighteen years.

"Yes, it happens. We've been through this exact scenario in the program before. Well, not with readings this high."

"They're high?"

"The highest level of connection we've ever seen. The AI did its job pairing you. That much is clear."

That shocks me. I thought everyone experienced their Sympathetic deeply. Well, maybe not the *love* and *sex* part. But the depth of connection part.

To learn that we're unique? That's new, and very unsettling, too.

"What happened to the others?" I ask, though I'm not sure I want to know. "When they broke up?"

She sets her lips into a thin line. "That's why I'm giving you this warning today. We're not just talking about simple heartbreak here. Or them discovering your infidelity . . ."

"He would never . . . I would never . . ." I stammer.

But then I remember how Major Apollo made me feel.

My body responded even when my brain screamed to resist. And then there's Drae. He's had plenty of girls fawn over him. I remember how it was in high school with him and his popular friends. He could've dated any girl.

But for some reason, he caught feelings for me, even though I hated his guts. And then we got paired together. And now, he's back at college with a million other girls and parties and more. I trust him, but there is temptation. I already felt a taste of it with Apollo.

General Titan reads my expression. "I won't sugarcoat it . . . it could *shatter* his mind. Or vice versa . . . he could . . ."

"*Shatter my mind*," I choke out. The words feel like sandpaper in my throat.

That hangs in the air for a long moment. I knew something like that could be bad. But I didn't know how bad, or how dangerous it was for us.

To fall in love.

"Like I said, after I saw your neural scans, I had to caution you. I don't think this will happen with your pairing."

"But it's happened before?"

She nods. "Sadly, yes. Even our most intensive rehabilitation programs couldn't bring them back. Their neural scans showed severe brain damage."

"Brain damage?"

"Yes, the scans almost resemble late-stage dementia. That's how severe."

Her words echo through my head again. *Brain damage . . . shatter his mind.*

But I clear my expression. I can't let her in. "Yes, General. Thank you for the warning. But . . . our relationship . . . it's not against the rules, is it?"

"No, but it's strongly discouraged. Emotional connection and openness—yes. That's the point of the program. But don't confuse that for . . ."

"*Love?*" I say with a wry twist to my lips. "Look, this is a total head screw."

She raises her eyebrows. "How so?"

I decide to risk speaking freely. "You put an implant in my neurons. Jack it straight into somebody else's brain. How am I supposed to stay neutral? And you said it yourself. Our connection is rare. The strongest you've ever seen. Major Apollo said it, too."

"Yes, it was key to stopping the Astrals. It's why you're stationed here."

"Exactly. And Drae . . . me . . . we're not like that . . . we'd never . . ."

The words sound silly even to my young ears. If it were Rho saying that, I'd point out her checkered dating history, how fickle an organ the human heart can be, and how most marriages end in divorce, and give her a reality check.

But my heart protests against my head. It tells me . . . we're different.

We have to be.

Because the alternative . . .

Shatter his mind.

The emotions must be playing out over my face. The general shoots me a sympathetic smile. "Look, your assignment here is critical," she says, sensing my worries. "We're facing another impending Astral invasion."

"We stopped them once, but we didn't destroy them. They'll try again."

"Exactly. So, we can't have you getting too distracted, or worse . . ."

"General Titan, I promise to keep my emotions in check. I appreciate the warning, but you can trust . . . us."

"Let's hope so," she says, but she doesn't sound convinced. "The fate of humanity may depend on you both."

That's the last thing she says before she dismisses me. She also says that she'll issue orders for the postmaster to monitor us more closely. Luckily, that's Anton—and I can trust him completely.

Haven put him here for a reason. Now, I realize just how important he is. However, we'll just have to be more careful and avoid triggering more warnings. I'll have to try to control myself. *Easier said than done*, I think as I stumble out of her office.

The green arrows appear again, summoning me to my barracks finally. My body feels weak, as if sapped of all energy by the sudden gravity, not just of the base—but the gravity of his heart pulling me deeper into this love.

This love that could also be our destruction, as I've just learned. I do trust him; I have to . . . but doubt lingers.

We're young. We're dumb. We just saved the world. But our future feels so unknown. With deployment, my biggest worry was staying alive. And now?

Everything just got a lot more complicated. He's at college, around a lot of temptation. And then there's me. My heart was locked in an iron vault before he breached all my defenses. Scaled my walls and invaded my heart.

And now—I feel like I can't trust it anymore. Like it could rebel again. Fall in love when I strictly forbid such a thing. The questions linger, worrying me. How can I trust him? But more importantly—how can I trust myself?

I think of Major Apollo again. How forbidden and terrible to consider doing anything with him, not to mention that he wouldn't return my attraction. There's zero chance of that. So, why does my heart beat faster around him? Why does it want me to self-destruct and implode?

And worse, shatter Drae's mind.

That's impossible. I would never do that to him. So why do I feel so unsure?

CHAPTER 12

DRAE

Watching my back, I hurry from the library with the precious book tucked into my bag. Willow's confession swims through my head. She's recruiting for . . .

The revolution.

That means the Resistance isn't just operating in the shadows anymore. They're planning for outright revolution. Maybe even to overthrow the government. And they're actively recruiting on campus for the cause.

That's enough to rattle me.

Clearly, Trebond has plans she hasn't shared with me. That troubles me. Something else is bothering me, too. Willow wasn't supposed to tell me. One thought rushes through my head—

Can I really trust my old professor?

Regardless, this is more dangerous than I realized. My sneakers churn the paved walking paths. Memorial Glade spreads out before me. Straight ahead, the Campanile towers over me, keeping time. The clock face shines like a beacon. Evening is falling, letting stars emerge.

I remember the first challenge that Rho and I completed there, back when we didn't know it was a test to see if we could be recruited to the Resistance. Back when we thought it was a Berkeley secret society. Oh, we were so naïve.

That makes me miss Rho. Being able to talk to her about . . . well . . .

Everything.

Not to feel so alone in all of this. She would help me think through it. Analyze and break it down. Willow is supposed to be my confidante now, but suddenly, I'm questioning everything.

Was that secret a true confession?

Or is that a tactic?

To get me to trust her . . . Trebond echoed that in her message . . .

Trust Willow.

But suddenly, I feel like I'm being manipulated. I'm suspicious of everyone and everything.

I glance around as a chill envelops the air. The campus doesn't feel welcoming anymore. Security bots swarm the footpaths, scanning students. But more than that, any student could be on any side. They could be spies.

Now, I see signs of it everywhere. The wind kicks up, sweeping through the buildings. A flyer flutters up to my foot. It's in a pastel shade of green.

I reach down and sweep it up. I scan the hand-copied print. It's funny how the more advanced tech got, the more we've gone back to old forms of communication. For one simple reason.

They can't be hacked.

There's a corny graphic of an alien. The bubble-shaped head and elongated eyes perched over a thin-lipped mouth.

ANNIHILATE THE ASTRALS!
Join the Anti-Astral movement!
7PM @ Founders' Rock

It's hardline pro-war propaganda. The meeting is tomorrow night. The language worries me, seeming to advocate for genocide. I look up to see where it came from, but come up empty.

This campus no longer resembles an idyllic university—it's a war zone. I can feel tension simmering in the shadows and electrifying the air. The security bots patrolling. The warring pamphlets.

Anti-Astral and *Disarm the Stars*.

I tuck my head down and take the route back to my dorm, feeling uneasy.

This college is a battlefield.

One thing is clear. Kari's not the only one on the front lines now.

I am, too. And so is every single student enrolled here.

I hurry into the common room. My new roommates, Sylvia and Theo, crowd the ragged futon. She has thick black glasses and blunt-cut bangs. They contrast sharply with her cherubic face. He's tall and lanky with a sloucher vibe.

But they're both whip-smart and not to be underestimated. I don't know them well, but it's been a relief housing with them after what I went through.

I was transferred here after the whole incident with Jude and Loki.

They glance my way at the sound of the door snapping shut behind me.

"Gaming, wanna join?" she says, tipping back her enormous headphones.

"Just tore this team a new one," Theo says with a smirk. He has earbuds in.

I suspect there *might* be something romantic between them. But I haven't wanted to rock the roommate boat.

"Ha, they're no match for my space warlock," Sylvia adds. "Total losers."

On their tablets, I spot a popular fantasy multi-player game. Their cartoonish avatars swarm the surface of a deserted moon, battling space monsters and aliens from a rival team.

"Thanks, but I'm more old-school," I say, already slinking toward my room. "Two-dimensional comics are my jam."

"Yeah, remember?" Sylvia quips. "His girlfriend is Estrella Luna."

"Oh right," Theo says. He glances my way. "Drae, you're an old soul."

"Yeah," she adds. "But I admire your devotion to post-war propaganda."

With that, I duck into my room and shut the door. I wish I could be more social with them. But I'm worried about getting too close to anyone these days. Clearly, what I'm involved in . . .

It's too dangerous.

I shut the door behind me gently, making sure that it clicks and locks.

Then I flick on my reading light and slip into the single bed. I retrieve the book that Willow gave me from my backpack. I feel a rush of adrenaline, wondering what this one contains.

Who else besides Trebond could have a secret message for me?

I flip through the pages. They flutter in front of my face, smelling bookish.

It falls out.

I see the signature immediately. It's from Rho. That makes me sit up.

She's Kari's best friend from high school, but after she enrolled at Berkeley with me, we became best friends. Actually, the truth is that she threatened me. She wanted to be kept informed about Kari since we got paired together.

I think . . . *on actual pain of death.*

Anyway, we both ended up getting recruited for the Resistance and going to space to avert the war, but Rho fell hard for a feisty Raider who was Kari's father's second-in-command named Gunner. Once everything was over, she decided to stay up in the stars.

I haven't heard anything since I came back Earthside. Between not hearing from Kari since her deployment and Rho since she stayed behind, I feel like I'm in the dark. I read the note eagerly.

Dearest Drae, ahoy!

A report from sailing the star-seas! You're probably wondering about me. Am I still alive? Are we still friends with me in the stars? Did the Raiders eat me?

Pssst . . . they're vegan, remember?

That's just propaganda. And you're back in propaganda-land a/k/a the California Federation, so don't forget what you've learned. I'm finally having adventures like I read about in my books. Kari's family has welcomed me into their little Raider family.

It's especially cute to see Bea with her dad finally. She's like a mini Captain Skye, always ordering me and Gunner around (for the record, yes . . . we're still . . . smooching).

Anyway, I guess I miss you. I asked Trebond to get this message to you at Berkeley. Don't rub it in . . . or it'll ruin my rep. Hope you haven't forgotten about me.

Your starless friend,

Rho

P.S. Don't you dare break Kari's heart! Not now that you've done the impossible and cracked it open! Or I'll murder you.

P.P.S. That threat is real! I have space pirate friends. Fear me, Draeden Rache!

P.P.P.S. Be careful. We hear a lot up here. Rumblings of Proxy tensions . . . the Astrals coming back . . . none of it is good . . .

Stay safe, dearest friend!

I set down the handwritten pages. My heart races faster after reading that last part. Oh, and the part about breaking Kari's heart. It's like Rho can see through me even from space.

How is that possible? I guess that's what it means to be true friends. They can sense your feelings and predict your actions even when you're far apart.

Guilt rushes through me for lusting after Willow (unintentionally . . . it was like my body responded even though my head was screaming, *Noooooo!*). But I'll do better next time. I promise myself. Keep my starless thoughts in check and turn that part of myself off.

But doubt creeps in anyway. Around her, I felt like my old self again—the cocky Ringer who got everything handed to him on a silver platter. Seeing Jude made me realize how far I've come, and how much I've changed.

Kari changed me . . .

Our love changed me.

I don't want to blow it. I don't want to break her heart. Not when the fate of the universe depends on her service. Not when she's the only thing I care about in this whole blasted universe.

I don't want to fall back into my old ways. I didn't like myself before. I was a coward, and I treated people badly.

My greatest fear is reverting. That the change is only on the surface. That I can't truly change. That once set, humanity falls back into predictable patterns ingrained in us since birth, maybe programmed in our primitive DNA. The Astrals saw that and tried to use it against us. And it almost worked.

Almost.

We came so close to being destroyed and losing everything we hold dear.

I set Rho's message aside. Her friendship makes me think maybe these are only worries and they're not true.

But as I fall into a restless sleep full of fragmented dreams—where Kari is always just beyond my reach, screaming my name and clawing at my flesh, while Willow beckons me with sultry kisses—I worry that I'm going to blow it.

And destroy us both.

CHAPTER 13

KARI

I head to the barracks, following the green arrows, still plagued by worries over Drae and our bond—the strongest they've ever seen. General Titan said that it spiked recently. That means, right after we consummated our love.

That alone makes me shiver with desire, but also shrivel with shame. That others know—or at least suspect—what we did on that unaccounted-for day.

Including my superior officers.

I wonder how much Major Apollo knows about our relationship, which sends my mind spiraling down a darker path. I fight to banish those thoughts and tamp down my reckless and impulsive emotions, even though they refuse and run wild anyway.

I hope I'm not losing it. I hope these aren't the first symptoms of space trauma. Or maybe this is just how being in love feels. Like you're in over your head and know you're going to drown, but you want to keep swimming anyway. I wish I could ask Rho about it, but that's just not possible right now.

I find my barracks. It's a compact room with a bunk bed, dresser, lockers for our belongings, and a small bathroom off the side door. The privacy is a nice perk.

The overhead lights dim, and I realize that it's already late on base.

I collapse on the naked mattress on the lower bunk, letting out a moan.

"That bad, huh?"

Luna leans her head over from the top bunk. She had clearly crashed out under her blanket. She blinks at me sleepily. So, that part hasn't changed.

She's still on top of me. *Literally.*

Just like back at basic training.

"Did they brief you?" I ask, flipping over and rubbing my tired eyes.

"Roger that. Secret moon base. Abandoned alien settlement outside our doorstep. We don't know shit about them. And they're going to kill us—unless we change that. And fast."

"That about sums it up."

"Did I miss anything?"

"*Anton.*"

She sits up straighter and looks worried. He was her battle buddy.

"Is he okay?"

"Yes—and he's here." Quickly as I can through my exhaustion, I tell her Postmaster Haven had him transferred here and that he's now the postmaster of our secret base.

"So . . . we're all here?"

I nod. "Random coincidence."

"Nothing is random," she parrots back. "You know that. I know that. That leaves only one question. Why us?"

"Because we saved Earth. He said we're more open-minded and suited for intel."

She snorts out a derisive laugh. "I wish I believed it worked that way. But something tells me—it's not that simple. Nothing at Space Force is."

"You're right. Everything is a complete and total mind fuck?"

"Yup. Pretty much. I just wonder what this specific mind fuck entails, so I can better prepare myself for it."

"With lots of lube," I joke back.

We both dissolve into punchy laughter. It's a crass joke, but crass jokes somehow make everything feel better when you signed your whole life away and have exactly zero control over it. We fall silent as the lights dim even more, signaling it's time to sleep. The moon has its own daylight and nightfall schedule, but we don't adhere to that. We keep to the twenty-four-hour clock back on Earth. It would mess with our circadian rhythms too much otherwise.

So that means our bedtime could be morning on the moon or the opposite. Sometimes it all aligns, and that feels special, like an eclipse back home.

Finally, Luna breaks the silence. Her voice comes out in the barest whisper. "Isn't it crazy how much everything has changed? Since we first enlisted?"

"*Crazy* doesn't begin to describe it. Bonkers. Insane. Unfathomable."

"You wanted front lines? You weren't afraid of . . . well . . . dying?"

"Dying still scares me. I'm human, right? But I was looking forward to turning my brain off and fighting. Waking up to the smell of blaster fire in the morning. Fighting is what I'm good at. Pretty much the only thing, really."

She rolls her eyes at me.

"Shut *the stars* up."

"What do you mean?"

"You're good at so much. What's crazy is that you don't even realize it."

"Intel? Get real! I'm way out of my depth here, and we both know it. You're so smart it hurts. This is your specialty."

"Well, I think you just might surprise yourself. Plus, the front lines . . . they don't matter anymore. The Proxy Wars are over. There's a peace alliance now."

"It's fragile, already fragmenting . . . from what I hear. I think the Astrals might be right about us. Humans are warlike at heart. We can't help it. We have to destroy everything we touch."

She leans down lower, so her torso hangs off the top bunk. She peers at me.

"Yes, but don't you see? That's why the Astrals might be a good thing!"

"Uh, how are kid-killing aliens who want to destroy Earth a good thing?"

She flinches at that. "Right, not the kid-killing part. But think about it. They gave humanity a common enemy to fight against. That's the only thing that ended the wars. Without them, we'd still be fighting . . . endlessly."

I want to disagree with her. I want to defend my own species. But looking back over our history, I can't do that.

Instead, I just nod sadly.

"But maybe we can do better. Be better. Grow. Evolve. Change."

I think of Drae and how much he changed since we got paired, from the privileged Ringer asshole . . . into someone I could fall in love with.

"Sure, okay," she says sarcastically. "Believing in that is like believing in . . ."

"*Aliens?*" I say with a good laugh. "Well, it turns out they're real. So, maybe my peace fantasies can be, too."

We leave it on that note. Better than to give in to the darkness, which feels more real and powerful right now, just like the void of space. But I remind myself that even in that dark vacuum, there are still glimmers of starlight.

I think about how my life could've taken a different turn. How I could be stationed in a dug-in trench on some forsaken moon with a blaster clutched in my hand and explosions blooming all around me and destroying everything.

But Luna is right. That world battling Proxies endlessly is over.

This is the front lines.

So, I still got my wish. Only it's not a battlefield fighting Proxies like I expected. The war effort has shifted that quickly. If what Major Apollo says is true, then intel is the *new* front lines.

We can't fight an enemy we don't know—and worse, can't even find.

We can't fight a ghost.

The bedtime warning goes out over the base. Harold also informs me. The lights are going to extinguish soon. I almost miss the drill sergeant chewing us out as part of our bedtime routine.

Almost.

At least it was a familiar routine. And now, I'm somewhere new and unfamiliar. It feels like starting over from scratch. Right before the lights go out, when I'm already drifting away, there's a sharp *rap* on the barracks door.

Luna jumps to attention, ready to fight, but then relaxes. She goes over and opens the door, revealing—

It's Major Apollo.

I'm shocked to see him. Only he looks almost ready for bed, too. His top few buttons are undone. I've never seen an officer not fully buttoned up.

My cheeks flush even noticing that. Luna goes to salute him, but he signals her at ease. His eyes find mine.

"Captain Skye, can I have a moment?" he says in a gravelly voice.

He's exhausted, too. I'm not the only one who had a long, stressful day.

My heart vaults into my throat. "Yes, sir. Is everything okay?"

I follow him out into the corridor. The barracks door shuts behind me. I can feel Luna's eyes boring through it, wondering what this is all about. I'm wondering the exact same thing. Is this about General Titan? And my Sympathetic? Ugh, why does everyone have to know?

But he surprises me.

"Sorry, I didn't mean to bother you. Just wanted to make sure you're okay . . . with everything . . ." He trails off awkwardly. I can tell he's uncomfortable.

I can also tell that his question is genuine. That shocks me more than anything I learned today. I'm used to my CO berating me. Not expressing concern for my well-being.

"You mean, the Astrals?" I guess.

He nods. "Some guardians. Well, the idea of aliens outside their doorstep . . ."

I let out a nervous chuckle. "Let me guess. It totally freaks them out?"

"Yeah . . . that. Exactly."

"I'm fine." I say it a little too curtly.

"Captain, don't lie to me."

It's a command; it sends a shiver up my spine. I feel like he's probing my mind again, rifling through my emotional state. But that's impossible. That only happens with Drae because of our neural links. I try to shake it off.

And focus.

But *something* about him makes it really hard. Maybe it's the unbuttoned uniform or the raw concern he's showing for me. Something I'm hungry for . . . something I've been hungry for my whole life . . . but it rivets me.

"Look, I'm not gonna lie," I try again. "I am freaked out. But I'm more freaked out if we don't do something to stop them. Does that make sense?"

He smirks. "So you're saying . . . one greater fear overrides the other fear? I like that. I knew you were different."

He gives me a conspiratorial smile that makes fire erupt in my cheeks, and now my body. Even my knees go soft.

I try to hide it, but I can't stop feeling that he's probing the inner sanctuaries of my mind. *Get out!* I think sharply.

He flinches back. It's subtle, but I notice it. That weird feeling also goes away in an instant. His eyes harden. "Get some sleep, Captain," he says in a curt voice.

"Yes, sir," I reply in an equally curt voice. Two can play this game.

"Tomorrow is about to get . . . *freakier*," he adds in a confiding tone.

"What do you mean, sir?"

He hesitates. I know they prefer to brief you in the morning, so you don't spend the night tossing and turning with worries about the assignment. "Your first reconnaissance mission is coming up," he finally says. "I thought it was too soon. But I have been overruled."

"Andromeda?" I guess.

"I can't say . . . it's classified. Above your ranking. But . . . you're smart."

His eyes probe mine. *His meaning is clear.* He said that she was under pressure to come up with new intel. Clearly, that pressure got worse.

"Sir, where are you sending us?"

"A reconnaissance mission to the Astral settlement. Or rather . . . what's left of it."

"Who is going?"

"You and Starfire," he says. "My team has been out there too many times with no results. Frankly, we're at a dead end. We need fresh eyes on it. And, well, you're both fresh."

What he really means is—

We're both green as the stars.

I have a million more questions that want to tumble out of my mouth, but he stops me.

"Captain, you'll get your official briefing in the morning."

That's when the lights go out and darkness engulfs the corridor. But I can still feel him standing there, watching me in the dark. His voice whispers out.

"Captain, dismissed. Try to get some rest. I mean it. The settlement . . . well . . . you'll find out. Seeing the images is one thing, but experiencing it in real life . . ."

"It can fuck with your head? Pardon my language, sir. But I'm used to that."

"Ah, basic training?" I can hear the smile in his words. "That is a mind screw. But it's just human psychology. The difference is—this isn't human."

His words hit me hard. My lungs constrict, forcing a sharp intake of breath. He leaves me like that, standing in the dark, wrestling with dread.

This isn't human.

I return to our barracks with my heart pounding from that. The door shuts behind me and clicks. Luna is still awake and waiting for me. She sits up.

"Uh, what was that all about?"

Her curiosity feels heavy in the air. I try to act nonchalant as I climb into the lower bunk, even though my heart is racing. It's not just the Astrals—it's him. But I don't want her to know that.

"Oh, Apollo just gave us a heads-up. They're deploying us to the Astral settlement on a reconnaissance mission. We'll get officially briefed tomorrow."

The darkness and silence swirl around us for a long moment.

"But why would he warn you?" I can hear the suspicion thick in her voice.

"I guess he was worried about how I was dealing with . . . well . . ."

"Aliens?"

"Yeah, that."

We both crack up in the dark. It sounds so preposterous when you say it out loud like that, but it's also the truth.

"Well, what about you?" I ask her in the dark. "Are you worried about it?"

It's another minute before I hear her response. "I probably should be . . . the whole situation is pretty scary, after all. But the truth is . . . I think I'm excited."

"Of course you are," I deadpan.

"We're some of the first humans to have contact with aliens," she says softly. "And, well, I don't know if I've ever been the *first* to do anything."

That's the last thing she says before we both try to fall asleep. It's important to be well-rested after our trip and with the reconnaissance mission coming up.

But tomorrow looms in my mind like a flashing neon sign. I'm restless, tossing and turning, fighting myself in the dark.

When I finally do drift off, I fall into that old black hole dream again.

I'm falling, spinning, flailing, being crushed under impossible gravity, struggling to breathe. I feel a scream on my breath before I plunge deeper into the endless void. Through the singularity, something appears.

This is new. This is not part of the nightmare where I get crushed to death.

It's them.

The Astrals. They look like light. Like prisms. They dance and undulate. They chant together in a choral voice.

Find us. Find us. Find us.

Before it's too late.

Explosions rock through my dream, ripping me back awake. I sit up and gasp for breath. I'm panting and gulping down oxygen like water.

My heart races then slows when I realize it was only another nightmare. I lie back down, feeling cold sweat slicking my flesh and the rough sheets.

My last conscious thought before I'm swept away back to sleep is—

The Astral settlement awaits us.

PART 2

PARALLAX

To know your Enemy, you must become your Enemy.

—Sun Tzu, *The Art of War*

CHAPTER 14

KARI

"No, don't . . . stop . . . let me go!"

I wake from a horrible nightmare where faceless aliens possess me—taking over my body and forcing me to turn on my own guardians and blast them, then my friends, even my family. I'm fighting back, thrashing around in my bunk.

Luna peers over the edge of the bunk, looking worried.

"Uh, you okay down there?"

I crack my eyes open. "Is it morning already?"

"More like . . . the approximation of morning," she says as the lights fade up. "Who knows where the suns are in the sky . . . or if they've even risen?"

"Good point," I say, stretching and feeling the tension in my body. "It could be the middle of the night out there."

I rise and go through my morning routine, putting on my uniform and shoving on my boots, washing my face, and brushing my teeth, but the nightmare remains strong in my mind. That feeling of being helpless and manipulated by those more powerful than you.

But isn't that my life now? I wonder if that's what triggered it. But something about it felt so real . . . then it hits me.

Space trauma.

That chills me to the bone. But I don't want to endanger my service, so I can't seek medical help or let anyone suspect.

"You ready for this freaky mission?" I say, remembering Apollo's late-night visit.

"As ready as I'll ever be to confront aliens," she quips, running one hand through her shorn blonde hair. "So . . . not really. But what choice do we have?"

"Spoken like a true guardian."

We both chuckle, then head out to the mess hall to scarf down bland rations. Unlike the giant cafeteria on Ceres Base, this is a much smaller dining room. It's mostly officers and scientists in lab coats, and the food is slightly more upscale.

Emphasis on the . . . *slightly.*

I wonder what else on this base is different. I scan the scientists and spot the woman in the lab coat from yesterday.

A shadow falls over the table.

"How'd you sleep, Captain?"

I look up—and my eyes fall on Major Apollo. He looks like he already knows the answer to that question, and more, like his sleep was about as bad as mine.

"Like normal, which means . . ."

"Total shit?" he finishes for me.

He gives me that smile again, the one that feels almost secret. I feel a shudder.

Why does he affect me this way?

Luna looks up and sparks to attention, trying to salute him, but he waves her off.

"At ease, Private." He sits next to us, which is unusual for a superior officer. Even his posture is relaxed as he leans back.

"How's the nosh?"

"Well, better than Ceres Base," Luna says right away. "These taste like actual sausage, even if they're totally fake."

"I'll give your compliments to the chef," he says, making us laugh . . . since the chef is a bot racing around the kitchen.

My cheeks warm in a way that spreads out to my entire body. I clear my throat, hoping Luna doesn't pick up on it.

"So, is this our official briefing?" I ask, choking down the last of my eggs.

Well, synthetic eggs.

He shrugs. "No, it's unofficial." That smile again. "But I figured I'd come get you, rather than have you summoned."

"Now, that is unusual," I say.

"Very," Luna says, glancing from him to me, clearly wondering if there's something more going on here that she doesn't know about. But I look away.

"Well, this is a small base. I like to think we do things a bit differently here."

"Harold will be disappointed," I add. "He loves any opportunity to boss me around . . . or tell me . . . *You're late!*"

"Harold?" he asks.

"Oh, that's what she named her neural implant. Don't ask . . ." Luna provides.

"Yeah, I figured you knew. Isn't that in my psych profile? Or more like . . . *psycho* profile?"

"Well, it was a pretty thorough report," he says, shaking his head in amusement. "But I guess they didn't cover that part."

"Maybe you can add to it?" I say, returning his smile. "Now that you're getting the chance to study me up close."

Another heated moment passes. I feel his boot edge near mine under the table.

But I jerk back and sit up straighter.

Surely, I'm just imagining things. I'm still discombobulated from my nightmare and missing Drae like a hole in my heart.

He also straightens up, turning more formal. "Well, better get this over with," he says, standing up from the table.

He gestures for us to follow him. The bots whisk our trays away. I glimpse a door at the back of the mess hall. It swings open as an officer emerges, revealing a dimly lit space with lounge chairs and small tables, and if I'm not mistaken, some kind of bar tended by bots.

"What's that?" I ask, nodding to it.

"Officers' lounge," Major Apollo says. "I take it you weren't briefed on that perk."

"I didn't even know we had those."

"Well, this base is full of officers and military scientists, so the little reminders of Earthside can make being stationed in such a remote place more bearable."

"Wow, I didn't think Space Force cared," I say, marveling a bit. "You make it sound like they almost have a heart."

"Almost," he says with a grin.

He leads us through the base toward the docking bay. The skylights lining the corridors beam purplish light down on us. The crystalline trees sway gently, caught in some lunar breeze. I wonder if they tinkle and make noise like wind chimes.

This really is an alien world . . . and we're about to learn about the former inhabitants.

My heart thumps faster at that reminder. In my mind, the Astrals are this nameless, faceless threat—like in my nightmare—lurking in the shadows, preying upon our greatest fears and weaknesses—on humanity's sins.

That makes them terrifying and hard to fathom. I don't know what to expect from their abandoned settlement, or what clues it might reveal about these aliens.

But then I remember something else—*We're the aliens here . . . if this was their home.*

We reach the docking bay. It's mostly deserted, but a smaller ship idles, being charged up. It's a sleek vessel, armed with blasters, and suited for quick, over-surface travel. I'm guessing that's our ride.

"You ready for this, Captain?" he asks as I slip past him.

It's whispered when I pass, as if only intended for my consumption.

Another secret between us.

A tiny, inconsequential gesture, easy to dismiss, but I feel something pulsing between us, something growing stronger. This time, I know it's not my imagination. There's a spark, like strange alchemy, something almost chemical.

But why?

Luna follows my lead, entering the docking bay.

Major Apollo pulls out his tablet and flicks through some intel. "You've both been briefed on the nature of our mission here," he briefs us in a formal tone.

"Yes, sir," we both say.

He nods. "Today, you're being deployed on a reconnaissance mission to the abandoned Astral settlement. It's located on the far side of the lunar surface."

"Roger that. Who else is coming with us?" I ask, glancing around for more guardians.

"Just the two of you," he says. "It's partially for you to get familiar with the terrain. But more than that, you have something that my team is lacking."

That surprises me.

"And what's that, sir?" I ask.

"Fresh eyes," he says. "We've already picked it apart and haven't come up with much. We've been running around in circles. But maybe you'll have more luck."

"Let's hope," I agree.

"The ship is preprogrammed on autopilot to fly to the location," he goes on. "So, you don't have to worry about that."

He hands me a tablet. "This has GPS three-dimensional mapping of the settlement hard downloaded onto the devices. You can use it to guide you."

"Yes, sir," I say, taking it.

He hands one to Luna also. But then he hesitates. "One more thing—try to rely on your other senses. Not just the tech."

He points to the tablets for emphasis.

"Why is that?" I ask.

"Just keep your eyes and ears open—and report any anomalies. Temporal shifts . . . strange energy fields. Anything like that. Your suits are hardwired with recording tech, so we'll be watching you."

"Recording?" Luna says. "Won't you be monitoring us live . . . in real time?"

He shakes his head. "It doesn't work."

"Sir, what do you mean?" I venture, feeling a pinprick of fear.

"We don't know why—but once you enter their settlement, our tech has a tendency to go . . . well . . . a bit haywire."

"Haywire?" Luna says.

"Is that the technical term?" I add, trying not to sound snarky, but failing.

"In fact, it is," he says, matching my tone. "Look, we don't know why. But our tech glitches. It won't transmit. Any communications distort and drop out. Imaging gets distorted. Even your neural implant is likely to go . . . offline."

That means no Harold. That's fine by me. But the rest of it concerns me.

"So, it's basically a dead zone? That's what you're telling us? For all intents and purposes, we're on our own out there?"

"Exactly," he says. "They're trying to get to the bottom of it. But once we're back on base, it works perfectly. Look, we wouldn't be sending you if it wasn't critical. And if we didn't think you were up for the challenge. One more thing . . ."

What other crazy shit could he possibly reveal now, when it's too late to turn back?

But I force that away and keep it to myself, instead replying, "What's that?"

"The settlement . . . has a tendency to reject . . . certain people."

"Reject them?" I say, surprised.

"We don't know why. Maybe it's some kind of forcefield. It's almost like . . . if it doesn't like you . . . or senses a threat . . ."

Apollo trails off.

"Who has it rejected?" I ask, my mind reeling. I think about the possibilities . . .

General Titan pops into my head right away. She had a creepy energy to her.

"Right, I can't disclose specifics," he says with a curt nod. "Just stay alert out there. I have a hunch you're different." He nods to Luna. "Both of you."

I trade a worried look with Luna, then turn back to Apollo. I lower my voice. "Sir, what's out there? Is there something you're not telling us?"

But he demurs and doesn't elaborate. "Just be careful," is all he will say.

He backs away, leaving us to our mission. But I study his face—chiseled and so handsome—and now etched with worry. I can tell he's afraid for us.

The ship taxies over, fully charged. I feel a shudder of adrenaline at everything I just learned. Not only does the settlement glitch out our tech, but it also has some kind of protective field that . . . rejects certain people . . . and keeps them out.

That all amps up my jitteriness. I realize that I shouldn't be surprised. If anything, I should expect the unexpected. We know almost nothing about the Astrals, but we know that they're technologically more advanced than us.

Of course, their settlement would have protections on it. It also makes sense that their tech and defenses would be different than anything we've ever encountered.

It also occurs to me—this is part of why they chose us for this mission. Apollo said it himself in our first meeting. I'm different, and so is Luna. We're also the only ones who saw through their artifice and discovered their plan. If we hadn't acted, then they would have succeeded.

They're counting on us. We don't have a choice. We need to find actionable intel.

This is my duty . . . my sacrifice.

Blood and stars.

"You ready?" I ask Luna.

She snaps a salute. "Always."

Then she frowns at me. "What's that weird look on your face? You look all squinty, and your face is crunched up." She pantomimes my expression. "Are you having a stroke?" she adds.

"Fine. You caught me showing emotions," I grumble, blushing. "You don't have to rub it in. I just want to say, I'm glad to have you here with me."

She staggers back like I blasted her. "Ah, it's like you care."

"Shut *the stars* up," I say. "You know I do. I'm just really bad at showing it."

She shrugs. "You've gotten better . . . since . . . well . . ." She makes a kissy face.

"Ugh, don't remind me."

But it's true. Something about Drae and our connection cracked me open, and now that my heart has been breached, all sorts of feelings I'd previously buried keep spilling out, even though I hate it.

We suit up in deployment suits and grab our helmets. The door to the ship hisses open, beckoning us to board it.

Luna turns more serious. "Well, nothing like a close encounter with dangerous aliens to make you emo."

"First of all, we don't know their true motivation. Asteroid fires, we know almost nothing. Maybe they have a reason."

"To hate us? And want to destroy us?" She frowns. "Nice try, but no way."

I know she's right; they killed our kids. But something bothers me about all of it. Earth is a tiny planet in a giant universe. Why go to all the trouble for us? We're basically tiny pinpricks in the vastness of the universe, barely even noticeable, like gnats of the cosmos.

The logic is missing. What's their true motivation? That's what we need to learn. I'm determined to find something new. Something that will help us win this war.

Outfitted, we return to Major Apollo, who is busy tapping on his tablet. I glimpse him finalizing our orders.

"Good luck out here," Apollo says, dismissing us. "Remember, the clock is ticking. We need new intel—and fast."

That's the last thing he says before we slip on our helmets, feeling them click in and seal as fresh oxygen circulates. We board the ship and take our seats in the cockpit. This ship could comfortably accommodate about six guardians.

But no more.

It reminds me of the smaller, faster postal ships that ferret our communications packages. Luna sits to my right. Before I can think—or more accurately, worry—Harold pings me. *Kari, prepare for blastoff,* he communicates.

A countdown appears on the console. The ship pilots itself, shifting into gear.

We taxi into the airlock. The exterior doors wane open, revealing the surface.

Major Apollo's voice echoes through my head. "Good luck out there!"

Then, with a great thrusting of engines, our ship carries us into the amethyst skies.

CHAPTER 15

DRAE

I wake from a terrible nightmare.

One where I was stranded on a strange lunar surface, but there wasn't enough oxygen, and the skies were tinted purple like Willow's hair.

I was looking for Kari.

Not just looking, but frantically searching, screaming her name.

Until my last gasping breath.

I blacked out, then—

I woke with a sharp inhale, feeling that strong sense of longing stabbing at my heart. I don't know where she is or when I'll hear from her again. I run a shaky hand through my hair.

It's getting longer by the day, but I'm letting it grow out more. For Kari, of course. Even remembering that makes me blush and drives heat to my body.

But I don't have time to get lost in memories of her. Memories that don't go cold or fade, but grow sharper. It's strange, as if the neural implant changes my brain chemistry and focuses it—

On her.

I try to snap out of it; I have classes. I just hope to hear from her soon.

I bolt out of bed and throw on my clothes from the chair at my desk. They're not clean exactly, but they're not laundry-worthy either. At least not yet.

I sniff the armpits just in case and decide they'll do. I grab my backpack and slip into my sneakers.

My first class is Federation History, a required core for all freshmen. It's not my favorite class by any means, but I like the professor. He has a wicked sense of humor that keeps me entertained through the lectures.

I shoulder my backpack and head into the common room. Theo and Sylvia look like they are in the middle of some kind of heated argument. But they step apart the second they spot me.

"Oh, hey," Sylvia says, looking down. "Didn't hear you come in."

She tucks a pastel flyer behind her back. They're all over campus for both sides. So, I wonder why she'd hide it.

"Trying to sneak up on us?" Theo adds with a genial shrug. But his attempt at humor sounds strained.

My suspicion grows stronger. But then I remember my theory . . . that something romantic has developed between them. They were probably bickering over something silly and didn't want me to find out or get involved.

"If I was *sneaking*, I didn't do a very good job of it," I reply with a smirk.

"Good point," Theo agrees.

"Yeah, you need to work on your sneakiness," Sylvia adds with snark.

Our usual banter lightens the mood.

"See you after class?" Theo asks.

"Maybe we can recruit into our gaming cult," Sylvia adds with a snort.

"Or reverse that," I say, heading for the door. Or I'm going to be late. "And I'll get you into my vintage comics."

I hurry across campus for the building that houses my class, bolt through the doors, and down the hall. The lecture hall welcomes me with that smell of books and chemical cleaners, along with some teenager aromas. I choose a seat alone in the back.

A few minutes later, Jude and his new crew barge into the lecture hall.

"Jude, lead the way," a hulking guy says with a clap on his back. "You're the king of campus. That party last night!"

"Yeah, you were something else," a slim girl with blonde nano hair says. "Sorry, your charms don't work on me."

"Give me time," Jude says with a leering smile. "I'll grow on you."

"Like a fungus!" the bulky guy jokes, then raises his hands. "Just kidding."

For a second, Jude looks pissed. He hates being the butt of jokes.

Clearly, the new crew hasn't learned about his famous temper yet. But I see him calm his expression and control his anger. However, it's still there, simmering beneath the surface and waiting to explode. That guy better watch his back.

"Who cares? How many girls wanted to talk to you?" the bulky guy's friend says, trying to smooth it over. "There was a line out the door!"

"Yeah, I had to play bouncer," the first guy adds. "All those frosh hotties. Or it would've been a mob scene."

The tension dissipates with them all orbiting around Jude like dwarf planets encircling a fiery hot sun, their speed and axis determined by his mood.

They make a show of finding their seats in the front, clutching expensive faux-coffee drinks. The bulky guy spots me in the back. He elbows his friends. They toss insolent stares my way. I can see them snickering and whispering at my expense. They're not subtle about it.

I sink lower in my seat, clutching my backpack to my chest. I shouldn't care, but my cheeks burn anyway. At least Jude didn't try to sit next to me today.

I've got that going for me.

The lecture hall is one of the bigger ones on campus, but I'm sitting alone. I miss Rho again. Her letter made that ache worse, though I'm thrilled to know how she's doing on the star-seas. Sometimes, I wish I'd stayed up there, too. Left college and Earthside behind.

But that would have meant leaving the Sympathetic Program and abandoning Kari, too. I couldn't do that to her. Trebond also made it clear that I was needed down here as a Resistance operative. That we're important.

I expect Professor Wembley to emerge. He didn't push us like Professor Trebond did in Great Books, but he's got a dry sense of humor that can turn dark and subversive. I appreciated his interjections while teaching federation-approved history.

But instead, another figure approaches the lectern and prepares to teach. I take in his short stature and bushy mustache, along with his silly bowtie that makes him look like a little boy more than an actual teacher.

I'm shocked by who it is—

Mr. Egbert.

He was my high school history teacher. What's he doing here?

This can't be happening. I thought I escaped him. He's not a college professor. He can't be qualified to teach at Berkeley. In the front row, Jude breaks into a triumphant grin.

So, that's why they chose those seats.

I'm horrified as his nasal voice rings out through the auditorium. "I'm sure you've noticed the recent turnover in professors," he begins his lecture in a smug voice.

Muffled whispers ripple through the lecture hall, then fall silent.

The smile vanishes from his face. "Let me make one thing very clear. Our federation takes your education seriously. Recently, I headed a program to review all instructor employment files, grading, and course syllabi."

More whispers cut through the hall, but he keeps speaking over them. I can guess who put him in charge of that program—Jude's father, Mr. Luther.

"Unfortunately, we've had to root out some Resistance sympathizers among the faculty," he continues darkly. "Those who don't support our military efforts in the stars. Historically speaking, this sort of dangerous, radical thinking has run rampant in higher education. As a history teacher, I know."

He swipes at his tablet as information about the program projects on the large screen behind his lectern. The Earthside Federation flag flies over bold letters, "Protecting Education from Resistance Sympathizers."

I feel sick as my stomach twists. So, this isn't just happening in my classes, but across campus and at other schools. I hear Professor Trebond's name tossed around by students in low voices. It created a big stir on campus when they tried to arrest her, but she escaped and went into hiding. She's a fugitive now, and the head of the Resistance movement on Earth.

"Ah, yes . . . that's right," Mr. Egbert says, hearing Trebond's name. "Some have been arrested, but others, like that notorious *former* professor, managed to evade the authorities. If anyone has information leading to her arrest, I promise there will be a great reward."

He swipes again, and a number appears to message with information.

Bribery, I think. I wonder who else has been targeted recently by Mr. Egbert and his organization besides Professor Wembley. He did have a transgressive streak, but I've never heard Trebond or anyone in the Resistance mention him.

But even the wording is dangerous. Not just actual Resistance operatives, but "sympathizers"—as in anyone who doesn't teach propaganda or harbors reservations about our war efforts.

I have a hunch about how much of the "rooting out" is based on real evidence, rather than gossip and accusations from students like Jude complaining that they didn't like their teaching or get high enough grades.

"However, make no mistake," Mr. Egbert drones on. "There is no greater reward than protecting our great federation, especially with the Astrals threatening our very existence."

That creates a hush. The Astrals are the new front in the endless war.

"We can't have radicals shaping the impressionable minds of our most promising youth. You represent our future. That's why we've brought in more trustworthy instructors, even some teachers from our lower schools."

He smiles brightly. "War heroes and Space Force veterans like me."

That produces clapping. He tips his head toward Jude in the front row.

"I must say, I'm so pleased to see some of my best students from high school here. I can't wait to continue your federation-approved education."

Jude basks in the praise and attention from Mr. Egbert.

But that attention doesn't reach me in the back row. The snub feels intentional, even though I'm hiding. I have a feeling it's meant to affect me.

That only makes me feel sicker. Of course Jude made this happen. It has his name written all over it. Back in high school, Mr. Egbert always gave us top grades even when we barely paid attention in class or did any homework.

Then something darker occurs to me. I flash back to the threats Jude made on his tablet yesterday. And what Willow said about the increasing Resistance activity on campus. Maybe Mr. Egbert was put here for another reason.

I scan for Jude again. He catches me latched onto him. His eyes sharpen, as his lips curl back. He mouths—

We're watching you.

That threat sinks in.

Mr. Egbert isn't just here to teach us—he's a spy. He said he was a veteran. He has military training. For all I know, he could have been in intelligence.

It all makes perfect sense now.

I shudder, feeling the chill work its way through my whole body and settle into my bones. The campus feels less safe by the minute. As the usual state-sanctioned propaganda broadcasts across the screen and Mr. Egbert launches into his lecture, a thinly disguised version of the same censored history lessons he taught us in high school, I have one thought—

None of this is a coincidence.

It's all carefully orchestrated with one purpose. To root out the Resistance by quashing our activity on campus.

Somehow, I make it through the rest of class, slumped down in my seat. Jude jokes with his friends and barely listens to the lecture. Not that anything is new, nor does it matter. It's the same dull messaging repeated over and over.

Finally, it's over. I bolt from my seat, and I'm the first one out of the lecture hall. My mouth tastes like metal. I wanted to escape my past, but now it's haunting me like a vengeful ghost.

Jude is back, now Mr. Edgar. They're spies, I realize. All spies.

Here at Berkeley for me—and all of us who want to "Disarm the Stars!"

I should feel afraid, but instead, I feel more radicalized than ever. I remember what Trebond said in her message. I'm supposed to report on any suspicious activity or developments on campus. Well, if I'm a spy . . . then maybe I should start acting like one.

I pull out the flyer I found from my backpack for the Anti-Astral rally.

It's tonight. At seven o'clock. Founders' Rock.

Should I go?

CHAPTER 16

KARI

The trip is nothing short of spectacular.

I almost forget I'm on a mission—a possibly dangerous one.

Unlike the bulky transport that brought us here, this sleek ship skirts just over the lunar surface, giving us a front-row view of the moon.

Ten minutes to target destination, Harold chimes in helpfully. My heart skips.

"You registering this?" I say, pointing to my eyes and out the bulbous cockpit.

"How could I not?" Luna says, equally transfixed by the landscape. "Now, this is what I imagined when I enlisted."

We move at high speed. As promised, the shuttle follows its preprogrammed route. The ride is smooth and exhilarating, giving me a rush of adrenaline. Below us, the alien landscape unfurls like a story.

We fly over thick, crystalline forests with tendrils growing out and stretching up toward the sky, casting kaleidoscopic prisms over everything. They even refract into our ship and dance over us. The whole place feels mystical and strange.

And so very alive.

I can see why the Astrals had a settlement here. The two suns cross overhead in a cosmic dance, eclipsing each other, as they do a few times a day by our Earthside clock. Trickles of liquid—I don't know what element—flow over the surface, coalescing into rivers.

The whole place has a magical feel. The tapestry of color alone makes Earth seem grim and dusty, even though it's not.

We approach a mountain range in the distance that juts up into sharp peaks blasted with snow and ice at the tips.

Suddenly, the ship flies right at a mountain. The sheer cliffside jumps out.

"Watch out!" I start—

But then the ship plunges downward, following the cliff into the earth.

We plunge downward—and keep plunging deeper and deeper. The light doesn't diminish; instead it runs through crystal veins in the rock like LED lights. The farther we venture into the cave systems, the brighter the veins grow. I don't know how it works, but it looks like they're channeling in the energy from the two suns and diverting it into the ground.

"Did you get a load of this?" I say, pointing to them. "So much light . . ."

"Yeah, it's like a dance party." Luna thumps her head in a silent rhythm.

All joking aside, it's truly spectacular. That's when the ship abruptly jolts to a halt. Outside the cockpit, there's a gaping opening leading into a cave system.

The shuttle door *hisses* open.

Arrival . . . at . . . destination . . . Harold tries, but his voice glitches out into static.

That freaks me out. Harold annoys me on a daily basis, but the absence is worse. It's like any connection I had is gone.

Likewise, the instruments on the ship go simultaneously haywire. The compass spins through numbers, while the instruments flicker and glitch. The strangest part? It's in rhythm with the light pushing through the crystal veins.

"Shit, it really is a dance party," Luna quips, trading a freaked-out look with me.

"Then let's dance," I say, checking my blaster, as she follows my lead.

"Locked and loaded," she agrees.

"Roger that," I reply. Our robotic voices come up amplified by the suits.

My breath hisses in and out of the ventilator in my suit. At least the life support appears to function just fine. It occurs to me that it's selective about what goes on the fritz, and what keeps going. I make a mental note of that as we approach the opening to the cave system. Luna checks the GPS mapping. The hard download means it keeps working.

I wonder how much of that Major Apollo was supposed to disclose—and how much was above our pay grade. Regardless, I feel like a Space Force guinea pig being thrown off a cliff.

It's fly or die time.

"What is this place?" Luna says as we venture into the cave system.

The GPS beeps, leading us deeper. The walls are lined with the crystal veins, pulsing in light of all colors. We don't need our headlamps and can see perfectly, even though we're deep underground. I'm tempted to try to pull up my instruments to scan if they'd even work, but I resist the urge. I remember what Apollo said . . . trust your other senses.

We step through the entrance and something invisible *whooshes* behind us.

I draw my blaster and flip around—

"Who's there?"

Then I slowly lower it. Luna lowers hers, too. "I think it's the forcefield."

"Well, it didn't reject us."

"Worse," she says, approaching it. A strange ripple of energy runs down it. "I think it sealed us . . . inside . . ."

"Are we trapped?"

She tries to breach it, but it flings her back, like bouncing off elastic. It doesn't hurt her exactly . . . but it's a strong push.

"Shit, that's uncool." Luna frowns.

"Very."

I approach it, but as soon as I reach my hand out, the same thing happens. It flings me back into the cave system.

Then, stranger—

The lights start pulsing in a manner that beckons us inward and deeper.

But I hesitate. I glance at Luna.

"Major Apollo didn't warn us about the forcefield trapping us. Why not?"

"My hunch—I think he didn't know about it. I bet it hasn't happened before."

"So, you're saying . . . this weird alien tech *wants* us in here . . . and only us."

"Well, he said that it *rejects* certain people. I'm wondering how many they tried sending down here who got . . ."

"Bounced out?" I say, jerking my head to the forcefield. "Like unwelcome party guests?"

"You said it first." Luna pauses for a moment. The lights reflect off her visor.

"What is it?"

"Well, it doesn't make sense. But look at the lights? They're talking to us."

"You see that, too?"

"Can't miss it."

"Thank the stars," I say with a deep exhale. "I thought I was losing it."

"If you're losing it," Luna says, "then we both are. Anyway, I don't think we have a choice. We have to follow it."

I check my vital signs. Then something strange happens. The reading that shows the ambient atmosphere goes from *RED* to *GREEN*. A pleasant beep goes off.

"Are you seeing that?" I ask.

"Yes . . . the atmosphere changed."

"To accommodate us," I say, double-checking the reading. "Think it's safe?"

Before I can unlock my helmet, it does it for me, controlled by some other force.

It's like a glitch.

Only, it seems intentional. My helmet decompresses and releases. I have no choice. I shrug it off and take a breath.

"Okay, I'm not dying."

Luna takes her helmet off, too. We both breathe tentatively, then more relaxed. The sensors weren't lying.

"We can breathe in here," I say. "But how? That should be impossible. How could the atmosphere change so suddenly? Not just change—but become something life-supporting for us."

"The possible is possible here."

Truer words could not be spoken. "Should we . . . continue to the party?"

We follow the lightship that leads us deeper into the complex cave system. It reminds me of a more organic version of the arrows back at our home base.

Different rooms branch off, all carved out of crystal and rock, all illuminated by the veins of light channeled from the surface. Some rooms have those trees.

I don't know if it's the trippy light show, or not having my helmet on, but I start to hear things. *Whisperings* that echo from the cave. Shimmers of light brush past me, almost like ghostly apparitions.

I come to decide—

They are ghosts.

And I'm seeing the past. I can't explain it, other than to say, I feel it in my bones. I remember Apollo mentioning something.

Temporal disturbances.

That means . . . time. I didn't understand the meaning fully, but now I do. He meant like time fracturing—

And letting me glimpse the past.

The visions of light resolve into . . . *children*. Only, it's like the light is bending itself into something I can comprehend, changing to communicate with me. I stumble upon a larger room—and it's filled with the light-children. They huddle around crystals jutting out of the floor.

They're computers of some kind, I realize. The next room hosts a garden. The light-people harvest food to consume, more like energy than the plants we consume on Earth, but it's their form of nourishment. The light-children giggle and play, rushing past me. I feel their heat and speed like a warm breeze on my flesh.

They are so alive.

This whole colony beams with the light-people and their light-children.

What happened to them? Why did they abandon this settlement?

I know I should check on Luna, but I'm so captivated by the light-people that I grow distracted and forget her location.

I enter a room that seems to be some sort of control room. All the light feeds into this space, flowing into a large, crystal structure that juts out of the floor.

COME, COME, COME!

I approach it, awed by the streams of light running through it like liquid fire.

TOUCH IT!

Voices echo to me. It sounds harmonic, like many singing at once. The melodies blend and undulate, hitting inhuman notes that shouldn't be audible to my fragile ears, but I hear them anyway.

I know it's dangerous to touch anything down here. I'm supposed to observe and report back. But I can't help it. My arm reaches out anyway, despite my mental objection, but then, even those melt away, seduced by the voices.

My hand touches the crystal—

And suddenly, it grows over my arm, wrapping around my suit. I try to scream. But the liquid crystal flows down my mouth and through my whole body.

I'm paralyzed and helpless.

Suddenly, I get that brain-sucking feeling that I only get when my neural link jacks in for a warp mail exchange.

Nooooooo!

I try to scream, but my mouth is frozen. That's when the onslaught of images hits my brain. I see the past in full detail now. The light-children run and flee as rocks cave into the tunnels. Their high-pitched screams rattle the crystals.

They start shattering.

The whole place is shattering, collapsing, as more rocks rain down.

Their shrieks pummel my ears—

PLAGUE ON THE UNIVERSE!
SPREADING TO INFECT!
KILL THE VIRUS!

Fear rushes through me, along with a surge of adrenaline, and then—with all my force—with all my willpower—I yank my hand back, breaking the connection.

The voices die out.

So do the images.

But there is still so much light. I see spots in my vision. I spin around—

And someone rushes at me!

I pull my blaster, my finger on the trigger. The adrenaline makes it twitch.

I'm about to blast them.

But a breathless voice reaches me—

"No, stop! Hold your fire!"

CHAPTER 17

DRAE

I creep around campus, cutting through the footpaths and back passages that separate the stately buildings, heading for Founders' Rock.

I know the spot. It's a natural rock outcropping covered in moss, where the founders of the school met back before the Great War to dedicate the campus. Not only is it important to the college, Rho and I also tracked the clues to this spot for our secret initiation into the Resistance. But now it's being used for another purpose—an Anti-Astral rally.

I'm wearing a gray sweatshirt with the hood pulled over my head. The flyer is stuffed into the front pocket. My heart beats faster in anticipation. I'm a student, but I'm going as a spy. I plan to report anything I learn to Willow.

If this campus is a battlefield, then I want to help the right side. I also have a selfish reason, though I haven't told anyone. I keep it to myself, hoarding it in my heart like a beacon of hope.

Disarming the Stars and finding a peaceful diplomatic solution like Trebond wants would mean that Kari could come home sooner. I fear the alternative—the Anti-Astral movement—would mean only endless war that puts her and all of humanity in danger.

I know there's a chance Trebond is wrong. That the Astrals are just as warlike and bloodthirsty as humanity. But I have to hold out hope for peace.

What other choice do I have?

A future of endless wars fought in the stars that will leak back Earthside isn't the future I want to build. I can already see the signs of military trickling back home. The security bots on campus. Sure, they're only armed to stun and detain, but how far are we from arming them with blasters?

Based on how fast everything on campus is escalating, not very far.

I head for the corner of campus where Founders' Rock juts out, shrouded with moss and shaded by leafy trees. This area has a wildness to it that beckons to California's past. It's a landmark where the twelve trustees stood to found our college. According to college lore, they read a passage from Bishop Berkeley's verse: "Westward the course of the empire takes its way."

That's who inspired the name of the college, and the quote couldn't be truer today. We were the first to launch our own Space Force, sending our soldiers to the stars. The head of the Earthside Federation heralds from California. We're still leading the way.

The moon creeps out, just a sliver of delicate light. The campus looks shadowy and dark. I do my best to avoid the security bots. Even though they'd probably just scan me and release me, they give me a bad feeling.

I can't believe how much has changed over the last few weeks since I first arrived on campus. The school looks more like a war zone every day. I notice metal bars have been added along the main footpaths, so students can't step out of the way of the bots.

We're being controlled, closely herded, and watched. There are two underground factions breaking out in the wake of the Astrals. The secret flyers peppering campus portray the two sides. Disarm the Stars and Anti-Astral, the hardliners who advocate for war and genocide against the invaders. The closer I get to the rally, the more afraid I start to feel.

First, I notice that the security bots thin out. Where are they? A few students join me, heading for the rally. I see them holding flyers. Everyone looks a little jumpy. The tension is palpable. We don't make eye contact, maybe fearing being caught and forced to ID the other attendees. Gatherings like this rally are supposedly forbidden due to the dark history of colleges like Berkeley harboring extremists and anti-war protestors.

As I reach the periphery of the crowd gathered there, I spot shadowy figures start to hear chanting. About thirty students gather around Founders' Rock. Most are dressed like me in sweats with hoods, but some are wearing navy and gold robes with peaked hoods.

That surprises me. Where did they get those?

Suddenly, I realize that the Anti-Astral movement is more organized than I first realized.

They hold torches, thrusting them into the air.

"*Astrals must pay!*"

"*They want to destroy us!*"

"*Humanity must fight back!*"

Their chants echo out, growing louder as more students join their ranks. I sidle up to the side of the gathering, trying to see over the hoods and torches. The crowd has an erratic energy running through it, both explosive and forbidding. I feel a jolt of adrenaline when I see who's leading the rally.

Jude and his cohorts.

Of course, I should have known. They're all wearing those robes and carrying torches. They parade through the crowd, which parts for them, and approach Founders' Rock. Someone else is following them . . . it's Mr. Egbert.

Standing with him, I spot Professor Goode, who replaced Trebond. Even some faculty are supporting this rally.

That chills me even more.

I keep expecting security bots to storm in with their riot shields up and break up the rally with tear gas and stun guns. But the rest of campus remains suspiciously quiet. Too quiet almost.

The meaning is clear—the government is condoning this rally. Not outright on the newsfeeds, but they're permitting it to exist, not rushing to detain these students and shut it down. I don't know if it's the whole fed or just the hardliners. The ones my father warned me about, like Jude's father. I'm also not sure if this goes all the way up to Secretary-General Andromeda.

Jude reaches the monument and scrambles up the rocks, climbing on top. His boots tear into the moss. He stands up and gazes out over the growing crowd of students with their torches and cloaks. Our college mascot, the grizzly bear, marks the lapels.

They wave U of Berkeley flags and California Federation flags. But I notice the absence of the new Earthside Federation flag, the one that has Earth surrounded by Mars and a halo of stars to represent our interstellar outposts.

Mr. Egbert hands him a torch, which Jude hoists aloft. Cheers break out from the crowd. He raises his voice—

"Annihilate the Astrals!"

The chants break out again, repeating what he said. I mouth along, not wanting to get outed as a spy.

He stands, holding a torch, relishing the crowd at his fingertips. The firelight flicks at his robes and sends sparks shooting into the air like tiny comets, giving him a demonic appearance.

"Exterminate the Astrals!" he preaches to them. "Save humanity!"

Everyone goes wild, but he gestures for them to listen. I notice Mr. Egbert slipping him something. Then I realize what it is . . . notecards with his speech.

He's nothing more than a puppet.

Jude clears his throat, then launches into his speech, reading off the cards.

"The Astrals threaten not just the stars, but Earthside too!" he says in a booming voice. "Never forget the Golden Gate Attack! And how they killed our innocent kids on that bridge!"

Boos ring out. I feel a stab of sadness.

The attack is unforgivable. I have a moment of doubt, wondering if Jude—or whoever wrote this speech for him—is right about the Astrals and war is our only option.

"We cannot afford to wait," Jude continues, reading the cards. "The Astrals are coming for us—a second invasion is inevitable. We have no choice but to destroy them first."

He pauses, raking his gaze over the fiery crowd. "And everyone who sympathizes with them—and the extremist Resistance movement."

More boos now, but also angry threats. "Exterminate the Resistance!"

A frenzy seizes the crowd around me. Some pushing and shoving breaks out with a girl falling to the ground.

There's a violent air to it all.

"To Disarm the Stars would be to surrender to our enemies! We must do everything we can to destroy them . . . before they can destroy us first!"

The crowd reaches a fever peak. I can tell he's finished reading his cards. That's when he nods to Mr. Egbert, who disappears behind the monument.

A second later, a group of Jude's crew emerges, dragging someone with a bag thrust over their head. They pull her onto the rocks next to Jude.

"This freshman is a Resistance operative!" Jude says, pointing at the hooded figure. "We caught them distributing pamphlets on campus and recruiting for the extremist group."

My mouth goes dry—

Is it Willow?

I remember what she said about recruiting for the cause.

The crowd surges around me. I'm pushed forward, as if they want to exact vigilante justice on the poor student. Jude pulls the hood of her head, revealing the freshman's identity.

I recognize her right away.

Sylvia.

My new roommate.

I can't believe it; I stagger back in shock, but the crowd pushes me forward again. She looks terrified. Her eyeliner is smudged from crying, while her lower lip trembles.

Jude reaches down and gets handed something that he then holds up over the crowd. It's a stack of Resistance flyers printed with "Disarm the Stars!"

"Look at this filth she's been posting all over campus," Jude sneers.

He holds up the illegal flyers, then starts shredding them and casts them off, where they flutter down like snow over the frenzied students and catch in their torches, going up in flames.

"*Annihilate her!*" someone yells behind me. The crowd picks up that chant, making Sylvia cower in fear.

Even Mr. Egbert looks a little taken aback at that and signals to Jude to cut it off. But I can tell Jude enjoys it. He resists stopping them, and the chanting continues for another heart-pounding minute. I'm actually afraid that they might follow through on their threats.

"I agree that she deserves the same fate she would bring upon humanity," Jude says finally, glaring at Mr. Egbert. "But let us not forget that we're a federation of law and order."

The crowd surges again. More boos echo out.

"Oh, don't worry," Jude said with a sly smile. "I didn't say she wouldn't be punished."

A hush falls over the crowd.

I feel a jolt of fear. Sylvia tries to stay strong, but tears leak from her eyes anyway.

"She's going to be expelled and detained for questioning," Jude proclaims. "Earlier, I spoke with the dean . . . personally. He wasn't on our side at first, but I was quite persuasive, shall we say. We cannot allow this filth to spread on our campus. We must stamp it out now."

The crowd goes wild. Jude grins in the torchlight, enjoying the seditious reverie. He shoves Sylvia, who slips and falls to the ground. His crew yank her back to her feet. I can see blood trickling down her knee where she scraped it.

They parade her through the crowd. I'm half-afraid vigilante justice is about to break out as they surge around her.

But they just jeer and taunt her.

"Resistance sympathizer! Pacifist Scum! Pro-Astral Lover!"

She reaches the back of the crowd. Her head lolls around, her gaze finding me. Our eyes lock together for a second.

Hers widen in recognition. Fear has made them look teary and glassy.

I flinch toward her, wanting to help. But she shakes her head and mouths—

Don't do it . . . save yourself.

Before she's dragged away.

So, I stand there, paralyzed and helpless to do anything. I feel like a coward. But she's right. If I try to protect her, I'll just out myself, too. I'm outnumbered, and they'd arrest me.

Now, security bots appear, careening down the path, but not for the rally.

They're here to arrest her.

One of the bots detains her, latching restraints around her wrists. She struggles weakly, and they stun her.

Her body goes limp, slumping forward. The bots carry her away.

All I can think—

That could've been me.

Suddenly, I remember the argument I interrupted between Sylvia and Theo earlier today. I thought it was just a lover's quarrel, but now I realize it was related to her activities on campus.

But there's more—

Her message to me was clear. She saw me at the Anti-Astral rally. But she mouthed, "Save yourself." So, that means she knows I'm with the Resistance.

She's another one of Trebond's operatives planted on campus. My new roommates aren't a fresh start like I thought. They were put there for me.

To watch me.

A shudder works through me. I feel manipulated and more paranoid than ever. Now, it's not just Jude I'm worried about, but can I trust my old professor?

As the crowd starts chanting again and calling for genocide, I realize that I don't have a choice. If we're at war, then both sides have to take risks, and some of those have dangerous consequences.

Even so, I feel chilled by everything that just unfolded. I'm afraid for Sylvia and what lies ahead for her.

I back away, hoping to make a quick escape. Drinking and debauchery have broken out as thumping music blasts out of a portable speaker with somebody in a hooded robe DJing. The rally is already morphing into a celebration party. That sickens me to my core.

I just want to go back to my dorm. Write out a message for Willow to deliver to Trebond. I turn to make a quiet exit, when suddenly—

I bump into somebody.

They were clearly watching me. They're wearing a robe and holding a torch. The light falls over his face.

"Oh, you came to my rally," Jude says with a devilish smile. He looks sweaty and jittery, amped up on adrenaline. "And all this time, I thought you were a Resistance sympathizer."

I try to control my expression, so I don't give away how freaked out I am.

"Uh, it was . . . surprising," I manage, not meeting his eyes. My voice wobbles, coming out weak and uncertain.

He points his torch toward the security bots carrying Sylvia away.

"Surprising, huh?" he prods me. "You mean . . . that part about your new roomie? You know, Drae . . . I can't help but wonder something."

"What's that?" I choke out.

"Why didn't you report her yourself? You had to have suspected something. Sharing that small dorm room . . ."

I flinch back. "No, I swear. I had no idea . . . I barely even knew her . . ."

That part is true.

But my heart pounds. I wonder if Sylvia said anything when they caught her—and how much she really knows.

Jude studies me. "You know what they say . . . the company you keep . . ."

He's not looking at me but at Sylvia. The bots round a bend and disappear with her. He leans toward me. The heat from his torch singes my cheeks.

"Be careful, Drae. I don't have proof, but we're watching you. You're going to be next."

With that threat, he backs away to join the party, pumping his fists in the air.

I swallow hard. That was close. I can't believe Jude is leading the Anti-Astral movement. I'm guessing this was part of his deal to return to campus. They already arrested my roommate.

He's right. If I'm not careful—

I could be next.

CHAPTER 18

KARI

"Kari, stop!"

Her voice cuts through my panic and disorientation. My pupils dilate and focus.

It's Luna.

I almost blasted her to pieces.

Quickly, I lower my blaster, doubling over and starting to hyperventilate.

"Kari, it's okay," Luna says, running over to me. She disarms me, knocking my blaster to the floor. "Just breathe . . ."

"I'm sorry . . . I'm so sorry . . . I don't know what came over me . . ."

Tears gush down my cheeks. My whole body feels liquified. I still remember that crystal forcing itself over my body and down my throat. Was any of that real?

The lights hum, then dim.

Are they speaking?

But whatever possessed me appears to be gone now. I flex my arm and crack my knuckles. I take a few deep breaths to calm my system, but I'm still jittery.

"What happened back there?" Luna asks, wheeling around to inspect the room. "Was somebody else in here?"

"No, not in the present."

She cocks her head. "I can't explain it . . . but it was like I could see the past. I could see them . . . they're not like us."

"You *saw* them?"

"Well, more like their ghosts," I say quickly. "Look, I know it sounds crazy."

"Just a little."

"But bear with me. They're like these light-beings. That's the only way I can explain it. And they lived here, but something happened to drive them out."

"Something?" Luna says skeptically. "Can you be any more specific?"

I shrug. "I heard them screaming. There were explosions . . . the tunnels started caving in on their kids . . ."

"You saw all that?"

"Well, I think I did . . ." I trail, off uncertainly. Now that I'm saying it out loud, it does sound a little crazy.

No, more like *a lot* crazy.

Silence engulfs us. There's only the strange humming of the light veins.

"Did you see anything?" I ask, hoping that I'm not alone in this insanity.

"Uh, aside from the dance party? I can't say I had any hallucinations."

"Is that what it was?"

Luna shrugs. "Blast it, I don't know! We took our helmets off. Anything could be in this atmosphere, stuff our sensors don't even know about. I'm just saying . . . it's hard to verify what you witnessed."

"Roger that," I say with a grimace. "That's a nice way of saying . . . I am crazy."

"Hey, I would've said cracked up. You know, more of a temporary situation."

I manage a smile. "Temporary? You're saying I'm usually levelheaded?"

"Don't push it, Skye."

"Duly noted, Starfire."

It sounds stupid, but the banter and joking around helps me feel better. It brings me back to myself. I appreciate Luna more than ever. But then worry rushes back in. "You're right . . ."

"About what? You being cracked?"

"Yes, that. Nobody is going to believe me. I can't prove . . . well . . . any of it."

I double-check my recording systems, but they're completely unresponsive.

"You get anything recorded?"

"Negative," she says, checking. "I tried the playback, but it's all blank or static."

"Same here. I got nothing."

"You really saw all that?" Luna says. "Swear it on blood and stars?"

"I did . . . do you believe me?"

"Yeah. Of course," she says without hesitation. "But will Major Apollo?"

Silence engulfs the room, but then the humming kicks up as if confirming my deepest fears. The cacophony pitches up.

"I doubt it," I say with a sigh.

"What's going on between you two?" Luna asks. "I picked up on something."

"It's nothing," I say sharply. *A little too sharply.* "Sorry, it's just that . . ."

"Being with Drae opened you to actually feeling things?" Luna provides. "Like obvi! And now you get a hot commanding officer who also expresses that he cares about your well-being . . ."

"Yeah, about that," I say, blushing hard and feeling called out. "You're in intel, but you should be in PSYOPS. I guess he stirred up all my major daddy issues."

"Hey, you said it," she says, play-punching my shoulder. "But yeah, it's a textbook case. You got the hots for him."

"Ugh, barf."

"I saw how you looked at him. It's different than Drae though. This seems more . . . physical . . . and lustful . . ."

"Ugh, double barf," I say again.

"Just be careful," Luna warns me. "I get why you got triggered. We're also young and inexperienced. And he is super hot. But it's not you that I'm worried about."

"What do you mean?" I say with a rush of concern. My heart thumps harder.

"It's him."

"Why do you say that?"

"He's into you," she says. "I'm pretty intuitive, and even I could sense it."

"You could feel that?" I say in a strangled voice. Now, I'm blushing hard and embarrassed. "I didn't realize it was that obvious . . ."

"Feel it? Who couldn't?" She kneels down and stretches her legs. "Anyway, I think our light show wants our attention."

She nods to the veins of light.

They've reversed course, flowing through the veins and leading us back the way we came. Their harmonious humming rises up.

"Unless you want to find out what happens to guests who overstay their welcome?" Luna adds, straightening up and dusting herself off.

"No, thanks," I say right away. "I had enough close encounters for one party."

"You can say that again."

"So, what are you going to tell Apollo?" she asks as we prepare to leave.

I shake my head, feeling even more upset. Not only can I not prove anything, but also I could be in big trouble over it.

I meet Luna's gaze. "If this gets out—that I almost blasted you—I could be removed from duty. And my weapon could be confiscated."

"Yeah, you're not wrong."

"But maybe I should turn myself in. Confess everything . . . request a medical review and leave of absence . . ."

Luna goes to retrieve my blaster and hands it back to me. "That's not happening. Not on my watch, Captain."

We head back through the cave system, following the light show. Everything I witnessed runs through my head again. It remains crystal clear in my mind, but impossible to explain in any words. At least, not human words. The caves hum back to me, still seeming to communicate. I shudder and rub the back of my neck with my neural link stub. I remember how it felt like it jacked into my brain directly. But how?

I'm left with more questions than answers. I doubt myself, but at the same time, I feel truth resonating inside me.

Something happened down here.

Something bad.

It drove them away. They didn't leave this settlement peacefully. I remember the high-pitched shrieks and rocks tumbling down. I wonder what happened here.

Maybe it was a natural disaster.

I remember the cryo-volcano on Ceres that almost killed us, spewing out ice and mud that flowed like lava after us.

Something brushes past me—

Another shimmer of light.

It flickers and giggles.

I pivot and jerk my head around, but it's already gone, vanished down the tunnel. Luna watches me carefully.

"Did you see that?" I ask. I point down the tunnel.

She shakes her head. "I mean, I see a lot of strange stuff down here . . . but not ghosts . . ."

I let out a defeated sigh. "I guess just being around all this Astral stuff . . . well, it's getting to my head."

"That makes two of us."

We reach the entrance to the cave system. The forcefield lies straight ahead.

We try to breach it, but it bounces us back. We fly back from the entrance.

"Shit, we're still trapped," Luna says, skidding into the dust and crouching.

I also go flailing around, and then struggle to recover my footing. I brush myself off. "No, there's a reason."

"Wait, let me guess—did you get another message from the alien ghosts?"

I shake my head and tap our helmets.

"No, it's protecting us . . ." I say. "We can't breathe out there, remember?"

Luna gives me a long, hard look.

"You really do seem to understand them," she says, replacing her helmet.

"More like—they really do seem to understand us," I say, doing the same.

She turns back to me. Her voice comes out from her helmet, sounding robotic.

"Just remember . . . they used that knowledge to try and destroy us."

"The GGA, the flyovers . . ." I trail off.

That hits me hard. I feel it down to my bones, and it darkens my mood. The connection and empathy I felt for them evaporates, replaced by cold, hard terror.

The way it trapped us down here and lured us deeper. How the Astral tech possessed and manipulated me.

The sheer power of it all.

I turn back to Luna. "Well, we learned one important thing on this reconnaissance mission."

"Oh, what's that?" she replies.

"We're in deeper trouble than I thought. To put it simply—*We're fucked.*"

She lets out a snort laugh. "You can say that again, Captain."

We traverse back through the cave system to the forcefield, and this time, it lets us pass through the veil, spitting us out on the other side. The forcefield reseals.

I try pushing my hand back through it, but then—it flings me back toward the ship, which also starts powering up.

I skid over the ground and land on my knees right in front of our ride back.

The door *whooshes* open.

"Heard! Time to leave," I say, backing away and gesturing for Luna to hurry.

Clearly, we did overstay our welcome. Or maybe it got what it wanted out of me. I saw things, but I also learned the power of their alien technology and just how dangerous the Astrals really are.

Everything on the ship seems to be coming back online, especially once we ascend out of the cave system and whiz through the lavender skies. The suns sink in tandem, dimming into the horizon.

"Major Apollo was right," Luna says, gesturing to the ship's instruments. "They're still a little glitchy. And my neural implant is still MIA . . ."

"Mine too. I'm okay with that interference," I quip with a grin.

"Oh, you don't miss Harold?"

"He's named Harold—for a reason."

That makes us both laugh, but then Luna turns serious.

"Why do you think Apollo sent us down there? It was almost like . . ."

The instruments glitch and flicker as we fly over the mountain range.

"A science experiment?" I say, feeling chilled that we're being manipulated.

Luna frowns. "Yeah, a *mad* science experiment."

"And we're the test subjects?" I reply. "Well, whatever we do, we need to get our stories straight about what we saw. I double-checked. The recording is static. There's no record of our mission."

Silence falls over the cabin. There's only the soft hum of the thrusters. We bank over the mountains and sail low across the surface, skirting the forest.

Finally, I break it. "Do you trust him?"

"Not even close," Luna says right away. "But that's sort of my job . . ."

"Intel? Trust no one?"

"Exactly! You're learning. My dad was intel. I'm sort of a military intel brat."

"Ha, that tracks!"

She smiles, but then turns more serious. We're nearing the base.

"I agree with you," she says softly. "Until we figure out what's really going on here, the less we say, the better . . ."

I nod. "I say we stick to the facts. We made it through the forcefield. We didn't get rejected. The atmosphere adjusted to accommodate us. We saw the light show and followed it into the cave system . . ."

"And that's it?" she says.

I nod. "We got a bad feeling and decided to head back to base. The forcefield let us leave. It could have stopped us probably. But it didn't."

What runs through my head—they already showed me what they wanted me to see, so there was no reason to detain us. But we can't tell Apollo that . . . yet.

"So, that's our story?" Luna says, thinking it over. "Roger that. My lips are sealed . . . but think he'll buy it?"

Fear stabs me, but we don't know who we can trust yet. This is highly sensitive.

"Well, we have to be pretty convincing. And make sure that our stories match."

"Yes, Captain." She shoots me a conspiratorial smile. "Remember that I'm special ops for a reason. Acting is a huge part of intel. My parents taught me that."

I feel relieved, but only a little.

"Let's just hope it works."

And that's when everything, including my neural implant, comes back online.

CHAPTER 19

DRAE

"No, don't blast me!"

I scream that at Kari. She's aiming her weapon at me. Fear lights up her eyes. It's like she doesn't recognize me.

We're in some strange cave system. The crystalline walls radiate purple light. She's cracking up, I realize.

It's a bad case of space trauma. From everything she's been through.

"Kari, it's me . . . Drae," I plead. I take a step toward her. "I love you . . ."

But she narrows her eyes.

"To the stars and back," I finish.

"No, you don't! You're a liar!"

She pulls the trigger—

A hot blast of energy fires out right at me. Pain explodes in my chest, while smoke hits my nostrils. It's me that's burning. My own flesh set ablaze and blackened, while my heart stops.

I bolt upright with a scream on my lips as a brain-sucking feeling hits me.

"Noooooooo!" I gasp aloud.

I'm sweaty and breathing hard. My chest aches like I got blasted. I run my hand over my flesh, but it's normal.

I blink hard in the sunlight filtering through the dorm room window. The trees aren't crystalline and alien.

They're also *normal*.

That was only a terrible nightmare. It's not real; none of it was real.

I exhale slowly, trying to calm the racing of my heart. It doesn't fully work. The physical shock still grips me. It looked and felt so real, even down to that brain-sucking feeling I only get when my neural implant connects.

It felt like we were connected.

Even though that's impossible. She's deployed to interstellar space light-years away from Earth. Plus, the implants don't work that way. We jack in at the post office and record our messages, which are then delivered and experienced in a mail pod. We did discover that when we were in close proximity, they could jack in and connect directly . . . and, well . . .

I blush as desire seizes ahold of me, remembering what happened after our minds melded together.

That finally relaxes me a little. Enough to shake off the strange nightmare anyway. Plus, Estrella is already reminding me about class.

I dress quickly, grab my backpack, and prepare to enter the common room. But my heart sinks. Memories of last night's Anti-Astral rally hit me hard.

Like that blaster in my dream.

Sylvia, I whisper.

I haven't seen Theo since I got back. He was asleep, and I didn't have the heart to tell him. Plus, I'm not sure I want it to get out that I attended the Anti-Astral rally. For one reason—

I don't know who I can trust anymore.

It turned out Sylvia was secretly working for the Resistance and knew about my involvement, too. That means Trebond planted her as my roommate. Theo didn't get arrested.

He could be Resistance, or simply an innocent freshman trying to get his education. Either way, I'm not sure I can trust him. And that makes me sad.

Quickly, I jot down a message for Trebond. *My roommate Sylvia arrested and getting expelled. She's one of your operatives? Jude leading Anti-Astral rallies. Professor Egbert and Goode involved.*

I stop writing, feeling the impact on all of it. But I add one more sentence.

Things on campus feel . . . dangerous . . . like a ticking time bomb . . . no one is safe. We have to be more careful.

—Your old student

I sign it that way and slide it into the book, *A Wrinkle in Time*. I'll drop it off with Willow on my way to class.

I take a deep breath, still feeling shaky from my nightmare, and step into the common room. Theo is there, slumped on the ragged futon as usual.

Only, he looks . . . crestfallen. That's really the only word for it. His tablet is open in his lap with the game he used to play with Sylvia cued up, but he's not tapping at the screen manically like usual. I can see his avatar standing there listlessly, as other avatars surround her.

And kill her.

"SLAYED," reads the screen in bloody splatter over the bloody avatar.

"Uh, you okay?" I ask him cautiously. I don't know how much he knows. "What's going on?"

He tilts his head toward me. "You don't know?"

I shake my head. "I was holed up studying in the library until late. I guess I came home and just passed out."

I feel bad for lying to him. But I have to be careful right now.

"Right, I figured." He snorts. "You and your books. Sylvia didn't come home. I thought she had a study date."

"What happened?" I ask carefully, trying to act like I don't know anything.

"I only found out this morning after frantically texting her friends." He lets out a quiet sigh. "They took her."

"They? Who . . . took her?"

"The security bots. They arrested her for being a Resistance sympathizer. I hear she's going to be expelled, too."

"That's . . . horrible. Did you know?"

He purses his lips, then glances around as if we're being watched. "No, I didn't . . ." But he hedges.

"What . . . tell me."

"Yesterday, I caught her with some flyers. You know, the ones posted all over campus? Disarm the Stars?"

"Yeah, I've seen them. Everyone has, right?"

"We had a fight about it," Theo says. "I'm sorry we kept it from you. Our relationship . . . well . . ."

"You caught feelings?"

He looks saddened and crumples into himself. "Yeah, and it felt like . . . she was the one . . . maybe. We didn't say *love*, but it was going that way. She wasn't like any girl I've ever met."

"And now you feel betrayed?"

I'm getting the feeling that Theo is innocent in all this, blissfully so.

"Yeah, I mean . . . I keep my head down. My mom is a fed, you know? I try not to get caught up in that political stuff. Pro-Astral, Anti-Astral . . . I don't want to ruin my future . . ." He winces at that, then adds, "Tell the truth. Does that sound . . . horribly selfish and cowardly?"

"Not at all," I say quickly. "My dad is a fed, and my mom is a war hero. It's too dangerous. You can't be too careful."

He reminds me of . . . who I used to be . . . before Kari and the Resistance.

I pat him on the shoulder awkwardly. We've grown closer over the last week and a half, but we still barely know each other. He flashes a guilty look at me.

"I just wish she'd listened to me," he says in a shaky voice. "I told her that stuff was dangerous. I said maybe if she turned herself in and confessed, they'd go easier on her . . . a suspension . . ."

"You did the best you could. She was her own person. She made the decision. She knew the risks . . ."

I have to stop myself from saying more and revealing what I know.

There's a sharp *rap* on the door.

Theo ambles up to answer it, while I hang back. "Sylvia Lawson's room?"

Two fed agents stand at the door.

"Yes, but they arrested her already," Theo says in a fearful voice.

"We need to search the premises," they say, pushing the door open. I notice that they're in protective vests with batons, stun guns, and tear gas.

They immediately begin ransacking her room, then sifting through the common room. They're destructive and sloppy about it. The book with the message feels like it's burning a hole in my backpack. I clutch the straps tighter.

Luckily, they don't seem interested in my bag. They also take our statements, asking where we were last night and what we knew about her activities.

"Nothing," I stammer. "I've only been her roommate for a little over a week. I barely even knew her . . ."

They nod. "We know your mother. Don't worry . . . we believe you, kid."

They turn to Theo.

I give him a hard look. *Don't say anything*, I mouth to him. But he collapses under the pressure.

"I only . . . found out yesterday . . ." he confesses. "I caught her with some flyers. I tried to stop her . . ."

They zero in on him now.

"Why didn't you report her?"

"I hoped she'd turn herself in," he starts, making it worse. "I wanted to give her a chance to do the right thing."

"Resistance sympathizers must be turned in," one agent barks.

"You know the law," the other adds.

"Put your hands behind your back," the first one says, pulling out restraints.

"Wait, where are you taking me?" Theo says, sounding terrified. He's shaking. "Am I under arrest? I swear, I didn't do anything wrong—"

"Right, you're not being arrested . . . yet," the officer says. "But we are taking you downtown for questioning."

"But I didn't do anything!" he pleads desperately, but they don't care.

They drag him toward the door. The only upside is that they're not focused on me anymore, even though I'm the guilty one. That makes me feel worse.

"Don't worry," I tell him. "You didn't do anything wrong. Get a message to your mother! She'll get you out . . ."

"Drae . . . I'm sorry . . ."

That's the last thing he says before he's taken away. He feels bad for not going to the authorities about Sylvia.

But I'm the real criminal here.

One thing is certain. Our dorm already feels emptier, and no one is safe.

I wait a few long moments for the agents to clear out, then stagger into the hallway, feeling upset and rattled.

A snide voice echoes down the hall. "Did you enjoy your visitors?"

I jerk my head around. The door down the hall is cracked open.

Jude peers out at me. Behind him, I hear rowdy voices and sounds of drinking games and loud music.

"What . . . are you doing here?"

He closes the distance with a red plastic cup in his hand. He looks a little hungover from the rally last night, but already a little buzzed, too.

"I *live* here," he says, sauntering closer. I can smell the booze on his breath. "We had such a sweet setup in that triple until you decided to ruin it."

The sharpness in his voice snaps at me. His casual friendliness melts away.

It's all ire and venom now.

"Couldn't just enjoy the ride, could you? We could've ruled this school together. That park vermin infected your mind," he says, tapping his neck. "You ruined everything!"

He means Kari and my neural implant.

"Don't call her that. I already told you! She's a war hero now . . ." But I clam up. I'm not supposed to talk about what she did, how she saved everyone . . . including this asshole.

"Oh, so they say," he says. "But I'll find out the truth about both of you. I know you're hiding something. Keeping secrets. You're both traitors. And I'm going to find out."

"What are you talking about? I went to your rally last night! If I was on the other side, why would I do that?"

He looks confused for a moment but quickly recovers.

"You're a spy."

I fight to keep my expression even. I can't let on just how right he is.

"That's pushing it, even for you. We've known each other since we were kids. My dad's a fed, and my mom's a war hero. It wasn't my choice to participate in the Sympathetic Program. But I'm doing my patriotic duty . . ."

"Nice speech," he says, slow clapping to mock me. "I'll get proof."

He leans closer. I can feel his hot breath on my neck and smell the booze. "Watch your back, Drae. You tried to replace me? Well, I got your new roommate arrested. Now you know how it feels. One by one you're going to lose everyone you care about . . ."

I grab his collar. I don't know if I'm triggered and it's PTSD, but I want to punch his face again and again. Everything in me boils into rage.

"You're a coward and a bully," I spit in his face. My cheeks flame with heat.

Suddenly—

The door down the hall bursts open, and his new crew emerges.

"Jude . . . everything okay? You need backup?"

They're all hulking figures. Big, strong, and brutish. They all glare at me.

"Yeah, everything is fine," Jude says, raising his hands over his head like he's innocent—and like I started it. "Just can't be too careful these days."

I'm still clutching his collar. I quickly drop my grip, uncurling my fists.

But it's not easy.

"Who are your new . . . friends?" I manage to choke out.

He shrugs and takes a sip of his cup. "My dad pulled some strings. Had some of his coworker's kids transferred here. These are my new friends. From good families. Rufus, Lionel, Thad . . ."

I back away, trying to calm my temper. They're all Ringers with parents who work at the fed with our fathers. I realize . . . they were selected to act like his personal bodyguards.

"Nice to meet you—and welcome to Berkeley," I manage, though my heart beats wildly. I dig for my old politician charm and flash my signature smile.

Then I rush away, feeling like the coward I used to be.

CHAPTER 20

KARI

We get back to base without incident, though I'm still rattled from my close encounter with the Astrals. As soon as we land, they remove our suits, and we have to go through decontamination because . . . well . . . *aliens*. It's a lengthy process, and I feel sprayed down, raw from being scrubbed over, and limp by the time they finally spit us back out the other side.

"Well, I was thinking I needed a new haircut," Luna says, feeling the back of her newly buzzed head. It's shorter than normal, cut to the bone, but it suits her angular face.

"I think I'm good on showers for a week," I joke back. "Pretty sure all bacteria were eradicated from my body. Nothing was left alive."

We return to the barracks, careful not to talk about everything we saw out there. But worries run through my head anyway. The more I learn about the Astrals, I realize how little we know about them.

What kind of technology was that? How did it adjust the atmosphere? What happened to their settlement? Why did they abandon it? What made them flee?

I remember the rocks tumbling down and the tunnels caving in on them. I'm left with more questions than answers. Not just about them, but about our base, too.

All I know—more is going on here than meets the eye.

And whatever it is . . . it's dangerous. And worse, Luna and I are caught in the middle of it. She climbs onto her rack and flops down with a squeak. I do the same, casting myself down on my rack. My whole body feels like jelly, like it's been thoroughly used up.

I have the urge to confess to Luna and tell her everything—about the weird attraction I have to Major Apollo, and General Titan, and the Sympathetic intervention. How I could shatter Drae's mind if I'm not careful. But also about the secret lab that I stumbled upon.

But secrets are dangerous. She's already keeping quite a few for me.

Compartmentalization is something big in intel. Keeps parts of your life separate. The less anyone knows, the easier it is to keep secrets . . . well . . .

Secret.

Plus, I don't want to worry her about my relationship with Drae. I've already involved my friends more than is normal. My thoughts drive to Drae back on Earthside. Did he receive my exchange?

I do a mental calculation. Still two more days at least. My heart aches. Another five days to wait to hear back from him. That sounds like an eternity. My heart sinks at that news.

Before I can wallow too much, or drift into a restless sleep, there's a noise.

It's a sharp *rap* on the door.

Still feeling a bit bleary and overwhelmed, I stagger up to answer it.

I'm met by those aquamarine eyes. It's Major Apollo. They seem to shift color depending on his mood, or maybe the angle of the light. They're mesmerizing.

They bore into me.

"Sorry to barge in, Captain," he says. "But I got an alert that you were back on base and clear from decontamination."

"Yes, sir," I say, stifling the urge to yawn. I feel completely wrung out.

"I know you're probably tired, but I need to debrief you right away."

"Of course, sir," I say with a nod.

"As expected, all the recording and transmission cut out as soon as you got in proximity to the Astral settlement."

"You were right. Everything went haywire. Did it record anything?"

My heart skips a beat while I wait for his response. If it did, then our cover story might be screwed. But then he replies—

"Nothing. It's all static. Both the ship's cameras and the ones in your suits."

I release my breath.

"The neural implants?" I feel Harold stirring in the back of my mind.

"Nope. They went offline, too."

"The limits of technology. So you're saying there's just our observations?"

He nods. "That's why it's important we do this now . . . before you . . ."

"Start to forget?" I quirk out a smile. "Close encounters with alien life are not something you tend to forget."

"Well, the human mind is prone to subjectivity, and memories fade. Eyewitnesses are known to be notoriously unreliable. But it's all we have."

I notice his emphasis on *human*.

I wonder if other species don't suffer from our memory problems. Is there any way to really know or verify that?

"Let's get this over with," I say. He waits while I return to get ready.

I brief Luna on the situation.

"He's here . . . again?" she says. "What does he have against electronic alerts?"

I just shrug. "I don't know . . . maybe he prefers in-person interactions."

"I think maybe he prefers . . . *Kari* interactions," she jokes back. She raises her eyebrows suggestively.

"Ugh, stop . . . it's important. He needs to debrief me before I start to forget. The recordings all dropped out back there."

She drops the interrogation. Quickly, I shove on my boots and straighten my uniform. I had hoped to have more time to calm down and collect my thoughts before the debriefing, but I know that's the opposite of what they want.

They want me fresh and less likely to be able to cover anything up.

As I prepare to leave, I wonder if there's some truth to what Luna said about Apollo. Regardless, I don't have time to waste. He's standing right outside that door. For some reason, that gives me a rush of adrenaline. My heart rate ticks up. I feel both excited and nervous.

I can't decide if that's a good thing or a bad thing. And which might be worse.

"The atmosphere inside the settlement . . . *adjusted* for you?"

Major Apollo levies that question from across his desk in his office in my debriefing. He sits up straighter and looks eager with his fingers poised over his tablet, but I know this debriefing is being recorded. Maybe even broadcast live for General Titan to observe.

"That's certainly new intel," he continues. "What else happened?"

Now, I get the feeling they expected us to fail. Get rejected like everyone else who tried to enter the settlement. But I keep that to myself, unsure if I can trust him.

"Yes, sir," I say, keeping my answers short and clean. "But I don't have any idea . . . how it did it . . . or even why . . ."

I trail off and bite my lower lip. His eyes probe mine, and I get that adrenaline rush again. *Tell me, tell me, tell me—*

Everything.

I feel him pushing me to confess, to spill my guts, to confide in him.

I pinch my skin to snap out of it. I'm sure it's some kind of interrogation technique. Some kind of good cop, bad cop . . . General Titan being the bad cop. Step one is to get a guardian right out of basic to trust you. Breach protocol and cross boundaries. Show up at her barracks in the middle of the night. Step two, act like you *fucking* care. Like she's not just a number in a uniform, but an actual human being who deserves . . . love. My thoughts derail right there.

But it works. My heart beats faster. The heat flushes me, and I feel slightly dizzy.

Blast him to the stars—he's too good at this.

My lips remain sealed.

"Look, I get it," he says when I don't cough anything up. "It does a number on your head. Close contact with aliens."

"Yes, sir. That's correct."

My words and body language remain stiff and unyielding. He runs one hand through his blond hair and lets out a long sigh. Our eyes lock again.

"Listen, I'll tell you something I'm not supposed to," he goes on in a low voice. "You're the first ones to enter that settlement. Others have made attempts, but *nobody* has succeeded in getting past that forcefield. They even used blasters."

I flinch. "They tried to blast it?"

"Yes, and it almost got them killed."

"What happened?"

He sets his lips into a thin line. "The forcefield deflected the shots back at them. Almost like it was . . . *personal*. Like it was aiming right for them. You gotta admire it almost, if it wasn't so infuriating—and worse, dangerous. Even deadly."

"How so?" I ask, trying to keep him talking.

He frowns. I can't help but notice even that looks attractive on him.

"Well, it's one hell of a defense system. It acts intelligent, maybe even sentient."

That's another way to say . . . *alive*.

"Sir, that's above my pay grade. But it is alien technology. Anything is possible. What else did they try to get past it?" I take a risk now. I drop the name. "Surely General Titan didn't stop there?" I add quickly. "I'd think breaching the forcefield would be a top priority."

He raises his eyebrows. "I didn't realize you were acquainted. The general tried EMP weapons, hacking, explosives, and radiation pulses, but nothing worked. Part of the problem is that all our electronics and systems go on the fritz down there. And, well, almost all of our tech is based on electricity. Nobody has managed to make it through that blasted barrier . . ."

The silence descends, hard and fast and loaded.

"So, you were saying—we're the first?"

"Not only the first. But based on your account . . . it just let you through? And then adjusted the atmosphere to make you and Private Starfire more comfortable?"

"Right. That about sums it up. Sorry, I don't know the technical term for it."

He leans forward. Intensity crackles between us in the recirculated air. "Captain, I don't think there is a *technical* term. These are all big firsts."

I feel the impact of that. The *first* to have contact with the alien settlement. "Is that why you sent us in alone?"

He looks pained. "Right, I wanted to brief you. Trust me, I did. It killed me to keep you in the dark . . . but that's what we signed up for. I was overruled."

I take another risk. "By General Titan? Or Secretary-General Andromeda?"

His silence is answer enough.

All the way up.

I let that sink in.

"Captain Skye, what else did you see down there? Don't leave anything out. It's important—I need every single detail. You're the only humans who have laid eyes on the interior of that settlement."

I look into his eyes, and he looks so earnest and frightened for humanity, but I can't tell him everything. Not only do I not trust *them*—they've proven they're keeping things from us—but I made a deal with Luna. We got our stories straight, and now I have to stick to it.

I clear my throat and expression, projecting neutrality. Even though, underneath my calm exterior, my heart is pounding, and my palms are sweaty.

"Yes, sir. From the beginning?"

He nods and poises his hand over his tablet. "Whatever you know, whatever you saw down there, even the smallest detail, it could be the thing that saves us."

That makes me feel even worse. I remember Luna reminding me about the GGA and what they did to our kids. But I stick to what we decided.

Quickly, I tell him about our electronics going on the fritz as expected, then how the forcefield let us into the settlement, the crystal veins pulsing with light that lit our way into the caves, the strange temporal disturbances and how it felt like time was bending.

I finish by saying we got a bad feeling and booked it out of there. I don't tell him about the ghosts, the voices, connecting to the crystals, or almost blasting Luna.

"Sir, it's hard to put it into words . . . what we experienced down there," I conclude my recounting of the mission, trying to look vulnerable. "I'm not a writer or a poet, or very good with words. And I suspect that's who you'd need to describe it properly."

He smiles at that. A softer moment passes between us, before he turns more serious. "You can confirm it was uninhabited? Did you see any . . . *bodies* . . . anything like that?"

"You mean, you sent us in thinking that live aliens could be down there?"

He looks hurt again. "What we don't know far outweighs what we do."

"No, sir . . . no dead bodies or live aliens. I'm pretty sure I would've led with that."

What I don't say is—

I saw them; I saw their ghosts as time bent; they were light-people; there were children playing; they were happy and thriving . . . until something terrible drove them away.

Is that what he's digging for? What does he know that he's not telling me? But I clam up and keep my expression neutral. I'm not sure how much I can trust him . . . yet.

"Anything else you'd like to report? Any idea why they abandoned that settlement?"

I flinch slightly. Did he read my thoughts?

But then I remember that's impossible. It's just an obvious question.

"No, sir. That's a mystery. But clearly something did . . . I just don't know what."

He scrutinizes me for a long moment. *Too long.* I stay strong; I don't flinch. It's not easy though. Finally, he lets out a deep sigh and sets his tablet aside. He looks stressed out.

"Well, we need more than that," he says. "We're running out of time."

My heart jumps faster.

"Right, I know. But I can't help if you don't tell me what's really going on."

A long moment passes between us. "Captain, it's not that complicated. Space Force is still run by hardliners who love military solutions. They want to annihilate the aliens."

I take that in. "Yes, of course. They wanted that interstellar war between the Proxies. But sir, we know so little about the Astrals. Think about it! From their perspective, humanity looks like a threat to the universe with our violent tendencies. In fact, that's what they used against us."

"Yes, our violent history. Forever wars. Genocides. Colonization. Slavery. All taken together—it's a damning indictment. Humanity has so many sins, including the ongoing ones."

I'm shocked he admitted that.

"Sending our kids to the stars to die?" I say, knowing this is dangerous territory.

He doesn't respond, but I go on.

"Sir, I know I'm just a lowly grunt, but military solutions don't seem to really solve anything. They just lead to more need for . . . military solutions. Have we considered another route? Maybe looking for a more diplomatic solution?"

I sit up straighter, feeling the need to continue. "Sir, if we could only find some way to communicate with them. Even get them a message. Open diplomatic channels with them . . ."

"You don't sound like a grunt," he says softly. "You sound wiser than your years. I'm afraid to report that while Space Force has changed since you uncovered the invasion plans, it's not as much as we both might like . . ."

I nod, but I still feel crestfallen. It must show on my face, though I try to hide it.

"Of course, sir. I know that. And you're right. This is what we signed up for."

"They want a military solution, not diplomatic. If you're looking for that, then I'm afraid you shouldn't have enlisted."

He's right, but I can't shake what I saw down there . . . the school . . . the young ones . . . something happened to drive them away. But I also know what they did to our kids on that bridge. Suddenly, something else occurs to me. Maybe they're more like humanity that way . . . capable of both creation and destruction? But which powerful impulse wins out?

I remember how the crystals possessed and controlled me. The strange message—
PLAGUE ON THE UNIVERSE!
SPREADING TO INFECT!
KILL THE VIRUS!

My flashback makes me flinch. But leaves me confused. What does it mean?

I have the urge to tell Apollo. Maybe he can help me decode it.

But I catch myself. I have to stay on the same page with Luna. I'm sure she's getting debriefed shortly. Apollo gives me a hard look. Almost like he . . . *knows*. Or at least suspects.

His eyes linger on me. They seem to trace the curve of my jawline. The swoop of my neck down to my starched uniform. Over my chest in a way that makes me shiver with desire.

Why does he have this effect on me? I wonder with another deep shiver.

I shake it off quickly, trying to keep it together. It's just errant adrenaline from the mission. I'm still jittery and twitchy. After all, I almost blasted my friend to smithereens. I have to stay focused. I can't let him crack me open so I break down and spill my dark secrets.

I'm still harboring so many.

"If you think of anything else, please report it right away," Apollo says, before he dismisses me from his office—and from his powerful grip on me.

I stagger up and head for the door, feeling more worried than before our debriefing. Questions circle through my head. Will Major Apollo find out what I'm hiding? And worse, relieve me of duty?

CHAPTER 21

DRAE

I burst outside into the sunlight, still heated from my run-in with Jude. I'm breathing hard like I just ran a marathon. I double over and try to catch my breath.

I need to go to the library and return the book to Willow with the urgent message for Trebond about the rally last night, even though I'm starting to feel like they're already one step ahead, and I'm the one in the dark. But suddenly—

I can't breathe.

It feels like everything is closing in on me. The sun feels too hot. Security bots roam the campus, even more than yesterday. It feels more like a military occupation every day. I notice more metal scaffolding on the buildings. Is it to protect us—or control us?

The crowded walking paths bustle with students and security bots. I start to feel jittery and paranoid. One thought races through my head like a blaster shot—

They're coming for me.

Once I think it, I can't un-think it. I jerk around and spot one. It seems to lock onto me.

Then I look the other way—

And another bot is targeting me.

It's only a matter of seconds before they turn their sirens on, wheel over with a great *whirring,* and detain me for questioning. Or worse—arrest me.

They already took my roommates.

Jude said they were watching me. My lungs constrict like in my nightmare where Kari blasted me. I gasp, trying to draw in air, but my lungs spasm and won't breathe. I crack my eyes open. The bots approach me, coming from either side. There's no escaping them.

Even if I could run, they'd stun me.

I hyperventilate at that thought, feeling even more trapped. Still, I want to run away, leave everything behind. I can't stay here . . . college is turning into a war zone.

How long before Earth rearmament happens? And the bots go from stunners and rubber bullets to real blasters?

I hear rumblings around campus, and on the newsfeeds, the ones my mother watches on repeat from her recliner with her whiskey on ice and her pill bottle.

I sink to my knees, my lungs gasping for air but unable to breathe it in. Why can't I breathe? Why am I suffocating?

The urge to flee is so strong.

And more—

I feel so alone. Rho is gone, and I don't know when I'll hear from Kari again.

Both gone.

Far away in the stars.

I should've stayed up there, too. I take one staggering step forward, trying to shake off the anxiety gripping my body.

The bright sunlight contrasts with my panic, only amplifying it and paralyzing me. They took my professors and then my roommates, now Jude is across the hall.

He's terrorizing and stalking me.

I can't stay here.

I'm about to tell Estrella to summon my transport so I can leave college—

But she pipes up first.

With the one thing that stops me dead in my tracks, keeping me from running.

Drae, incoming Sympathetic exchange. Please report to the post office right away.

My heart thumps in my chest, while oxygen rushes into my lungs like a cool breeze. I gasp in deep, calming breaths that chase the anxiety away. My limbs unclench and come back to life, releasing me so I can stand up straight again.

It's Kari.

I finally received a new message.

The panic leaves my body, almost like it was never there. She's my lifeline, my reason to stay here and fight back.

I blink, and my vision clears. The bots I thought were coming for me—whiz right past like I'm not even there. They have another target. A student farther down.

They screech up—

And scan them. The student drops their bag, and flyers spill out onto the lawn. I glimpse Anti-Astral propaganda.

I squint at their face, wondering if they were at the rally last night, if that's what radicalized them to post those. The bots also scan the flyers, and then they *beep*—

"Scan complete. Continue on your way," the bot barks in a robotic voice.

They switch off their sirens and leave the student in peace to collect the flyers.

That chills me. If I didn't already suspect that the fed government was supporting the Anti-Astral movement, that's all the proof I need. They released the student after scanning the flyers.

If those had been *Disarm the Stars* flyers, their fate would've been different.

I'm sure of it.

Hastily, I add to the secret note for Trebond, then tuck it back into the book.

I need to get to the post office, but as much as I want to forget everything else, this can't wait. Quickly, I stop by on the way, leaping up the steps two at a time.

I burst into the busy, air-conditioned lobby and scan for Willow. She's behind the front desk. Is it my imagination, or does she look . . . paler than normal?

She locks onto me—and I hurry over.

"Returning it so soon?" she asks when I slide the book toward her.

"Well, it was such a good read," I reply, glancing around to make sure nobody is watching. "I couldn't put it down."

"Of course." She runs her hand over the worn cover of *A Wrinkle in Time*. "One of my favorites since I was a kid."

"Right, I can see why. Now it's one of mine, too." I lean in closer and lower my voice. "I took a lot of . . . *notes*. You'd probably like to read them right away."

Her eyes sharpen. She sets her lips.

"Of course. Thank you for the return."

Subtly, she slides the book under the desk. I need to get to the post office, but I hesitate. My eyes linger on her carefully.

"No more recommendations today?"

"Not today." She flashes a tight smile. "But give me a day to think about it."

That means—

No new messages.

After everything that happened at the rally last night and today with my roommates, that triggers my alarm bells.

Why wouldn't Trebond send me a message? Even if it's just to stay put?

Unrest is clearly spreading through campus. I can feel it like electricity sizzling in the air everywhere I go now.

But I don't have time to worry about that. *Kari, Kari, Kari* . . . beats my heart emphatically, urging me to hurry.

I nod a quick goodbye to Willow.

"I'll stop by tomorrow," I say, backing away. "To see if you got new books in."

Then I bound down the steps with my heart thumping wildly in my chest.

All I can think about is . . .

Kari.

I rush across campus, not even noticing the multiplying security bots or the pastel flyers peppering campus like warnings. The propaganda has turned darker and more dangerous. They contain crude drawings of Astrals getting blasted with skulls and crossbones.

I hit a logjam at the scaffolding that now lines all the walking paths, but instead of weaving around, I stay in line and file along like a good, law-abiding student.

I can't afford to get stopped.

Finally, it clears. Estrella helps me find a shortcut that's not crowded.

I make it to the post office and check in.

"Draeden Rache . . . I'm here for my Sympathetic Exchange? I got an alert."

"Yes, right this way, Mr. Rache," says the postal worker. I vaguely recognize her, but it's been a while since I've visited the post office. "We've been expecting you."

My heart beats faster as we pad down the corridor. She takes me back to my usual mail pod. The door cracks open.

"Have a good exchange, Mr. Rache," she says with a placid smile.

Then she hits the button.

The pod closes and seals shut, as the meditative music fades up, along with some soothing aromatherapy. The lights dim to pitch darkness. It's all meant to relax and ease me into the experience, but my heart hammers even faster.

I have so many questions—

How is Kari? Where in the stars did they deploy her? What's her new mission?

But most of all—

Does she still love me?

Bold words flash in my retinas.

INITIATING SYMPATHETIC EXCHANGE

That's accompanied by Estrella's voice. *Calibrating neural link*, she communicates in a pleasant tone. *Connecting now.*

I get that brain-sucking feeling in the back of my head. It used to freak me out, but now I ache for it. It means one thing.

I'm connecting to her.

Then suddenly—

She's standing right in front of me.

CHAPTER 22

KARI

I head back to my barracks after my debriefing with Major Apollo with more questions than answers. I feel even more confused and unsettled than before. A million questions fire through my brain.

But one pushes to the front—

Why . . . us?

Why did the forcefield let us through? Now, I have confirmation of my suspicions that it rejected everyone else. So, what makes me and Luna different? Once we got inside, why did it single me out and show me all those things?

Luna said she didn't see the ghosts. I'm also the one who connected with that Astral computer terminal—if you can even call their tech that. It sounds so pedestrian. The limitations of human language and thought occur to me now. I can barely voice what I experienced down there, let alone explain it. The *why* questions haunt me. I wish I could talk to Drae about this.

Frustration surges through me at our separation. At the lag time. At the distances of interstellar space. After we got paired, I would've prayed for as much distance between us as possible. But now that's changed. Everything has changed.

This most of all—

I need him.

That hits me like a gut punch. I've never needed anyone before. My father, but after he deserted, I learned that you couldn't depend on anyone else. You had to take care of yourself. Other people disappointed and abandoned you.

Drae, I need you, I whisper to nobody.

The silence fills in, along with worries about the fidelity of his heart. The quiet is broken up only by the smack of my boots. The corridors remain deserted, imbuing the base with an empty feeling like a haunted house. The lab was busy, but it's secret—and I'm barred from entry.

Again, I wish I could talk to Drae about all of this. But I don't even know if he's gotten my exchange yet. Any response is still days away from being delivered. Who else can I turn to?

My father.

Maybe he has some new intel on the Astrals that could help us. He deployed his Raider fleet all over the universe, looking for signs of the Astrals, their home world, or other settlements. I can also tell him what I discovered here.

I should go back to the barracks and make sure Luna's debriefing went okay. I'm sure they took her right after me. But instead, I reverse course and head in the other direction. Harold shows the route and projects it in my retinas as I'm still learning the base's layout.

Green arrows illuminate along the floors, directing me. I remember the veins of light in the Astral settlement, how they beckoned me deeper into the caves. Their technology echoes our own, but it's also so different. I'm still learning, decoding, searching for an answer to solve this problem, one that doesn't lead to—

Another Great War.

But Space Force is still dominated by hardliners who favor military solutions over all other options. Apollo told me that, but the flicker in his eyes, the empathy etched into his face—it revealed something. We might be more aligned on this than I thought. But that's dangerous territory. He could lose his ranking.

We both could.

Or worse, get dishonorably discharged and shipped back Earthside to the Park, the housing development where I grew up that's populated by those who couldn't hack it—deserters and their families.

I reach my destination and rush into the post office lobby. I feel a rush of familiarity. It only grows stronger when I spot Anton behind the counter. Bots zip around him, beeping in annoyance.

He scowls as one nudges his boot.

"Sorry, I'm not like you," Anton says. "I'm fast for a human though, if you must know. Just slow for artificial intelligence."

They beep back loudly.

"They driving you crazy?" I ask with a teasing smile. "Need some company?"

He looks over with relief.

"Thank the stars," he says. "And yes . . . *certifiably* crazy. Scram, bots!" He shoos them away. "She's here for me. Got it?"

They beep and protest more, but take the hint and scurry into the back.

"How can I help you, Captain Skye?" he says, slipping into postmaster mode.

"I need to send a message."

"Who's the recipient?"

I hold his face, then utter the code.

"*Jack Sparrow.*"

His eyebrows raise, but he remains composed. "Of course. Let me look up where he's stationed currently."

"I need to send him a message once you locate him. It's . . . urgent."

"Of course, Captain."

He taps at his watch. It looks like a relic from before the wars, but it's actually a key that all the postmasters and their workers get. It allows them to communicate on private channels that aren't monitored by Space Force.

I know Anton rigged his to send messages to my father on his Raider ship. I wait while he fiddles with the dials, manipulating the levers on the dial.

"Anything else?"

"Uh, I know it's too early."

"Yes, any communication from your Sympathetic is still several days away from being delivered. I can confirm that he received your most recent message."

"He did? Did he reply yet?"

"He's likely there as we speak," Anton says, making my heart leap. "But with the lag time, it's impossible to verify the timeframe of events back Earthside."

"Of course, thanks."

But he can see the worry written on my face, plain as a communication package.

"Care to step into my office?" he says. "Maybe I can assist you further?"

"Yes, that would be great."

"Right this way . . ."

Anton leads me past the room with the pods into an office that I didn't even know was tucked back there. This base is full of mysteries. An officers' lounge. Secret labs.

I can't help but wonder—

What other mysteries is it hiding?

The office is cozy and filled with old furniture that looks like it would belong in an antique shop, not a Space Force base. Unlike the hard-edged plastic chairs and desks in Major Apollo's office, everything here is soft and worn and slightly dumpy.

But as I sink into the armchair by the old-fashioned desk that looks like it was fashioned from actual wood (though that could be only an illusion), I feel myself relax. Some of the tension finally melts away.

"Comfortable?" Anton asks. "I quite like the furnishings. Postmaster Haven had them sent here along with me."

"The more I learn about the postmasters, the more I realize I don't know. This is quite unexpected."

He leans and lowers his voice. "The furniture serves another purpose."

"What's the that?" I say, catching how his energy has become secretive.

"They have sensors embedded that interfere with any . . . *recording* devices."

"Really? That's genius. Does Space Force know about it . . ."

"Not to our knowledge," Anton says. "They turn a blind eye to the postmasters. They depend on us too much for everything. They don't want enemies."

"So, communication is the true superpower?" I joke back. But I mean it.

"Anyway, this is a safe space. You can tell me . . . *everything*. The postmasters are on your side even more than you know."

"How so?" I ask, my heart beating faster. My question hangs in the air.

"We don't want another war," he replies. "We'd prefer another solution. If we can help facilitate that, then we will."

"So, why are they helping me?"

"Because you're the one who prevented the last war from happening. I know that most civilians—and even most guardians—don't realize how close we came to the brink of war recently."

"That's true," I say, still feeling unworthy. I know I'm only a lowly guardian caught in a big escalation. "But it's becoming clear that there's a lot going on here that you don't know about . . ."

"Yes, and I'm hoping you'll tell me."

I want to tell him, but I hesitate. "We should summon Luna. This involves her, too. We were all deployed here together."

I realize it's time to come clean . . . about *everything* . . . to my friends. And I can't do that without Luna joining us.

Suddenly, there's a *rap* on the door. That's accompanied by annoyed *beeps*.

"Let me through already!" a familiar voice gripes. "I'm supposed to be here!"

"Is that . . . Luna?" I say in surprise.

Anton cracks one of his lopsided smiles. "I sent her a message to meet us back here. Great minds think alike?"

"You can say that again."

I feel gratitude for him and his quick thinking and action. But most of all, for having people I love and trust with me.

"Come in!" Anton calls.

The bots beep, but all her to open the door. She thrusts it open to more complaints. "Feisty little suckers, aren't they?" she says, shoving it shut on them.

"You can say that again," Anton says with a laugh. "Welcome to my domain."

She surveys it with an appreciative smile and flops into the other chair. "Nice digs, Ksusha. So, what did I miss?"

It almost feels like old times back at basic training. *Almost.* There are still three gaping holes—Nadia, Percy, and Genesis. But it's better than nothing.

"Did they debrief you already?" I ask her quickly.

"Sure did. It was short and sweet though. I stuck to the story. Played dumb. I'm good at that." She forms a blank expression. "Yes, sir. No, sir. Uh, I guess that's above my ranking. I don't know."

"Who conducted it?" I ask.

"General Titan," she says. "I guess she summoned me right after they took you."

"Titan is important," Anton says. "She runs the whole operation here."

"Yeah, and she's a real piece of Space Force work," Luna says with a grimace. "Real tough. Tries to trick you into trusting her and spilling your secrets."

"You stonewalled her?" I ask.

"Like a pro," she says with a wink. "My parents are both former special ops. And I say *former* lightly. Sometimes I think they're still active agents. Anyway, how do you think I survived childhood?"

That makes us all laugh. "Did they good cop, bad cop you?" I ask.

"They used every PSYOP tactic in the books," she says with a grimace. "And even some off the books. Trust me, it's a minor miracle I survived to adulthood."

"Yeah, I wouldn't want to try to crack you in an interrogation," Anton adds.

"Why did I get Major Apollo?" I ask curiously. "I'm higher ranked, so why would the General interrogate you?"

"My guess is that General Titan thought Luna would be easier to break," Anton says, thinking it over. "Little did they know . . . she's like an iron safe."

"That's true," I say, nodding along. "Also, it's possible that . . . well . . ."

I blush and trail off.

But Luna jumps in. "That Major Apollo has a *special interest* in Captain Skye here."

"What do you mean?" Anton says in confusion. "What am I missing here?"

Luna makes a kissy face, which makes Anton cringe back. "Ugh, no way . . ."

"Yeah, tell me about it," I say, feeling even more embarrassed. "Not only is it unprofessional, but there's Drae . . ."

Anton grasps the challenges. "That's . . . messy. Do you trust him?"

"Not entirely," I say, biting my lower lip. "Something is *different* about him."

"Are you special ops now or aren't you?" Luna challenges me.

"Yes, I guess so."

"Then he's a potential asset," she goes on. "He's a mark. This attraction—or whatever in the stars it is—is something you can use against him."

"What do you mean?" I ask, feeling my cheeks burn hotter.

"Well, if it was me," Luna goes on, "I'd get him alone out of a work setting. Get him to confide. Spill his deepest secrets. I'm guessing he's got a lot of them."

"More than you know," I say in a soft voice. "This whole base is full of them."

As quickly as I can, I fill them in on everything, starting from the beginning. Keeping things to myself is only going to sink me. It's become clear I need their help if I'm going to survive this mission.

I tell them about the secret lab. General Titan's intervention about the Sympathetic Program and my relationship with Drae.

Anton looks shocked. "So, you're saying . . . if you're not careful you could shatter his mind?"

I nod quickly. "That's why this Apollo thing is . . . dangerous . . . like walking a tightrope . . ."

"I'm so glad my Sympathetic is just friendship vibes," he says, absorbing that. "I had no idea that could happen."

"Hard same," Luna echoes. "They don't tell you that in your orientation."

"But there's more," I say, and then tell them everything I learned in my debriefing. This time, I tell them about what I didn't tell Apollo. The way the Astrals showed me things—echoes of the past—and let me into their computer systems. The message screamed at me at the end.

PLAGUE ON THE UNIVERSE!
SPREADING TO INFECT!
KILL THE VIRUS!

"Asteroid fires, what does that mean?" Anton asks, frowning at the cryptic message.

"And why did they pick you?" Luna says. "I agree, they let us both in. But obviously, I wasn't their target. I didn't see any of that stuff . . ."

"Kari, it's clear they've chosen you," Anton agrees. "To communicate . . ."

"But why?" I ask, feeling rattled. "And what else do they want from me?"

None of it makes any sense. In frustration, I lean back and gaze at the ceiling. Anton's office has skylights like the other officers. The suns are both starting to set, casting the sky into twilight, while the trees shimmer with dimming purple and pinkish light. This singular moon is so beautiful and full of life—albeit strange, alien life—that I start to wonder something.

I ask the question I keep coming back to after the mission to the settlement.

"So, why did they leave their home? What happened that drove them away?"

Anton shrugs. "We don't know. There are many possibilities. Both natural . . . and unnatural. We know so little about them."

"Well, there's something else bothering me," I confess. "Don't you think it's a coincidence that we happened to stumble upon the abandoned settlement?"

"Major Apollo said they traced elements from the GGA explosive device," Luna says. "And that led them to this moon. It seemed like a reasonable explanation at the time."

"All the way out here in interstellar space? This small moon orbiting a planet? Also, this base . . . it feels like it's not new construction . . . like it's been here longer."

"You're right," Anton says, sitting up straighter. "It's like finding a needle in a haystack. The universe is so vast. It's not impossible—anything is possible, of course—but it's highly improbable.

"Occam's razor again?" I ask, knowing how that helped save us last time.

"You're both right," Luna says. "I didn't think to question the backstory. Rookie mistake. It holds up if you don't look too hard. But there are too many leaps in logic that don't quite add up."

I nod, thinking fast. "So how did Space Force *find* the abandoned settlement?"

They both look stumped.

Suddenly, something occurs to me. Any official records would be highly encrypted and lock us out, just like that secret lab. *Access Denied* would be the least of my problems if they caught me trying to snoop through the classified records.

But what if there's another type of record that they haven't considered? Records that fall outside of their purview—because they don't control that part of Space Force?

"Anton, does the post office here have any archives or records they keep private?" I ask him, keeping my voice low. "Can we access the earliest communications sent from the base?"

He looks at me in amazement. "That's brilliant. I can't believe I didn't think of it, but you're right. The first thing they'd do when installing a new base—no matter how top secret—is set up the post office."

"Exactly," Luna chimes in. "Because Space Force can't do *anything* this deep in interstellar space if they don't have the ability to effectively communicate."

Excitement grips me.

"Anton, doesn't the post office keep archives of all communications?"

He nods. "They sure do."

That's the answer. I bolt to my feet. Luna and Anton follow my lead.

"Well, that's our solution. We should be able to find out the history of the base—and what really happened out here."

Anton grins and rubs his hands together in anticipation. "Oh, goody. My favorite! I love archival research."

"A study project?" Luna says. "Now you're thinking like an intel operative."

"Let's do some digging," I say as Anton leads the way to the private archives. "We've been one step behind since we got here—let's try to get one step ahead for a change."

CHAPTER 23

DRAE

The blackness drops away as amethyst light berates my senses. Slowly, the strange landscape fades into view, bathed in purplish light and peppered with crystalline trees that sprout into a forest.

I'm staring deeply into her eyes.

Kari, I whisper.

But she stares back at me blankly. She doesn't respond; she can't hear me.

This is only a recording.

All I can do is experience her message. I feel her thoughts, her emotions, and her heart beating wildly and uncaged. She hasn't spoken a word yet, but I know one thing with certainty. The knowing of it is as crystal clear as the grove of trees surrounding us and casting off prisms that dance over the glittery surface.

She still loves me.

I can feel it pulsing out from her mind and her heart like a warm blanket wrapping around my body on a cold night, like the heat from a smoldering fire that's ready to reignite and burn hotter if only I'm there to provide the spark.

I want to spark her so badly.

I want to draw out that fire again, even if it burns me. I'd welcome the pain.

But underneath her love for me, I feel her anxiety and fear radiating out in rhythm to her pulse. Wherever she is—whatever she's doing—she's afraid.

Deeply so.

In a way that I've never felt in her. She's so brave and stoic in situations where I'd run away like a coward.

But there's more. She's worried that I don't feel the same way about her. Her insecurity flares out in a sharp burst that breaks my heart, as her emotions flood into my brain through the neural links.

Of course I miss you . . . I try to say, waiting to reassure her. *More than anything. I think about you all the time.*

But my words can't be received that way. She's only a recording—a vision captured from the past and replayed now, light-years away—though so lifelike and inflected with depth and emotion. It's hard to take my eyes off her, but I drag them away to inspect her environment and discern any clues. The amethyst light filters through the clouds, where two suns perch in the heavens. The crystals grow everywhere, sprouting from the ground and catching the light, transforming it into prisms. Rainbows dance at our feet.

But something startles me. This is the same landscape I saw in my nightmare last night. The one where Kari blasted me. Even down to the purplish tint and the slant of the light shining through those crystalline formations sprouting up around us with their prisms.

How is that possible?

A strange coincidence?

It has to be.

I think back to the dream, looking for some anomaly, but the details match. My memory of this dream hasn't faded. It's still crisp and fresh. That's also strange . . . usually dreams dissipate in the breaking of dawn, unable to withstand the onslaught of morning.

But not this one.

Before I can think through it more, Kari finally starts talking. Her message sounds urgent. She tells me that she's stationed on a remote moon base, deep in interstellar space. Only it doesn't have a name.

The whole operation is top secret. She tells me about the Astral settlement and the need to produce actionable intel. And fast. How Secretary-General Andromeda's position grows weaker by the day, as the old proxy tensions start to resurface.

I knew about Andromeda, but I'm stunned about the Astral settlement. I'm also surprised that it's not redacted from her message, but then she tells me about the postmasters convening about us, even transferring Anton to her base and making him the postmaster there.

How they're protecting us. How important our connection remains. She also tells me about the intervention by General Titan, how if we're not careful, if we break each other's hearts, then it could shatter our minds. It's happened before.

That shocks me. I knew we could hurt each other. That comes with the territory. We didn't mean to fall in love. Well, I've loved her since high school, but more in a *crushing-on-the-girl-who-hates-you* way.

I never dreamed she'd love me back, or that we'd fall for each other in space, in the middle of stopping a great war, only to be separated again under the threat of another invasion and worse. But now—

We could shatter each other's minds?

The fear I see is reflected plainly in her eyes. The timer ticks down as she finishes briefing me. I see her eyes flick to the diminishing numbers. Her face falls.

She speaks in a pleading voice.

Drae, I miss you . . . I need you . . . don't forget about me . . . because . . .

Two seconds. One second left—

I love you even from these distant stars.

That's when the communication cuts off. My heart drops like a stone, as the brain-sucking feelings pull me out. Everything goes black.

The blackness fades as the lights dim up slowly, while I reorient to my reality.

I'm sitting in the mail pod. I never went anywhere, of course. I'm stunned but also crestfallen. I can't believe it's over and cut her off. I can't believe that . . .

She's gone already.

That message was too short, and most of it was taken up with briefing me on intel that's critical to share with Trebond and the Resistance. What she told me flashes through my head. I can't believe that we've located an Astral settlement.

That's major news.

But the last part hit me hardest. She said that our connection was so strong, that we have to be careful, or we could shatter each other's minds, only it cut her off before she could explain more.

That definitely wasn't in the Sympathetic Program orientation.

I do remember something about being careful to tell the truth (or your neural implant will shock you). But nothing about actual brain damage. I trust Kari to the stars and back—but can I trust myself?

I remember how I felt around Willow. Can I control myself? Can my heart remain steady and faithful?

Or will it betray me?

Before I can process everything, the lights are already dimming down.

I have to record my response to her. When I checked in, they told me that the lag time was about three days because it was being expedited. I'm guessing that's thanks to Postmaster Haven. Even so, that's a long time. Longer than we've ever faced.

I start to panic and freak out. I need more time to think. I'm not ready to record my exchange. But I can't stop what's already been set in motion.

Estrella's voice pipes up.

Initiating Sympathetic Exchange.

The timer in my retinas cues up.

10:00 Minutes

That's when the lights dim to black as I'm sucked into another reality.

My consciousness fades up. Pale moonlight cascades down over me, casting long shadows. I glance around.

The area looks wooded with tangled branches scratching at the moonlit sky.

I feel a jolt of fear.

Where am I?

I look down at the moss under my boots. That's when it hits me. I'm standing on Founders' Rock. The same location as the Anti-Astral rally—the same spot where Jude made his hate-filled speech.

Interesting that my mind is projecting this environment as the backdrop.

I wonder what it means?

But the timer is already ticking down. I need to get talking—and fast.

Kari . . . I miss you . . . more than you can ever know.

My voice comes out halting, filled with yearning and desire.

I knew leaving you would be hard—but I didn't realize it would be this hard.

I know my life seems easier on the surface. I'm at college back Earthside, and you're fighting a war up there. But it's harder than it looks.

Everything is supposed to go back to normal, but nothing feels normal anymore.

Look, it's probably a coincidence . . . but I think I recognized the landscape from your exchange. The crystal trees, the purple light. I can't shake the sight of it.

That's the moon where you're stationed?

I run my hand through my lengthening curls, feeling self-conscious. But I force myself to confide in her anyway.

It's going to sound crazy . . . but I saw it in my nightmare last night. You were so upset.

I don't know what you were seeing. I don't think it was me . . . but you blasted me. I'm not sure if it was even real, or if I'm . . .

Losing it.

But this dream.

It's strange and unnatural.

It doesn't fade with waking.

Then everything crowds into my brain, so I start talking, everything spilling out.

Things are so tense on campus right now. Jude is back at school and tormenting me. Receiving your exchange today is the only thing that kept me from running away.

I brief her on everything going on. The Anti-Astral rally. The professors being replaced by federation puppets like Mr. Egbert. How Trebond isn't just talking about Resistance anymore—but outright revolution. My new agent handler . . .

Willow . . .

My voice catches on her name. I didn't mean to mention her. I worry my attraction can be felt through the neural link—and that Kari will pick up on it.

I clear my throat, and try to clear my mind. It was only a flicker.

A hot second of hidden desire.

That flashed through my mind.

But that weakness, coupled with her insecurity . . . I worry that I just blew it.

Kari, I'm sorry . . . I stammer, trying to backpedal. *I swear . . . it's not anything real. Nothing like what I feel for you.*

The lame excuses tumble out, one by one, spilling like poison from my lips.

I barely know her.

It was just a reaction.

I can't always control how my body responds.

I'm under a lot of pressure.

Finally, I stumble upon the truth at the bottom of the deep, dark well.

I'm too young and too dumb and have too many bad habits that I still need to unlearn. Space junk from my past, from hanging out with Jude and Loki, from high school. Maybe even from my parents.

Please, forgive me . . . I'm not perfect. I'm a mess. That's the truth. I'm barely holding it together. I love you so much, too much. And I'm so scared that I'm going to mess it up . . .

And destroy . . .

Us.

That's my greatest fear.

I sputter to a halt.

I feel my cheeks burning and tears streaming down my cheeks. Humiliation and fear grip me.

Anyway, the dream thing.

That's impossible, right?

It felt like we were connected through our neural links . . . in real time. Like when I saw you in person on your father's ship. But we can't do that. Not at this distance. Not with this lag time.

But in the dream . . . it felt like I was right there.

Beside you.

With no delay.

Not like these recorded messages where we can only experience the past. A time capsule of you from three days ago. Even expedited by the postmasters, that's a long time to wait.

But I hope you'll wait for me.

I hope you can forgive my mistakes.

The truth is . . . I'm so afraid. I don't know who I can trust down here. Trebond and the Resistance. Willow told me that they're keeping things from me. Controlling the intel flow. I feel manipulated by them, like I'm in the dark. Just like you feel about your superior officers.

What does my mom always say?

It's an old military saying.

Same shit.

Just a new location.

The timer has almost ticked down, and I wish I had longer. I stammer out—

But I know one thing—

I can trust you.

Always.

Please forgive me.

The timer ticks down and cuts me off. As the brain-sucking feeling sweeps through me, and the lights go dark, I know those words are true. I can trust Kari. What terrifies me is this—

Can I trust myself?

Or did I just ruin everything?

CHAPTER 24

KARI

"Are you sure this is it?" I ask, feeling like this tunnel could lead . . . *nowhere*. The dark beyond gapes at us. "This is the way to the archives?"

Anton had to open the door using his special key—the antique-looking wristwatch that only postal workers have. The entrance itself looked nondescript, shoved in the back of the post office.

"Seconding that," Luna says. "Looks like a good place to dispose of a body."

"Look, I'm not going to murder you," Anton says with a sly smile. "But I am going to take you to a secret place that only the postmasters can usually access. Technically, I am breaking the rules."

"See, that sounds murder-worthy," Luna quips. "The postmasters are freaky."

Anton shakes his head. "Haven gave me special permission to do whatever is necessary. This falls under . . . *necessary*. It's my judgment call. Now, come on."

Suddenly, I get the feeling that Anton and Haven talk more than I realized.

All the postmasters do.

I hesitate, but Anton waves for us to follow him anyway. Lights flicker on as we step inside, sensing our motion. They make me think of the crystal veins in the Astral settlement. As we continue, more lights flicker on ahead, while those behind us extinguish. Darkness licks at our heels.

We move through the corridor in a pocket of light, which feels almost like a living thing. Ever since the Astral settlement, I keep sensing the aliveness of photons, in the brilliant prisms they cast over the surface, at how light dances.

I shake my head to clear it.

That's not true—light isn't alive.

It's a particle. Physics proved that a long time ago. Anton could explain it. But it's also a wave sometimes, I remember, and it behaves differently when it's observed. That's also proven by quantum physics. We learned about it in school.

So, maybe it is sentient and alive?

More lights flicker on ahead. I try to focus on the mission, not chase the questions running in circles in my head. But it's true—since the reconnaissance mission and what I experienced in the settlement, I feel different . . . changed.

But I keep that to myself.

Under my boots, the tunnel tilts down, like we're going deeper underground. Just when I start to worry, we reach a larger cavern carved into rock. Smaller crystal veins run through it, not as large as down in the Astral settlement, but enough to give the cavern an otherworldly vibe.

The overhead lights illuminate and cast a soft, warm glow in contrast to the rest of the base. The sconces look old-fashioned, like they were lifted out of historical photographs from pre-war. But it's the walls that really catch my attention.

I can't believe my eyes. They're lined with floor-to-ceiling bookshelves that display leather-bound books. There must be hundreds, maybe thousands of tomes.

Real books.

Or at least, they look like it. This archive is more like a library. I approach the nearest shelf and scan the books.

Some titles I don't recognize, but the few that I do have been banned.

What are they doing here?

Anton notices me staring. "Welcome to our archives. It's a pet project of Haven and the postmasters. They don't just store records for each base. They also save books that . . . well . . . aren't allowed back on Earth anymore," he says tactfully.

"But isn't that risky?" I ask, pulling one off the shelf. *Stranger in a Strange Land* reads the gold-embossed title stamped into the leather cover. I flip it open.

Dust dances out of the pages, which are yellowing. Crazier yet, the type looks handwritten, like the book was copied. I've heard of that happening with banned books. Uploading anything into the computer networks is too risky.

The safest way to preserve and reproduce banned books from the few copies left in the world is to copy them by hand, a tedious and labor-intensive process. Not to mention, one that remains highly illegal. I stare at the words, painstakingly scrawled onto paper.

Anton shrugs. "Well, think of it this way. They're banned back on Earth, right? But nobody said anything about outer space. We're not even in our solar system out here. The rules don't apply."

"But why go to all this trouble?" I ask, still not getting it. I like some comics. But reading isn't really my thing. I'm partially dyslexic and always struggle in school.

"The postmasters have their own reasons," Anton says. "That far predates my existence on this astral plane. They don't always share them. But in a basic sense, the postmasters love reading. You could say they're closet book addicts."

"That tracks," Luna says, running her hand down the spines. "You're all nerds."

Anton beams at that. "Thank you. I take that as the highest compliment. Plus, when you're stationed out in the middle of nowhere, there's not much else to do. This is our source of entertainment."

"And Space Force doesn't care?" I ask, still feeling worried over all this illegal literature. "Back Earthside, this would get you tossed into a space prison camp."

Anton approaches the bookshelf, then turns back. "They turn a blind eye to most of the postmasters' extracurricular hobbies, like saving books. Mostly, they think it's just one of their quirks, nothing dangerous. Plus, the postmasters are too powerful and important to Space Force."

"That's right," Luna agrees. "The postmasters operate independently within Space Force. If they stop delivering our communications, then Space Force becomes inoperable. If you can't communicate, then you can't do shit."

That makes us laugh. But it's true.

Anton approaches an antique typewriter perched on one of the shelves.

A bronze owl statue keeps watch over it. "Postmaster Ksusha," he identifies himself to the owl. It hoots back softly.

"Now, you're talking to an owl?" Luna says, arching her eyebrow at it.

The owl hoots at her, but not in a friendly way. Then it turns back to Anton.

"He doesn't trust you," he says.

"You speak owl?" I ask.

The owl swivels its head around in a circle and flaps its mechanical wings.

"In fact, I do. Look . . . he's asking for the password," Anton says as his watch lights up, the dial spinning. Then he taps out the code into the typewriter's keys.

They *clack, clack, clack.*

I see the mechanical gears and innards shifting around like a complex puzzle.

"Let me guess . . . this is all more of Postmaster Haven's antics?" I say.

"Indeed," Anton says. "He has style. I wish I could've shown you the inside of the post office on Ceres before you left."

"It is a bit over the top," Luna says, moving closer to inspect the mechanism. "But a lot of tech has reverted to older analog systems. Harder to hack."

"That's smart," I say. "The further we advance, the further back we have to go to protect ourselves and our secrets."

The owl hoots again, and then—

The bookshelf in front of me cracks open with a groan, and swings inward.

It's a secret door hidden in the bookshelf.

I can't believe my eyes. Anton grins.

"Pretty neat, huh?"

"And nerdy," Luna sighs. "But yes, I admit it's a nice touch. Very secret agent."

"I thought you'd appreciate it," Anton says. "I didn't want to ruin the surprise."

"All the post offices are like this?" I ask, taking it all in. I feel like I've stepped into a book with the library and typewriter.

"Yes, in fact," Anton says. "These offices are for the postmasters only. Over the years, they've overhauled the specs and decorated to suit each of their individual tastes."

"It feels like something from the past," I say, marveling at the intricacies of design. "That must be on purpose."

"Yes, they don't want us to forget the past and what the postal system was built upon. Long before we had computers and airplanes, or even cars and trains, there was always the mail system. Back in time, they even used horses to deliver the post."

"Horses? I don't believe it," I say.

"It was called the Pony Express," he says. "I've seen the pictures. Haven has a particular fascination with that time period. He collects the memorabilia. As long as humans have had language and writing, they've had to communicate with each other. Even before that, they used ancient cave paintings to tell stories. The images were meant to convey meaning."

"And now, Sympathetics?" I say, thinking it over. "And warp mail?"

"The conduit and location may change—but it's all the same," Anton says in a solemn voice. "We deliver the mail."

"To the stars and back!" Luna and I say together, the official slogan of the Space Force Postal System. But it's true.

"Come on, the archives await!" Anton says, leading us through the secret door.

Now, we enter the real archives. Boxes line the shelves, filled with digital records. Anton gets to work, sorting through them.

"We're looking for anything pertaining to the origin of this outpost," I say, following him to the back of the room. "What really happened at this base."

We pass rows of shelves, heading for the back, where the earliest records would be housed. Anton rounds the corner.

But then comes to a halt.

"This is where they should be . . ." he says, trailing off. "But it looks like they're missing. That's really weird . . ."

That's when I see it—

Four empty shelves. The whole back wall. Dust motes scurry under them.

They've been missing for a while too.

"Could someone else get in here?" Luna asks. "Besides the postmasters?"

"Not that I'm aware of," Anton says, biting his lower lip. "But this is above my station. I'm pretty new here. Before me, this post office was mostly run by . . ."

"Bots," I finish for him.

Then it hits me. I turn back to Anton. "That's right. These security systems are analog and can't be hacked, right? The owl, the typewriter, the library door?"

"I know they seem quirky," he replies. "But that's precisely why we use them."

"But the bots aren't analog," I say, thinking of the annoying little droids. "They can be hacked, I'm guessing."

"You're right," Luna says, picking up the tangent. "Either somebody hacked them to destroy these records. Or the order came from . . ." She trails off, but then adds, "Someone in charge."

"No hacking needed then," I say, pacing around. "But why? What was down here that they didn't want anyone to find? What happened at this base?"

My questions hang in the air. This is a dead end. It only raises more questions.

"Are there any other records?" I ask in frustration. "Maybe duplicates?"

Anton shakes his head. "For security reasons, they wouldn't keep copies. This base has the top security clearance. Remember, it doesn't even have a name."

We all feel deflated. I stare at the empty shelves, desperate to know what they're hiding. But then, Anton perks up.

"What is it?" I ask him.

"They may have destroyed the *official* records. But what about the Sympathetic exchanges?" he says, leading us into another room. "Those are kept separate."

"Of course," I say. "Any guardian stationed out here, even at the inception of the base, would have to communicate with their Sympathetic back on Earth."

"Exactly," Luna chimes in. "It's a mandatory program. And this moon base wasn't built until after the program."

The new room also has shelves, but these are marked with names. These are all the guardians who sent exchanges. Anton starts going through the records manually.

"Major Apollo told you they traced signatures from the Golden Gate Attack back to this moon outpost?" he asks, going through the files. "That's how they discovered the Astral settlement?"

"Exactly," I say. "They got lucky because the odds of finding it were low."

"Really lucky," Luna adds. "That's like finding a needle in a haystack . . . only harder. One tiny moon in the vastness of interstellar space? What are the odds?"

"Not non-zero," Anton says. "But pretty damn close. Infinitesimally small."

I take that in. "So, you're saying . . . his story doesn't add up. It's suspicious?"

Anton shrugs. "Weirder things have happened. But our little friend Occam would have some serious doubts."

At the time, I didn't think to question what Major Apollo told me. When your CO briefs you, it's not your job to ask questions. That can get you tossed out.

Your job is to say, "Yes, sir!"

And follow orders.

Anton slips on a visor and starts reviewing the recordings. The names of guardians and their civilian counterparts whiz past on the visor's readout. I wonder how many of them remained lifelong friends . . . if they survived their deployment. Did any fall in love?

My heart skips a beat, thinking of Drae. And how strong our connection has grown. Worry creeps in, too. I'm still waiting to receive his first exchange. I yearn to hear his voice. To see him. Feel him. Experience the tumult of his emotions again. The lack of contact and information terrifies me. It feels like he got swallowed by a black hole, and not even the barest hint of light can reach me out here. He's at college, surrounded by distractions and temptations.

General Titan's warning about the danger of our connection flashes in my head.

Can we maintain our love—or will we destroy each other?

My heart beats faster. I love him so much it hurts. But love isn't enough. I know that, too. Love didn't keep my parents together after my father vanished. That terrifies me.

A few minutes pass while we wait for Anton to review the exchanges. "I've got something," he says finally, sliding the visor off. "It's not what we expected . . ."

His vision refocuses on us, and when it does, he looks afraid.

"What is it?" I say, feeling worried. "Spit it out already."

"Well, it turns out that this base is older than Apollo told you," he replies. "And there's more—it wasn't even our base in the first place."

"Wait . . . what do you mean?" I ask, shocked.

He takes a second to respond.

"This base belonged to our former enemies—the Siberian Federation."

"What do you mean?" Luna says. We exchange a confused look. "How is that possible? Then how did we get it?"

"Simple. We fought them for it," Anton explains. "The origin of this base was—a Proxy War," he goes on, flipping through various exchanges. "We dug in, using trench warfare to push them out. You can't see the trenches now because the forest must have grown back over them."

"Trench warfare?" Luna says. "Then, it must have been bloody and drawn out. That method was outlawed years ago."

Anton nods. "Maybe even outlawed because of this battle. Steep casualties on both sides. The guardians who survived and took over the base for Space Force talk about it in their exchanges. Many of them suffered terrible injuries and lost limbs. They were never the same after."

"Space trauma?" I ask.

"The Sympathetic Program is the only thing that saved most of them," he goes on. "Having someone to talk to . . . confide in . . . give them something to live for."

That hits all three of us. Now I realize why the base has such a different feel from Ceres Base. We didn't build it.

We took it.

"I can't let you experience them fully," Anton says. "Some things are sacred. But I'll play some audio." He turns up the sound in the visor, so the tinny voices from the past echo out.

I had to blast him . . . in the face . . . no choice . . . he snuck into my trench . . . [sobbing, wracking gasps] . . . we finally took their base . . . that's why I can send an exchange . . . we took over their comm systems . . . you probably thought I was dead . . . sometimes I wish I was.

Anton cues up another one.

Finally, we firebombed the whole moon, rooted them out . . . and stormed the base . . . the whole surface scarred and damaged . . . crystals shattered into oblivion . . . whatever life existed here . . . none of it survived . . .

Anton hits pause on that.

I imagine our munitions scouring the surface, igniting it into a blazing inferno, so we could storm the base. The shards of crystal breaking into a million pieces, scattering over the dust. But it did regrow. Those shards must have been seeds.

They regrew over the bloodshed, absorbing the terror that they witnessed.

We listen to a few more exchanges, each heartbreaking and terrible. This Proxy war was erased from the official records, but their memories live on.

Luna sits back. "But what was the purpose? What were we fighting for?"

Anton sorts through the exchanges. "Mining operations mostly—those crystalline veins. This moon has valuable resources for warp fuel and critical components. We were running low and needed it to continue our expansion."

"The crystal networks," I say, feeling it in my bones. "The same tech that powers and runs through the Astral settlement."

"Yes, I'm guessing so," he agrees.

"When did this happen?" I ask.

Anton does a mental calculation.

"About five years ago . . ."

"I mean, everyone knows we fought the Proxy Wars against the Siberian Fed for centuries," I say, stumped. "So, why erase this battle from the records? Why try to hide what happened out here?"

My question reverberates through the room, then dies out. Silence rushes back in, thick and consuming. There's only one answer—and we all know where it leads. And it's not good.

"The Astrals," Anton says. "After we seized the base from the Siberian Fed, I'm guessing we resumed the mining operations. We explored the surface, digging deeper . . ."

"We stumbled upon it by accident?" I say. "That's what you're saying?"

He nods. "Exactly. We didn't know they were here. Also, we didn't discover their settlement recently. We knew about it long *before* the Golden Gate Attack."

"Right, and that explains how they found the Astral settlement so fast. They didn't have to look for it, they only had to confirm that it was the same aliens behind the attack."

"Yes, they probably matched the trace elements from the explosive device to the rare elements on this moon," Anton goes on. "I think that part is true. Then they deployed us here."

"Reconnaissance," Luna says. "To learn about them—so we can destroy them."

"So, they've been lying to us this whole time?" I say, feeling betrayed by Major Apollo. "I know we're low-level grunts. I assume they don't tell us everything. But to lie to us?"

"Well, I don't trust anyone in the first place. That way, you're never disappointed. I was raised by spies, remember?" Luna adds with a smirk. "Guess they rubbed off on me."

"But something still doesn't add up," I say, pacing around. "A *big* something."

I turn back to my friends. "Why didn't they want this intel getting out? Someone with power went to the trouble of destroying all these records and lying to us. They hid all evidence of the Proxy war for resources. The exchanges are the only reason we discovered the truth."

"Exactly," Anton says. "They probably didn't think anyone would dig this deep. Or maybe it didn't occur to them that there would be Sympathetic exchanges in the archive."

"But why bother to hide it?" I ask. "Why not admit that we'd already had contact with the Astrals? Sure, they wouldn't want it leaking out on the newsfeeds. But why keep it from us?"

"That's the real mystery," Luna says. "Space Force has a lot of secrets."

"But our purpose here is intel," I point out. "This could help us find a way to defeat them faster. It's counterproductive to keep it from us. Not to mention, it makes our jobs harder."

I feel frustrated. I have a bad feeling about this—and everything happening on this moon. I think back to our reconnaissance mission and what I learned about the Astrals.

"The settlement . . ." I go on, digging into my memory. "I had strange visions when we entered it . . . like these temporal distortions where I could see the past overlapping with the present. I saw them . . . they were peaceful. They had children. They were growing things . . ."

I trail off, feeling a rush of emotion flood through me, transport me back.

"Are you thinking what I'm thinking?" Anton asks in a worried voice.

Luna meets his gaze. She looks troubled, too.

"I think so—and I don't like it."

They both turn to me. It takes a minute to find my voice. The recordings from the visor reverberate through my head, coupled with my visions from the settlement, both terrible and true.

"What if the Astral settlement wasn't abandoned when we came here?" I say in a shaky voice. I swallow hard. "What if . . . we're the reason why they left?"

That sinks in . . . slowly. Painfully.

Luna sets her lips. "The Proxy war."

I nod. "In the visions I had down there, something terrible drove them out. The ground was shaking, and the caves were collapsing. Their kids were running for their lives. Something drove them away."

Luna shoots me a look.

"You're saying, it was us?"

"The firebombing," Anton says. "We blanketed the whole surface to drive the Siberian Fed out of their entrenchment."

"Yes, and it turns out, they're not the only ones we drove away," I say. "My guess is—the Astrals weren't our target. We probably didn't even know about their existence. But they were here the whole time, living just under the surface. They were simply . . . collateral damage."

The implications topple through my head, one after the other, knocking down each flawed assumption, until the truth is the only thing left standing. Once I see it, clear as crystal, I can't unsee it anymore.

I look at my friends, all the blood drained from their faces. I'm sure my pale visage matches their own. This one realization changes everything we know.

I have to face it.

I can't hide from it.

Secrets are why we're in this mess in the first place. The Astrals are right about us. We are violent and prone to mass destruction. They know that about us—because they experienced it firsthand.

This must be why they let me into their settlement and showed me those visions.

This is what they wanted me to see. It's terrible. It's shattering. But what I fear most is—

It's all true.

I find my voice. It isn't easy. And it comes out strained. "What if the Astrals didn't invade us first? What if we've got it backward—and we're the ones who started this war?"

PART 3

SCISSION

*Let your plans be dark and impenetrable as night,
and when you move, fall like a thunderbolt.*

—Sun Tzu, *The Art of War*

CHAPTER 25

KARI

We started this war.

The heaviness sits on all of our shoulders. I can't believe what we just uncovered in the archives.

Suddenly, the strange messages that I received in the Astral settlement start to make a disturbing kind of sense. They reverberate through my head again.

I turn to Anton and Luna.

"The Astrals think we're a plague on the universe. That we're spreading farther out and infecting everywhere we go . . ."

"Can you blame them?" Anton stands up from his chair. "Look at what we did to this moon fighting the Siberian Fed. We obliterated their peaceful settlement."

We're still deep in the archives. Quickly, he inserts a drive to copy what we found. The Sympathetic exchanges download to the tiny device. Then, he puts the recordings back, covering up any evidence of our snooping through them.

This secret is too dangerous.

Even Luna agrees. "We killed their kids, so they retaliated by killing ours."

"You're right," I agree, feeling a hard pit form in my stomach. "The Golden Gate Attack wasn't a coldblooded, unprovoked incident—it was retaliation."

We all take that in.

"I agree." Anton nods. "Maybe we're not so different from the Astrals after all."

"What do you mean?" Luna asks. "They seem pretty *blasted* different."

"Think about it. You said it was retaliation? *An eye for an eye.* Doesn't that sound a lot like us? That never ends well. Violence just leads to more violence."

"Exactly!" The wheels turn in in my head. "Trebond and the Resistance are right. That's why we have to convince Space Force to try something other than a military solution. We need diplomacy."

Neither of them responds to that. We all know Space Force and how they operate.

It's like shouting at them to—

Disarm the Stars!

Not only is that never going to happen, not while generals remain in charge with their vast armies and weapons systems, but it would also get you dishonorably discharged, if not tossed into space prison camp. However, I have to try something.

I just don't know . . . *what*.

I wish I could talk to Drae, but I'm still waiting for his reply to my exchange.

Anton heads for the door. "Not to end this little party, but we'd better get going. Before Major Apollo or anyone notices we're missing and starts looking for us."

That snaps us into action. We've already been gone too long. We all get up to leave. But then, I hesitate—

"Listen, this is a dangerous secret," I say softly. "We need to be careful. More than ever. And gather more intel. I already sent a message to my father to see if the Raiders have discovered anything."

"What about Drae?" Luna asks. "We need to brief the Resistance ASAP."

I feel my heart lurch at the mention of his name. "I'm waiting for his reply to my exchange. It should be any day now."

"Yup, that's right. I'll make sure you're alerted the moment we receive anything from Drae," Anton chimes in. "The same goes for a message from Captain Skye."

Even though I'm still plagued by worries, we disband our little research party and depart from the archives and emerge back into the lobby. A few bots rush over and start beeping in annoyance at Anton. Clearly, his presence was missed. I just hope nobody else noticed.

Bidding farewell to Anton, Luna and I head to the mess hall. It's dinnertime by our Earth-synched clocks, which don't match the rising and setting of the two suns on this moon. My stomach should be grumbling with hunger pains. But all I feel is a sick emptiness that twists at my gut. I glance up at the skylights filtering down pale morning light through the crystalline trees, which sway gently in the soft lunar breezes coasting across the strange landscape.

Triggered by everything we just learned, a torrent of thoughts rush through my head. Most of all that we may have started this war—*even if it was accidental*—but now that the Astrals know about us and our violent nature, they won't stop. They think that we're a plague that's spreading and infecting the universe that must be destroyed at all costs.

And the worst part?

They're not totally wrong about us.

Frustration hits me like a blast radius. Anton said that maybe we're not so different from the Astrals. *An eye for an eye.* But not all humans think that way. We aren't all prone to violence. Trebond and my father and the Resistance, for example. They want to bring peace to the stars.

So . . . what if the Astrals are like that too? What if not all of them want to invade Earth and annihilate humans?

What if there are like-minded Astrals who think more like us? But the problem is, I don't have any way to test out that theory. I wish there was a way to communicate with them and tell them—not all humans are bad and warlike. But why would they listen to me?

I'm a Space Force guardian. I'm trained to fight and kill. I've always been a fighter, ever since I was a kid, brawling in the back alleys of the trailer park. And I have the scars to prove it. I have rage and hate and violence stored away in my heart.

But I've changed these last few months. Some of it is learning the truth about my father. I used to hate him more than all the stars in the galaxy. But it's not just my father. Now, I have love, too.

For one reason—

I have Drae.

He unlocked parts of my heart that I didn't even know existed. That I thought I'd locked up behind impenetrable walls. But if I can change, then maybe others can change, too. And that means there's hope.

If only I could find a way to talk to the Astrals and convince them that humanity made a mistake here on this moon, but that we deserve another chance . . .

But I know the odds of being able to get a message to them, let alone convince them, are slim to none. Maybe zero. Look at us? Once the gears of war shift into motion, they're like an unstoppable force.

The Astral invasion is coming.

It's not *if*. . . it's *when*.

I let out a frustrated sigh. We're almost at the mess hall. Luna gives me a look.

"Yeah, that," she says, echoing the sigh. "It feels hopeless, doesn't it?"

"Yeah, it does feel hopeless. But that doesn't mean there isn't still hope."

Luna frowns. "How do you mean?"

"Well, it's like a star. The light doesn't always reach us. Sometimes, it's blocked by orbital rotations and other celestial bodies, and we can't see it. But that doesn't mean the star isn't still shining."

"So you're saying, hope is like starlight?" she says. "That's damned poetic. I thought you were a soldier."

"Soldiers can be poets," I say. "Look at Sun Tzu. A whole book about war that reads more like poetry than battle plans."

We eat in silence. But I keep thinking of starlight and love and Drae, trying to beat back the darkness that descended when I heard those recordings in the archives.

A few more days pass like that. No news comes. No new messages from Drae, or my father. No new missions or briefings. It's quiet . . . almost too quiet.

Never trust that.

In my experience, that doesn't mean bad things aren't lurking in the periphery, waiting to ambush you. Finally, I get an alert, but it's not from Anton or Harold.

It's late, and there's a knock on the barracks door. Luna is already asleep. The lights have dimmed, mimicking nightfall.

I tiptoe over and crack it open.

A familiar voice echoes out. I can see his outline cast into the shadows.

"Captain Skye, may I have a word?"

I stare at Major Apollo. His hair looks rumpled, and there are creases on his face. His uniform appears wrinkled, and he missed a button on his shirt. In short, he looks like a hot mess. But that's weirdly alluring. I feel my heart thump faster.

"Sir, now?"

He nods. "Yes . . . in private."

That last part sends a shiver oscillating down my spine all the way to my toes.

"But sir, it's late?"

He shrugs. "I can't sleep. Looks like you might have the same affliction."

"Guilty as charged."

A smile cracks his lips. "Great minds think alike. Isn't that the saying?"

"More like . . . great minds *don't sleep* alike," I quip back, pushing at his boundaries. My heart hiccups in my chest.

This isn't how you talk to your CO.

Suddenly, I get that weird brain-probing feeling again. Like he's rifling through my thoughts, trying to crack the safe that holds my deepest, darkest secrets. *Get out!* I think in annoyance.

He flinches back slightly. His eyes break contact as the strange feeling slowly dissipates. Then he smiles at me. His eyes crinkle up at the corners.

"Captain Skye, follow me," he says, turning down the hall and not looking back. He assumes that I'll just hop to and scramble after him. And the problem is . . .

He's right.

This is all a bit unorthodox. His late-night knocking on my barracks door. Though so much about him has felt that way since I met him. Maybe that's just how he operates. He did say this operation needed open-minded guardians. That's why they targeted me. Well, then maybe that missive applies to him, too. Before I can think about it more, his impatient voice calls out.

"Hurry up, Captain. You're lagging!"

CHAPTER 26

DRAE

"Sorry about Sylvia," I say as we sink into the worn vinyl booths at my favorite pizza spot located right off campus. That means, it's all Berkeley students crowded into the hole-in-the-wall local spot.

The walls feature historic black-and-white framed photographs of the college and students from before the war. The campus miraculously survived to host more generations of students. And now here we are, still eating the greasy pizza.

The only difference?

It's all faux meat.

But it tastes real, and that's what matters. I glance at my roommate sitting across from me. My one remaining roommate after they arrested Sylvia. Trebond is working on getting her out. But I haven't gotten an update from Willow. Theo has been moping around the dorm room since he got questioned and released . . . I know they're probably still watching him.

Feeling paranoid, I scan the crowd for Jude or his minions. But so far, the coast is clear.

I breathe a sigh of relief. "Faux pepperoni?" I ask before ordering.

"*Double* pepperoni," he adds glumly. "I need it. And Sylvia isn't your fault."

A stab of guilt hits me. It's not directly my fault, but I'm just as guilty as her.

No, strike that.

I'm *guiltier* since I'm an actual Resistance operative. But I can't tell Theo any of this. It would only endanger him. Well, more than he already is . . .

I signal to the busy waitress, who looks like she's worked here as long as those old pictures have been hanging on the wall.

Once she races off to put our order in, after depositing two large waters, I return my focus to my roommate. I thought he needed to get out of the dorm tonight.

Maybe we both did.

"Listen, it's nobody's fault," I say, lowering my voice. The din of laughter and banter is a good cover. "These are difficult times. The campus feels like a war zone. She did what she thought was right. It's not like she killed somebody."

He looks skeptical. "Are you . . . a sympathizer?"

That hits me. Whatever they did when they retained him—it hardened him. I was expecting that, and now it scares me.

"Uh, no!" I backpedal. "My mom is a war hero. My dad works for the fed. Of course not . . . I support Space Force."

I default to my solid Ringer status as my cover. But my heart pounds harder.

"Sylvia's parents were vets, too." He swallows hard and sips his water. "That doesn't mean you're not . . . one of them."

Now I get it.

How he got out of there.

He cut a deal with them.

The deal? It's to spy and be an informant on campus—starting with his roommate, who is already under suspicion. Jude has his target on me, suspecting that I'm a Resistance agent. Willow warned me that government hardliners were planting spies all over campus. That they think the universities are hotbeds for harboring dissidents and anti-war sentiments.

"I swear, I'm not!" I say, my heart pounding. "Look, this is top-secret . . . but I'm in the Sympathetic Program. I'd never betray my pairing . . . or damage her enlistment."

That gets him. "Oh, I'm sorry . . . I didn't know. I'm guessing that explains why you disappear sometimes. It's for your exchanges, right?"

Shit, he's noticed my coming and going. So, he is spying on me . . .

Luckily, he doesn't know much about the program. Few civilians do. Nor does he know about the lag time and her deployment, and how it's not that often.

Luckily, our pizza gets deposited right then, adding a good distraction. Theo downs a slice, then a second one. He also seems to finally relax around me.

"You're a true patriot," he says between chewing. "Anyway, I should be apologizing to you. For putting you in danger . . . maybe even your Sympathetic."

If only he knew the truth.

Suddenly, I wonder again if Sylvia was just a student activist who recently got swept up in the movement—or if Trebond planted her there to keep an eye on me. I hope it's the former, but worry flickers in my heart, signaling the latter. Clearly, Trebond is keeping secrets from me.

I have to be careful.

More than ever.

"I should've known . . ." Theo goes on mournfully over the pizza. "Or at least turned her in after I found the flyers."

I force down a slice, even though my appetite has deserted me. "It's not your fault. She made her own choices."

Theo frowns. "Yeah, guess you can't trust anyone these days. Hey, can I tell you a secret? I miss her . . . even though she was a dissident. Is that fucked up?"

I reassure him that no matter what our head says, our heart is a different organ that doesn't always obey orders. That makes me think of Kari and her rebelliousness. But then I'm also forced to remember that exchange I sent her.

I haven't heard back yet.

I'm afraid of what I'll hear.

What if she doesn't respond?

That stops my heart cold. I hadn't considered that possibility yet.

Participation in the program is mandatory. But now I know that our connection poses dangers to both of us . . . and I might have just fucked up beyond any salvation. The worst part?

I don't know anything. And due to the lag time, it could still be another week.

Theo mistakes my distress for worrying about Sylvia. "I know you liked her too," he says, lowering his voice. "But I learned a lot when they took me in. We have to push her from our minds . . ."

"And our hearts?" I say softly.

"Yes, especially our hearts," he says emphatically. "The sympathizers . . . they're dangerous . . . they're infecting campus . . . we have to be careful who we trust, or they could get to us again."

"You're right—down with the Resistance. We fight in the stars . . ."

He narrows his eyes. Hate burns in them, something I've never seen in him.

"*Kill the Astrals.*"

His voice comes out a sharp hiss. They didn't just scare him down there—they brainwashed him. He's turned hardline.

I know I'm supposed to parrot the genocidal phrase. I try to form the words . . . but they fail me . . . nothing comes out.

Now, he looks suspicious. But before he can question me further, someone slides into the booth next to me. I jerk my eyes over. They land on Willow . . . looking as cute as ever. Her punkish bangs dip into her amethyst eyes, which match her hair color perfectly.

She flashes a sexy smile.

That makes me feel even guiltier about my message to Kari. Even the fact that I categorized her smile as *sexy*. Clearly, I can't be trusted . . . not around her.

"Mind if I crash your pizza party?" Willow says, helping herself to a congealing slice. "I had such a long day of classes—and now I'm starving . . ."

I give her a sharp look—*trying to warn her*—but she ignores me. Then, I get it.

She's been following me on purpose, spying on me. She saw things getting intense with Theo. She must have been warned about what they did to him when they detained him.

"Uh, we're kind of deep in the middle of something here . . ." I start, hoping to brush her off. My heart is thumping faster.

Theo is already suspicious enough. And now my agent handler is right here.

"No, please join us," Theo cuts in. "You're like a breath of fresh air . . ."

Ugh, he's into her. Worse, he probably thinks she could help him get over Sylvia. Now, I'm both worried—and I feel strangely jealous and protective over her.

She scrunches up her nose.

"Poor boy. Too much studying?"

"Something like that . . ." he mutters. "More like . . . I had feelings for this girl . . . and let's just say . . . it didn't work out."

Now, she pats his hand sympathetically. My jealousy grows stronger, despite not wanting to have these feelings. They resist my attempts to quash them into nothing.

Willow brightens. "Well, then some other girl will be the lucky one . . ."

She's actively flirting with him. I wonder if this is just part of her training taking over to distract him from me. Or if she's actually into him . . . or maybe both?

Theo grins. "Drae, who's your friend? I don't think you've mentioned her before."

He turns his smile back on her. Before I can respond—probably in an awkward and hostile way that will potentially blow her cover—Willow thrusts out her hand in greeting.

"I'm Willow! Part-time librarian, full-time student, at your service," she says cheerfully, spouting out her cover story.

I study her countenance, searching for the lie buried under her upbeat energy and crooked smile. But she doesn't crack. She's good at this. Way better than me.

"Exactly, she's my . . ." I start then trail off, unsure how to explain how we met.

"Study partner," Willow says. "I'm helping him with his reading list."

Theo accepts that. He's so thoroughly charmed by her that he doesn't even think to question anything. I breathe a sigh of relief, despite my surge of jealousy.

It's just an act, I reassure myself.

He shakes her hand, lingering a little too long over it. "I'm his roomie."

The banter takes over from there, with Theo and Willow flirting. It ends with him asking for her contact, which she gives out, before he begs off. He's under a strict curfew as a condition of his release.

"I can go back with you." I start to get up. But he generously waves me off. I have a feeling it's in no small part to the heavy-duty flirt fest courtesy of Willow. He doesn't want to seem uptight in front of her, or like he's trying to stop our party.

"Nah, she's your study partner," he says. "I'm sure you've got reading to go over. I'll tell you one thing. He takes his reading seriously. He's always holing up in his room with new library books."

That makes my heart stutter. Half of those books contain . . . *secret messages.*

"I hate to break it to you," Willow says coyly. "But we're both major book nerds."

Theo blushes at her confession. "Well, you are the part-time librarian."

She winks. "Maybe full-time one day. You never know. A girl can dream?"

But then he turns more serious, checking the time again. He promises to message her soon for a proper hang.

Willow keeps that smile plastered to her face until he exits the buzzing restaurant and vanishes down the street.

Then she drops it instantly.

Like flipping off a switch.

"Yeah, so I think you already figured it out. But you can't trust him anymore."

"Yeah, you saw that?"

"And heard it."

She taps her ear. I'm guessing she's got a concealed listening device in her ear.

"You're spying on me?" Feeling betrayed, I lower my voice. "You planted bugs? Seriously, where are they . . ."

She nods to my backpack. "In the books, of course. You never go anywhere without them these days."

I take that in. And I feel foolish. Of course the Resistance is keeping tabs on me. I should've already put that together. I really suck at being a secret agent.

"Look, don't be upset," she goes on. "You're too important to Trebond. This is for your own protection and safety . . . things are heating up on campus . . ."

"He cut a deal, didn't he?"

She nods. "He's one of them now."

"How did they turn him so fast?" I say, still a little shocked over it. "He's even talking genocide now. Before, he wasn't even political. He was just an ordinary student crushing on his roommate."

"Right. They have new techniques. And we hear . . . they're giving them neural implants . . . that they use to control them . . . even their thought patterns."

My mouth drops open. "That's got to be illegal and against the peace treaties."

"*Illegal* implies that they enforce the laws. Remember how he recalled his curfew out of the blue? He wasn't even looking at the time. I think it's his implant."

"Of course," I say right away. Only civilians who participate in the Sympathetic Program get them. And of course, guardians in Space Force. So, I'm very familiar with the reminders.

And the enforcement of them.

You get *shocked* if you ignore the warnings. No wonder he got going so fast.

"Plus, it's a requirement of his release," she continues. "So they can track him. Make sure he doesn't try to run for it."

"So, things are worse than I thought." I start shredding the paper napkin between my fingers, feeling the grease staining it.

Willow nods. "Look, you need to do better at controlling your emotions around me. The look on your face?"

"Well, you were hardcore flirting with him," I say, backpedaling. "It was way out of character. You're usually different."

"No, I was *hardcore* doing my job," she snaps back. But I see the color in her cheeks. So, she is a little embarrassed.

"Trebond teach you that?"

"Among other techniques."

"What about me?" I say, feeling betrayed. "Is that what you did to me?"

She looks hurt. "No . . . you're different. I have real feelings. But I'm probably being unprofessional. I should recuse myself from being your agent handler—"

"No, don't do that."

Her eyes widen. "It's not smart."

I hold her gaze. "Look, I've lost everything that I care about . . . you're the only friend I have left on this campus."

Until I say those words, I don't realize how true they are. Losing Rho has been harder than expected, coupled with Kari's interstellar deployment and the accompanying lag time. I was leaning on my new roomies, but now that's gone, too.

"Don't worry," Willow goes on. "We're trying to get Sylvia out of detainment."

"Where did they send her?"

"They have these new camps for suspected dissidents. No hearing or trial . . . they're off the books too . . . out in the Mojave desert at an old military base."

That hits me hard.

"Tell me the truth. Did Trebond plant her as my roommate . . . to watch me?"

Willow looks taken aback. "Not that I know of . . . Look, I get it—you don't trust us anymore. You know we have secrets. But here's what you don't know . . ."

"Oh, and what's that?"

"Secrets keep you safe."

Her words hang in the air before they dissolve back into the ambient noise.

"That's also something they teach you," she goes on. "It's to protect you. Welcome to being an operative. The less you know, the less danger you're in."

I give her a questioning look. I want her to drop the mask for real—and let me in.

"And what about you?"

The moment stretches and lingers.

"Who is keeping you safe?" I add in a soft voice. We lean in closer to each other. Closer still. I feel a flush of attraction despite my best wishes to the contrary . . . I can't help it. I know I suck.

Kari doesn't deserve me.

But it's like this magnetic force pulling me toward her. I can almost taste her breath. Her lips glisten in the low light.

"So, then tell me the truth," I demand. "Why did you come here? You're spying on me? Is this part of it . . ." I mean, the closeness. The making me trust her . . . want her . . . desire her . . . "Is it all some act?" Hurt trembles in my voice.

"No, I'm not on assignment," she finally says. "I wanted to check on you after I heard about your roommate. Sorry, please don't tell anyone. Trebond would be mad . . . it's risky . . ."

I reach out and clasp her hand.

"This is the truth?" I ask.

"Yes. It could get me in trouble."

I see the fear in her eyes.

Either she's an incredible actress—or she's telling the truth. Still, I hesitate, unsure if I can trust anything she says.

"Swear it on all the stars in the galaxy?" I press her. Our eyes lock.

"And the moon and the planets."

Now we're centimeters apart, speaking of the cosmos and how we're intertwined, two beings swept up in the gravity of the moment, orbiting each other as everything else in the universe dissolves away.

I lean in to kiss her.

Our lips.

They brush.

Lightly, softly, tentatively . . .

I breathe her in like oxygen. Like I didn't even realize how I was suffocating. Like she might be the only thing keeping me alive right now . . . but that's when—

I see . . . *him.*

Standing across the restaurant. Staring at us. A cruel smile stretches his face.

I jerk back from Willow.

"Wh-what is it?" she hisses.

Then she sees him too. He's watching us both. "Hurry, let's get out of here."

CHAPTER 27

KARI

At first, I expect Major Apollo to lead me to his office, where we do our briefings. But instead, he takes me up to the docking bay, then over to a ladder grafted into the wall. He starts climbing, leading me up. We emerge into a rooftop deck covered with a dome. I can tell this is where the air traffic controllers direct the ships to land. However, it's empty right now. This is a small, secret base. Very little traffic comes through our docking bay. I wonder what we're doing up here, but then he gestures to the dome overhead. Through the panels, the two suns begin to rise from opposite corners of the sky and beam light upon the lunar surface.

"The best place for sunrises," he says in a dreamy voice. "Insomnia has some perks."

"How do you keep track of the lunar time?" I ask curiously. "Our Earth time is so out of sync with any place we're stationed. I always feel like I'm in a temporal distortion."

"My neural implant. I overrode the settings to make her tell me the true lunar time." He shrugs and taps the nape of his neck. "I call her . . . *Mother* . . ." he quips.

"Mother?" I say with a snort.

"She's the great connector. Just made sense in the moment." He cringes after he says that. "Ugh, I know what you're thinking. Maybe I have Mommy issues?"

"I can't really judge. I've got . . . *Harold*." He starts to pipe up, but I mute him. "See, told you . . . he has no sense of timing. Oh, and zero sense of humor."

Now it's his turn to tease me. "Guess we both need a psych eval."

"You can say that again. Wait, haven't you read my file? It was pretty thick."

"Sure did. It had some fun diagnoses."

"Wait, don't tell me. I prefer to think I'm a special kind of fucked up that hasn't been discovered yet." This time, I don't hold back. "*Unidentified Fucked-Up Object.*"

That sends him. Laughter tumbles from his luscious lips, deep and true. I join him, letting my guard down more.

"Well, unlike Harold," he says once he manages to get a hold of himself, "you've got a definite sense of humor."

I arch my eyebrow at him.

"Is that an *official* diagnosis, sir?"

He nods. "I'll make a note in your file, Captain. You're never safe around me."

You can say that again.

That flashes through my head as I feel my body warming up in his presence.

I know it's dangerous. We're alone up here. Anyone sane is still sleeping. This base is so unpopulated that sometimes I forget where we are, or why we're here.

Right now, it feels like we're floating in space in our own little universe.

He sits in a chair and pats the spot next to him. The suns are cresting the ridges. The kaleidoscopic light show is about to peak.

I know I should cut this short. Beg off and ask to meet later . . . when it's less . . . intimate . . . just *less* of everything.

But I don't do that.

I sidle into the console chair next to him. I peer at the instruments, but the screens are dark. The radar doesn't show anything for one reason. There's nothing else out here. Whatever alien life was here—we obliterated it in that Proxy war.

He reads the look on my face. "The desolation of interstellar space?"

"It's not desolate," I reply, meeting his intense gaze. "Or at least, it wasn't."

He looks pained, like he's fighting with himself over his true feelings. I guess my CO isn't a robot like most of the Space Force officers. Or maybe, he's not as good at acting. Then another thought occurs to me. A dangerous one. Maybe it's something else altogether.

He's dropping the mask—

And letting me in.

My heart beats faster. A long moment passes as we watch the sun climb higher and erase all the stars from the sky. I remember what I said about hope being like starlight. How even when you can't see it, that doesn't mean it's not shining.

"You said you wanted a word, sir?" I venture. "Are there any new updates?"

"No, and that's the problem. Aside from you getting into that Astral settlement."

"What was the reaction?"

"Well, they didn't believe it at first. There's no proof, aside from your word. And Private Starfire. Just like you said, all the instruments cut out as soon as your ship descended into the caves."

I snort. "Not surprised. Permission to speak freely?"

"Granted."

"Assholes."

That makes him smile again. "Well, those *assholes* made me send a few guardians down to try again. See if it was a fluke, or if they could gain access."

"What happened?" I ask, genuinely curious, though I can already guess.

"Uh, let's just say . . . their access was denied. And not in a very nice way."

I shake my head. "So, now do they believe us? About what happened?"

"I'd say . . . they're less skeptical. But there's a wide gap between that and true belief. Plus, I think you're full of shit."

I'm taken aback. "Wh-what do you mean?"

Now, he turns his gaze on me. His eyes blaze into me like the twin suns cresting the sky with burning light. "You said as much as you needed to, but you're holding something back."

I get that probing, brain-sucking feeling again. But I fight it off.

"Something important," he adds. "But I can't force you, and I don't have proof."

That sits with me. I want to tell him suddenly, confess everything. But I bite my tongue. It's not just my ass on the line. It's Luna, who covered for me. Anton, too.

What if Apollo gets us in trouble?

"You don't want to narc and get your friends in trouble," he goes on. "Well, you asked for an update. The Earth Federation alliances are shakier than the newsfeeds are reporting. Every day that Secretary-General Andromeda doesn't have actionable intel, her rule grows weaker."

"Has anyone else turned up anything on the Astrals?" I ask.

He shakes his head. "We're scouring the universe for something . . . *anything* . . . but the settlement on this moon is all we have. No new attacks, either in space or Earthside. It's like they're *fucking* ghosts."

"Isn't that good news?" I ask, then immediately regret it.

"Not really. We know they're coming for us. We know they got through our Earthside defenses like they were nothing. So it's like . . . we're sitting ducks."

He's right—how do we fight a ghost? I remember everything I saw in the caves. The light-beings. They are ghost-like.

He sits there, looking so hot. That's the only word for it. The more he mopes, the more attractive it is . . . I can't explain it. We're close, only inches apart really.

My heart beats faster and faster. I should leave this right where it is—and give him nothing. But all I can think about is hope and starlight. And that I need to do something and take a chance, even if it backfires and gets me in deeper trouble.

Everything is on the line.

He's right. We're vulnerable targets. We're the only ones they let into the settlement. The Astrals wanted me to see all of that. They had a message for me. That led me to the archives and the big discovery. The Astrals are trusting me.

So, that means—

I have to trust myself.

"You're right . . . about me."

He perks up. "Which part? Your un-diagnosable psych problems? Or your sense of humor? Or is it . . . *your secrets?*"

That stops my heart.

Freezes it right there in my chest. I can't explain it, but it's like he can see inside me to my very vulnerable core. But Drae is the only person who can do that. Even my family can't pierce my emotional armor. Okay, maybe my little sister has had her moments of melting my heart. But that's different. This is something else altogether. And it's far more dangerous.

"It's the secrets . . ." I whisper, barely a breath from my lips, barely audible.

He leans closer. "You can trust me."

Also, barely a whisper.

We're so close right now. I can see every worry line and crease on his face.

He's my CO. I repeat that in my head like a command. I have to be careful. I can't blur these lines. I can't afford to be feeling this way about him. I can't afford to *feel* anything like this for anyone other than Drae. But that doesn't still my heart.

I take a deep breath. He leans over and rests his hand on my knee. I feel it warming my flesh through my uniform. But I don't move to push it away. He squeezes gently.

"Kari, you can trust me," he says, using my first name. "You don't have to be alone in this. Maybe I can help."

My mind races. I can barely think straight with him so close. But I come to a decision. I decide to do something that goes against all my old instincts.

I decide . . . to *trust*.

"Look, I didn't tell you everything that happened inside the settlement. Partially because I couldn't explain it really."

"So, there was more."

It's not a question. I nod slowly.

"I had visions of . . . *them*. I can't fully explain it . . . they lived there. They were peaceful, full of life, in sync with their world. Then something terrible happened . . . when I was down there, it was like time bent . . . and I saw it happen."

"Temporal distortions?" he says. "That's not imagination. We can document that. It's part of what makes our tech go completely haywire."

"Yes, it was like . . . I could see the past . . . but only because they let me see it."

"Let you? What do you mean by that?"

I nod. "They *wanted* me to witness it. They had a message. Something about a plague infecting the universe . . . like a virus that had to be destroyed . . ."

Their messages shoot through my head in all their intensity. I jerk back. He also looks pained, like he could hear it.

But that's impossible, of course.

"A virus . . . what does that mean?" he asks. "You're sure you heard it right?"

I shrug. "Temporal distortions. Weird alien mind messages. Who can be sure?"

"Point taken," he says with a smirk.

Then seriousness descends again.

"Anyway, I was scared to tell you. I was worried you wouldn't believe me. Or worse, that it would lead to a psych eval."

"Your concerns were valid," he says, not gaslighting me, which I appreciate. "Just look at how they made me deploy more guardians down there, who were blown back from the forcefield the second they tried to breach it . . . and injured."

"They got hurt?" I gasp.

"Two are still in medical with burns. Almost like sunburns . . . radiation."

"Light. They use light. It's their technology, maybe also a weapon."

"We need to investigate that theory further. But light can time travel. It can bend reality. It changes direction depending on being observed. That's the core tenant of quantum psychics. It can travel either as a photon or a wave."

"The way you describe light," I say in awe. "It's almost like . . . it's alive."

Now he meets my gaze. "Who are we to say it isn't?"

That question hangs in the air. I think of the Astrals again, how they shimmered and beamed around, interacting with the crystals. I watch the suns shine through the crystalline trees, painting the surface a multitude of colors. No wonder they felt at home on this moon.

It's the light.

"Is that . . . everything?" he asks, watching me closely. Following my gaze.

I'm scared to tell him the next part. But I've come this far . . . I don't have a choice.

"Something happened to them down there," I force myself to continue. I watch the light dance, and it gives me courage. "I grew suspicious. You said it yourself. They're like *fucking* ghosts. So it's a pretty big coincidence that we just happened to stumble upon their abandoned settlement on this moon when we haven't even known of their existence for very long."

He frowns. "You're right. It's a big *fucking* coincidence."

"Also, what's their motivation for attacking us and invading Earth? Of all the two trillion planets in the observable universe? Why target our home world?"

"Another great mystery," he says. "Like the true nature of light."

But I shake my head adamantly.

"My friend taught me about Occam's razor. The simplest answer is usually the right one. That's too many coincidences."

"What do you mean?"

"Sir, what if it's the other way around? What if this moon and that settlement . . . are the reason behind everything."

That's when I tell him what we found in the archives. I spill it out in a race of words and breath. When I finish, he looks like a ghost. All the color has drained from his face.

"You weren't kidding about those secrets," he says finally, still shocked.

A long moment passes, and neither of us says anything.

"Sir, did I just make a big mistake and end my military career?"

My words hang in the air like a bomb about to detonate. When he doesn't reply at first, my heart drops through my chest. But then, he looks at me with newfound respect.

"Not even close. I think this is the moment your real career in intel started."

I shouldn't bask in his praise; we have way bigger problems. But I can't help it. I light up under his light like those trees.

"Right, I'm telling you because I need your help," I say quickly. "If I'm right that we started the war, then their attack wasn't unprovoked. That's why we need to push for a diplomatic solution. We need to find a way to open communication channels with them."

"Diplomacy? Look, don't get me wrong. Despite the recent reforms, military hardliners still control both the fed government and Space Force. They won't like that idea."

"What about Andromeda? She's behind the reforms—she wants change."

"Listen, I'm not supposed to tell you. But she's barely holding on. Even mentioning *diplomatic solutions* would get her overthrown. She'd sound weak and like she sympathizes with the Astrals. And worse, like she might actually agree with . . ."

He trails off, but I fill it in.

"*The Resistance.*"

He nods. "Look, we're a military state. And military states default to . . . war."

"But war just leads to endless war . . . forever war."

"Right, I hate to point out the obvious," he says, sounding pained. "But you enlisted in Space and trained to fight and become a guardian. You know what you signed up for . . ."

Frustration bubbles up in me, boiling over and scalding me. I made a big mistake confiding in him. He's just like everyone else. He won't fight to change anything.

It's hopeless.

That's when he says something that startles me. It's so soft that I can barely hear it.

"*Captain Skye, don't give up on starlight.*"

"What did you just say?" My heart lurches in my chest.

"Sorry, don't listen to me. Too little sleep messing with my head."

That's the moment when it feels like the spell breaks. He stands up and straightens his uniform. He clears his throat roughly. "Captain, don't worry—your secrets are safe with me."

"Is that all, sir?" I ask, gaining my feet.

My knees feel wobbly. Actually, scratch that.

It's my whole body.

But he steps closer to me. His eyes probe my face as if searching for an answer to the meaning of existence. He leans even closer. "You were right about me   I'm on your side."

My heart leaps up at those words.

"And there's more," he adds. "I don't know how yet . . . or if there's any chance of success given the current state of our affairs. But I'm going to try to help you."

"You . . . are?" I'm stunned by this.

"First, we need to find a way to communicate with the Astrals. Then we can take that to General Titan and push for diplomacy. That's our best shot."

I take that in. He's right. If we go with hypotheticals, we'll just get shot down.

Literally.

"But how are we doing to do that?" I say, feeling stumped. "They're aliens."

He shrugs and gives me a look. The look lingers, making my heart thump. "They already let you into their settlement, right? You heard messages from them. Maybe you can find a way?"

I look down. "Easier said than done."

"True. But I know this—you're our best shot." That's the last thing he says before he gently dismisses me. "Get some sleep, Captain. We both need to be well rested for what's next."

He's right. I can't afford to be tired or dulled. Everything is on the line now, and our chances of success are slim to none. But at least I'm not alone in this anymore. I've got Anton and Luna. My friends are with me. And now, Major Apollo. We've got something else, too.

It's starlight, as old and bright and endless as the universe.

A glimpse of a time before any of us even existed.

CHAPTER 28

DRAE

Willow grabs my hand, and together, we flee from the pizza spot and out into the dark night. A smile lights up her face. She tugs me along into the shadowy campus.

We take the back alleys to avoid the Fed Patrols. Willow moves smoothly and confidently, already knowing the best secret routes to get around campus.

"Come on, slowpoke," Willow teases me.

I feel her hand gripping mine.

"What's the rush?" I joke.

"Oh, just your psychotic former best friend stalking us," she shoots back.

"In my defense, I'm sort of used to him being a total asshole at all times. Too bad you didn't get to meet Loki, too."

"Why . . . is he worse?" She frowns, and I want nothing more than to make her smile again. "I've read your file."

"Not worse exactly. Just like a different flavor of asshole. But double the fun."

"Yeah, too bad I only recently transferred," she says, smiling again.

It's her cover.

"Is it weird . . . that it feels like I've known you longer?" I ask suddenly.

"Well, in my case . . . I knew you . . . before I knew you . . ." she admits.

"You did?"

"Your file, silly. The Resistance keeps tabs on all their agents. And, well, I sort of asked Trebond if I could be assigned to your case and be your agent handler."

That surprises me. And makes my heart beat faster. "You requested me?"

I match her gaze. We hold each other for a moment that only deepens.

She bites her lower lip. "Yeah, I guess something about you stood out."

"My irresistible good looks?" I say, tossing my longer hair back dramatically.

"Oh, shush!" She play-punches my arm. "Plus . . . I'm sapiosexual . . ."

"*Sapio* . . . what?"

"It means I'm attracted to intelligence. Not physical appearance."

"You like book nerds?"

"Ha, I guess so. Anyway, it was my idea to make the library our point of contact—and how we trade messages."

Her *knowing* me before she knew me affects me in a way I can't explain.

"And what did you think when you finally met me in person?"

"Let's just say, you didn't disappoint." She gives me a shy glance. "And, well, maybe you do have some irresistible good looks that even I couldn't ignore . . ."

She trails off, but I take a step closer.

"Oh, do I? Ms. Sapiosexual?"

Something about the danger. Something about our shared secrets. Something about how it binds us together . . . and makes my heart skip a few beats.

But I like the risk. I embrace it.

Blood rushes to my head like a drug.

The Campanile looms over us like a sentry, keeping watch over everything. The stars burn brighter in the absence of moonlight. However, I pull my gaze from them and their beauty.

I don't want to be reminded.

I'm still caught up in the moment and don't want to think about what I did and the damage it's going to cause.

"Well, it's a lot of things," Willow says, turning and grasping my hand. She leads me into another back alleyway that cuts behind the stately academic buildings. "The biggest thing?" She turns more serious suddenly. "It's your devotion to our cause. It's never been more important to fight for peace . . . and to Disarm the Stars . . . and bring our brave guardians home."

Guilt stabs me hard. Willow said she's read my file. So, she knows about my participation in the Sympathetic Program. But I'm guessing my file doesn't mention what *really* happened between me and Kari in space . . . how we broke the rules . . .

How we fell in love.

"I couldn't agree more," I say softly, not wanting to dwell on that. "The Sympathetic Program is what got me to join the Resistance in the first place."

We reach Willow's dorm. Now we're standing under the eaves in the starlight.

"I know you're worried about your Sympathetic fighting up there," Willow goes on. "But we'll figure it out. Trebond is smart . . . smarter than anyone I've ever met. And more join our cause every day. We'll put an end to the endless wars . . ."

I take in that reminder of why we're risking everything for this cause.

"And then Kari can come home."

The words leave my lips. Willow seems to shudder under them. And just like that, I'm sucked back into this moment. My heart beats faster and faster.

I'm about to pull back and cut this off before it gets worse, but then she leans in closer and closer. I'm lonely. *I'm so lonely.* She places her hand on my shoulder . . .

The old me would kiss her. The old me *wants* to kiss her . . . blast everything else. Her purple eyes enchant me deeper. The taste of her calls to me. I lean in . . .

The wanting.

It swells and blots everything else out. I don't care about anything else but her. Heat flushes my cheeks, then my whole body, while gooseflesh pricks at my skin.

She leans in closer.

I can smell her now.

Our lips are about to brush together, yearning for more . . . when suddenly—

A cruel voice echoes across the glade.

"Got a new girlfriend?"

We jerk apart, both scanning for the source of it. Even though I already *know*.

Jude steps into a pool of lamplight.

He's sneering. I recognize the twist of his lips. He's enjoying this.

"None of your business," I say, stepping in front of Willow protectively.

But we both know it's bad that anyone catches us together. Especially . . . Jude.

"How would the Park Rat feel?"

That's when I hear the slurring. He's drunk. That makes him unpredictable and twice as dangerous. He must have followed us here, even though we took precautions to avoid the main campus. I find my voice, but it's shaky. The problem? He's not wrong about what he saw . . .

"Again, none of your business."

"Oh, really?" He takes a few steps toward us, savoring my humiliation. Then he sneers at me again. "I thought you were only into deserter spawn? What would your Sympathetic think about . . . your new friend?"

Willow's breath catches in her throat behind me. She takes a step back.

"What does he mean?" she hisses in my ear. "What's he talking about?"

But I can't respond to that yet. It's too complicated, and I don't want Jude to know that he's landed a good blow.

"Look, she's just a friend," I say, trying to keep my voice even but failing miserably. "She's my study partner . . ."

There's a long pause. Then he grins.

"Oh, the fluorescent nerd's replacement?" He knows Rho's name, but he refuses to say it. "She should know . . . you're not very loyal. Just ask Loki."

Willow takes another step back, distancing herself from me. She squares her shoulders and faces him. She doesn't shrink back. She holds her space. That seems to intrigue him.

"Oh hello there, and who are you?" He leers at her, clearly finding her very attractive. Her feisty attitude becomes even more of a turn-on. "I haven't seen you around campus."

My heart drops. Is he going to figure it out? That she's a Resistance operative? And put it all together . . . Rho's absence . . . Willow's subsequent arrival at college . . .

"Well, I could say the same thing about you," Willow says, pursing her lips.

"Transfer student?" Jude asks. He's suddenly even more suspicious.

She crosses her arms. "Yes, that's right. I also work at the library part-time."

"Book nerd, too? No wonder Drae likes you. You know what they say about reading too many books. It's dangerous . . . can't be too careful these days."

"Depends on your taste in literature," she interjects. "*The Space Force Diaries*, for example, is my favorite book."

He lights up. "Oh, really? My father is interviewed extensively in that book."

She drops the steely vibe and starts fawning over him. "No way. Really? Wait . . . are you . . . Jude Luther?"

Jude smirks. "Guilty as charged. He's my father. He's quite important . . ."

"Oh, I know! I'm such a fan."

She reaches into her bag and pulls out a copy of the book. "Wait, will you . . . sign it for me? I mean, I know you're not technically in the book . . . but still . . ."

"Well, he is my father," Jude says, puffing up under all her praise. "So, it's basically the same thing. Wanna know a secret? He's gonna run this fed one day."

He winks at me, making sure I overheard that.

So, that's their plan?

I would bet anything that his hardline father is already working to undermine Secretary-General Andromeda and plotting to overthrow her. Stoking the Proxy tensions and pushing for war.

Willow flinches but hides it. I can tell she picked up on the implications, too. Luckily, Jude is busy pulling out a pen and scrawling his name down in looping cursive in her book.

Patriotic literature, I think.

Nice touch to keep her cover safe. Inside her bag, a few flyers tumble out. For a split second, I freak out, thinking it's Resistance propaganda. Jude reaches down.

The way his eyes narrow—I can tell that he's thinking the same thing.

His fingers close around the pastel-colored paper. He scans them quickly. I brace myself for the fallout, remembering my roommate and what happened to her.

But then Jude smiles.

"Be careful being seen with these." He hands them back to her. "It's still technically against the rules."

That's when I glimpse the bold print—

"KILL THE ASTRALS!"

It's hardline pro-war propaganda. Why does she have that? Then it dawns on me.

Also part of her cover.

Like the patriotic book in her bag. In case she gets caught . . . they won't suspect that she's Resistance with that stuff.

That's brilliant. And nefarious.

Not dropping her act, she starts shoving the flyers back in her bag.

"Oh, please don't turn me in," she says, acting all flustered and scared.

Jude appears thoroughly charmed now, even though he saw me kissing her a moment ago.

That doesn't faze him.

Willow gives him a frightened look, but he reaches out and pats her arm.

"Don't worry. Your secret is safe with me. We share the same sentiments." He lowers his voice, glancing around. "Don't worry, my father is going to fix it."

"Really, he is?" She keeps her voice low and leans into his touch. "When will true patriots be safe to speak the truth?"

He smiles in a creepy way.

"Soon. Very soon now."

That chills me to the bone. But Willow keeps up her act. She admires his signature in her book, then carefully stows it in her bag with the Anti-Astral flyers.

"You have no idea what this means to me! I'll treasure it always. I promise . . ."

That's when I see under the signature—it's his number so she can message him.

"Don't be a stranger," Jude says. "And take my advice. Stop hanging around this loser. He's not like us—he can't be trusted. You're clearly too good for him."

He says that loud enough to make sure that I hear it. I wince, but I know she's working him, pumping him for intel. She gives him a flirty look.

"Thanks. For everything."

I'm still too shocked to do anything but appreciate her acting and spy skills. Right before this, she had me enraptured and falling for her. And it all seemed so real.

But now I wonder, is that an act too?

Can I even trust her?

Suddenly, a group of girls cuts across the glade toward the dorm. They're dressed in tight clothes and giggling, clearly returning from a frat party.

They pick up on the tension.

"Everything okay out here?" one says when they spot Willow with two guys.

I'm standing with my arms crossed, glaring at Jude. I didn't even realize I was jealous. It's all an act, my head argues. But my heart flares, making me feel upset.

The girls fan out and surround Willow, but she shrugs and tries to brush them off.

"Oh, it's fine!" She slings her bag over her shoulders. "These are just . . . my friends . . ."

Still, the girls sense something is off. They stay put and don't break off into the dorm. I wonder if they know about what happened and why Jude left campus.

From their narrowed eyes, I'm guessing so. Maybe they knew the girl.

Jude takes the hint.

He raises his hands and backs away from Willow in a harmless gesture. "Just making sure my *friends* got home safe."

As he brushes past me, roughly side-swiping my shoulder, he hisses, "*Just watch yourself.*"

Then he makes a *message me* gesture to Willow before dissolving into Memorial Glade and disappearing into the shadows.

He was alone tonight. That's unusual. I wonder where his protectors are—and why he was following me on his own. Regardless, it can't mean anything good.

The whole night took a dark turn when he turned up. But who am I kidding?

I'd already chosen the shadows.

As I leave Willow safe with the gaggle of girls, I gaze up at the night sky. I wonder if Kari got my exchange and when I'll hear from her again.

I'm losing it without her, I realize. I need that connection. Or I fear what could happen. Even worse, I fear I already messed it all up. Why is it so hard to do the right thing and just walk away?

Not only did I blow it with Kari potentially—well, more than I already did—but I almost blew Willow's cover, too.

Only her quick thinking and planning, plus her top-notch acting skills, saved us. Jude responds to flattery. And he likes cute girls who fawn over him. She must have known that also . . . from his file. I know she read it, just like she read mine to prepare for this operation.

Even as I doubt everything that I feel for her, everything that drew me to her in the first place, my heart still beats faster at the thought of her. I fight my desire. But I'm losing the battle.

I glance back—and Willow meets my gaze. She's standing in the entryway as the girls filter into the dorm one at a time, tramping in their platform heels. Sadness sweeps her features into oblivion before she turns away and enters the building, swallowed by the light.

The door shuts behind her with a decisive . . . *thud*.

CHAPTER 29

KARI

After the midnight sunrises and spilling my secrets to Major Apollo, I finally fell into a fitful sleep. It was plagued with nightmares of the Astrals—light-beings—assaulting me and screaming about murdering their kids.

I wake with a start, then, blurry-eyed and fuzzy-brained, go through my morning routine on autopilot, finally finding myself in the mess hall with Luna. Breakfast is usually my favorite meal, but today it curdles my stomach.

Luna notices. "Everything okay?"

"Fine," I say, trying to avoid the inevitable confession.

"Does this have anything to do with your little midnight field trip?"

"Uh . . . maybe."

My cheeks color. I look down at my congealing eggs and faux bacon.

"Let me guess. That knock? Could it have been our hopelessly handsome CO?"

My cheeks color more.

"Maybe," I hedge again.

Luna sighs deeply. She leans closer to me and lowers her voice.

"Don't look now—but he's watching you." Immediately I jerk my gaze, making her roll her eyes. "I said . . . don't look."

He sees me—his eyes lock onto me. The corner of his lip curls into a smile.

I get chills. Whole-body ones. The kind that you can't ignore. Luna notices.

"So . . . what the fuck happened last night?" Luna demands. Now she sounds worried. Like extra worried. Not good.

"Nothing . . . like that," I say quickly. Then, finally, I confess to telling him the secrets we discovered in the archives.

She's silent for a moment.

"You told him?"

"Well, I thought we all agreed that we need help. We can't solve this problem on our own. We need people within Space Force to support diplomacy—not more forever wars."

"You're right," she admits. "But how do you know you can trust him?"

That's where I stumble. I don't know, but how do I tell her that without freaking her out? Or worse, freaking myself out? The truth is—it could be a horrible mistake. But my gut rebels and argues with my head. *Trust, trust, trust . . .*

Those words hit me.

I look over—and Apollo has his gaze trained on me. His eyes look pleading.

I turn back to Luna.

"I don't know, but something inside me tells me that . . . he's different," I say at last. "That he's more like us . . ."

"So, it's a feeling?"

"Basically."

"Not very scientific."

I nod. "But science can only explain so much. There's more we don't know."

"Anton would probably agree with you," Luna says. "But that doesn't make me feel comfortable. I prefer facts."

"Me too. This feeling stuff . . . it's pretty new for me."

Luna nods. "You've changed . . . since you and Drae . . ."

"Ugh, don't remind me!"

"Just be careful."

"What do you mean?" I say as a jolt of embarrassment rushes through me.

She tilts her head toward Major Apollo, who keeps furtively glancing our way from his table, where he's eating with General Titan and the science officers from her team.

"Look, I may prefer facts," Luna says in a low voice. She locks her gaze onto me. "But even I can feel the sexual tension simmering between you and our CO from over here."

"Shit. Is it that obvious?"

"Maybe not to someone who doesn't know you. But I'm not that someone."

She's right—she knows me.

"What about Drae?" she asks.

"I confess . . . it's been hard," I say, my heart sinking. "The lag time is harder than I thought. I'm still waiting for his response to my first exchange. The truth is . . . I miss him like a blast to the chest."

"Right. And Major Apollo . . . is right here?" she says in a knowing voice.

"Yes, and the temptation is worse than I imagined. Before Drae, I never had crushes or feelings like this. My best friend Rho had a new boyfriend—or girlfriend—every other week in high school. While I felt . . . *nothing*."

"Not even for Drae?" she presses me.

"Oh, I felt for him." I snort. "I hated his guts to the stars and back. He tried to kiss me once, and I punched him in the face."

That makes Luna laugh. "Oh, right. I forgot about that. Then you got paired?"

I nod. "Exactly. I was *forced* to communicate with him—and more than that—to experience his side of things. And it turns out, he was hopelessly in love with me the whole time. But he was such an asshole and a coward back then."

"Ringers," she quips. "So, you're saying . . . the Sympathetic Program actually works. It changed you both."

"Exactly. And, well . . . the rest is history. But now we're separated more than ever with all these big feelings on the line."

"And now there's Major Apollo."

"No, it isn't like that," I protest and struggle to explain it. "I admit it—I have a special connection with him. I've felt it since our first day on base. But it's totally different than what I feel for Drae."

"How so?" she presses me.

Both our eggs have turned cold and unpalatable.

Neither of us seems to have much appetite now.

"Drae has my heart and soul. It's like this incredible mental connection," I try to explain. "But with . . . *you know who* . . . it's like this full-body response . . . like an energy exchange."

"That makes sense. And it's not weird at all. You've got the hots for him."

We both laugh.

"Guilty as charged."

"He's a pretty attractive specimen of a human male. My advice? Just don't go catching feelings, too. Or it could turn out bad . . . for everyone. Especially the one you really love."

Her advice resonates. I struggle with how my emotions seem to have been unleashed, unbolted, ever since I crossed those boundaries with Drae on that ship.

And now that they're out, I can't seem to stuff them back into their iron cage. They're wreaking havoc on my mind and my body, and I'm afraid of what I might do. I promise myself to be more careful around Major Apollo. I just hope trusting him with that secret intel wasn't a mistake. It's not just my sorry ass on the line—but my friends too. I can't afford to hurt them.

"Let's hope you did the right thing," Luna says as we clear out trays and head out. "And we can trust him. You are right—we can't do this alone. We need help."

I glance back. His gaze remains directed my way, casually, as if he's just looking out into space. But I know the truth. It's not my imagination either.

He's watching me—he's been watching me—maybe since I first arrived on base.

I don't know whether to be thrilled at his interest, like my racing heart demands, or terrified, like my head is warning me.

Or maybe both.

The confusion lingers for the rest of the day, dissolving into more nightmares the second my head hits the pillow.

I dream of the Astrals as they're tending, growing, and nurturing their world, then, abruptly, explosions and blaster fire rain down over their peaceful civilian settlement.

I wake breathless and sweaty, tangled in my sheets. Harold pings me the second consciousness floods my body—

"Kari, you've received a new message from your Sympathetic. Please proceed directly to the post office—"

I don't wait for him to finish. I leap out of my rack and start shuffling into my uniform and yanking on my boots.

"You . . . okay?" Luna mumbles from her top rack. She slouches over the side, her hair rumpled from her pillow.

I wave her off. "Go back to sleep, Private. It's just my Sympathetic."

"You got a new message?"

"Yeah," I say as my heart beats faster in anticipation. "It's about time . . ."

"Good luck," she says in a chipper voice. But it sounds forced.

I hurry from our barracks, but I can't ignore the way her worried eyes linger on me.

The pod seals around me, erasing Anton's visage from my view. Then blackness descends, followed by that brain-sucking feeling. It envelops me and transports me. The next thing I see—

It's Drae. He's standing on this mossy rock formation in a tree-filled glen.

I absorb everything he communicates to me. That Jude is back on campus. That knocks the breath out of me. I feel his fear and paranoia. He keeps talking, briefing me on everything going on at college.

The campus unrest and Anti-Astral rally. The way they targeted his roommate and arrested her.

How Mr. Egbert is a professor now—and worse—helping Jude and the Anti-Astral movement. I can't believe our old high school teacher is at Berkeley. According to Drae, they're purging professors accused of being dissidents and replacing them.

I thought he would go back to a more peaceful Earth for now. But it's the total opposite. It's worse than I thought.

All of this upsets me.

But then I get to the rest—

He stumbles over his words. But once he says her name—*Willow*—he can't take it back.

His emotions flood through the neural link. It's sickening.

His desire, his lust for her.

Before I know it, I'm blinking back tears. My chest aches like I just got stabbed.

This girl . . . the agent handler.

Willow.

That's her name. The cause of my pain and heartbreak. He quickly apologizes for his runaway emotions, but he can't hide the truth of how much he desires this girl. It throbs through the connection like a heartbeat, subtle but steady and undeniable.

I know it's like my attraction to Major Apollo, but Drae has a history. He's dated more girls than I care to guess. He has more experience and, therefore, more tendency to stray and fall back into his old habits, which he admits. He's also at college.

My greatest fears are coming true.

That's all I can think now.

Temptation is everywhere on that campus. I remember what Luna said about proximity and our long-distance struggles. I know Drae is apologizing for everything, but I can barely hear him through my sobbing. This is why I avoid relationships, why I stuff down my emotions.

Only I'm trapped in this pod.

And I can't do that anymore. The exchange ticks down to . . . *nothing*.

Finally, I'm released from my purgatory and expelled into the light.

My respite is short-lived. Now I have to record my replay to be whisked away to him and warped back Earthside.

The neural link sucks me back into another world, plunging me onto the lunar surface. The trees sway and tinkle their crystal in the gentle winds.

But I barely notice it.

I'm fighting back tears, winded, and utterly blindsided. I can't believe I trusted him. I don't speak; I let my thoughts cascade out and bombard the recording.

Willow.

How could you?

I loved you.

Past tense. It comes out in past tense.

So much sad.

Too much sad.

Betrayal. Everything with you . . .

Mistake. Regret. Hurting.

So bad.

I wish I could form words, or communicate better, but my heart feels like an open wound gushing blood onto the battlefield, spilling out my life force.

You stole it.

I glance at the timer. That orients me and grounds me. Our love was accidental; there are bigger things on the line now.

I force myself to brief him, so the Resistance can know what we discovered.

I take a deep, shaky breath.

Force the words out.

I wish I could say more, but we have bigger problems. We've uncovered secrets at my base.

Quickly, I tell him about the Astrals and what we discovered about how we started this war. How this moon was the location of a Proxy war that's been deleted from the archives and records on purpose . . . so nobody would know the truth.

There's still time left. Too much time. But I can't talk anymore. I'm too hurt. My heart lurches in my chest, fighting me.

Harold cuts in. *Kari, you have to be honest about your feelings in your exchange.*

I know the rules—

But it feels like it will kill me.

I don't care that the timer is still loaded with precious minutes. Or that I still love him despite this heartache. Feelings . . .

They're just feelings . . .

I tell myself that, but it doesn't lessen the pain. In a panic, I disconnect the exchange. *Harold, pull me out! Now!*

I scream it at the top of my lungs. My tearstained face is the last thing that Drae will see. But that's what he deserves.

I told him to protect my heart. He promised. And he broke it.

The exchange dissipates in the blink of an eye, and it hurts worse coming out than usual, almost like a knife to my skull. The blackness fades into light as I tumble from the virtual landscape back into reality, disoriented and upset. My head splits with pain.

The door cracks open.

I'm gasping for breath, trying to control my emotions. Anton rushes over. He's rubbing my back, trying to calm me. I know he was observing that . . . so he already knows . . .

"I'm so sorry," he says. "About what happened in your exchange . . ." He trails off, but worry lights up his eyes.

What else is there left to say?

He's not Drae. He didn't do it.

But then panic grips me like a vise. I try to fight back against it, using all the tools I learned in basic training to calm my mind. Finally, my breathing slows. The anxiety lessens. Some rationality creeps back in. I try not to think about the girl. It's not her fault either.

She doesn't know about us. It's only one person's fault. And that's—

Him.

I used to hate his guts. Then I fell in love with him. What am I worried about?

That I'm back to hating his guts again.

How fast can the pendulum swing back? How fast can we revert to our old ways? I thought he changed. No, more like . . . we changed. Both of us changed.

But now I realize that maybe he never changed at all. Maybe it was all . . .

To quote something he said once in an exchange that pissed me off . . .

Temporary insanity.

That must be it, I decide. Falling in love with me? It was temporary insanity.

None of it was real.

My head feels fractured, like it's splitting into pieces. A part of me is still back there with him, and a part of me is back in reality . . . and they're at war with each other. Suddenly, I remember what General Titan said about the dangers of falling for your Sympathetic.

These were only thoughts—desires—not actions. I can't imagine what would happen to me if he really cheated.

I try to shake it off. But it doesn't work.

Not really.

"I'm fine," I say with tears in my eyes. "I'm probably . . . overreacting . . . he didn't actually cheat on me . . . or do anything."

I want to add—*yet.*

It's been several days since he recorded that exchange. Anything could have happened since then, and I have no way to know about it.

"Of course, that's possible," Anton says. "The program amplifies your feelings due to the neural links. Anything you experience in there will be stronger."

"You can say that again," I say with a wince. "*Stabbing-me-in-the-heart* stronger."

He winces at my deadpan. "Yeah, that about sums it up. That's why the program advises against romantic entanglements. Most pairings remain . . . only that . . ."

"Friend-zoned?" I quip.

He nods. "We're not supposed to discuss our Sympathetics . . . but that's definitely the situation with mine."

"That's lucky. Our situation has always been complicated. We started as enemies. And then, we sort of blasted right past the *friend* part and into the danger zone."

"Once that happens, it can't be undone. They become a part of us. And you become a part of him. And you're . . .

"Stuck together? With our brains neurally linked basically . . . forever?"

"Basically. Unless you die."

"Even if we hate each other?"

He frowns and scratches his head. "I guess so. A lot of married couples would tell you that's often the case. But they didn't really cover this in my orientation."

"Ugh, kill me now," I mutter under my breath. I pry myself out of my pod.

My legs feel wobbly, while my head pounds like the blazing stars.

"I'd better get back to my barracks and collapse in my rack feeling sorry for myself . . . for the rest of my tour of duty." I try to force a smile. Then I add, "*No, scratch that . . . for the rest of my life.*"

"Well, you just described heartbreak perfectly," Anton says. "On the upside, at least you're feeling something. And that's better than never feeling anything."

"Yeah, tell my heart that."

I turn to leave, but Anton stops me. "Wait, I know you want to throw a big pity party. But I can't let you leave yet."

"What do you mean?" I scowl back, my heart dropping in my chest. "Don't tell me I have to finish that exchange?"

My time wasn't up yet. I asked to be pulled out early. Technically, that violates the rules of the program. You're required to stay in there for the duration. But I was hoping they'd make an exception.

"No, not that," he says. "I gave you an exception . . . due to the circumstances."

Relief floods me. But it's immediately chased by curiosity. "Then, what is it?"

"Let's just say, it might be the one thing that will cheer you up," he says with a smile. "You've got another message."

"I do? Wait, is it . . ."

He nods and whispers, "Your father."

"Well, what're you waiting for?" I say, reaching my hand out to receive it.

But he shakes his head. "It's not that kind of message."

I frown at him. "What do you mean?"

"This one is a special delivery—it's being sent . . . in person."

I give Anton a sharp look.

I'm confused, but then——

"You mean, he's *here*?"

"Yup, he surprised the stars out of me, too," Anton confirms. "I was expecting a normal message. Not an actual visit."

I bite my lip. Anxiety floods through me. "But why would he risk that? Venturing into Space Force territory? That's pretty risky, even for him."

"Right. It must be urgent." He shrugs helplessly. "Sorry, that's all I know."

Then he looks down at his watch. The one the postal workers have. He perks up.

"We have to hurry if we're gonna make the rendezvous with his ship on time. Oh, and we have to be very careful."

"Oh, you think?" I retort. "Just some Raiders in our immediate vicinity? The sworn enemies of Space Force?"

He grins. "Yes. That. Exactly."

"Guess I need to put my new special ops skills to work." I follow him into the secret passage that leads to the docking bay, where the postal fleet awaits.

Anton darts ahead of me, leading me toward a small, idling ship. "Yeah, so act like a spy already—and let's blast off."

CHAPTER 30

DRAE

The campus is burning. Flames lick up the library steps. But what's on fire?
Books.

I realize it's all the books burning. Remnants of civilizations that have risen and fallen, preserved in written words on pages of flammable paper. They die on the steps of the memorial to their existence.

Now, I see the rest of the campus. And it's mashed with crowds chanting "Kill the Astrals! Death to the invaders!"

Jude leads them, screaming into a loudspeaker, his voice amplified and stoking the rage. His minions run into the library, emerging with more books to burn. Then I hear it—the screams.

It's Willow.

I burst into the library to save her from the fire, sprinting up the steps over the charcoal remains turned black with burning. But the lobby fills with smoke.

I cough, choking on it.

Then I see her—

Behind the desk. I run to her and grab her hand. "Let's go, we have to get out!"

But she clamps her arms around me and anchors me in place. I try to struggle and pick her up, but she holds me tighter.

That flirtatious smile lights up her face. The one she used on Jude last night.

His lips part—to kiss me.

I try to break free and drag her from the library, but she's impossible to move. She embraces me as the library goes up in flames. The fires singes my flesh—

I wake up screaming—"*Noooooo!*"

But it comes out only a soft gasp. I'm sitting in the morning sunlight in my bed. It was only a nightmare. Still, it takes a long moment for my breathing to return to normal. The dream replays in my head.

I don't have to wonder what prompted it. Everything from last night comes crashing back through my head with a vengeance. Willow . . . the desire . . . and Jude crashing our private moment.

I feel guilt coupled with relief that more didn't happen between us. I have Jude to thank for that. I also remember how she turned her charms on him.

How that made me jealous.

Even though I'm not supposed to have those feelings at all. I'm in love with Kari. I can't stop loving her even as I struggle to control my reckless desires, even as I fuck up everything that we believed in.

Maybe that's why my nightmares have been getting worse. More vivid. They come every night and only fade with my panicked waking. But I feel rattled all day. I'm not sure what to do about them.

I could talk to a doctor. But they'd probably just point out that my fears are embodied in those dreams. That it's everything I'm most afraid of happening. Doesn't take a psych degree to know that much. The simple conclusion?

I'm breaking under the pressure. Unraveling and falling to pieces.

I wonder if Kari got my exchange yet. That strikes terror into my heart. And more so, will she even reply to it? I'm terrified of what she'll say—but I'm more terrified she won't say anything at all.

That would be worse.

Her anger and her tears would be better than her silence. Her silence would feel like the void of outer space—empty, soul-crushing, and devoid of emotion.

And it would be all my fault, too. I have zero excuse for my mistakes.

The only thing I know for sure?

I don't deserve her.

I never have.

I cross campus with my bag slung over my shoulder, still feeling terrible. The sunlight only makes it worse. Even as fall consumes campus in a pantomime of winter's arrival, it won't get truly cold. This is California. The land of sunshine.

The contrast only darkens my mood further. I long for cold and gray, like the June gloom that consumes Lompoc, pushing summer off until almost fall.

Fed Patrols stop and scan me, before barking, "Proceed to class." Then speeding off.

Every day, it seems more of them crawl around campus. I wonder how long before they start to outnumber the students, or even replace us altogether.

Bots are easier to control. They don't rebel and post anti-war propaganda. They don't complain when their favorite professors are replaced with fed puppets. They smile and answer questions perfectly and say, "Please and thank you."

But you know what?

They're also lifeless and can't think for themselves. Quickly, I scan the newsfeeds. More reports of tensions in the government and Secretary-General Andromeda's struggles to maintain control. Last night flashes through my head again—and what Jude said.

He told Willow that his father was going to take over and change things.

That terrifies me. But it's also big intel that we need to report to Trebond.

That means—

I have to go to the library. And face her, even though I don't want to . . . in fact, it's the last thing I want to do right now. Guilt twists my heart and makes my stomach lurch. My head is filled with turmoil.

The jumbled emotions swirl around.

But too much is on the line.

And Willow is my point of contact. I duck behind a building to scrawl a quick note, then tuck it into a library book that's due back. Then I change course and head there. It might make me late for class, but needing to return books is a good excuse.

And Fed Patrols don't read.

Neither does Jude.

The chances of them searching through the pages are close to zero. That's a safer way to communicate than electronic communications, which can be hacked.

My heart stutters as more Fed Patrols zoom past. But they don't stop me this time. I scan the bustling campus for Jude. The threat of him remains fresh in my mind, like a bad dream that I can't seem to shake. The kind that follows you everywhere you go.

But I don't spot him anywhere. The closer I get to the library, the safer I start to feel. Books are basically his archnemesis. It reminds me of a comic book where the superhero has a built-in weakness, like an Achilles' heel, that the supervillain uses to destroy them.

I climb the steps and rush into the lobby. That's when I spot him.

Jude is sauntering out.

Weirder yet, he has a book clasped under his arm. What in the stars?

"Wh-what are you doing here?" I stutter before I can stop myself.

"Oh, just stopped by to see your little friend," he says with a lascivious grin.

I snap my gaze to the front desk. Sure enough, Willow is back there helping a student check out a stack of books. She furtively glances my way, then frowns.

Dark fire burns in my heart.

"She's my friend—not yours."

"Feeling a bit possessive?" Jude enjoys making me squirm. "And I thought Ringers weren't exactly your type."

I know I should play it cool and act nonchalant. The last thing I need is for Jude to grow more suspicious and discover the true nature of our relationship. But I can't help it.

"What do you want with her?" I blurt out. It comes out louder than intended.

"Figured she could recommend some federation-approved reading."

"Since when do you read?" I can't keep the ire out of my voice. I know what he really wants and that makes me angrier.

"Only if it's approved," he shoots back. "That's where you and I differ . . ."

He holds the book up and flips it open in my face. I smell the fragrance of paper. Space Force guardian pictures flutter past my eyes. It's the second book in the *Space Force Diaries* series. Basically, propaganda.

Not big words. Lots of pictures.

Just his type of book.

Abruptly, he snaps the book shut in my face with a *smack*. Then he backs away.

"Anyway, see you around," Jude says before he leaves. "And I'm definitely going to see your friend again soon."

That burns my heart. I feel the heat creeping up my neck singing my flesh.

But I have to control my temper. I can't let myself become . . . well . . . like him.

I worked so hard to change and distance myself from my bad habits from high school. I tried to get away from my friends. But they keep following me.

And now, I can't trust myself.

I force myself to complete my errand. I wait in line to speak with Willow. It only takes a few minutes, but it feels like forever. Finally, I reach the front of the line and slide the book onto the counter.

"Jude came to see you?" I hiss.

"Yup, he sure did," she says, keeping her voice pleasant. "It's a library . . . that means it's open to all students."

I frown, not buying it. "He's not really a library guy."

"Right, I also messaged him this morning," she admits. She scans my return. "That might have had something to do with his recent change of heart."

"You . . . what?" My heart drops. "He's dangerous! Why would you do that?"

An awkward beat passes.

I can tell she doesn't want to have this conversation. And I'm making a scene.

"Look, I'm not leaving until you tell me the truth. What's really going on?"

She sighs heavily. "Because it's my job," she whispers. "That's why . . . remember how much he told me last night? Imagine if he starts to trust me—"

"But he's my enemy."

"Spy 101. Keep your friends close—and your enemies closer." Off my stunned look, she adds, "Besides, this comes top-down. From the Old Lady herself."

"Trebond ordered you to . . . get close to him?" I snap. "And just how close?"

I remember how she flirted with him last night, turning on all her charms. Charms I know too well because I fell for them, too. Suddenly, I feel foolish.

"Look, you don't want to know. But yes . . . basically what you're thinking. But Drae, listen . . . it's just an act . . ."

Her expression pleads with me. But she's such a good actress. I don't know what to believe—or who to trust.

"Are you so sure?" I huff. "What about with me? Was that all just an act, too?"

Hurt stings her face. She flinches. "No, it's not like that . . . you're different," she backpedals.

I can't keep the ice out of my voice. "I bet you told Jude that, too."

Tears sting my eyes. I have to get my emotions in check before they ruin everything. First, I'm blowing things with Kari . . . and for what? Someone I can't even fully trust. I realize I need to leave.

The line is queuing up behind me. We're just lucky it's a library, so they remain a respectful distance back. Most have their noses buried in books while they wait.

I point to the returned book. "That's an important story. You should take a look. You won't be able to put it down."

Willow flashes a tight smile.

"Already beat you to it," she says. "It's a real page-turner. Full of urgency."

I decipher that. She already told Trebond what we found out. That makes me feel useless—and out of the loop.

"Of course. You're a fast reader. I should've known you'd jump all over it."

I don't mean to insult her, but that's how it comes out. I turn to leave, simmering in a swirl of black emotions.

But she stops me.

"Wait, I have a new book suggestion for you . . . it just came out."

I hold my hand out for the book. But she shakes her head and taps at her computer. "The problem is that this particular book is on backorder. You need to pick it up in person."

In person.

My heart lurches. That can only mean one thing—Trebond wants to meet. Suddenly, I turn more alert and focus on the mission at hand. Somehow it puts everything in focus.

"When do I pick it up?" I say in a casual voice.

She taps more, then looks up. "Tomorrow evening. I'll go with you to make sure you get the right book."

Now she doesn't trust me.

Or maybe it's Trebond who doesn't trust me. The problem is? I have no way to know for sure until tomorrow. The line grows impatient behind me, but I have one more burning question.

"What's the book about?"

Willow gives me a warning look, but then she gives in.

"Our little friends in the stars," she whispers, looking a bit jumpy. "But that's all I can say for now. The story is being kept under wraps. All I know is—there's a big twist."

I leave the library with my heart beating faster. Trebond wants to meet in person. Willow is coming with me. Something new has come to light about the Astrals. And it's something big.

But what could it be?

CHAPTER 31

KARI

We blast off in the postal ship. Anton has me stowed in the mail storage compartment, just in case. But a postal ship doesn't draw security attention.

I'm still only beginning to grasp the full power and extent of the postal system. They have their own fleets of small, super-fast ships fitted with warp drives. Their own headquarters hidden within our bases with secret rooms, tunnels, exit points, including access to the docking bay. They also have their own communication network that's heavily encrypted, only accessible by the postal workers and postmasters. They're all trained guardians, and their ships also have state-of-the-art defense systems and weapons to fight off Raiders and other Proxy threats.

"Okay, you can come out now," Anton says as we clear the airspace. We sail into the upper atmosphere and slide by the planet that it orbits, encircled by those glittering rings.

"Where is the rendezvous point?" I ask, sliding into the copilot's chair.

"Dark side of this planet," Anton says. "That remains . . . *nameless* to us. But I'm betting the Astrals have a name for it."

"True. They had a settlement here."

"His ship is cloaked in the rings. The dust deflects any radar or sensors, rendering them basically invisible."

I feel a secret thrill. "I haven't seen my father in person . . . since . . . well . . ."

"We saved the world?"

"Yeah. That."

"Well, buckle up," he says, kicking in the thrusters. "We'll be there soon."

I feel the blast of acceleration slingshot us forward, as my sling chair adjusts to counterbalance the drag on my fragile human body. In the grip of propulsion, my heart thumps faster and faster.

The distraction is only temporary. My father. Sneaking off base. Luna and Anton are going to cover for me, so hopefully my absence isn't noticed. Officially, I'm assisting the postmasters with a secret project. Like I said, they have a lot of pull.

That buys us time.

But not endless time. That saddens me. As excited as I am to see my family again—I'm just as saddened to know that I'll have to leave them again.

Feelings bubble up. I can't stop them. They flood over me. *Drae.* That exchange threatens to reply in my head like a bad dream. His attraction to that girl. Anger sparks in my heart like a flashpoint, but then cools into sadness. So much of it.

But I can't risk dwelling on him. I have to push it away and focus on my mission. I have to find out what my father and Raiders have discovered about the Raiders—*if anything*—and share our intel.

And I have to do it all—

With a broken heart.

I fight my feelings. I try to stuff them down. But I worry I'm regressing into my old ways. Turning twitchy and angry.

Waiting to run away.

My usual M.O.

Wanting to escape anything that makes me feel . . . but the problem is that . . . what I really need to escape is myself. I'd made so much progress, or so I thought. I believed that I'd found my person—my real sympathetic. Someone who knew all my flaws and saw my rough edges, but loved me anyway. Now, I know the truth.

One bad message has the power to destroy everything.

And that scares me.

Because I can't just run away from him. We're paired together with neural links implanted into our delicate brains and hardwired into our central nervous systems. But it's not just the program.

What really scares me is how much I need Drae. No, *needed*, I correct myself, switching it into the past tense.

I can't trust him anymore. I made a mistake letting him in. I remember General Titan's ominous warning. I have to be stronger now and shut him out.

For both of our sakes—

Or it could shatter our minds.

My thoughts break as we sail into the glittery space dust, and it swallows our ship.

Suddenly, we start spinning and lock onto the Raider ship, which emerges out of stealth for a split second, glimmering under the glow of the two suns encircling the planet in orbit. We're hidden behind the rings on the dark side, shielded from the moon where our base is located.

Our ship shudders as it locks into place, and the sickening spinning stops abruptly. My chair undulates against it.

"Welcome home," Anton quips, unblocking his harness. He knows my family lives on this Raider ship now.

So technically, it is my . . . home.

We trek to the door, which hisses and cracks open. We enter the airlock into a burst of vapor clouds. The other door opens to the Raider ship. Before the vapor can clear—it's pierced by a familiar voice.

"Kari, I grew two inches!"

I don't wait; I run toward the voice and sweep my little sister into a tight hug.

I feel her bony shoulders. While I'm taller and thicker, Bea is built like a fragile bird. But she's stronger than she looks. And she's not lying. She has grown and feels heavier, too. Tears prick my eyes.

My little sister is growing up—she's nine and had her birthday last month—and I'm missing it. But I try to hide them.

"You miss me?" I sniffle.

"Like, Captain Obvious," she jokes back. "Now, ask me something harder."

"You miss Earthside?"

She juts out her lower lip. "Nope. Good riddance. I never really fit in down there. Plus, Ma is so much happier."

"With Dad?"

"It's like she's . . . finally free."

I take that in. My tears don't stop, but they turn joyful.

Anton joins us, waving to my little sister, who blushes at the attention.

Bea leads us into my father's Raider ship. I remember it from when he saved us back on Ceres. And saved my battle buddy Nadia's life with his medical bay.

We step into the ship, and it's like a homecoming. Rho rushes over with bright pink nano hair and eyes. That punk vibe complements her new Raider chic. She left college after she met Gunner, my father's copilot, and fell hopelessly in love.

She doesn't greet me so much as word vomits at me in her usual rapid-fire style.

"Kari. I need the life update. This minute. Did Drae mess everything up?"

I can't hide my sadness. "How did you know?"

"Ugh, I knew it! Gunner, I told you he'd fuck it up and break her heart!"

"Predictable!" Gunner says, emerging into the corridor. "Earth scum of the male variety always finds a way to suck bad. Maybe you should consider switching teams?"

I want to laugh and cry, but most of all, I needed that. To feel seen and validated.

"So, what happened?" Rho says.

"He didn't do anything . . . yet," I say carefully. "But the neural links make it so I feel his emotions—and you can't lie."

"It's someone else, isn't it?" Rho says with a sigh. "It's always someone else."

My cheeks burn. She's so much more experienced in relationships than I am. Drae is technically my first love. Actually, he's my first kiss. First sexual encounter.

My first everything.

That makes this so much harder.

"You never forget your first heartbreak," Rho says, reading my mind.

"Or your first true love," Gunner says, thrusting her arm around Rho, making it clear that's hers. It would be annoying if their feelings weren't so genuine.

"Who's the temptress?" Gunner says, stroking her blaster. She leans in with her rum breath. "Do you need me to . . . you know . . . pay a little visit Earthside—"

"Ugh, stop that." Rho slaps her hands way from her blaster. "You're not murdering Drae. Well, not yet . . ." She turns her gaze on me. "Who is the girl?"

"Her name is . . . Willow. She's his agent handler and a Resistance operative. I guess she's posing as a student and librarian, but that's all I know. She works for Trebond."

His desirous feelings for her flood through me again, drowning my heart. I can picture her through Drae's perspective. Pixie cut, punk-meets-Goth aesthetic. I blurt out—

"And she's . . . really *freaking* cute."

"Seriously, I can blast her for you," Gunner says. "I've done it before."

"Ugh, it's not her fault!" Rho says, but then hardens. "Not that we know of . . ."

"Look, you're strong and resilient. Stronger than heartbreak. Stronger than alien invaders. Stronger than your asshole drill sergeant who tried to break you down."

I nod, even though I don't believe it.

That all sounds easy compared to affairs of the heart.

"Crushes and lovers come and go," Rho adds with a knowing look. "Trust me, you've seen it happen to me a hundred times. But not best friends. I'm not going anywhere."

That's when everything in me deflates.

I crumple up and let the tears flow, and Rho hugs me just like all those times I hugged her back in high school when her relationships inevitably went south. That's friend karma. Her one hug feels like the hundred I've given her after she got her heart broken or broke someone else's heart, and it does soothe me. My brain feels less shattered. And my heart?

It keeps thumping insistently, telling me that I still have people to love.

"You know what? This is bigger than my best friend abilities," Rho says, and steers me into the interior cabin. "For something this catastrophic, you need your mother . . ."

The cabin door *whooshes* open.

And there she is . . . waiting for me with her secret smile.

"*Kari*, my brightest star," Ma breathes into my hair, and hugs me like she never wants to let me go again. That's what she used to call me as a little girl who dreamed of enlisting and blasting off the stars, so she could see them for herself.

When we separate a good minute later (and I have to admit that Rho was right about needing my mother) I notice some positive changes. Back Earthside, she raised us as a single mom after my father deserted, working the night shift in the factory, a life that wore her down.

But now, after a few weeks in space, she's filled out and grown stronger, dressed in a pirated Space Force uniform, the usual Raider regalia. The biggest change?

Her smile doesn't have worry lines. It's as if being in zero-G erased them.

But I know the truth.

It's because of—

"Captain Dad!" Bea announces like a tiny first mate, snapping off a salute.

Our father strides into the cabin in a swirl of scarves and bluster. He looks every bit like the Raider captain with long, black hair tied into a ponytail and a thin mustache and beard, and twin blasters. We have the same eyes. And just like that, my little family is back together.

"Kari, you're a sight for sore eyes," he says in a boisterous voice. He gives me a fierce hug that threatens to crack my ribs. "Guess it takes a full-blown emergency to reunite us."

"Ugh, I know! I guess impending alien invasions have their upsides."

Everyone laughs, but there's an underlying seriousness. However, we all need to forget that for a moment and take the time to be together without death and destruction breathing down our necks, without feeling my heart shattering from the fallout of my message from Drae.

For if we can't have this—family and friends and feasting and drinking and banter and love—then what are we fighting for? My only regret right now?

I wish this moment didn't have to end. I wish I could stay up here in my father's ship in suspected animation—and I didn't have to crash back down to reality.

And face what *he* did to me.

At that reminder, I down another shot and try to forget all about his existence.

It doesn't work.

Not really.

After a vegan feast for the ages, thanks to Gunner and her cooking, easy conversation floats around the cabin, maybe thanks to a healthy dose of Mrs. Smee's rum. The engineer sits, happily drunk and dozing, at the end of the table.

But her rum is still wide awake, and winding around the cabin for pulls.

"Do you miss Earthside?" Anton asks Rho, fascinated by her choice of a Raider lifestyle over studying at U of Berkeley. "What about all the books and the library you left behind?"

"You're one to talk!" Rho shoots back. "You enlisted . . . you could've enrolled in college. All that knowledge could've been right at your fingertips. What made you do it?"

"I wanted to see the stars for myself," he says in that dreamy way. "Enlisting was the only way to land a ticket."

"Nothing compares to them, does it?" Gunner says. "Except for you, of course."

They kiss softly, tenderly. My heart swells for my best friend. She's happy.

Then Rho leans in toward us and whispers in a low voice. "And you never know. Maybe your father will give Gunner and me our own ship one day—"

My dad overhears and cuts in. "One day . . . far, far away!"

Jeering laughter explodes in the cabin.

I feel cheered up from the inside out. Maybe it's the rum talking, but I know it's not the only reason for it. For once, I can forget about Drae and my heart shattering into pieces.

This moment.

This levity.

It's everything I need.

I never want it to end. But every good dream has to burst and dissolve into reality, and this gathering is no different.

Anton breaks it first. "Look, I hate to stop the party, but we have to get back soon," he says, glancing at his watch. "Luna said the coast is still clear . . ."

"But for how long?" I add, knowing it will only stay that way for so long.

That's the thing with Space Force. Once you enlist, they control your life, your every breath, when you wake up, when you go to sleep, what you eat, how much you eat . . .

My father catches my eye.

We need to have a serious meeting before we head back to base. It's hard to leave them, but I hug every last person in the cabin. My eyes blur with tears as Dad leads me away.

"It's not goodbye," my dad whispers in my ear.

"See you later?"

"Exactly."

We enter his private quarters, but now I can see my mother's touches. Evidence of her return to his life, almost like little love notes scattered around his chamber. Her colorful scarves strung up on the walls. Her new uniforms—smaller than my father's and adorned with colorful feathers, shiny beads, and handmade patches—hanging in their shared closet.

And the beds. Two twin-sized bunks pushed together, almost like two halves of the same heart coming together. That makes me smile. But it quickly fades as seriousness settles over us like a dark cloud. I have to brief my father on everything we learned. This is critical intel for the Raiders and their allies in the Resistance back Earthside, who also need to know ASAP.

I'm not sure whether my exchange to Drae or my father's speediest ships can reach Earth sooner. As much respect as I've gained for the postal service, I'm betting on my dad. I remember how Mrs. Smee's experimental warp booster tech saved us. And now, it just might have to again.

I tell him about my mission to the Astral settlement. This time, I don't leave anything out. I tell him the weird parts. The temporal anomalies. What I heard and saw and experienced in there.

His expression turns from curiosity to shock, then hardens into anger when I tell him what we discovered in the archives about the true origins of the secret moon base—and most importantly, how the Astrals didn't invade us first.

We started this war.

His anger flickers across his handsome face like a solar storm then settles into a deep knowing. "Of course we did," he says in a dark voice. "Well, this changes everything."

His words hang over us. A long moment passes, long enough to feel strained. Somehow, my father knowing and confirming my worst fears . . .

Well, it makes it all real.

"I know . . . The Resistance is right. They've always been right . . . if we had *disarmed the stars*, then the Astrals would still be living peacefully on that moon . . ."

"Yup," he confirms. "And those kids on that bridge would still be alive . . ."

I hold out the drive that Anton made for him. "Here's the evidence. You need to get that to Trebond right away. Your ships with their warp boosters are faster than the postal service."

He accepts the drive. But a heaviness tenses the air.

"We need to find a way to talk to the Astrals. Some way to communicate with them. Another Great War will only lead to . . ."

"More war," he confirms. "Plus, they're more advanced than us. If we try to face them head-on without the element of surprise that we had last time . . ." He trails off.

But I pick up the thread. "Then it will be the end of us."

"But how do we open diplomatic channels? That's the real trick." My father scratches his beard. "You said . . . you saw things when you were down there?"

"When I was in their settlement, it was like they wanted me to find the truth about what happened to them. That's what led me to search the archives."

"It sounds like they want to talk to you," he says in a thoughtful voice. "That worries me, but it also gives me hope."

That's when I remember what I learned from Drae's exchange. Not the part that set me off like a ticking time bomb—the more important part I almost forgot. This is why falling in love is a bad idea. It distorts all your senses and warps your logic, making you lose sight of things.

"Listen, in my last exchange with Drae, he said something weird," I say, thinking back. "He said that he's been having nightmares—and he *saw* me on the moon where I'm stationed."

My dad shrugs. "Well, that's not that unusual. I dream of you all the time. Our dreams are manifestations of what we love . . . but also what we most fear . . ."

"Of course. That's not the weird part. He said that he had this dream *before* he knew where I was deployed. Before that first exchange."

My dad sits up. "Wait, you're sure?"

"Well, it could be a coincidence," I say, backpedaling. "But he recognized the landscape from my exchange. He also . . . saw me draw my weapon and almost blast someone . . ."

"Did you . . . ?"

I feel shame. "Yeah, in the settlement when the Astrals were distorting my perception. I almost blasted Luna."

"And Drae saw that in a nightmare?"

"He said it was like he was right there in front of me with zero lag time."

Neither of us has an answer.

All I know is that strange things are going on, and I don't know what it means.

"I'll send a message to the Old Lady and report back," my father says, interrupting my runaway thoughts. "Sorry I don't have more intel for you today."

"Right. It's okay." I pause, then meet his eyes. "So, why'd you come in person? We thought you had important intel."

He gives me a soft smile. "Sorry to disappoint you. But your old man wanted to visit you. Is that okay?"

"More than okay," I say, knowing that seeing my family and friends is the only thing keeping me together right now.

"Don't worry," he says, patting my shoulder. "We won't give up. We're Raiders for a reason; we're survivors."

"I love you," I say, but then I feel that sadness creeping in. He studies me.

"What else is going on?" he presses. "I may have been absent these last many years, but I'm still your father. I can tell when you're upset."

"It's Drae," I say, my voice catching.

"Did he hurt you?" He looks suddenly incensed. "That *blasted* yellow-bellied scoundrel! I'll blast him! Then I'll have my medics revive him and blast him again!"

"Dad, calm down!" I say, even though I appreciate the overprotectiveness. I wonder how my growing up might have been different if he had been around. "Besides, he's no use dead," I add. "That's the problem. I don't want to need him, but I need him . . . and I hate feeling weak."

"Right. It's like they're ruining your life, but you still love them." He gives me a look. "You're describing *real* love."

I drop my face into my hands in a display of exaggerated agony.

"Ugh, why does it have to hurt so bad? And how do I make it stop?"

Dad pats my leg. "Well, fess up. What did he do?"

"He didn't *do* anything," I say quickly. "At least, not yet. Because of the neural links, I'd know. You can't lie in the exchanges. But he had thoughts . . . about someone else . . ." I trail off, my cheeks flushing. "But with the lag time . . . that message was recorded three days ago."

"Right, so you're worried that something could have happened since then. Did he know it was wrong?"

"Yeah, he apologized right away. But it doesn't matter . . . it still hurt me."

"I see," he says with a helpless shrug. "Well, he's a young lad. We make a lot of mistakes. Asteroid fires, I'm shocked your ma has put up with me for so long."

"But that's the thing. The long distance. Being so far apart. You and Ma were separated for years . . . and look at you now! Like two lovebirds. How did you keep the love alive all this time?"

"Guilty as charged." Now it's his turn to blush. "What can I say? She brings it out in me. Makes me act all mushy and turns me into a hopeless romantic."

"I get the good times. But how do you overcome the bad and the sad?"

"And the mad?" he adds.

Yeah, he's definitely my father.

He knows me.

"Yeah, that," I say in exasperation. "All the dumb feelings I'd rather avoid."

"But you can't avoid them. Once you've fallen for someone like you and Drae, you're stuck with them. I wish I could tell you it gets easier. In our world, it doesn't . . . it requires a lot of grace and forgiveness. And communication."

"But I don't want to talk to him ever again. I cut off the last exchange early."

My dad nods. "Look, he's going to make a lot of mistakes. It comes with the territory. You both are. You'll see . . . you're not perfect either, daughter dearest."

That hits me like blaster fire. My cheeks flame again, only this time it's because of . . . Major Apollo. Yup, that's the worst part of how I feel about Drae.

I'm a total hypocrite. Because I have the same errant thoughts. The wandering attraction to my CO. How is that different than Drae and his interest in Willow?

But I'm not ready to face that.

I'm not ready to admit that the Apollo thing is real. And I can't give in to it.

Dad goes on, oblivious to my internal struggle. "You're both young and fighting against something big and hard. The question is—can you live with what he did to you and still love him anyway?"

"I don't know . . ." I say.

And it's the truth.

He doesn't press me further. But he does stand up. Time is running short.

He palms the drive, flashing it at me. "I'll make a copy to keep just in case. Then I'll send Gunner and Rho with my fastest ship Earthside to alert Trebond." He holds out his arms for a hug. "But I'm afraid, my dearest daughter . . . it's time for you to head back to base."

I blink back tears and hug him back.

"Remember, it's not goodbye," he reminds me. "It's see you later. Just promise you'll stay safe down there . . ."

His worried tone jerks me. I search his eyes and see the concern in them.

"What do you mean?"

"Just that . . . Space Force isn't as united as they want everyone to think."

"Secretary-General Andromeda?"

"That's all I know. Just be careful."

With time running short before our absence is noticed, my father leads me down the corridor to the airlock, where Anton is waiting in our ship with the engines already fired up to carry us back through the space dust to our base. As the Raider ship fades away, dissolving back into stealth mode, my heart contracts. I just hope he's right. And there is a *later* . . .

For us to see each other.

CHAPTER 32

DRAE

"So, is this your ride?"

Willow saunters up to my transport in her pink skort and flouncy top. It's idling right in front of Sather Gate. The night air hasn't turned cold yet.

But the fog should be rolling in soon.

Keep this professional, I remind myself.

I can't afford any more mistakes like the other night. Not when Kari's heart is on the line—and maybe the whole universe, too. Now, I understand the wisdom of the Sympathetic Program rules advising against romantic entanglements.

But what is done—

Cannot be undone.

However, I can take accountability and tamp down my impulsive feelings. I strive to keep my voice sharp and emotionless.

"Yes, that's right," I say stiffly.

Willow frowns at me. "Are you getting sick? Coming down with a cold? Your voice sounds kind of scratchy . . ."

My cheeks burn. "No, I'm fine. Just we'd better get moving. We don't want to miss the rendezvous."

I ask Estrella the time—just after 7 p.m. Then I mute her for the duration.

That's when Willow passes me a device to slip over my head. This blocks the neural implant, temporarily interfering with the connectivity. It'll just look like a glitch in the system.

The implants are for the Sympathetic exchanges. They're not supposed to actively monitor us, but we can't be too careful meeting in person like this.

The sun is sinking into the horizon, and soon night will fall. We clamber into the backseat of my transport. The car is self-driving, so I give the destination.

"The Golden Gate Attack Memorial," I say, feeling the impact of those words.

It's the scene of the crime. Where it all happened—and the Astrals blew up that school bus of kids. The Resistance uses the monument as a perfect meeting spot. People come and go to pay their respects at memorials. That makes it a great cover.

The transport picks up speed, levitating a few feet over the ground and silently propelling itself toward the city. San Francisco lights gleam in the twilight as if beckoning us into their fold. High-rises jut out, trying to touch the heavens.

It's almost all new construction from after the war. Most of the city was leveled to dust. First, they had to remediate the radiation, and then they could build on top of the rubble, covering up the devastation. I wonder how many bodies are buried under the newly laid foundations. The whole place is a graveyard, and since the GGA, I figure the dark waters of the bay claimed just as many bodies as the soil.

We sit in uncomfortable silence. I'm squirmed over by the window, as far from her as possible in the cozy backseat. I try not to notice her soft breathing. How her skort rides up slightly, revealing her sleek, toned legs. How the heat seems to waft off her pale skin.

She shoots me a sharp look. "Seriously, cut it out."

"Uh, cut what out?"

"This!" She gestures at me dramatically. "You're acting super weird."

"I don't know what you mean," I say in that formal voice, making her scowl.

"And that gravelly voice. Drop the act—and get real. What's going on?"

I freeze like a deer in the headlights. "It's nothing . . . I told you already . . ."

Her expression sharpens. "Is it what happened yesterday with Jude?"

That's when her eyes widen. "Oh no . . . wait, it can't be . . . Drae, are you jealous?"

My cheeks burn hotter. I cross my arms against her accusation. "No, I'm not . . ."

"You are."

I let out a deep sigh. "It's more like . . . I feel protective. I know how dangerous he can be, especially to *attractive* girls."

My voice catches on attractive, drawing her attention. "Oh, am I then?"

"Attractive? Like, obviously. You already know that. And you wield it like a weapon." Anger leaks into my voice. "It's what you're doing to him—and to me."

She shakes her head in disbelief. "So, which is it? I'm a helpless damsel in distress? Or I'm a femme fatale tempting and preying on the weak hearts of men?"

"When you say it like that, it sounds bad," I say weakly. "But you're twisting my words around. It's not like that."

Willow scowls. "I'm just weaponizing the male gaze and throwing it back. It's not my fault patriarchy still has a stranglehold on most of our culture."

She bats her eyelashes and pouts her lips—and I know it's an act—but it also works. Lust simmers under my skin, rushing through my body like fire.

"See . . . that's how it works," she says, snapping back to normal. "Seriously, you should read some books on feminist theory. Not all wars are fought with blasters. We have to use every weapon."

"Even if that means getting close to my enemy?" I shoot back. "Someone dangerous and connected? Whose father is plotting to overthrow the secretary-general?"

"Especially then." She softens slightly. "Look, this is war . . . only now it's not just being fought in the stars, but back on Earthside. Even on our college campus."

Her words sink in. I soften too, dropping the act. "I get it . . . I mean, my brain understands . . . but my body . . ."

She smirks, raising one eyebrow at me. "Has a mind of its own? Oh, I noticed your strong reaction to me. Part of my job is to notice that stuff. Don't worry. I'm used to it."

"Now I feel foolish," I say, stewing in my humiliation. "My emotions are all jumbled. They've been jumbled . . . well, since this all started. It's not just because of you . . . it's also my Sympathetic."

She looks shocked. She searches my face for the truth.

"Wait, you and her . . . you're in love with her, aren't you?" Her face falls at that revelation. "Fuck, how did I miss that? I scoured your file. I studied your every move in person, too."

"Well, it's supposed to be secret," I remind her. "It's probably not in my file, though Trebond and Xena probably know. It's also really complicated. She used to hate me in high school, but then when we started communicating through the program that changed."

"Wait . . . she hated you? And then you got paired together?"

I nod glumly. "Yeah, and I deserved it. I was such an entitled asshole back then. And now, I'm worried I'm turning back into one. That I didn't really change, not permanently."

"Drae, you're a lot of annoying things. But I know you better than just about anyone. I practically got my undergrad degree studying up on you for this sensitive mission."

I feel a rush at that confession. "A bachelor's degree in . . . *little ole me*?"

"Ugh, don't let it go to your head." She slaps my hand in faux punishment. "But like I said. You may be a lot of super annoying things—but you are not an entitled asshole."

"Ha, Kari would beg to disagree," I mutter. "I'm pretty sure she's right, too."

Willow surprises me and shakes her head. "Being a spy requires studying people. It's basically my specialty." She holds my gaze for another heart-stopping second. Then she goes on. "Drae, you're actually one of the most sensitive people I've ever met. That's probably why the Sympathetic algorithm chose you for the program. And why you fell in love with her."

Wait, I'm sensitive?

Thoughts rush through my head like a Category 5 hurricane. I've been believing what Kari said about me, beating myself up over it this whole time, trying to change and do better for her. But what if she's wrong about me? Meanwhile, Willow had to study up on me. I believe her about that part. Plus, would an *asshole* feel so guilty and shameful over their mistakes?

No, they'd be like Jude . . . remorseless and doing it all over again . . .

She's right. I'm not like him. I know that in my heart.

I do make mistakes. All the *fucking* time.

Lately, my life is like a stellar minefield leftover from a Proxy war. But I hate myself for it. And no matter what happens, I try to do better. Even if I keep failing over and over again.

Willow places her hand on mine, drawing me back to the present, back to this transport and the dark night enfolding us and the exhilarating propulsion carrying us to a secret meeting.

"You're wrong about one thing," I tell her. "I didn't fall in love with her in the pods. I've always been in love with her, ever since I noticed her back in school."

"That long?" she says,

I nod slowly. "That long. I loved her even when she hated my guts. I loved her even when she swore to never speak to me again after graduation. But then, we got paired together. And over time, I guess, I won her over. But now she's deployed, and the lag time is really hard."

"Drae, you don't give yourself enough credit." Her voice sounds low and raspy right now. "For how good your heart really is . . . for what an amazing person you are . . . even if you do make mistakes."

I look down in shame. "It's not good enough. Growing up, my mother made it clear . . . that I never did anything right."

"And now, let me guess?" She squeezes my hand. "Kari makes you feel the same way? Never good enough?"

That hits like a punch.

I can't even respond. Tears prick my eyes. Damn, she's good at this spy stuff. She has figured me out. Maybe even better than I figured myself out. If this is all an act though, she deserves an award. I've always put Kari on a pedestal. However, now I can see that Willow made a valid point. Kari has never made me feel good about myself. Around her, I always feel lacking. Almost like I'm the cold expanse of space that's going to dampen her fiery sun.

That messy swirl of emotions? It amplifies now, clouding my thoughts.

All I know is—

Willow understands me better than anyone ever has.

And she's only known me in real life for a few short weeks.

"Maybe you're right," I say, forcing my voice out. "But I made promises to her. And ever since I got back from space, I've done nothing but fuck up and betray her."

"And I helped you," Willow says, but I shake her off adamantly.

"It's not your fault. You didn't know."

"So, you make mistakes? Newsflash—you're human. At least, last time I checked. You're not a heartless alien who would blow up a bus of kids. Humans make mistakes. Look at our history! It's basically hardwired into our DNA."

"Still, what I did isn't right."

"Did you apologize?"

"Of course! The second I realized what I'd done . . . but she's angry. I don't know if she will ever forgive me . . ."

Willow sets her lips. "Then that's on her. Forgiveness isn't earned. It's given with grace and understanding. It sounds like an impossible trap she's set for you to fall into..."

"What do you mean?"

"Withholding forgiveness?" she says in a judgmental tone. "Blaming you for every problem in your relationship? But you know what? She's human, too. I'll bet anything that she's going to make mistakes. You don't know who's up there in space with her!"

"Wait, what do you mean?" Suddenly, I feel panicky, like I can't breathe.

Willow folds her arms. "How do you know? She could be doing the exact same thing. You said yourself that the lag time is crushing. You're just as much in the dark as she is..."

"You think... she'd cheat on me? No, she's not like that. It's me... I'm the problem..."

"Drae, I hate to break it to you," Willow says. "But you're both young. And in every relationship, you're going to mess up. It pretty much comes with the territory. The question isn't if you're going to mess it up. It's when and how much." She pauses and squeezes my hand. "But can you forgive each other when you do? Because it's going to happen, no matter how hard you fight it."

Her words hang in the recirculated air of the transport. We don't speak the rest of the way. For what is there left to say?

But for once, I don't feel like beating myself up like I've been doing. Finally, I see myself and my situation a little more clearly. Before, Rho was my biggest confidante when it came to Kari.

But Rho is her best friend and hardly an objective witness. If Kari and I break up, Rho won't hesitate to pick her side. And my friends? Jude and Loki are the worst when it comes to girls. I might need to brush up on some feminist theory, but they need to go back to kindergarten.

But Willow is an outsider. She didn't grow up with us. She grew up in a Resistance bunker, fighting her whole life. She has a unique perspective because she did study my file, and now she knows me.

Maybe she's right.

More right about me than anyone else has ever been... maybe since I was born to a mother who didn't want to be a mother because she was too damaged by space trauma and her secrets to love anyone, let alone her squalling baby.

The Golden Gate Bridge materializes before us, rising out of the sloping hills and standing over the dark waters of the bay. My transport takes the exit for the memorial constructed on the banks.

The white marble obelisks appear, each standing for one of the fallen kids and the brave bus driver, who also lost her life in the attack and drowned in the bay. That's because not all the bodies were recovered.

Because not much was left of them.

As my transport slows, Willow reaches over and gives me a look. "Asteroid fires, you're a better spy than I realized. At least when you want to be . . ."

"What do you mean?"

Our eyes lock.

"You didn't want me to know about your relationship with your Sympathetic—so you hid it from me well. I didn't even guess. If I knew, I never would have . . ."

"Deployed your weapons on me?"

Now it's her turn to blush. "Yeah, that. I would've kept it professional . . ."

Electricity flickers between us, making it clear that's going to be a struggle. Now that we've drawn our weapons, the war in our hearts has already broken out—and it won't be ended quickly or easily . . .

Or without collateral damage.

She clears her throat, pulling away. But the electricity still flickers. "We still have to work together. This is what we signed up for. So, you're stuck with me . . ."

I nod my agreement as we jerk to a halt in front of the monument and climb from the transport. But what I don't say is that no matter what, I'm stuck with my Sympathetic, too.

That's also what I signed up for.

The impossibility of the situation threatens to overwhelm me. But I don't have time to dwell on that now. The roaring of a school bus breaks the silence, then the headlights pierce the foggy darkness, lighting it up. My heart thumps faster. Willow nods to the school bus.

"The Old Lady . . . she's here."

The bus jerks to a halt. It's old and it sounds like it—and smells like it—as diesel exhaust pollutes the misty air. Only the poor kids have to ride the school buses. Ringers like me get their own transports. Yet another way our world legislates and enforces unfairness at each turn.

The door *cranks* open. Behind the wheel, I spot Xena. She's the second-in-command. The bus drivers are all aligned with the Resistance, and they can move freely around the federation without drawing suspicion. They all look the same, and nobody notices the drivers.

A figure parades up the aisle and steps out into the headlights. They shine on her from behind, creating a dark silhouette.

It's Trebond. My old professor and the head of the Resistance on Earth. Her voice echoes out, strong and determined.

"New information has come to light about the Astrals. Our Raider friends paid us an emergency visit Earthside yesterday. Your Sympathetic discovered something."

"Wait, Kari found something?" I ask right away. My heart beats even faster.

"What is it?" Willow adds.

We wait in anticipation. My mind races, trying to figure out what it could be. There's a long pause. And then—

"Kari learned that we started the war with the Astrals. Not the other way around."

CHAPTER 33

KARI

I wake from a horrible nightmare about Drae. He's *kissing* her. Their arms are locked around each other, while riots break out and the whole campus burns. They walk hand in hand in the chaos as if immune to the destruction breaking out.

I'm watching them like a ghost. But she sees me suddenly. She locks my gaze.

He's mine, she hisses at me.

Her arms wrap around him like she's ensnaring him in her web of deceit.

Then the skies light up. Without warning, the Astrals invade Earthside, raining down fire and terror from the skies. And then the whole planet burns.

REVENGE. REVENGE. REVENGE.

That word reverberates through my head. I wake with a start, breathless and breathing hard. It takes me a moment to adjust back to reality and realize that—

It was only a dream.

But still, it feels so real. My nightmares are getting worse. Again, I worry about space trauma. Or could it be something else? Something to do with . . . *them*?

I've felt jumbled ever since I entered the Astral settlement. My dreams are sharper—clearer—almost more real. And the terror that grips me is stronger, too.

It doesn't fade with waking. I still feel the intensity radiating through my body.

I sit up in my bunk and stare into the partial darkness of my barracks. It's barely morning, but this is how I've been waking lately. Too early, thrashing around in my rack, just grateful not to wake Luna, who is snoring above me, still wrapped in the peaceful solitude of her mind.

I let out a shaky breath that I didn't even realize I'd been holding.

So much has happened lately.

The last few days since I snuck out to meet my father on his ship have passed in a blur. No news, which should be a good thing, but makes me more aware that time is ticking down—and we're stumped.

But I hate sitting around and doing *nothing*. I feel like I'm going crazy. My mind keeps creeping back to Drae and his betrayal. Even if it was only a *mental* betrayal, it still makes my heart ache.

I need to do something, anything, to stay busy and get my mind off . . .

Him.

I don't even want to think about his name. Instead, I summon my implant.

Harold, can you see if Major Apollo can meet with me?

Yes, Kari. Sending a message now.

A few tense minutes pass while I pull on my uniform and boots, leaving Luna to finish sleeping in . . . for now. I know it's early, but I also know that Apollo seems to have nearly as much insomnia as me.

Finally, the response comes through. *Affirmative,* Harold communicates.

When and where? I think back.

Another short pause, then—

Meet him at his office in ten minutes.

I arrive at his office right on time. The lights on base are just starting to brighten, heralding the breaking of day. Or rather, the fake day that our clocks demand.

I feel jittery, almost nervous, and there's a sick feeling in my stomach. The sunrises we shared on the roof deck rush through my head again. The way he leaned into me . . . my confessions. His confessions to me. The tenor of his voice, and the tremble of mine.

Our shared secrets.

They're our secrets now.

I feel another shudder, this time more like desire, rippling through my body. I try to stifle it, but when I push the door open to his office, his smile beams at me.

And that doesn't help.

He looks a bit tired, ragged even, but excited to see me. I know this is bad . . . I shouldn't feel this way about my CO. On the upside, it's a good distraction. At least I'm not thinking about Drae anymore.

"Sir, good morning." I pop off a formal salute, but he waves me off.

"Have a seat, Captain."

He leans back in his chair and regards me with those eyes that seem to probe every inch of me. I follow his direction and slide into the hard, plastic chair.

A heated second passes before he continues to address me.

"You requested this meeting?"

I don't hold back; I blurt it out. "I want to return to the Astral settlement. For another reconnaissance mission."

He raises his eyebrows. "So, you're assigning the missions now?"

"Sorry, sir. If that violates the chain of command . . . it's just that . . . I've been thinking . . ." I trail off, looking down.

"Go on. I'll allow it."

"Since we talked . . . the other day . . ." My cheeks redden, but I gloss over the details. "You're right. We need to find a way to communicate with them. They let me into their settlement. I heard messages. Maybe the answer is going back there."

He takes that in. "Is that all?"

"At the very least, I want to confirm the theory that we started the war. And that what happened down there, on the first mission . . . wasn't a fluke . . ."

"That you didn't imagine it?"

"Exactly. That's one way to put it."

He smirks at me. "Or put another way—to prove that you're not crazy?"

We both smile at that. I guess it's become an inside joke. My mental instability. Dark humor is one of the only things that got me through basic training.

I clear my throat and break eye contact, but feel him studying me anyway.

"Well, if we're going to build any support for diplomacy, it would probably be good to prove that I'm *not* crazy."

He nods. "But none of our instruments work down there. The strange anomalies block them. Nothing can record you."

"Yes, that's why I can't go alone. I need witnesses."

"You and Luna?"

I nod. "Oh, and one more person. Postmaster Ksusha."

"You want the postmaster to join you? That's a highly unusual request. I'll remind you, this is a military operation. And a highly sensitive one at that."

I bite my lip, trying to ignore the way his eyes track over me just then. Like they're probing every inch of me . . .

"I know, sir. But we went through basic training together. He's just as much a guardian as the rest of us. And, well . . ."

"Let me guess. He sees things differently, too?" He folds his arms over his chest. "Level with me. That redacted stuff in your file. Does he have something to do with that?"

I clam up and keep my mouth shut. But that's answer enough.

"I see . . ." He shakes his head. "You're full of secrets. But I'll allow it. You have three days to prepare and get your team ready for the mission."

"Thank you, sir," I say, but really I'm thinking—

What choice do you have?

CHAPTER 34

DRAE

I stare at Trebond in surprise, still struggling to absorb the shocking news.

"What happened?" I force out in a worried voice. "What did Kari find?"

We're standing on the banks of the bay with the iconic, rust-colored scaffolding of the Golden Gate Bridge towering over us. Fog rolls through like smoky fingers clawing at it, trying to pull it down. Xena clambers out from her bus and joins Trebond. Her short-cropped hair, sun-varnished face, and toothless smile complement her stocky frame, giving her a disarming appearance. She may look like a harmless bus driver, but she has twin blasters under her uniform. Trebond exchanges a look with her as if they can communicate without words.

"Apparently, there was a Proxy war over the moon where she's deployed," she finally replies. "A few years ago, we fought the Siberian Fed for control of it. It turns out the moon has valuable, rare minerals that we need to power our warp drives."

"This is about Astral settlement, isn't it?" I say, remembering our exchanges.

"Well, it turns out we didn't know about them," Xena chimes in. "When we invaded, there was a huge battle. They were collateral damage at first, but then when we discovered their existence . . ."

"Let me guess," Willow says with a dark expression. "We killed them?"

"More like obliterated them," Trebond confirms. "*Blast first, ask questions later* should be the Space Force motto. Turns out it was a peaceful, civilian settlement."

"First contact . . . and we kill them?" I mutter under my breath. "Figures. No wonder they think humans are prone to violence and tried to use that against us."

"That also explains the Golden Gate Attack," Willow says, glancing between us. "It was retaliation then. *An eye for an eye.* We killed their kids, so they . . ." She trails off, looking at the monument with the kids and their bus driver's names on the marble pillars.

I feel it in my whole body like an electric current. Each name etched there feels like a blast to the heart. Silence descends over us as the fog rolls through our bodies like ghosts.

"So, it turns out the Astral attack wasn't unprovoked," Trebond finishes, bringing our briefing to a terrible conclusion. "It was retaliation for what we did to them."

"Yeah, and that also explains something that's always bothered me," Willow says. "Why target humans and Earth out of all the billions of planetary systems in the universe?"

I nod. "They had a reason. A big one."

"The sad part?" Trebond sets her lips. "They're not wrong about us . . . our propensity toward violence almost got us killed last time. We stopped it . . . but just barely."

I meet my old professor's gaze and find my voice. Doubt and fear dissolve so that it comes out clear and strong. "If this is all true, then it changes everything."

Trebond nods. "Now you understand why we had to meet in person. And the urgency. We only got the intel last night."

"And Kari has proof?" Willow says. "We can't afford mistakes. This is major, and the hardliners will want to bury it."

It makes me uncomfortable to talk about Kari with them. I wish I could keep it separate, that it wasn't so messy. However, there's nothing I can do about it.

"Indeed. In fact, they already tried," Trebond says. "Somebody erased all the official records. Even the base itself doesn't have a name, officially speaking. Same thing goes for the moon. According to Space Force, it's like they don't exist."

"They really tried to hide a whole Proxy war?" I say, processing that. "I'm not shocked, but that's a big cover-up."

"And they thought they'd get away with it, too," Willow adds. Anger filters into her voice. "The *blasted* arrogance."

"So, how'd they find proof?" I ask. "If they erased any evidence of it?"

"Thanks to Kari and her postal friend," Trebond says. "They found another way."

"Anton?" I ask, remembering our adventures together.

Xena nods and holds up a small drive. "They had to dig into the Sympathetic exchanges. Only the postmasters can access those encrypted archives. I guess Kari and Anton figured it out."

"Of course, they did," I say, smiling despite the circumstances. "They're two of the smartest people I've ever met."

"Saved by the post office again . . . really?" Willow raises her eyebrow.

Even in dark times, a little lightness goes a long way. It helps you remember that you're still human, prone to mistakes, but also capable of more than simply our worst impulses.

Then Trebond turns more serious. "Anyway, this makes our core mission to find a diplomatic solution more critical. The Astrals aren't the invaders after all. We are . . ."

I nod in agreement. "The Resistance was right this whole time. So, what do we do now?"

Xena pipes up. "Right, luckily we've got a lead on security footage from the GGA that the feds tried to bury. Our operatives inside got a tip. The contact has agreed to meet."

"Yes, and that's why our time is short today," Trebond says apologetically. "We have to get going. Things on the ground are changing fast—and up in space, too."

I have a million questions left, but I also know when to keep my mouth shut.

"Just keep your eyes and ears open," Trebond goes on, backing away. "Tensions between the hardliners and old Proxy factions in the Earth Federation are growing stronger."

"It's not just them—it's happening on campus, too," Willow says. "There's elevated activity led by Jude and the Anti-Astral students. They're planning more pro-genocide rallies as recruitment tools. Even some campus militia drills. The planted professors are helping, too."

She glances at me, then adds in a low voice—

"Last night, I learned that weapons are being smuggled onto campus . . ."

That shocks me. "You mean, blasters?"

Xena nods. "Confirmed. We tracked some shipments from Jude's father . . ."

So, Jude and his minions are armed and more dangerous than we thought. But something else troubles me. Willow said . . . last night . . . I feel a hot surge of jealousy. That also means she's been getting cozier with him than I realized. I shoot her a disturbed look.

She still won't meet my eyes, but she goes on.

"Yeah, Jude let that slip. Then he clammed up before I could get more out of him about their plans. And trust me, I tried . . . *everything*."

I don't have to ask what everything means. The whole idea sickens me to my core. But I'm also not surprised it worked. He loves to brag about his power and influence, and he loves nothing more than an audience. Especially a cute, flirty girl. It's his biggest weakness. He can't keep his mouth shut, even about sensitive intel.

Clearly, Trebond knows this. That's why she gave Willow the assignment. I just wish that it didn't make me . . .

So jealous.

"But that's illegal," I blurt out before I can stop myself. The words sound foolish. Even to me.

"Since when has that stopped them before?" Xena snorts. "You know the long game they're playing? His father wants to break Trantor's Peace Treatise. They've been clamoring for Earth rearmament."

"Yes, and they're working to push Secretary-General Andromeda out," Trebond says. "She's more centrist than we like, but she's better than the alternative. Luther is using the youth movement to increase popular support for what he's planning behind the scenes."

"That explains what's happening on campus," I say, putting the pieces together. "And it's not just UC Berkeley. It's probably the other colleges around the California Federation."

Suddenly, something else occurs to me. "Wait, what about Loki? Is that why he didn't come back to Berkeley like Jude? He transferred to UC Santa Cruz . . ."

I trail off, searching their faces for answers. But Willow looks down and won't meet my gaze. I'm right—and they already know about it. And they've been keeping it from me.

"Drae, you have to understand," Trebond says. "We didn't want to worry you. We needed to keep you focused—"

Suddenly, an alert grabs her attention. She scans her neural readout, then snaps into action. "It's the security footage. From the GGA attack. The contact is ready to meet."

She signals to Xena, who is already clambering onto the school bus and sliding behind the wheel. She cranks up the engine, spilling out black diesel exhaust that mixes with the fog, tainting it . . . almost like my heart feels tainted now. Willow salutes them as they roar off into the distance. Then she follows me back to my transport, which promises to carry us back to a campus that's becoming more like a war zone every single day. But the bigger war—

Is being fought in my heart.

And right now, I feel totally betrayed.

CHAPTER 35

KARI

"Buckle up," I tell my team after we board the ship. "And hold on tight."

We blast off as the ship autopilots us back to the Astral settlement. Our return goes about the same. The instruments go wild, glitching and flickering, then cut out the second we land. Our ship also cuts the engines. The barrier sizzles with electricity, daring us to try to enter it.

The only difference this time?

Anton is with us.

"That thing looks . . . *dangerous*."

He leans closer to it, the barrier buzzing just beyond his helmet. Luna shoots him a look through her helmet.

"It is dangerous," she barks, yanking him back. "Be careful . . . it let us through last time. But I can't speak for you."

"Me?" he says, sounding offended. "I'm the least threatening one of our group. I'm a *freaking* postal worker. If the Astrals are going to let anyone in . . . it's got to be me."

Luna sighs. "Oh, and I'm scary?"

"Yeah, a little," Anton says, then backpedals. "Actually, maybe a lot. Let's just say, you got special ops for a reason."

Before they can launch into one of their famous bickering fests, I cut them off.

"Relax," I say, taking a few steps toward the barrier. "It's going to work."

It sizzles again and flickers, snapping in and out of visibility. That dissolves all of my false bravado. This mission was my idea, so if anything goes wrong and they get hurt, then that's on me. But I have to act brave. I have to be a leader now. Even if I'm beyond terrified.

"Remember, a lot is on the line," I continue. "We have to find something we can use to communicate . . . or, well . . ."

"We're fucked," Luna supplies.

Anton makes an exploding noise. "Aliens invade . . . *boom* . . . Earth is destroyed. And humanity is wiped out."

"Yeah, something like that," I agree.

Breath hisses out of my deployment suit, filtering through my mask. Despite the ship cutting out, the suits still work.

That's how I know the security system is intelligent, making decisions about what to allow to work, and who can be permitted within the settlement's vicinity.

"Ready?" I say to them. "Remember our core mission. Once we're inside, stay together. I need you to be my witnesses . . . if anything happens. Is that clear?"

"Roger that, Cap," Luna says. "Only, I'm a little fuzzy on how to do that. Last time, things got a little funky in there."

"Funky?" Anton says, flanking us. "Uh, that doesn't sound reassuring."

"*Funky* is about the best way to describe it," I supply. "Look, it's not too late to back out now. You're the postmaster. You're not special ops. You didn't sign up for this."

"What . . . back out now?" he says. "Where's the fun in that? Plus, I needed to get off base. It's just me and those bots in there, and they're not the best company."

Luna snorts a laugh.

"Understatement of the century. They're basically tiny, annoying jerks."

"Yeah, they make Harold seem enjoyable to converse with," I add.

We all revel in the moment of levity. But then electricity sizzles through the barrier, driving home the danger. That barrier could just as easily refuse us this time, as allow us back inside the cave.

"Well, it's now or never."

I take a deep breath; it hisses through the vents in a rush. Then I shut my eyes and think hard—*Please, let us in, let us in, let us in*—as I force my legs forward to stumble forward.

I pass through the barrier, feeling the electricity run through my body.

But—

It doesn't hurt.

And it doesn't expel me.

I pass through unharmed. *It let me in.* Luna is up next, and she also passes through just like last time. Anton is last.

"Please, alien overlords, don't hurt me," he says as he runs through it.

The electricity ripples—almost like it's laughing at him—but lets him through.

"Well, that was a trip," Anton says, adjusting his suit. "Definitely a new experience—entering an alien settlement. Actually, I got it backward. More like, we're the aliens here."

That's when our sensors beep, turning to green. Once again, the atmosphere adjusts so that we can breathe in here. Anton strips his helmet off, testing it out.

"By the stars, I don't believe it . . ." he gasps.

We follow suit, ditching our helmets.

He turns to us. "Seriously, how is this possible?"

"That's the great mystery," Luna says. "And what we're here to find out."

The cave system extends in front of us. Veins of crystal illuminate it, carrying light from the surface underground. Anton continues to be mesmerized by each new discovery.

"This really is something," Anton marvels in a dreamy voice. "I wish I could record it, or take a picture. Their tech is simply . . . incredible. It's not like anything I've ever seen before."

"We can't record it," I remind him. "That's why you're both here."

"We're the witnesses," Luna says. "That's the best we're going to do."

Anton nods. "Humans are subjective and unreliable, at best. But you're right."

"Yeah, and we're lucky it's not short-circuiting us, too. I heard that's what happened to the other guardians."

"Yeah, they ended up in the infirmary," Luna confirms. "I asked around base. One was even in a coma for over a week."

"Okay, you left that part out," Anton quips, sounding freaked out. "When you talked me into this crazy-ass mission."

"You said it yourself," I shoot back, waving for them to follow me. "Selective amnesia . . . my memory is unreliable. I can't be held accountable for my serious lapses."

"How'd you know it would let me in? Sounds like it's . . . well . . . unpredictable."

I let out a sigh. "I didn't."

"Gee, thanks," Anton grumps.

"But I hoped that it would," I go on quickly. "For one simple reason."

He tramps behind me. "And what's that?"

"Because I asked it to . . ."

"You asked it?" Luna says. Now she sounds skeptical. "How did you do that?"

"Look, I know it sounds crazy." I plow forward, leading them into the settlement. "I can't really explain it. But the last time we were here, it was like it wanted to talk to me. And it wanted me to see things." I turn back to them. "So, when I went through the barrier, I asked if it would let you through, too."

"You. Asked." Anton looks amazed.

I shrug. "And I said the magic word."

"And what's that?" Luna asks.

"*Please.*"

I continue into the cave system and lead them deeper into the settlement, but I hear Anton grumbling, *"Oh, she said . . . please . . ."*

We keep going farther, and it keeps blowing Anton's mind. He's a total nerd for anything like this. We're some of the first humans to have actual contact with intelligent alien life. That's the long way to say—

This is a big fucking deal.

The farther we venture into the abandoned settlement, the more time seems to distort. I see the light-beings running through the tunnels, flickering like laughter, and swirling around us. I follow them as if some force is taking over and drawing me inward. Vaguely, I sense Luna and Anton behind me. But their words don't reach me. Just the sense that they're talking, but that our language has lost all meaning here, or I've lost the meaning, and light is the only language.

The language of light.

I find myself back in the room with the crystal tech. The interface juts out. I come to a halt right before it. I know my friends are right behind me, but I can't hear them.

And I can't speak.

But I have enough sense to make a choice. *I want to talk to you . . . please.* I think that, only not in those words. It's more like projecting an emotion, like through the neural links in my exchanges. The feeling carries the meaning to them. I understand it now.

Please, show me the truth.

I want to see it . . . I'm ready for it.

I reach my hands into the crystals, and they melt away like water then reform over my hard, snaking up to my chest, then enveloping my whole body.

Suddenly, they invade me; I can't breathe.

I want to—*scream!*

No, let me go . . . I take it back!

But I'm helpless. And that's when I feel my neural link connect to them. Memories invade my mind like an assault, colors and sounds and sensations—and I realize that this is how they communicate.

They are all linked together.

They all share this link. They feel what the others feel. They don't always agree, but they share their minds and thoughts.

Again, I relive the war.

But this time, I witness the invasion of the settlement. Guardians charge into the caves with their blasters drawn.

Our guardians.

Their uniforms clearly read "California Federation Space Force."

They attack them; they blast everything that moves, everything they see that scares them or that they don't understand. The Astrals weren't prepared.

They didn't know we existed.

They didn't know our nature.

Now, they do.

HUMANITY . . . VIRUS . . . PLAGUE ON UNIVERSE . . . MUST DESTROY!

The guardians keep blasting the Astrals, but our blasters don't hurt them—they absorb the energy. They feed on it.

But the crystals are different. They shatter and start collapsing. The Astrals scream and contort. It's like their life energy is tied to the environment—the harm to it kills them, too. They're connected not just to each other but to everything. The guardians catch on. They stop blasting the Astrals directly and instead turn to the caves themselves and plant bombs.

They retreat and detonate them.

Everything starts collapsing around me. I want to scream and throw my arms over my head to protect myself, but it's only a memory.

The shards flicker and fall over me harmlessly.

But the Astrals flicker out. Before they do, they send out a call to their people.

EARTH. EARTH. EARTH.

KILL. KILL. KILL.

VIOLENT. DANGER.

This call to invade us goes out, wide and clear. The memories—the images I witness—are broadcast out. This is the moment the war began. Right here.

I struggle to hold on and communicate with them. *We're not all bad! Some of us aren't like that! We're different! We want peace . . . we want to stop all the wars!*

I plead with my mind, with my emotions, through the neural link.

But they scream back at me—

KILLERS! VIOLENT! PLAGUE!

And suddenly, I'm expelled from the mind-link. I feel that sucking feeling that I get in my exchanges, only more violent. It feels like my neurons are being fried.

The electric shock shoots through my body as the crystals release me.

I fly back. Across the cave.

I hit the wall. Hard.

I crumple to the ground. My brain short-circuits. I convulse, frothing at the mouth, and flopping around helplessly.

That's when the world turns dark—

And I black out.

CHAPTER 36

DRAE

I never understood the statement *the silence is deafening*. Until right now. Willow and I ride in the transport in silence—*the kind that's louder than talking*—heading back to Berkeley. I still can't help but feel totally betrayed. I feel so foolish at how much I've trusted her and how stupid I've been. How left in the dark. How completely manipulated . . .

Not just by her, but Trebond too. They've been withholding intel and controlling me this whole time. And I fell for it. Finally, I can't keep it bottled up anymore.

I try to keep my voice even, but ire burns into it.

"You lied to me."

It's a simple statement.

Not a question.

"Drae, stop acting like a petulant child," she shoots back. "That's part of the deal. You signed up for it, remember?"

She's not wrong. Back in the beginning, my professor manipulated both me and Rho into thinking we were being tapped to join a college secret society, only to learn it was the Resistance.

I did know what I was getting into, but that doesn't make me feel any better. Or make me want to trust her ever again.

I seethe for another moment, then latch onto my next explosive thought. "Jude? Really?"

"Do you want details?" She rolls her eyes. "I was trying to spare you . . ."

"No, ugh . . . I don't. Trust me, I already know enough *details* about him to last me the rest of my life. Maybe eternity."

She can't help it. She snorts a laugh.

"Eternity? Asteroid fires, you make it sound like you and him . . ."

I raise my hand. "Strictly bromance. Not romance. Not that I have a problem with that . . . but seriously . . . gross . . ."

She sighs heavily. "Trust me. It wasn't my choice. But they're secretly arming students! Breaking the Peace Treatise!"

I want to argue, but she's right.

That's big intel. And she got it.

"Drae, do you know what that means?" she goes on in a heated voice.

"We're in more danger than we realized," I admit, running a hand through my hair. Silence simmers between us again, but it's lost some of its edge, even though I want to hold on to my anger and resentment. Some rationality creeps into my brain. She did what she had to do.

For all of us.

I seize onto another terrifying idea. "So, Loki is doing the same thing at UC Santa Cruz? That's why he didn't transfer back like Jude? Asteroid fires, I bet his father has planted operatives at all the colleges. All the kids of the Ringers who work at the fed."

Despite my anger, that chills me.

"Affirmative," Willow says. "You understand why the campuses are ground zero for our Resistance operations now? And why you have become so important to us?"

"Yeah, I get it—even if I don't like it," I say in a tight voice. My whole body feels tense. "That's why I'm risking everything to help you! But seriously, you could've trusted me and told me the truth . . . not frozen me out and left me in the cold."

I feel foolish. I feel angry. I feel jealous and grossed out. All at the same time, no less. And I know all these emotions are totally wrong and messy. And that I'm betraying Kari, too.

I'm a total disaster.

But I can't help it. Can't rein myself in. Can't seem to simmer them down.

"Drae, I'm sorry," she says in a soft voice, scooting closer. So close.

"How sorry?" I huff.

"Really, really, really . . . sorry."

"*Three* reallys? Is that a lot?"

"You tell me."

She lays her hand on my arm again, and this time where our flesh touches, it burns like pale fire. She gives me a pleading look—her purple eyes flicker with unnatural light—but I wonder if she's just manipulating me again.

"I think I need . . . four."

"*Really.*"

That humor. That smile twisting her lips and lighting up her amethyst eyes. I can't help it—I lean into her touch.

Confusion rushes through me. Over Kari and what she said about us being wrong for each other. Over Jude and her seduction of him. Over my trust issues.

But something else is stronger—

My thumping heart.

The way she makes it flutter to life around her. The way her touch burns me.

I want to burn, I realize.

I want the flames to consume me. I can tell she does too. Her lips part slightly.

They beg me to—

Kiss them.

I still have my implant muted and blocked. There would be no record.

I'd have to control my thoughts next exchange. If there even is another exchange . . . if Kari gave me a chance . . .

But I can't pull back. I lean toward Willow to kiss her, deeply, but then—

I stop myself. I douse the flames. I do it. I resist the temptation. Disappointment floods Willow's face, twisting into pain, but she doesn't protest. She pulls back from me and grants me that grace.

Silence descends on us again, hard and fast. This time it's not fueled by anger, but sadness at all that could have been. At the reality we face now, where she knows the true nature of my relationship with Kari, and I know the lengths she's willing to go to to acquire intel from my worst enemy. We're nearing campus. Soon, we'll have to part ways altogether.

"When are you seeing *him* again?"

I can't help how it comes out. All teenage petulance. She called me a child earlier. So, I guess that's what I am now.

She winces. "Tonight. Frat party."

"Figures. Is he pre-partying?"

"Of course. What's new?" She sighs. "You used to be like him, didn't you?"

That question hurts.

"Unfortunately, before books and college and all of this . . ." I wave my hand around the cabin to mean the Resistance. But I don't give voice to the one thing that changed me the most, that I thought altered the very nature of my DNA.

Kari.

Why won't I tell Willow the truth about the full extent of my feelings for her?

Why am I still hiding and hoarding it in the depths of my heart?

Is it because I'm afraid to scare her away? Because I still want something to happen between us? Or because Kari belongs to me, and I don't owe anyone else an explanation?

Oh wait, I know . . .

It's because—I'm a coward.

Just like I've always been.

"Well, be careful," I say, trying to keep it from sounding . . . jealous. "He's dangerous . . . you're playing with fire."

"No choice. You heard Xena? She confirmed the weapons shipment."

Suddenly, I remember my nightmare about the campus erupting in violence and burning to the ground. Now, it seems like it could actually come true.

"We have to do something," I say, giving her a look. "We can't just sit around and let him destroy our school."

"Well, we're already gathering intel," she says. "What else can we do?"

Frustration surges through me. I search for answers, clawing at anything.

"If Jude is building an army, then maybe we need one, too?"

"Right, I hear you. But the students we're secretly recruiting? They're pacifists.

They're not fighters. And worse . . . they're privileged like you . . . no offense."

That makes me feel shame. But I'm forced to agree. My mom may be a war hero, and that bought me the privilege to avoid enlisting and enroll in college instead.

"You're right about me. And probably them. But you're a fighter . . . you could teach us. Not with blasters like them. There are other ways to defend yourself."

"Like self-defense? I don't know."

She chews at her lip, but I push her to consider what I'm saying.

"Listen, you said it yourself!" I whisper in her ear. "We're recruiting *helpless* students. We can't lead them to the slaughter and leave them defenseless. We have to train them."

"You don't know what you're asking!" she shoots back. "I grew up as a Resistance fighter. I'm only posing as a student for the cause. For them, it's the other way around."

She play-punches me, making me flinch—and proving her point.

"They're soft . . . like you."

"Point taken," I say with a wince. "But if I can learn and change, then so can they. Plus, you're not giving me credit. I already saved the universe once."

"I know—I read your file. Drae, you're not a fighter. Neither are those students."

Maybe I am way off base here. But I can't shake the feeling that something bad is coming to our school—and Jude is leading it straight for us.

I let out an exhale. "Look, I know Trebond is in charge—but this is our school. These are our friends and classmates. We need to take matters into our own hands, even if it's dangerous."

"*Super* dangerous. You're right about Jude. Not to mention the illegal part."

"The way I see it—people will get hurt either way. At least if we train them, then we can give them a *fighting* chance. Pun intended."

I can tell Willow sees the logic. She finally relents and gives in.

"Okay, I'll alert Xena. She's in charge of operations, training, and munitions. Trust me—we need her help if we have any chance of pulling something like this off."

Before I can reengage my implant and go back online, she flashes me a worried look.

"We'll have to be careful though. Jude is watching us . . . closely."

CHAPTER 37

KARI

"Kari . . . please wake up!"

Desperate voices reach me in my fugue state. I hear my name. I don't want to wake up. I want to succumb to the blackness that has swallowed me whole. But I force my eyes to crack open.

Only a slit of light hits them.

I see blurry faces. They slowly, painfully, resolve into . . . my friends.

It takes me a moment to remember their names. Part of me is here, and I know that, but part of me is still connected to those other minds. The screaming ones . . . the angry ones.

The Astrals.

That should shock me. But I only feel an overwhelming sense of peace. Being with them, intertwined with them, feeling the singular pulsing life of a multitude, changed my perspective. Only for a moment, but it felt like a lifetime.

Temporal distortions.

They must experience time differently. I want to stay in this contemplative, free-floating mental state, but my name jerks me out of it again, and slowly, like a dream that resists all waking, it fades.

"I'm alive . . ." I croak out.

My whole body aches. Every single inch of it. Like I got electrocuted.

Probably because I did.

I cough hard and sit up, instantly regretting it as my head spins violently.

"Here, take this," Anton says, shoving some pills in my mouth, followed by water from his satchel. I swallow and feel temporarily worse before they kick in.

The dizziness fades away. "What the hell did you give me?" I manage.

"Anti-nausea meds." He turns to Luna. "She's already cursing. That must be a good sign, right? She's not gonna die."

"Confirmed," I say. "Not dying . . . yet. But I think I came close," I try to joke.

But their ashen faces tell me—

My gallows humor is not appreciated.

"Too soon?" I say in a feeble voice.

"You think!" Luna snaps. She's usually so calm and collected that it catches me off guard. "Kari, we thought you died! That's seriously not funny!"

"Yeah, that." Anton crosses his arms. "I mean, you basically just connected to some crazy-ass alien tech. See those crystals? I can't explain it, but they enveloped your entire body."

I glance over at the crystal formation jutting out of the center of the room.

"Really? That's what it felt like. I think it . . . accessed my neural link . . ."

"Wait, you could communicate with them?" Luna says, shocked. "You did it?"

"Uh, sort of . . ." I say with a grimace. "It's hard to explain. Plus, they were seriously pissed off. Like nuclear-level-supernova pissed off. And honestly? I don't blame them."

"What did they say?" Anton asks.

"Well, they showed me what *really* happened to their settlement." My heart sinks even remembering it. "Our guardians invaded their settlement . . . and figured out how to kill them."

"Like on purpose?" Luna says, glancing at Anton. "Wait, I thought it was an accident? That they were just collateral damage from the Proxy war with the Siberian Fed?"

"Part of that is true," I say. "We didn't know they were down here. But once we found out, we ambushed them. Only our blasters don't work on them. They're these energy beings."

"I thought you said we killed them?" Anton asks.

"No, they absorb the blasts." I think back to what I saw when I was jacked in. "But the guardians figured out that if they destroyed the crystals veins," I say, nodding to the formations, "then it killed the Astrals. It seems their life force is connected to the environment."

"Whoa, that's *huge* intel," Luna says.

"Let me get this straight," Anton says. "The first sentient alien life we encounter—and we immediately try to blast them, then ask questions later? We don't attempt to communicate with them, or at least study them scientifically?"

"Space Force doesn't like to ask questions," I remind him. "They prefer to kill on sight. Remember the Raiders? And how they brainwashed us into thinking they were dangerous savages when really they're resistance peace fighters?"

"You're right," Anton agrees. "They don't like anyone different from them."

"So, what did you say to them?" Luna asks. "Did you communicate with them?"

I frown, trying to remember. "Sort of . . . it gets fuzzy. But basically, they screamed at me—kind of as a hive mind—and called humanity violent and a plague on the universe."

"Hive mind?" Anton says.

"Whoa, that sounds . . . intense," Luna adds. "So, what did you tell them?"

"Well, I tried to convince them that not *all* humans are bad and violent," I reply with a wince. "Some of us want peace . . . but let's just say they didn't like that very much."

"Is that when they electrocuted you?" Anton says.

"First, they screamed at me again—*Earth, Earth, Earth!*—confirming they're planning to invade again. And they're not giving up. They want to destroy us."

"Sounds absolutely delightful," Luna quips. "Very pleasant species of aliens we decided to piss off down here."

"Yup, and then they electrocuted me," I say with a wince. My body still aches. "But I'm counting that as a win."

"A win?" Anton says. "How so?"

"A near-death experience?" Luna says.

"Exactly! *Near death.* I didn't die." My friends don't look convinced, but my thoughts are racing. "I'm convinced they could have killed me . . . if they wanted."

"True," Anton says. "They let you live . . . for now. What does that mean?"

"It means . . . this was our first conversation. They had to yell at me. Basically, they need to vent . . . a lot. We're their sworn enemies. Now, they're watching me to see how I react."

Anton scratches his head. "Like a scientific study?"

"Exactly. That's what I would do." I think it through. "They don't trust us, right? They're testing me to see if what I was telling the truth—that not all humans are violent. That some of us want peace."

"That's really smart," Luna says. "Very high-level special ops mind-fuckery."

"Fuck, I like these Astrals," Anton says. "Even though they want to kill us. Kari is right. Why else would they let us into their settlement? And show her that?"

"I have experience communicating with my enemies," I joke. "Look at Drae?"

"Truth," Luna says. "Enemies to lovers? Shows anything is possible."

Suddenly, I feel a pang of sadness. I don't say it out loud—because I'm not ready to face it. But now, I'm worried we may revert back to enemies. Not just worried . . . petrified.

"So, what do we do now?" Luna asks. "We did acquire some valuable intel."

That question hangs in the air. We all think it over. But I already know the answer. It's pretty crazy, but what choice do we have? "We learned that they're interconnected—and they've chosen me to communicate with them. So I guess I'm like the alien ambassador now."

"Alien ambassador." Luna snorts. "What does that make us?"

"My cohorts?" I say.

"They're expecting you to take that intel and try to use it against them," Luna says. "If your theory is correct . . ."

I nod. "So, we have to do the opposite. Plus, I have a feeling that intel is actually a trap."

"How do you figure that?" Luna says, scrunching up her forehead.

"Well, why show me their major vulnerability and reveal it so easily?" I say in a careful voice. "If they don't trust me? I could use it against them. That would be like suicide."

"Yeah, you're right," Anton says. "It wouldn't be smart—and we know they're crazy smart. Think about their first invasion plan? Even if the crystal veins were their vulnerability, they probably fixed it. If we tried to use it against them, I'll bet anything it wouldn't work."

"And worse, it might backfire," Luna agrees. "And kill anyone who tries."

"Yeah, just look at that barrier," Anton says. "Also, what they just did to Kari."

I groan. "Yeah, that hurt like the stars. But you're both right. So, we have to do the opposite of what they expect. Prove not all humans are warlike and violent."

"Sounds easy. What's the opposite?" Luna asks. "What's our plan then?"

"Let's see," I say, thinking it over. "We have to react with peaceful intentions now. We need to take this intel back to Major Apollo. Build alliances internally and try to convince the Earth Federation to support a diplomatic solution."

"I take back what I said about . . . *easy*," Luna says. "Diplomatic solution? That's trying to convince them to . . . Disarm the Stars. That's never gonna happen."

"Yeah, Occam's razor dictates that it's unlikely they'll go for that," Anton says. "The fed is controlled by hardliners."

Luna nods. "Plus, our old Proxy enemies are looking for any reason to overthrow Secretary-General Andromeda. I hear her tenure is shaky . . . at best."

That all makes me want to give up. But I know I can't . . . or we're dead anyway.

"Hey, your friend Occam isn't always right," I say, forcing a grin. "*Usually* correct doesn't mean *always*. There are exceptions. And this is one of them."

"You're an optimist now?" Luna says.

"No choice," I say in a sardonic voice. "But seriously, they're already trying to communicate. That's a good sign. Why do that if they don't want a diplomatic solution?"

"Why pick you?" Anton says.

"Simple," I say. "Because we're the ones who stopped the war last time. They know that. We advocated for peace."

"That all tracks," Luna said. "Space Force won't want this intel out there. It's like the Raiders. They need all the Astrals to be seen as dangerous invaders."

"You're right. They'll fight it. That's why we need to find more guardians like us," I say. "Who are open-minded and see things differently. I say we start with Major Apollo."

I ignore Luna's pointed look; she knows that there's more to our relationship than simple chain of command. But fire finds its way into my cheeks anyway, giving me away.

"He's a good start . . . if you can convince him to support diplomacy," Anton agrees, then frowns. "But he's not going to be enough. We need more reinforcements."

"Well, who else do we know?" I ask.

"My parents," Luna says. "They're still active in special ops, even though I'm not supposed to know that. They're good spies, but I'm better. They'll listen to me."

"And my parents," Anton says. "They're veterans. But they'll listen, too."

I nod. "That's great. We have my father and the Resistance down Earthside."

I feel buoyed, despite the terrible odds.

"But we need more inside Space Force," Anton says. "Active duty."

That's when it hits me.

"Yup, and I know just the people," I say, climbing to my feet though it hurts like asteroid fires. I start limping away. "We have to get back to base so I can put a special request in."

The upside of talking down here is that nothing can record our conversations. We reach the barrier—and pass through it harmlessly. I was holding my breath, not sure if the Astrals might change their mind about us after that whole *screaming-and-electrocuting-me* thing.

Luckily, they allow us to pass. Our ship immediately fires up, readying for the ascent.

"A special request?" Anton says, jogging to keep up with me.

We reach the ship and climb aboard, settling into the seats. I take the captain's chair, Luna the copilot's, and Anton rides in the jumpsuit behind us. It's a smaller, swift ship.

I seize the controls and push the buttons to take us back home. The autopilot and navigation systems kick in as the engines rev and start to levitate us upward rapidly.

I glance back, straining to speak over the roar of the engines. "I need to build our team. I've got you and Luna. But we're missing *three* guardians."

"Three," Luna repeats. "Oh . . ."

"You mean . . ." Anton adds.

It dawns on them both exactly who I mean. The three people who we've been missing since we deployed out here.

Excitement rushes through me at the thought of being reunited. Since I transferred to this moon, their absence has felt like phantom pains from a missing limb. I was obsessing about Drae so much that I almost didn't notice it. But now, I realize how important true friends are.

They're not replaceable even by the person you fall in love with.

Like Rho.

I just hope Apollo goes for it.

CHAPTER 38

DRAE

"Nooooo . . . *I'm sorry!*"
I wake sweaty and freaked out from another nightmare where Kari blasts me in the face. I don't have to wonder why. Yesterday, I received her reply. If you could even call it that.

Yeah, it was about as bad as I expected. No, scratch that. It was a million times worse. She barely said anything. Just relayed a quick briefing of what Trebond already told us.

She had to force the words out, too. But through the neural link—
I could feel . . . *everything*.
Her devastation. Her sadness and betrayal. And I could see the tears.
She tried to hold them in. But our bodies betray us. Our emotions hijack them. Something I know about all too well. It's a quick message—she requests to be pulled out early. That breaks me more than all her tears.

She doesn't even want to talk to me.

That's never happened before, not even when she hated my guts. We had to stay in the exchange for the duration. Those ten minutes could feel like an eternity, but we still endured it.

I'm shocked by how quickly it cuts off with her demanding to be pulled out. I don't even have time to think about what I'm going to say in response before I'm pulled into my exchange.

The timer stares at me almost accusingly.
But my head is swimming, and I'm drowning. My response is short.
I don't say anything.
Except for two words.
"I'm sorry."
I know there's nothing else to say. *I didn't mean it* will sound like I'm avoiding responsibility. *I love you* will sound like I'm deflecting and minimizing her pain, trying to gloss over my mistakes.

But I don't pull out early.

I stand there, staring straight ahead with tears in my eyes, letting my emotions roller coaster through me, so she can feel how devastated and disappointed I am in myself, too. So, she can experience the full extent of my recent transgressions.

There's no point hiding it from her, not with the neural links revealing our deepest, darkest secrets. And my implant waiting to shock me if I'm not fully . . .

Honest.

But I can't find words, so I let my emotions talk. She'll experience everything when she gets the message.

If she gets the message . . .

I know there's a good chance that I won't get a second chance with her. She's made that clear from the outset. That she was trusting me, but that if I broke her trust . . . then it was over.

Forever.

And I did. I fucked up. I know it.

All this roils through my head in a stream of consciousness for her to experience. I don't hold any of it back. One thought after another. Her message was so short that I wouldn't be surprised if she asks to nullify our Pairing. Even get paired with a different Sympathetic. She could probably use our romantic entanglement as a reason. Unlike when we first got paired and she was a new recruit, now she has a rank, so they might bend the rules and accommodate her.

Regardless, I force myself to stay in the exchange even though it feels like torture for one simple reason—this might be the last time I get to communicate with her.

Finally, as the timer ticks down, I say one last thing. I mouth the words—

Please, will you ever forgive me?

I leave the post office in a daze, feeling like all hope is lost.

Devastation grips me and won't relent. Kari sounded so hurt. So utterly heartbroken . . . and it's all my fault. I wish I could take it all back.

The worst part?

Since then, I actually kissed Willow. And I wanted to do more. If Jude hadn't interrupted us by her dorm . . . I don't want to think about it.

However, I can't stop thinking about something else. It's what Willow said in my transport. She was talking about Kari. She said that maybe we weren't right for each other in the first place. That after our Pairing, our minds got warped and twisted together.

That worries me. *I love Kari*, I remind myself.

But doubt lingers in my heart.

What if the Sympathetic Program brainwashed us?

Willow also pointed out that our relationship was toxic. How Kari always makes me feel not good enough for her, just like my mother did growing up in her long shadow.

I've never even stopped to consider that, probably because I've been crushing on Kari so hard since high school, desperate for any chance to win her over and get to be with her. Something that I never thought would actually happen, until a miracle occurred when we got matched at the Pairing Ceremony.

But maybe Willow is right about us. Maybe we aren't actually right for each other . . . deep down. Maybe it's just the Sympathetic Program controlling our emotions, making us feel things that aren't real, but are a product of the implants in our brains. And just like how we met, when she punched me in the face—

All we're ever destined to do is cause each other pain. I wince at that thought.

But I can't deny the power of it. And once I think it, it's hard to un-think it.

This sacrifice to be in the program and her lifeline back to Earthside . . .

It's a sacrifice of flesh and fury.

Love isn't strong enough to cover up how we began. In violence and pain . . .

Is that all we can ever be?

But I can't dwell on it. Tonight is too important.

It's our first training session.

I cross campus on autopilot, heading back to my dorm to get ready for tonight. I just hope it works. We used Trebond's technique of slipping handwritten letters under their pillows inviting them to the next stage of our resistance. I even penned a new riddle for them to solve.

The words run through my head.

All federations want me. Most people, too.
But for all their talk of hopes and dreams,
I'm diminished by what they do.
I'm a grand idea, a noble cause that hopes to one day stay.
If only you won't keep sending me away.

The solution is the password that will get them in. Even Willow said it was great. Maybe all that reading and studying books has rubbed off on me.

I just hope it works the way it did when Rho and I got recruited with a series of riddles and scavenger hunts to solve and prove our commitment to joining the cause. Jude is arming his followers with blasters. The Anti-Astral agitation on campus grows stronger every day. I scan the campus, counting the Fed Patrols. I lose count around twenty. They multiply daily.

The whole atmosphere at school feels like a bomb about to detonate. In the classes and lecture halls, the dorms, just crossing the walking paths, I can feel it sizzling in the air. I can't miss all the flyers posted. I notice the patrols taking them down . . . but selectively . . .

Only the Disarm the Stars ones.

That makes it clear who is behind Jude and Mr. Egbert and the Anti-Astral supporters. Who really supports them. This is bigger than our little college—it stretches all the way to the stars. But we're still ground zero for the coming war.

And make no mistake.
It is coming.

"Think anyone will show up tonight?" Willow asks, nervously pacing around the empty warehouse. "For our inaugural training session?"

My nerves jump into high gear at that thought. Sunset was a little over an hour ago. We're meeting tonight after dark at an abandoned warehouse off campus. Xena secured the secret location for us. She's standing outside, manning the door.

I watch Willow circle around me in loops. She's dressed in her Resistance regalia tonight—looking less like the student she's posing as and more like a fighter. Her pirated military fatigues grip her body perfectly, making her look even better. I've never seen her like this.

I try to keep my eyes off her but keep failing miserably. "We distributed recruitment letters using Trebond's secret student list. What else can we do now but wait?"

"And hope?" Willow adds.

"Maybe wish upon a star?" I say, joining her pacing around. We've laid out some dusty wrestling mats. Crates of training supplies are stashed in the corner, still unopened.

Just in case we don't use them.

So they can go back to Resistance headquarters, an old military bunker north of the city, where supplies are in short supply and desperately needed to arm our fighters . . .

Again just in case.

"So, solving the riddle gives them the special password?" Willow says, pulling out one of the invitations from her fatigues. She rereads the riddle I crafted.

"It's a bit dramatic. Don't you think?"

I scan the verses again, even though I've already memorized them.

All federations want me. Most people, too.
But for all their talk of hopes and dreams,
I'm diminished by what they do.
I'm a grand idea, a noble cause that hopes to one day stay.
If only you won't keep sending me away.

Willow purses her lips, and then it dawns on her. "Peace. The answer is . . . *peace*. That's clever. But will they figure it out?"

"Well, it worked on me and Rho," I point out. "Trebond's used it for years. She says it helps weed out those who lack curiosity and also can't think for themselves."

"Think it'll keep Jude and his minions away?" Willow asks, sounding worried.

"Yeah, because they can't *think*," I reply. "Truth is they can barely read. Plus, we've got Xena on security just in case."

Another long few minutes pass with *nothing* happening. The allotted time comes and goes, then suddenly, right when I think it's a complete failure—

Rap.

It's tentative, but definitely somebody knocking. Willow cracks the door open—and there stands a freshman girl I recognize from my Great Books class. She has long, red hair pulled back into a sharp ponytail. She's also wearing sweats. I recognize our college mascot of a grizzly bear, long ago extinct, printed on her yellow and navy sweatshirt and matching pants.

"Peace?" she says in a soft voice.

She holds up her invitation. I spot Xena standing guard across the dark alleyway, checking everyone who passes.

"That's right," I say, feeling a secret thrill. She solved my riddle. I nudge Willow and whisper, "*See, it's working.*"

She scowls at me and hisses back, "One little recruit doesn't mean anything."

But quickly, more Berkeley students trickle in, one by one. They're each holding invitations with the secret password on their lips. Hearing them say *peace* over and over again fills me with a strange sense of hope. Some also salute Willow and say, "Disarm the Stars!"

They all sound hesitant.

It's so new for them. They're used to hiding and lurking in the shadows, worried their sympathies and anti-genocide beliefs will be them expelled, or worse, tossed into the detention camps. I hear more are being erected every day.

Finally, after a half hour has elapsed and new recruits stop arriving, we check them against our roster. About 75 percent showed. That's better than we expected when we came up with this crazy idea. We beckon them to follow us onto the wrestling mats.

Xena joins us at the front. Nervous energy runs through the students.

"What happens now?" one asks. A boy in a tie-dyed hoodie with Berkeley insignia.

"Yeah, you gonna tell us why we're here?" the red-haired girl asks. "And why we had to wear these . . ." She points to her loose sweats. "This better not be a trap."

Nervous laughter ripples through everyone. But she said what we're all thinking. I raise my hands for quiet.

"No, I assure you this is very real—and more serious than you realize." My voice echoes out stronger than expected.

Something about my riddle working and this being my idea gives me courage.

"I'm sure you've noticed what's happening on our campus recently," I continue. They're all riveted. More hushed whispers and nods of agreement. "And how it's fast becoming a war zone."

Someone yells out. "Yeah, the Fed Patrols keep stopping us on the way to class."

"They take down our flyers—but not the Anti-Astral ones," another recruit speaks up.

"It's not fair!" yet another recruit yells.

They start chanting together—"*Disarm the Stars!*" It picks up volume, filling the warehouse with our united call for peace.

I let them go for a minute to build camaraderie, then signal for quiet.

"I'm going to tell you something top secret." I pick up where I left off. "The Anti-Astral students aren't just posting flyers and holding pro-genocide rallies."

I pause to let that sink in.

"They're being secretly armed by our federation government and holding militia drills," I go on, picking up steam. "They're preparing for a revolution. That's why we have no choice now."

I nod to Xena, who steps front and center. She punches her fist into her palm. Willow flanks her, taking a fighting stance.

"So welcome to the *Disarm the Stars Alliance*," I finish, raising my voice louder. "If they're breaking the peace treaties and smuggling blasters onto our campus—then we need to defend ourselves."

"Surely you don't mean to give us weapons?" someone yells.

"Yeah, that goes against everything we're fighting for!" the redheaded girl says to cheers of approval. "That would make us just as bad as them, wouldn't it?"

Willow nudges me. I'm losing them, so I quickly jump in. My heart beats faster.

"No, of course not!" I say quickly. "Our mission is the solution to the riddle—*peace*. These are dangerous times. But you're not alone. We're going to teach you peaceful resistance tactics today. How to defend ourselves—and disarm them."

That works. They immediately snap to attention. I can tell they understand the seriousness of what I'm saying. They've witnessed what's happening on campus.

That's why they're here.

I hand the makeshift stage—more like a pile of old mats—over to Xena now.

"Now is the first day of your training," Xena says. "Welcome to the Resistance. Thank you for coming and supporting our movement. Now, let's get to work!"

This draws cheers. These poor recruits have no idea what they're really in for . . .

"Not bad," Willow says after our last sparring where I land a single jab.

The fake blaster in her hand goes skittering across the dusty concrete floor. Around us, the warehouse is alive with grunting and Xena's voice barking out orders. Everyone is in various stages of running drills or wrestling together—or recovering, breathless, on the mats.

"For a green recruit?" I joke back.

"You're not *green*," Willow says, picking up the fake blaster. She shakes her head. "But you're not in fighting shape."

"I still disarmed you."

"'Cause I let you," she shoots back.

I can't tell if that's true, or if she's saying it to mess with me. But still, it eggs me on.

I raise my hands to spar.

"Go again?" I say, still panting.

She gives me a nod of respect. "But mark my words—you're not disarming me this time, Rache."

"Challenge accepted," I say with a grin, as I swipe my leg out trying to sweep her legs out from under her.

She dodges, then flips around and chops my back. She pulls the jab—

But not fully.

I wince and rub my back. "Okay, you don't have to rub it in. I admit it—you're kicking my ass."

A few hours later, under Xena and Willow's drill-sergeant-style coaching, we're all shaking and collapsing from exhaustion. One kid is even puking in the corner, while the redheaded girl rubs his back and waits to give him water.

Willow circles me for one last round, taking me down with a few well-placed jabs and a sweeping kick. I hit the padding with a groan, but I'm smiling. And she's standing over me, offering her hand. We're leveraged together as I find my feet, squaring my stance.

I've never been more impressed by her. The way she moves her body, teaching wrestling moves on the mat to disarm someone with a blaster. Xena also passes out defensive weapons from the crates developed by the Resistance that deactivate blasters and act as shields.

They won't work on more assailants, but it's better than nothing. And they don't violate the Peace Treatise. I'm grateful we have other options. That we can employ self-defense, and they won't be left completely vulnerable and exposed. But worry creeps in as I watch them. They're all so soft and green. But then I remember Kari and her friends, especially Anton. Apparently, he barely made it through PT. However, over time, they all grew stronger and graduated.

Maybe we all start one way from birth, but it doesn't have to be our destiny. Life twists and turns on you, but you can learn how to drive. You don't have to stay on autopilot and be at the mercy of fate.

You can choose.

And you can . . . fight back.

Never in a million years did I think I'd become a Resistance fighter. But here I am going through the same drills. I'm panting and my side hurts like I'm being stabbed, and Willow is laughing at me like starlight shining down, so I don't mind the pain.

I'd let her kick my ass a million times if it meant I could be wrapped up with her, sweaty and spent and utterly exhausted.

We return to campus in a pair, her and me, locked together and united in our purpose. I marvel at how we set this in motion tonight, and what it could mean.

I'm relieved we can fight back.

But I'm also afraid of what's coming next, like the bright afternoon that inevitably descends into the darkest, moonless, fog-laden night. Something bad is coming. I can't shake my nightmares.

And it's coming soon.

That snaps me out of my thoughts. It's getting late; I catch Willow's eye.

"Okay, that's a wrap on our first training session," Willow says, calling everyone together. "Great job tonight. Get back to your dorms safely. Walk in pairs, not all together. Remember rest and ice. Don't forget what you learned tonight."

"You grunts just might make decent Resistance fighters after all," Xena adds.

That provokes laughter. I worry we've scared them away, but they don't immediately disperse. The puke kid speaks up. "When's the next meeting?"

"Yeah, when do we get to practice again?" the redheaded girl says.

I notice them standing close together and secretly wonder if it's the beginning of something between them. Willow catches my eye—I can tell she's thinking the same thing, too.

Are they like us?

"Very soon," Willow says, dragging her gaze away. "In the next few days, look for another invitation . . . and riddle," she adds, winking at me.

A few groans leak out.

"Another one? That was hard."

"And they're only going to get harder," I say, stepping up beside her. It feels natural now. "Same goes for the training."

More groans, but also some cheers.

I smile at that. My body aches too. However, I mean it when I say—

"But it's all going to be worth it."

That gets a big round of applause, along with chants, "Disarm the Stars!"

They leave in groups of two and three, Xena timing them between exits so they don't draw suspicion. While the last students trickle out, Willow and I start straightening up and returning sparring gear to the crates in the corner. Her lithe, strong body in the fatigues makes me think of what she did to me on this mat. A shudder of desire erupts inside me like pale fire. If I didn't know better, I'd think she was a trained guardian. But then I remember how many Resistance fighters are vets, including Trebond. Plus, Willow was raised by her for this purpose.

To fight back.

I hope it doesn't come to that, and our campus remains peaceful.

But I have a bad feeling that it's about to explode.

And soon.

CHAPTER 39

KARI

When I return to base, I make a beeline for Major Apollo's office. I need to get him to approve my request for a team. After everything that's happened, I need support more than ever.

I also need to tell him what we discovered on the mission. The Astrals are connected, like they're neurally linked, and they want to communicate with me. Just that . . . well . . . they're still kind of pissed off over the whole *we invaded their settlement and murdered them* thing.

But he's not in his office.

Harold, what time is it?

The skylights overhead show only stark darkness poked through with shimmery stars. Several moons hang in the sky in various phases, from waning to waxing. A lone moon shines full, blazing its glory over the crystalline landscape.

But Earth time is different.

Kari, it's six p.m. Earth time.

Asteroid fires, I need to find him.

No need to curse, Harold replies in his usual stiff manner. *Typically, this is dinner time.*

Right. I should check the mess hall.

I mute Harold before he can try to give me directions since I already know the way.

My body is still sore, but I force my legs to carry me down the corridors. As usual, the base has this eerie empty feeling. I don't pass anyone. I reach the mess hall and peer around.

But the officers' table where he eats is empty. I feel deflated, and worse, stressed out. *Where in the stars is he?* This can't wait. I can feel it in my bones. The way the Astrals said—

EARTH! EARTH! EARTH!

They're locked onto us. The machinations are already in motion for their next invasion attempt. We have precious little time to convince them to choose diplomacy instead.

That's when my eyes land on—the officers' lounge. The door is closed, but I'd bet anything he's in there with the others. Technically, I am an officer, so I should be allowed inside. Only I've never exactly been to a bar or lounge in my life.

Feeling nervous, I push the heavy door open. It swings inward, revealing the dimly lit room. Faux leather armchairs are scattered around the room in different groupings. Some are occupied by science officers, while others remain empty.

Finally, I spot him.

He's sitting by himself, nursing what looks like a brown liquor over ice. I hesitate, wondering if this is a mistake. I'm still in a dark place over Drae and his crush on that girl. But somehow, that fuels me. If he can crush, then why can't I?

Looking isn't touching.

Yet, my brain argues. But I hush it like I muted Harold and force myself to cross the lounge to where Apollo is sitting. I wonder if some of this is revenge on Drae for what he did to me in that exchange.

My jumbled thoughts don't make anything easier, not with important things on the line. I halt in front of Apollo. He looks . . . well . . . as handsome and charming as ever. Those eyes do something to me that I can't explain. They look up—and probe into me.

"Fancy seeing you here, Captain," he says with a secret smile that penetrates me.

He sips his drink. A tense silence falls, then he breaks it.

"Please join me . . . have a seat?"

I slide into the oversized armchair across from him. The lamp on the small table casts off dim light that only adds to the atmosphere—and his alluring nature.

Ugh, why do I have to crush?

On him of all people?

"Business or pleasure?" he adds once I've settled into the chair, which feels far too large.

My cheeks flame at the question. "Uh, business."

His face falls. "Maybe we can do both," he whispers conspiratorially. "What are you drinking?"

"Sir, I don't drink."

While that's not entirely true—I've sampled my father's wares—I can't admit to that . . . I trust Apollo. But the Raiders are officially still our sworn enemies.

He raises his eyebrows. "Well, there's a first time for everything. The rum is an officer's perk. This vintage is particularly splendid. They really outdid themselves with this bottling."

"Rum?" I say in surprise. I lower my voice. "Raider rum?"

He swirls his glass, making the ice clink. "Of course, we have to confiscate it from Raider ships. Technically, we're supposed to destroy it. But why should it go to waste?"

"Of course. In that case, I'll have the same. The Officer's Perk . . . is that it?"

He grins. "I think that's what we're calling this vintage from now on . . ."

His eyes glaze over as he orders via his neural implant. A few seconds later, a bot delivers it with a few annoyed beeps.

Apollo scowls at the bot. "She's an officer! I know she's new here, but get it straight in your circuits."

The bot beeps in annoyance but deposits the drink on the table anyway, then zips off.

"Go ahead . . . try it."

I have to pretend it's my first time, so I make a big show of inspecting it.

"Bottoms up?" I joke, making a silly face.

"Sip it . . . slowly." He gives me an example as he dips his glass toward his lips, swirls it around his mouth, then swallows. "This vintage deserves to be . . . thoroughly enjoyed."

Shivers shoot up my body.

I know he's talking about the rum, but something tells me that he's really talking about other things too . . . dangerous and forbidden things . . . especially with him.

"Sip it slowly," I repeat, lifting my glass. I gently touch the liquid to my lips.

In the past, I've always pulled shots from a flask passed around the ship, usually instigated by Mrs. Smee. But this is different. The ice has cooled it to a thrilling temperature that mellows all the flavors, giving it more depth and nuance.

I sigh as it courses down my throat, relaxing muscles still sore from the mission. Tension releases me from its grip, and the anxiety needling my brain relents, too. Now, I see why the officers need a lounge, and why they keep the rum.

"Isn't it pleasurable?" he says softly.

I take another sip . . . slowly.

I feel his eyes watching me, tracking each movement and utterance down to my sighs. "*Pleasure* doesn't even come close. The vintage is amazing . . . not that I'd know the difference. Is everything else gonna pale in comparison now?"

Secretly, I do give my father credit. His rum is nothing short of delectable. I'll have to tell him the officers are fans. Even if they steal it from him.

But the Raiders steal our supplies first, so I guess that makes it even.

"But on to the business," I say, taking another sip and setting my glass aside.

"I know," Apollo laments. "Just, it's nice to forget for a little while . . ."

"That we're on the brink of war?"

"Yes, that . . . and . . ."

I take a brave step. "You're my CO?"

"That too."

Disappointment etches into his face, making him look horribly saddened. I feel myself deflate a little too. Fantasies are nice, but they have the power to destroy.

I learned that from Drae.

"The mission was successful," I say, trying to keep my voice steady.

He sets his glass down now.

"You found it?" He keeps his voice low. "A way to communicate with the Astrals?"

"Yes—it appears they've chosen me."

Quickly—and in a hushed voice—I brief him on everything that happened in the settlement. His eyes widen as I finish. Now, he's huddling close to me and whispering.

"Who else knows?"

"Just me. And Private Starfire and Postmaster Ksusha. I came here straightaway to find you."

"This is . . . *big*."

"I know, sir."

He takes a long swallow of his drink. "It could change everything. That's nothing short of a breakthrough."

My heart thumps faster.

"Exactly! We need to use it to push for diplomacy. They're waiting to see what we'll do now that I know about it."

"And you said . . . they're neurally linked?" Apollo says. "You're sure?"

I hesitate. "I mean, we're talking about aliens here. It's hard to be sure about anything that happened down there." I pause, searching my thoughts. I feel a certainty that I can't explain. "Yeah, it was like . . . I was one of them . . . it reminded me of the Sympathetic Exchanges . . ."

"The Astrals must have used their tech to tap into your neural link," he says.

"Except with them, there's no lag time. Remember all those temporal anomalies? I think they've figured out how to bridge space and time, so there's no delay."

He sits back. Downs his drink.

"That is big intel," Apollo says. "I'll have to send this up the chain to General Titan. She'll want to know right away."

I glance across the lounge—and that's when I notice her, huddled with some scientists. Her hair is pulled back into a tight bun. She sees me talking to Apollo.

I can feel she's watching me.

That gives me a bad feeling that I can't shake. When she warned me about the Sympathetic bond, she was trying to help me, I remind myself. And prevent me from getting hurt like I just did . . .

"Of course . . ." I say, but trail off.

"What is it?" he asks, noticing my hesitation. "You can tell me . . ."

"I can trust you? Are we on the same side? We have to use this to push for a diplomatic solution. At least try to open the channels of communication with the Astrals . . ."

"With you as the . . . alien ambassador?"

I blush hard. "Never thought that would be in my job description."

We both smile, despite the seriousness of the circumstances.

"Well, it has a nice ring to it." He takes another swallow of his drink. I follow suit, feeling the rum go to my head a little. *Liquid courage*, I tell myself. I need it to do this next . . .

"Sir, one more thing."

"Oh yes?"

"A special request," I venture. "I can't do this alone. And you said yourself that we can't trust the hardliners running things. I need to build my team."

"A team? You have Starfire."

"Remember all that redacted stuff in my file? Well, I didn't stop the Astrals alone. I had help. I couldn't have done it without my friends—I need them. They see things differently, too."

"So, you're saying . . . they're like you?" he prompts.

"No, sir. Not even close. We're all completely different. But that's how it works. We bring in different perspectives."

"How many are we talking?"

"Three, sir."

My words hang in the air.

Three faces flash in my memory—Percy, Genesis, and, of course, Nadia.

He looks skeptical, and I get the feeling he's about to deny my request. I realize how outlandish I'm being to demand three guardians be transferred to this top-secret base.

That doesn't even have a name.

"Look, you said you need results," I push him. "Well, then I need my team."

He scrutinizes me. "Who are they?"

I spout off their names. His eyes glaze over as he runs them through his neural link, probably pulling their files.

"But these are all low-level guardians. Engineering? Medical?" He looks up with a frown. "Only one of them is a fighter. Front lines. But she's just a body . . ."

I wince when he says that. He notices and backpedals, "Sorry, I didn't mean it like that. I see she was your battle buddy."

I nod. "She saved my ass in Basic more times than I can count. Also, I was going to be front lines . . . until my orders got changed."

He absorbs that. "So why these three?"

"Sir, because they helped me stop the Astrals once already. We're the only ones with that kind of experience. But also, it's like you said—they're low-level grunts."

"How exactly is that a good thing?"

"Sir, in this case, that actually is a major asset. They haven't been corrupted or jaded yet. Their minds are . . . *fresh*."

"I see. Like you?"

I get that strange feeling like he's probing my brain again. I break eye contact and try to focus on my drink. The ice clinks in the glass, but I still feel like he's trying to violate me . . . mentally.

"Exactly," I say in a low voice. "You said it yourself. There's a reason they deployed me here. Plus, we're the ones who discovered the invasion plans in the first place—and we stopped them."

"Well, if they're anything like you, then I'm forced to agree," he says slowly, making my heart skip a beat. "You can have your team. I'll put in the transfer orders—and expedite them."

Elation floods through me. "Thank you, sir."

"And Captain? Don't sell yourself short. You have the makings of a leader, even if you don't fully believe it yet."

"Sir, I do?"

"Have some *blasted* confidence. You just approached your CO and demanded he build you a special ops team. Now, what does that sound like to you?"

I hesitate. "A leadership decision?"

He winks. "Exactly."

I get ready to leave, but he stops me. His eyes travel over me in a way that pins me in that chair. I feel my heart race.

"Just remember—we're not all the same here either." He lets that sink in. "Even if we're wearing the same uniforms and clutching the same blasters . . ."

I get what he's saying. He's telling me . . . that he's different, too.

My father said something that sticks out in my memory. *Space Force isn't as united as they want everyone to think.*

I thought he meant the hardliners and Proxies at the time, but what if he also meant those who want peace? What if I'm not the only one inside Space Force fighting to avoid war?

I meet his gaze. Our eyes lock together—and for a moment—it feels like our thoughts do, too. It should be impossible . . . but it's like he's inside my head, and for a split second—

I'm inside his head, too.

Like being hit by blaster fire, I feel how intensely he desires me.

My whole body flushes and heats up with the wanting. My mouth goes dry, and my heart thumps faster and faster as my desire hits him like the floodgates opening, too.

I catch myself and startle back. How is this possible? Is it . . . the Astrals?

Did they do something to me? To my neural link? I haven't felt this way since . . . Drae on my father's ship . . . but it's been bottled up . . . maybe pent-up for too long . . .

He leans toward me. In the dim light of the bar, it almost feels like nobody can see us, like we're in a safe space that's our own little world. His lips are inches away.

Kiss me!

The thought hits me. I lean closer, closer, our lips brush . . . but then—

Suddenly, I feel General Titan watching me. I jerk my eyes over—and see her staring at me. Her eyes narrow to slits.

That brings me back to myself. I break the link—*No, get out! Dangerous!*

Apollo flinches slightly in his chair, but the feeling passes. He looks flustered too. He reaches over and downs his drink.

I shift back in my seat, too. I can't believe that almost happened. My heart is racing like I've just done a hard PT session. I stand up awkwardly.

"Sir, I should get back," I say in a shaky voice. "Luna's waiting for me."

But it's a lame excuse—and we both know it. He doesn't press me further. But he does look a little . . . disappointed. Then he seems to come to his senses, too.

"Captain, I'm granting your request," he says in a formal voice. But I can hear the desire tainting it. "Build your team."

"Thank you, sir," I say and pop off a salute. But my heart is still flushing my skin. That moment between us . . . the *almost kiss* . . . I push it from my mind.

"Just don't fuck it up," he adds with a sexy smile. "I'll report back on the intel after I brief General Titan and the team."

"Thank you, sir."

I leave the lounge through the heavy door, feeling flushed and dizzy, emerging into the stark lighting of the mess hall that blinds me, even though my heart beats emphatically, making me wish I didn't have to go.

I don't know if it's the rum on an empty stomach, or the Astrals scrambling my neurons, or being so close together. But it's intoxicating.

Or rather—he's intoxicating.

More than any drink.

And that's dangerous.

CHAPTER 40

DRAE

Campus feels as tense as ever on my way to class. The roaming Fed Patrols. More Anti-Astral rallies. The flyers. I pull one down from the wall in front of me and read the bold-faced print.

DESTROY THE ASTRALS!
GENOCIDE IS THE ANSWER!

This sort of pro-war propaganda is everywhere now; the Fed Patrols don't even bother taking it down. They're not even pretending to be neutral anymore. They've chosen their side.

But something else has changed over the last week. I feel stronger and less afraid, and I know the reason—

Our new DTSA group.

We don't greet each other outright, but I keep passing members cutting across the footpaths. We nod in understanding and acknowledgment, then quickly divert our gazes. But the quick moment—

I see you; you're not alone.
You're one of us.

Means everything.

It's not just my body changing and sprouting muscles I didn't even know I had. Especially my abs. Even my abs seem to have abs now. I've never been out of shape, but I've also never tried this hard.

I run my fingers over the hardening lines under my shirt and smile. This is thanks to Willow and her training techniques. She stopped going easy on me—and started fighting me for real.

I won't say the first day didn't have me limping to class and feeling like I got beat up in a back-alley fight. But by the next day, I already felt stronger and ready for more. No, more like—wanting and craving more. I can't get enough of it.

The training. But also—
Of her.

Our group has secretly met four times over the last week, and while my body aches, my mind feels sharper and clearer. My anxiety has also lessened. I think it has for everyone in our alliance. Why?

Because we're not alone in this fight anymore—and we're actually doing something about what's happening at our college. Not just cowering on the sidelines and hoping to avoid the collateral damage, at the complete mercy of our parents, professors, and federation, and worse, our fellow hardline classmates clamoring for the genocide of aliens that we know next to nothing about.

The one thing I do know, thanks to Kari, is that their attack wasn't unprovoked. We slaughtered them first. I'm not justifying what they did to our kids, but it changes everything.

If we keep trading violence for more violence, then nothing will ever change, and there will always be more kids dying, both down here and in the stars. If we want to change something, then we have to open the lines of communication.

We have to reach for empathy and understanding, for a peaceful solution.

And more—

Disarm the Stars.

That's the long-term goal. But right now, it's looking worse. The newsfeeds are chattering nonstop about Earthside rearmament in violation of the Peace Treatise. I talked to my parents last week, and my mother was practically gleeful at the prospect, which chilled me to my core.

I don't even bother trying to convince my parents otherwise. First, I have to keep my cover. My father works with Jude's father at the fed. The last thing I need is them opening an investigation into me.

My father will protect me, but only for so long until it threatens his position of power, then he'd turn me in. I harbor no illusions about how far his defense goes. And I know Jude's father is looking for any reason to get revenge on me—for what I did to his son when I beat the *living stars* out of him for assaulting that girl, and got him suspended from school.

Like father, like son. They're both vengeful and hold grudges. They're dangerous enemies to have now.

The other reason I don't try to convince my parents that war isn't the answer? Because they'd never go for it. They're too brainwashed and bought into the system. And I know—they'll never change. My mother spends her days drinking fed-issued whiskey and watching the news. She's practically salivating over the prospect of war like it's entertainment.

The problem is that I know she's not alone. Public sentiment is shifting under the nonstop footage of the terrorist attack of the bus plunging over the bridge.

And secretly, the federation is already breaking the treaty. I glimpse Jude across the glade with his minions. They're all dressed in baggy sweatshirts, and I can't help but wonder if blasters are concealed under them, and if they're already armed.

But I keep my head down and hold on to the one hope I have—another DTSA training session tonight. My heart rate quickens at the thought of Willow and the mat and her sweaty arms, and beyond my carnal yearning, the hope that this will get us ready for the real goal of our group.

Revolution.

Beep! Beep! Beep!

The alarms go off late at night, when I'm back in my dorm room and fast asleep after another hard training session, where Willow kicked my *stars-loving* ass.

All hell breaks loose on campus.

That's the only way to describe it. Faintly, I smell smoke and taste ash on my tongue. Something is burning. I jerk my gaze to the window. Flames erupt in the center of campus—it's a huge bonfire.

I scan for the Fed Patrols, but they're suspiciously absent from campus.

Why aren't they stopping it?

Earlier, the footpaths were thick with the bots, but now I don't see even one.

Then I realize the reason.

Students in those golden robes with peaked hoods parade around the blaze, throwing more tinder and stoking the fire.

"Death to the Invaders!"

"Kill the Astrals!"

"Genocide is the answer!"

I bolt into action, my heart jumping into my throat. The alarms continue, along with evacuation orders. I hear it over the loudspeakers and through my implant.

Estrella pipes up.

Drae, evacuate campus. Don't panic. Proceed slowly to the nearest exit . . .

I mute her quickly, then hurry to Theo's room to grab my roommate. But he's not in his bunk. It's close to three a.m.

Where could he be?

But I don't have time to worry about that. I have to get out of the dorm. I charge down the stairs, taking them two at a time and pushing through the other students, and burst into the night air.

The campus is in total chaos. Students evacuate from the dorms, pouring out into the streets. My heart hammers into my chest. Suddenly, I spot a DTSA member.

It's Ariel. The redheaded girl.

"Go to the warehouse!" I hiss in her ear as she passes. "Tell the others . . ."

I know it's a safe place. We can send Xena there for security just in case.

The girl nods and takes off, her hair whipping behind her. I see her pushing through the crowds of students, carefully targeting our members and whispering.

I scan campus for purple hair. The sea of bodies ebbs and flows with students streaming for the gates. But I don't see Willow among them. Where is she?

I dart closer to the bonfire, now climbing higher into the sky. It's set right in the middle of Memorial Glade.

"Death to the Astrals!"

"Annihilate them!"

The protestors' chants grow louder, fed by the frenzy of the fire and a night turned bright with burning. Two figures stand at the foot of the flames on a pedestal. They're hooded and robed, masking their identities, but I have a pretty good guess.

Jude and Mr. Egbert.

A lump forms in my throat, and I swallow hard against it. A voice echoes out behind me, making me jump.

"Drae, you wanna join us?"

I spin around, recognizing the voice.

Familiar eyes stare out from a golden, peaked hood. It's Theo, my roommate.

"Wait, you're with them now?" I sputter before I can control my surprise.

His stare turns hard, suspicious. "I'm on the right side of history," he spits back. "The question is—what side are you on?"

I make a snap decision. "I mean, of course I wanna join. Why do you think I'm here?" I backpedal, hoping he buys it.

His gaze softens. It works.

"Okay, I've got you! Over there." He points to a pile of robes that are being handed out on the lawn a few feet away.

Questions rush through my head while I wait. Did this riot spill over from another rally? That's my first thought.

But then I realize that it must have been planned. How else would Theo have known to be out here in the middle of the night otherwise? When I got back from training, he was in his room. He had to have snuck out on purpose without my hearing. Plus, they had robes ready to go.

This wasn't an accident.

I move forward in line with the other new recruits, then shimmy into the silken fabric, pulling the hood over my face.

I feel like a traitor in my enemy's uniform, but I don't have a choice.

I need to find Willow. I'm worried that she didn't get out in time. But I can't stand out here looking like I don't fit in and risk drawing more attention and suspicion.

The crowd swells larger and grows more frenzied. I lose sight of Theo in the mob. I marvel at how fast he went from protecting our other roommate when she had Resistance flyers and not turning her in—to joining the hardliners. How fast they brainwashed and radicalized him.

And so many others.

I count thirty to forty students. Maybe fifty. Way bigger than that first rally.

All in robes and feeding the fire.

"Watch out!" one barks, shoving me hard. He's carrying something in his arms.

More tinder is tossed onto the pile. What are they burning? I squint closer—then horror hits me like blaster fire.

Books.

They're burning books. My heart jumps faster. I jerk my gaze to the library. The Anti-Astral protestors broke through the doors. The lights are on inside, and through the large front windows, which are aglow, I glimpse a familiar face.

Purple eyes and hair catch the light.

Only, she looks terrified.

Willow is stuck in there. What is she doing in the library in the middle of the night? She's clutching a stack of books.

Of course—our secret messages.

She couldn't let them fall into the wrong hands. She had to save the books harboring the Resistance communications.

But now, she's stuck in there.

The protestors are guarding the door. That's when I see something in the upper windows—flames slowly curling toward the window, licking at the panes of glass.

The fire isn't just outside.

Someone set fire to the stacks inside the library. And Willow is trapped in there. I glance around helplessly, still expecting Fed Patrols to arrive and put out the flames. The alarms keep blaring into the fire-tinged night.

But nobody is coming.

We're on our own now. I should evacuate campus, but I can't leave her.

Without thinking, I jump into action. The library entrance is being guarded, but I slip through in my disguise. "Kill the Astrals!" I shout for good measure.

They don't even question me.

Even down here, I smell the smoke. Luckily, the hood covers my mouth enough . . . for now. But thick, black smoke is starting to billow down from the upper floors. More hooded figures race out with armloads of books. But I don't see her.

The sprinklers should kick on. But then I hear someone yell, "Somebody cut the waterlines! Everything is going to burn!"

The horror reverberates through me. This was meticulously planned. They set the fire—and also cut the water to make sure that the building burns down, so nothing is left but the ash of what once existed. This library has stood here for hundreds of years, filled with over fourteen million books. It also has paintings, lithographs, papyri, and video and audio recordings preserved in the archives. Many are pre-war relics, older than the brick and mortar that houses them—and they're irreplaceable.

Some may even be the last copies left in the entire universe.

But that's the least of my worries right now. There's also only one Willow in the entire universe, and I'm not letting her burn, too. But I'm running out of time to find her.

"Willow!" I yell, searching for her, straining to see through the smoke.

I bolt to the reading room where I saw her in the window. But she's not there.

"Time to get out!" another hooded figure yells. "This is the last haul!"

Caught in the stampede to get out, I dash back into the lobby, then duck behind the help desk, preparing to force my way upstairs to look for her, which is probably a very bad idea, but then—

I bump into somebody.

I spin around, half expecting Jude.

But I gaze into amethyst eyes.

It's her . . .

Willow is crouched behind the desk, frantically shoving books into her bag.

"What are you doing?" I stammer.

She looks up and freezes, raising her hands in surrender. I've never seen her look this afraid before, but tonight it's etched into her face like a terrible mask.

She backs away in fear. "Please don't arrest me! I work here . . . I'm just . . ."

She trails off, leaving me confused.

Why is she scared of me? Then I realize—she thinks I'm one of them. And I just caught her trying to save the books.

Not burn them.

"Willow . . . it's me!" I whisper, lifting up my hood to show her my face.

"Drae . . . thank the stars," she gasps, lunging for the books and forcing them into her bag. "What are you doing in here?"

"Uh, saving you . . . I think?"

"Saving me? Are you crazy!"

This was not the reaction I was expecting. "Maybe, but now isn't the time to discuss the status of my mental health."

That only pisses her off more.

"You should've evacuated!" she snaps. "Not risked your life to save me! You're too important to the Resistance—"

"No, I'm nothing without you," I cut her off mid-sentence. "And you're wrong about that. We're *both* too important."

She looks conflicted, unable to reply. The warring allegiances play out over her features—her fierce loyalty to the Resistance, her forbidden feelings for me—but then she flings her arms around me, catching me totally off guard with the uncharacteristic show of affection.

And this time, I'm sure she's not acting. It's too real with smoke breathing down our necks and danger at our backs.

I'm shocked, but I hug her back fiercely like she's the one thing that can still save me. I can feel her sharp shoulders. The way strong muscles cut around them. She fits inside my long arms perfectly.

Too perfectly.

I don't want to let go of her, but I pull away and gesture for her to hurry.

"We have to get out of here! They set fire to the stacks. And they cut the water-lines, so the sprinklers don't work."

"They're burning . . . the stacks?"

Her face crumples at that realization. The situation is worse than she thought. I grab her arm, pulling her toward the exit.

"The whole building is going to come down if we don't get out . . . now!"

But she digs her heels in. She clutches her bag to her chest like a life raft.

"No, we can't go that way—it's being guarded. We have to save these books."

"Listen, I love reading too—but it's not worth dying over," I say, but she stops me. "Forget the books! We've got to get out of here now . . ."

"No, you don't understand!" she hisses. "These have messages with intel for Trebond in them! We have to smuggle them out. We can't let them burn . . ."

That's why she came back for them.

She's right—we can't escape through the front entrance with those books. She's not wearing robes, and clearly she's hiding something in her bag. The lumpy forms can only be one thing.

We can't risk those secret messages falling into the wrong hands. Or being destroyed. Every bit of intel could make a difference with so much on the line.

More smoke billows into the lobby, choking us. My eyes sting, making it hard to see. She falls into a terrible coughing fit. I help her up. I look around in a panic.

Suddenly, another idea hits me. I grab her arm, pulling her the other way.

"Hurry, I know another way out."

CHAPTER 41

KARI

I wake from another nightmare of the Astrals screaming at me, then invading Earthside. Drae and other students run for their lives as the campus catches fire.

Everything burns.

He burns.

They all burn.

I jerk upright with a scream on my breath.

"Drae!" But it comes out in a hushed whisper. My heart pounds in my chest.

I may be angry with him—no, more like heartbroken and furious—but I still love him, and that combination is enough to make me wish I were still sleeping.

But reality can't be avoided.

I glance around to get my bearings. I'm in my bunk with Luna snoring above me. That's when everything that happened with Major Apollo in the lounge comes rushing back to me.

The . . . *almost kiss.*

Guilt singes my heart, but my cheeks flame with something else—desire.

I can't deny it any longer. I know that he feels it, too. But it's dangerous and has the potential to torpedo both our careers, and hurt someone who I still love, even though he's having similar thoughts about someone else, too. It's so messy . . .

I hear Rho's voice in my head. "Love affairs are always messy. Newsfeed alert—but that's what you signed up for when you unlocked your heart and fell in love."

She's not even here, but I know what she would say. We've been through enough dating vent sessions in high school that I can predict her advice perfectly.

Messy.

That's the word for this, I think as I sit up in bed, giving up on sleep. It's a lost cause. That's when Harold pings me. My heart skips a beat when it comes through.

Kari, you've received a new message from Major Apollo.

That status flashing in my retinas says URGENT. My heart skips another beat.

Harold, what is it?

There's a pause. Too long. Then—

Proceed to the Docking Bay immediately.

Why? I can't help the question.

I don't know, Harold replies in that annoying way. *The message doesn't say.*

That's when Luna leans over her bunk and dips her head into my view.

"Did you get a message too?"

"Docking Bay?" I say, already scrambling up to get dressed.

"Think it's . . . *them?*"

She sounds as excited as me, but also as apprehensive. I mean, it's been only a few weeks since we all saw each other, but already that feels like a lifetime ago.

"What else could it be?"

I do the math. The timing tracks. It's them. It has to be them! I tug on my boots and we both hurry to the barracks door and barge out into the corridor, where the lights are just brightening to signal day.

"This way," I say, leading her past the errant bots that scurry around.

They beep angrily.

But Luna grabs me. "I found a shortcut," she says, pulling me another way. We cut through the base with our boots slapping the floors in rhythm.

That's when I see her—

General Titan. She's huddled with some of her scientists, flipping through something on her tablet. She looks up suddenly, and her eyes land on me.

"Captain Skye, good job out there," she says with a respectful nod.

That means Major Apollo told her what we found. I halt and salute her.

"Thank you, General."

"This could make all the difference," she continues with a steely smile. "You'll be briefed further shortly. Dismissed."

With that, they continue down the corridor and disappear into the secret lab.

My heart is still pounding. Luna gives me a look.

"Does that mean . . . our secret plan is working?" she whispers.

"I hope so," I say, forcing a smile. But a sinking feeling haunts me anyway.

Why can't I think positively for once? Why do I always worry so much?

"Well, she gave you a compliment," Luna goes on. "I mean . . . a general knows your name! You know that's huge, right?"

She grabs my arm and pulls me down the corridor. We move at a rapid clip. We have to get to the Docking Bay.

"Yup," I whisper back. "But it's just because we got the intel she needed."

"Well, she's clearly pleased with it. It looks like they're working hard in that lab . . . what do you think they're doing?"

"I don't know. Maybe for a way to hone in the communication—so I don't get fried next time," I add with a grin.

"Yeah, not electrocuting you," Luna says. "I can sign off on that."

That's when Harold pings me again.

It's another message from Apollo.

Captain Sky, what part of URGENT didn't you understand? Where are you?

Someone is . . . impatient. There's a pause, then another part comes through—
Don't you miss me?

That makes me roll my eyes. But also feel that electric charge between us.

I send a message back.

On our way . . . we bumped into General Titan. She seemed pleased with the intel.

A response comes right away. *Captain, it's a major breakthrough. But don't let it go to your head. Let's hope General Titan backs our plan to open diplomatic channels with them.*

Then, he adds—

Now get your ass to the Docking Bay. I'm tied up in meetings all day. You and Starfire are the official welcome party. Don't fuck it up.

That makes me smile, but then I kick into gear. I made this special request, and now I better make it worthwhile and not a waste of everyone's valuable time.

A few minutes later, out of breath, we emerge into the cavernous space, right as a transport is exiting the airlock and docking. Luna is right behind me.

The ship lands smoothly.

A few seconds later, the door gapes open and emits a burst of vapor.

Luna tugs my arm.

"Think that's them?"

That's when we see them—

They emerge one by one. Genesis with Percy right behind her. The way they move together, I can tell they're thrilled to be reunited—and their relationship has more to it than mere friendship. Thankfully, it's survived their different MOS orders—hers to Medical and his to Engineering—and the lag time. Clearly, they've succeeded where Drae and I are failing miserably. But the sad reminder of our shortcomings doesn't taint my joy at their happiness.

Their eyes widen when they see us.

"Luna . . . Kari . . . is that you?" Genesis says, pulling Percy behind her. Her dark hair and eyes remain unchanged, and she's still got that bouncy personality.

Like the total opposite of me.

"Wait, are you the reason we got our asses shipped all the way out here?" Percy adds in a jovial voice. His large form and square shoulders are a welcome sight.

Then a third voice echoes out of the ship, "Yeah, to the middle of nowhere?"

Nadia steps down. And I knew I missed her, but I didn't realize just how much until this very moment. She spots me and shoots me a practiced scowl.

I notice that she has a slight hitch in her gait now. I wonder if it's a new injury sustained fighting on the front lines.

"Asteroid fires, I should've known this was your doing, Private Skye," she snaps.

I take a few steps toward her. "It's Captain Skye now."

That's when the scowl melts away.

"Captain? Well, clearly somebody fucked up on your deployment forms."

We both laugh. Dark humor.

Stars, I've missed her.

"You can say that again," I say, covering the distance to give her a hug. "This is way above my pay grade."

Luna comes up, and it's a big old welcome fest like old times back at basic training. For a moment, I forget about all my problems and bask in the purity of this homecoming moment.

"Twin sister dearest, you made it?"

Another voice cuts across the Docking Bay. We all turn to see Anton rushing in. A few bots scurry around his ankles.

"Guess you can't get rid of me," Nadia says, play-punching his shoulder.

"Stuck together since birth," he gripes. "I'm still the older one," he adds.

And then they soften and hug.

"So, wait . . . you were all deployed here together?" Genesis asks, putting it together. "And Kari got a promotion?"

"She's not the only one," Percy says. "Look at Anton's uniform . . ."

Nadia's mouth drops open.

"You're the . . . postmaster here?"

"Postmaster Ksusha, at your service," Anton says, popping off a crisp salute.

The bots beep their approval.

"Now, shoo . . ." he tells them. "Go unload their rucksacks from the ship."

They scurry off in a fuss, speeding over the transport to fetch the baggage.

"Guess I'm the slacker here," Luna says. "Still just a lowly private . . ."

"Oh please, you kicked all our asses in basic training," Percy says. "And you had to drag him along with you."

He jerks his thumb at Anton, who raises his hands in surrender. "Guilty."

"Yeah, you don't get special ops for nothing," Genesis says, then catches herself. "Wait, am I supposed to say that . . . out loud? Did I blow your cover?"

"Nope—you're all *technically* special ops now," Luna says with a grin. "Welcome to Captain Skye's team."

All their eyes find me.

"You are behind this," Nadia says, shaking her head. "I fucking knew it."

We settle them into the barracks across the way. I still can't quite grasp that my friends from my platoon are reunited again, even if it's on this *nameless* secret moon base with the fate of humanity at stake. It still feels like old times.

Our joking and banter fill the air of this empty base chasing out the ghosts. Is it the Astrals haunting it, or maybe the guardians slaughtered on the Proxy battlefield?

Or maybe all of the above.

I guess the stakes were always this high. When I enlisted, the Proxy tensions were at an all-time high in the wake of the Golden Gate Attack, and that was before we knew anything about an alien invasion. But not being alone makes it better—*less daunting*—and cheers me up in a way that I haven't felt since I got that last exchange. Maybe since I deployed . . .

Luna and Anton helped a lot. But now, with Genesis, Percy, and Nadia, it finally feels complete. Like everything makes sense. I smile at them picking their bunks.

"Hey love birds, you get the bunk bed," Nadia says. "I'm flying solo."

She flings her rucksack on the single in the corner. It squeaks in protest like it hasn't been occupied in a long time. *Probably because it hasn't.* Nadia aims her steely gaze at me. "So, battle buddy. Wanna tell us what in *the stars* we're doing all the way out here?"

"I was doing my medical rotation when they yanked me," Genesis adds, climbing onto her top bunk. "Something about . . . an emergency transfer?"

"Yeah, we all got pulled from duty." Percy sinks his large frame onto the lower bunk. It groans and sags down, drawing laughter. "They didn't tell us shit."

"Asteroid fires, when I boarded the transport," Nadia goes on, nodding to Percy. "And the first stop, this guy got on . . . and we about lost it. Then we placed bets on who was next."

"I won the wager." Percy smirks. "But it was a selfish choice. I hadn't seen Genesis since we deployed. And quite frankly, the warp mail wasn't cutting it."

She blushes. "Hard same."

That confirms it—they're weathering deployment and still together. Emphasizing that point, she pops her head down from the top bunk and flips down elegantly to land next to him. The thin mattress sags in his direction, forcing her to lean into his side. But I can tell she doesn't mind in the least. I pull my eyes away. Envy stirs darkly in my heart, but I quash it fast.

It's not their fault that Drae broke my trust—and my heart.

"Then we land here . . . on this weird moon," Nadia picks up the story. "And find you three waiting? Yeah, that was about as big a mind fuck as basic training. Does this base even have a *blasted* name?"

"Seriously," Percy adds. "Like I said, they wouldn't tell us *shit* from *shit*."

Genesis elbows him. "Show some respect to Kari. She's a *captain* now!"

"Sorry, Kari," he says, then grins. "But she knows I curse like a Raider. And she can't complain . . . 'cause she's got . . ."

A hard jab hits him again. Percy winces. He looks big and tough, but he's a real softie, especially when it comes to her. He zips his fingers over his lips.

"Right, shutting my mouth now."

"Foot in mouth disease," she quips. They fall silent, and all their eyes find me.

Even Anton and Luna wait for me to start the briefing like I'm the leader of this whole operation. And then it dawns on me—I guess I am. I'm not used to being in charge. More like, I'm used to being a grunt and following orders. However, I remember what Major Apollo said in the lounge. That I had the makings of a great leader. Maybe I had better start believing it, too.

I summon my voice and keep it even. "Remember how we saved the world?"

Nadia rolls her eyes.

"Uh, how could I forget?" She tugs open her uniform a little, revealing a jagged scar. "I got blasted to pieces."

"Yeah, that's pretty much a core memory now," Genesis says.

"Yup, it's seared into our neural synapses," Percy agrees. "You don't forget about thwarting a secret alien invasion."

I wait a moment, then say—

"Well, we have to do it again."

CHAPTER 42

DRAE

"Follow me . . . this way!" I hiss to Willow, grabbing her hand and pulling her after me and away from the lobby.

With smoke chasing us, we cut through the library, pushing through the door to the basement toward the secret entrance that Rho and I found on a scavenger hunt during our initiation into the Resistance.

We rush through the basement, packed with old, broken bookshelves. I spot the neglected door. The door doesn't close properly. It's easy to force it open. I hope that's still the case. With the fire blazing above us, I don't think we have time to head back the other way.

I give the door a hard shove—at first, it doesn't budge. My heart drops. If we can't get it open, then this basement is a death trap. But then, Willow adds her weight and pushes.

Together, we force it open.

We barely escape the library as flames spread through the stacks, igniting the books with savage ease. We huddle together and watch it burn, clutching the bagful of precious books we saved.

But inside the building, the books are all dying—*it's almost like I can hear them screaming into the abyss*—the words igniting and transforming into brittle charcoal that shatters in the hot winds sweeping the stacks, cast by the blaze.

Finally, sirens erupt into the night, not from the campus alarms, but actual firetrucks. The firebots roll out and get to work dousing the flames with chemicals, but the damage appears so extensive. The library might be a lost cause with all that dry tinder just waiting to ignite.

The newsfeeds also finally come to life with BREAKING NEWS alerts, almost like they were waiting for the protestors to finish what they started, giving them just enough time to burn everything to the ground. The realization sickens me.

Coordinated attacks erupt at college campuses over the California Federation.

Libraries raided and books burned in what appear to be coordinated attacks. Hardline Anti-Astral student groups claim responsibility, saying the books violated federation education standards and threatened our Earthside security. Secretary-General Andromeda calls for calm and requests Space Force guardians deploy Earthside to put a stop to the campus unrest. "We must protect our children from this heinous outbreak of violence . . ."

Stay tuned for breaking newsfeed updates on this developing situation . . .

"Coordinated attacks?" I whisper to Willow. "So, it's not just Berkeley. It's everywhere."

"Space Force guardians deployed Earthside?" she says in a shocked voice.

"Earth rearmament," I say, equally stunned. "That means . . . it's already happening. This was all planned."

I can't believe it. Now our attempts to train students and fight back seem silly and pointless. Black smudges grace Willow's cheeks. I have the urge to wipe them away, to erase all the damage that's been done. But it's too much.

I feel so hopeless.

We're standing by the outskirts of campus, standing in the shadows. We stash the books in the bushes while we decide what to do next. We're both in shock still. We've been outmaneuvered.

Between the alarms and sirens, the campus is anything but silent.

Willow is struggling to process what just happened. She looks shell-shocked.

Something about our little college, despite the recent unrest, made it seem like nothing could pierce our idyllic bubble, isolated from the wars raging beyond our atmosphere in the stars.

"I mean, we know they've been clamoring for it," she says finally with a sad shake of her head. "But we didn't think it would happen this soon. That it would be to protect us from the Astrals . . . we were prepared to counter that."

"But they used the student groups instead," I agree. "They took a line from the GGA . . . *to protect our children*."

"And who can argue against that?" she says helplessly. "It's evil but brilliant."

A recorded voice broadcasts over campus between the ongoing alarms.

Secretary-General Andromeda urges for calm and peace on campus, telling students to stop burning books and breaking into campus buildings. The flames have been doused, and the protestors seem to be dispersing, but in no hurry. They're not even afraid of getting arrested. They know they're being protected from the top levels of the fed.

I wonder about Andromeda's message. Did this take her by surprise? Was it orchestrated behind her back by Jude's father and hardliners to force her hand? Or was she in on it the whole time?

That's when a hooded figure approaches us, casting a long shadow.

He pulls back his hood, so we can glimpse his face. He looks pissed off when he sees me standing so close to Willow.

The scowl cuts around Jude's face.

"Still hanging with this loser? Next time, you should pick the *right* side."

Suspicion colors his voice. Willow had won him over, but now he's not sure.

I start to tell him off, but Willow pushes the bag behind us into the bushes and interjects herself between us. She plays into the act, trying to cover for us.

"Oh, it was pure chaos . . ." she gasps. "Thank the stars! Drae saved me . . ."

"Well, he does love saving damsels in distress," Jude says, flicking his tongue over his teeth. "It's his biggest weakness. Even better if they come from the Park—"

The secretary-general's message broadcasts over campus again, cutting Jude off and making him scowl. He grins at us. "Oh don't worry. That Astral sympathizer won't be around much longer. Things are already in motion."

"What do you mean?" I ask sharply.

But he just laughs darkly.

So, that means that Andromeda wasn't in on it. One thing is clear—this was his father's doing. She was probably resisting rearmament. They planned the campus riots to force her hand.

Worse yet—

This is only the beginning.

Another hooded figure approaches Jude and whispers urgently in his ear.

"Next time . . ." Jude says, raising his hands like a blaster and pretending to fire at me. "Come find me—not him."

Willow bats her eyelashes.

"Yes, of course . . . next time."

Jude still looks suspicious, but he hurries away with the other figure, who I think must be Mr. Egbert. Things are unfolding fast—and it's not safe here.

I jump into action, grabbing Willow's hand and scooping up the bag of books.

"We have to get out of here—and find Trebond," I say, summoning my transport to carry us away from campus, while the stench of smoke still hangs thick in the air, hovering over it like a dark cloud.

We rush into Resistance headquarters, housed in an old military bunker. We blocked my neural implant on the way over. Willow hands off the bag of books to a guard, signaling that they contain intel.

I grab her attention and whisper. Something is bothering me. I can't shake it. "We need to go back! I feel guilty just leaving our DTSA members behind."

Willow's face hardens. "They're not helpless—we taught them to fight."

"Yes, but this is bigger. They need protection. We can't just leave them."

She wants to object, but she grabs someone's attention. Here she's even more in her element, even though she's still clad in her civilian clothes.

She whispers heatedly in his ear, barking orders. I catch a few words.

"Send someone to the warehouse . . ."

He salutes her, then rushes off. But I feel better not leaving them hanging.

"The Old Lady was expecting you," another Resistance fighter says, leading us back to her office. I remember the familiar route through the abandoned military bunker.

Concrete floors and walls. Clunky desks and chairs. Nothing has any flair or hint of design, except the graffiti spray-painted on the walls that loudly reads "Disarm the Stars!"

We barge inside to find Xena and Trebond waiting for us . . . tensely.

"Asteroid fires, you're safe," Xena says, breaking from her usually stern persona.

She hugs Willow, then me. Trebond rises from her desk, all business.

"Remember our contact with the footage from the Golden Gate Attack? That the federation tried to hide?"

"Of course," we both say in unison.

"Did you find something?" Willow adds, trading a worried glance with me.

"A *big* something," Trebond says. She signals to Xena, who cues up the footage on the screen behind Trebond's desk.

The footage snaps out of static, resolving into a school bus idling in a parking lot by the bay. The Golden Gate Bridge can be seen in the distance.

Suddenly, a blur of energy rushes by the camera, distorting the footage.

"Is that the bus from the attack?" I ask.

"The very same," Xena confirms. "Now, watch what happens next . . ."

The blur of energy flickers, making the video cut in and out, but then the light transforms and shifts into human form.

It's the bus driver.

The driver glances around, then drags a duffel bag from the bus and tosses it into the bay, where it quickly sinks below the surface, clearly weighted down.

Xena freezes the screen. "That looks like our driver. But it's not them . . ."

"Then who . . . is it?" I ask, confused.

"Not *who*—but *what*," Trebond cuts in. "This driver isn't human—it's an Astral."

Shock emanates through us. Willow's mouth drops open. "Wait, you're sure?"

"Think about it," Trebond says, pointing to the screen. "How did they infiltrate Earthside? And plant that bomb on a school bus? All without being seen?"

"Ha, right?" Xena says. "I may not know much. But aliens walking around tend to get noticed. But not if they're shifters who can impersonate us."

"They studied us and knew we were prone to violence," Trebond says. "We now know they experienced it firsthand. They also learned how to mimic us."

She taps the screen. "When we got that last Raider intel, they said something strange that Kari told them. That the Astrals were more like energy beings."

I think about my freshman physics class. "So, you're thinking . . . they can bend light . . . change their appearance."

Trebond smiles proudly. "Makes sense, doesn't it?"

"What's in the bag?" I ask, nodding to the frozen footage. The dark water still ripples where it disturbed the surface.

"The *real* bus driver," Xena says, her voice wavering. "Who gave their life."

"The *brave* bus driver." Trebond pats her back. "The Astral killed them and dumped the body here. That explains another mystery that stumped us."

She pulls out a map of the bay. She taps the bridge, pointing to the shore where the GGA monument is erected. It's the same spot where we're standing right now.

"The kids' bodies were found over here, which makes sense given the drift and currents." Trebond points to another spot, far away on the other side of the bay. "However, the driver's body was fished out here over two days later. Nowhere near where the attack happened."

She looks up. "At first, we thought the body drifted. Currents can be unpredictable. But then we ran some simulations—and none produced this result. We just brushed it off . . ."

"But now, we know the driver was killed the day before the attack," Xena says. "We reran the models, changing the date to account for the time difference—and feeding this spot into the simulation." She purses her lips. "And *boom*—it came out perfectly."

I glance at the screen where it remains frozen on the Astral shifted into human form, struggling to process what I'm seeing. "So, if they can shift and impersonate us . . . and mimic our behavior perfectly," Willow starts, but trails off in horror. But I pick up the tangent.

"Then they could already have infiltrated Earthside . . . they could be everywhere."

"Exactly," Trebond says. Her face has a gray pallor that I thought was triggered by the coordinated campus attacks, but now I know the darker truth. It's this shifter discovery.

"This is the next phase of their invasion," Trebond continues. "We thwarted the first phase, but they were already working on phase two . . ."

"The fed government?" Willow gasps. "Space Force even? The Resistance?"

Paranoia hits me like a torrent.

"Wait, you're not . . . one of them?" I say, glancing from Xena to Trebond.

"Touché," Xena says. "We should be asking you the same thing . . ."

"Ask me something—anything—that only you and I would know," I counter.

"Drae, what was the answer to my hardest riddle?" Trebond asks with a wry grin.

"*Time.*"

Everyone relaxes slightly.

But then Trebond turns to Willow. She narrows her eyes. "What was the last thing your mother said to me? Right before she succumbed to her injuries from the mission?"

I'm stunned by the question. I knew her mother died, but I didn't realize it was in the line of duty. A tear runs down the corner of Willow's eye. Her voice comes out halting and strained.

"Train my baby girl to fight back in my place . . ." she stammers. "Don't fail me . . . I want her to grow up on the right side of history . . . fighting until her last breath for peace . . ."

Trebond sheds a few tears, then hugs her fiercely. "Thank the stars . . . we're human."

Silence rushes back in when her voice dies out.

A million questions race through my head—but most of all, this one. "What do we do now?"

Trebond holds up a tiny drive. "You ready for another mission with our friends?"

She hits a button on her desk. That's when two figures enter the office, dressed in Raider uniforms. I can't believe my eyes when I see the first one—

"Ready to hitch a ride to space?" Rho says, jerking her thumb at the other figure. "My girlfriend is the fastest pilot this side of the cosmos. Though I may be biased . . ."

"Again . . . you're serious?"

Rho flashes a wry smile. "Well, it turns out we didn't fully save the universe last time. It may need some saving again . . ."

Gunner nods to Willow. "You too, newbie. You're coming on this mission."

My heart beats faster, caused by a shot of fear. This time, it's not going to space that I'm afraid of—it's facing all the damage I've caused the person I love. My cowardice flares in my heart, telling me to run away. But I don't have a choice. I can't run away and hide in fear.

I accept the drive from Trebond—and the trajectory of my fate.

Even if I think I might be blasting off to my doom.

What choice do I have?

CHAPTER 43

KARI

"We started the war—not the other way around. We're the . . . invaders."

I watch my friends' shocked faces—Anton, his sister Nadia, Genesis, and Percy—as they take in my words.

"You're kidding me. Good one, Kari," Percy says. "Wait, this isn't a joke?"

Genesis elbows him. "Obviously not. Kari wouldn't joke about something like that. That's why she summoned us here."

Nadia lets out a slow whistle. "Wow. And I thought you just missed my witty comebacks and snarky putdowns."

"Well, I do miss those," I reply, unable to hide my smile. "But not enough to change your orders and warp you all the way out to this interstellar outpost."

"That's a relief," Nadia quips. "I was starting to worry you needed a psych eval."

"I could probably still use one," I say with a derisive snort. "But this is serious—and I need your help. All of you."

Then as quickly as I can, I tell them everything that's transpired since I landed on base. This time, I don't leave anything out. Luna and Anton pitch in, too. With each twist and turn, their eyes grow wider and their faces more shocked.

I can tell they want to ask a million—*maybe more like a billion*—questions. But I keep plowing forward to get it all out, and when I do, I feel lighter and unburdened, but also guilty for dragging them into this.

I finish by telling them the big intel. How I communicated with them. That they hijacked my neural link somehow.

"Wait . . . you talked to the aliens?" Nadia says. "And I thought this briefing couldn't get any crazier."

"Well, more like . . . they screamed at me and threatened me," I say in a sheepish voice. "As you can imagine, they're still pretty pissed off at us."

"Yeah, well . . . we destroyed their settlement," Genesis says. "So, the GGA was retaliation for killing their kids?"

"Wow, we're real bastards sometimes," Percy says, looking saddened.

"So, you see why they tried to cover it up," Anton chimes in. "They erased all evidence of the Proxy war fought here to win this moon from the Siberian Fed. But we found the original Sympathetic exchanges. They couldn't erase those."

Nadia arches her eyebrow.

"The postal service to the rescue again? Seriously, and I thought I'd see all the action on the front lines. Turns out, it's my nerd brother with his paper pushing."

We all laugh in a good-hearted way. Anton blushes, but even he chuckles. Nothing has turned out the way we planned. But maybe, just maybe, it turned out even better. I have to hope, right?

"So, you brought us here," Nadia says. "What's the plan?"

I clear my throat. "War is inevitable—a war that we're destined to lose—unless we can find a diplomatic solution."

"Yeah, if even half of what you said is true," Percy says, "humanity is toast."

"We still don't even know how they got by our Earthside defenses to plant that bomb on the bus," Genesis adds. "But clearly, they have more advanced tech."

"In the communication," I continue, "they also showed me a weakness. A way to hurt them . . . but I think they were testing me to see if I'd try to use it."

"Yeah, and I doubt it works," Nadia says. "I'm front lines. Remember all that *Art of War* stuff from Basic? Well, it's like the next level of battle strategy. That's what I'd do . . . see if they can trust us."

"Exactly," Luna agrees. "It's a clever ruse. I've got to hand it to the Astrals."

"That's why we have to push for diplomacy," I continue. "I briefed Major Apollo, and he took it to General Titan and the scientists on base. We think they're working on a way to communicate with them. Titan seemed . . . pleased . . ."

I trail off, hiding my misgivings. But Nadia picks up on it right away.

"Titan? You trust her?"

That hangs in the air.

"We don't have a choice," I say carefully. "I trust Apollo . . ."

Luna smirks. "Uh, Kari has a . . . special connection . . . with our CO . . ."

"Wait, what about Drae?" Genesis asks, then whispers, "Is Apollo a hottie?"

We all laugh at the two questions.

But then sadness envelops me and chokes off my voice. I have to force it out. It's not easy. "Honestly, I don't know what's going on with Drae lately. He's back at college. There's a lot of temptation. The lag time is killing us. Our last exchange . . . well, it didn't go well."

"Kari translation," Luna chimes in. "He's crushing on this cute Resistance girl. Kari got upset 'cause she could feel his emotions through the exchange."

I shoot her a look. "Gee, thanks."

"What?" she says with a shrug. "We're all friends here. They need to know the truth. You suck at speaking in . . . *emotion*."

I let my head sink into my hands. "Ugh, she's right. I do suck at it. And I'm guessing that's half our problem."

"Well, if it's any consolation, I've had to *hate* message Percy a few times," Genesis adds. "When he cheated on me."

"Wait, he cheated on you?" I say in shock. "I don't believe it . . . he'd never."

We all glare at him.

"In her dreams!" he exclaims. "She dreamed about it, then blamed me."

He gives us a helpless *my girlfriend is a little bit unhinged* look, then adds, "How am I supposed to control her dreams?"

"I don't know, but find a way," Genesis says, then laughs. "Anyway, the point is . . . relationships are hard. Add deployment and lag time into that mix."

"Yeah, it's a recipe for disaster," Percy says. "In a way, you saved us . . . now if she dreams about me cheating, I'm right here to reassure her that it's not real." He aims a look at Nadia. "And you're my alibi . . . that I never left the barracks."

We laugh, then sadness pours back into my heart. I feel so confused and lost.

"Can you forgive him?" Nadia asks.

"Look, I want to . . . it's not that different from cheating in your dreams . . . he didn't actually do anything . . . yet . . ."

The *yet* hangs in the air.

"But it still hurts," Genesis says, side-eyeing Percy. "Even when it's not real."

"And there's the lag time," Anton says. "The postmasters expedited their messages, but it's still almost a week. And a week can feel like forever . . ."

"Yeah, the last time I saw you feels like a million light-years ago," Nadia says. "But don't tell anyone I missed you. Gonna ruin my cred on the front lines."

"Exactly," I agree. "He didn't act on his impulses . . . *yet* being the key word. But it's been days since that last exchange. Anything could have happened."

That sinks in, and they all look saddened. But then Luna lightens the mood. "Yeah, Apollo is more than a hottie. He's like some kind of guardian god."

That brings *hoots* and *hollers* from my friends. We have real problems, but I feel cheered up by their pretense here. I have support now, too. I'm not alone in this.

I built my team.

But our homecoming is short-lived when an ALERT cuts across everyone's retinas. It's from the newsfeeds.

Anything we receive is dated a few days back, so it's not really *breaking*.

Coordinated attacks erupt at college campuses over the California Federation.

Libraries raided and books burned in what appear to be coordinated attacks. Hardline Anti-Astral student groups claim responsibility, saying the books violated federation education standards and threatened our Earthside security. Secretary-General Andromeda calls for calm and requests Space Force guardians deploy Earthside to put a stop to the campus unrest. "We must protect our children from this heinous outbreak of violence . . ."

Stay tuned for breaking newsfeed updates on this developing situation . . .

My heart drops as I scan the newsfeed alert. I can't believe what I'm reading. Sending in actual guardians Earthside? That would violate our peace treaties. And to the colleges? That means . . .

Drae.

Instantly, I regret being angry about our last exchange—about everything.

The anger in my heart dissolves into something else . . . fear. It grips me like a tourniquet. It won't stop squeezing.

Everything I was angry about suddenly seems petty in the face of this violence. Tears squeeze from my eyes. I should've sent him a longer reply. Not punished him with my silence.

I have so much more I want to say to him, but now will I ever get the chance?

Or am I already too late?

PART 4

METAMORPHOSE

It is easy to love your friend, but sometimes the hardest lesson to learn is to love your enemy.

—Sun Tzu, *The Art of War*

CHAPTER 44

KARI

All I can think about is—*Drae*.

I keep asking Harold for updates and scanning the newsfeeds, but the silence is deafening. The lag time is my enemy.

I rush to the post office anyway. I burst through the doors, my panic building.

"I'm such an asshole," is the first thing I say to a shocked Anton.

"Sometimes," he agrees. "But what is this about exactly?"

Quickly, I spill my guts. I tell him about Willow and how I didn't record a full response during my last exchange.

"Kari, calm down," Anton says. "It's going to be okay. We don't know anything."

"Yes, and that's what's killing me," I say, my breath catching in my throat. "Have you gotten any new packages?"

The way it works with interstellar communication is that any news or intel has to get loaded onto drives and physically warped on postal ships. Then when it arrives at the post office, the postmaster disseminates it to the base. We receive the alerts via our neural implants.

But first, it goes through the post office. This is ground zero for any information.

"Newsfeeds just came in," Anton says, holding up a tiny drive. "Follow me."

He leads me back to his office that looks more like a cozy study. Then he feeds the drive into a slot as a monitor descends from the ceiling and sparks to life. The BREAKING NEWSFEED ALERT plays over the monitor in gritty footage. Students are trashing campuses, breaking into libraries and setting fire to books in huge bonfires in the center of campus.

"Look, freeze it . . . there!"

Anton hits freeze. This footage is from UC Berkeley.

A student stands in front of a big rally, stoking their anger. They're all wearing navy and golden robes with peaked hoods. I remember Drae describing it all in our exchanges. They hold Anti-Astral and Pro-Genocide signs and scream slurs.

"Annihilate the Astrals!"

As the leader descends from the makeshift stage, he slides his peaked hood back for a split second. The firelight from the bonfire flickers and illuminates his familiar features.

My heart catches in my throat.

"Wait, rewind and play it back, then freeze when he gets off the stage."

Anton does as I request, pausing again.

"*Jude*," I hiss at the sight of him.

"You know that guy?" Anton says. "He looks . . . psycho. Pardon my language."

"You can say that again," I mutter. "Worst bully from my high school turned fascist leader of the Anti-Astral movement."

We finish watching, but there's precious little footage from Berkeley. And no sign of Drae, but he could be hiding or in disguise. Clearly, everything is getting worse Earthside. Worse, there's almost nothing I can do about it from up here.

"I need to send Drae an exchange," I say, standing up. "Make sure he's okay."

Anton nods. "I can put a request in."

He fiddles with his watch communicator, then frowns deeply.

"That's strange," he says slowly. "How is that possible?"

My heart thumps faster.

"What is it? Please tell me."

"I'm sorry, but you can't send Drae an exchange."

"What do you mean? I have to wait for his reply first?" That's the usual process, but you can always request to send an additional message. But Anton shakes his head sadly.

"No, the Sympathetic Program is suspended due to the campus unrest."

"Suspended? What do you mean . . . the whole program?"

He fiddles with his watch more. "Yes, it's an emergency order from the secretary-general. The campus post offices have all been closed to protect the workers and students. Campuses are on lockdown with students confined to their dorms under mandatory curfews."

"So, there's no way to message him?" I say, still shocked.

"Not through the official channels," he confirms. "The postal system was just updated. That's why I can't even put the request in for it. We can record something . . . but there's nowhere to send it."

That hits me hard. I sink back down into my chair, feeling the weight of it.

"Has this ever happened before?" I ask in shock. "Have they ever suspended the Sympathetic Program?"

"No way," he says. "It's the backbone of Space Force. Not even during the Golden Gate Attack. When bad things happen, we need it the most. That's the whole point of the program."

Fear jolts me like an electric shock.

"Then why are they doing this?" I manage. "It doesn't make any sense."

Anton thinks it over, then looks afraid. He meets my gaze. "The better question is—what don't they want us to know?"

"Ugh, you're right. It's our best connection to what's really happening back Earthside. This puts the majority of us in the dark. We're at the mercy of . . ."

"The newsfeeds," he finishes for me. "And we know they're basically state propaganda that can be manipulated."

"So, we're cut off."

He nods. "All of us."

"And Drae could be in danger. And I have no way to know if he's okay."

I look back to the monitor, where it's frozen on Jude's visage. He looks angry and determined—and worse—dangerous. The mob behind him follows his lead to burn the books. Things are going from bad to worse on Earthside. Violence isn't just erupting in the stars anymore, but back home. We're on the brink of rearmament. And now, I'm cut off from Drae.

In the dark.

Please, I hope you're okay.

That's my last thought before we both get pinged.

It's Major Apollo requesting to meet with my team.

"Kari, your Sympathetic is strong," Anton says before we hurry off. "Remember that, okay? He may not be a trained guardian, but he's still a fighter."

"I know . . ." I manage to choke out. But guilt twists at me. For that last message I sent him. For getting so angry at him for having errant thoughts and feelings about that girl . . . when the truth . . . that I don't want to admit to myself . . . is that I've been doing the same thing.

With Apollo.

And now, I have to meet with him. I can't avoid him.

I'm such a hypocrite.

"Welcome to our base," Major Apollo says, as my team files into the conference room and takes a seat. I slide next to Luna, while the twins are across from us. Rounding out our group, Percy and Genesis take the two seats at the end.

"I trust Captain Skye has already briefed you?" Apollo continues.

"Yes, sir," I reply. "My team is up to speed, including on the latest intel."

That's when there's a sharp rap on the door. Then it flies open, revealing General Titan. She strides in flanked by a team of scientists in white lab coats.

"General Titan?" Apollo says, clearly caught off guard.

He wasn't expecting her. But she quickly turns to me. "I wanted to personally thank Captain Skye for getting us this intel. They're connected . . . what do you mean exactly?"

"Yes," I say right away. "That's the best way I can explain it. They're all connected, almost like they all have neural links."

"And you could communicate directly with them?" Titan presses.

"Affirmative . . . only I don't know how I did it. And, well, they were pretty angry."

Titan nods. "Apollo mentioned that in his report." She taps her screen. "We tried to . . . replicate . . . your experiment. We sent a few guardians and scientists into the settlement."

"What happened?" I ask, feeling shocked. I remember how I flew across the cave when they shocked me. They didn't include me in the mission.

"Well, that's the problem," General Titan goes on. "The guardians we sent in, along with a team of scientists, they couldn't get past the security barrier."

I nod. "Are they okay?"

She sets her lips, while her scientists look sheepish. "Two are in the infirmary. But the good news is they'll live."

I'm not surprised, but I hide it.

"Captain Skye, I have one question," General Titan continues. Her steely eyes bore into me. "Why you? And your team? Why can you get through unharmed?"

Her suspicion hangs thick in the room.

"I wouldn't exactly say . . . *unharmed.*" That produces sounds of affirmation from my team. "They did a number on me. Like I said, they're pretty angry at us. For what we did to their civilian settlement."

"Yes, that was in the briefing," Titan says. "But we can't confirm it. That's classified."

That's a rebuke. I flinch slightly.

But they can't ignore me completely.

For one reason.

I'm the only one who can get in that settlement and communicate with the Astrals. And everything that's happening back Earthside and with Drae gives me the courage to speak up.

"With all due respect, the Astrals chose me," I continue, holding her gaze. "And I don't know why. But I do know this much. If we don't find a way to open diplomatic channels and negotiate a peaceful solution, then they will invade again. And this time, we won't be so lucky."

Silence falls over the room.

I can tell General Titan still has reservations. Her team avoids looking at me.

I think all hope is lost; she's going to deny my request.

But then, Major Apollo comes to my rescue. "General Titan, my captain has a valid point. These aliens remain a mystery to us. They're *alien* . . . for a reason. But if we don't open communication channels and start learning about them, then we've already lost this war."

"Major, don't state the obvious," Titan snaps back. "What do you suggest?"

"Look, we can't fight a war in the dark," he replies. "*Know your enemy and know yourself and you can fight a hundred battles without disaster.* But that's the problem, don't you see? We don't know our enemy at all. We've been going about fighting this war all wrong."

General Titan raises her eyebrow. "Sun Tzu?"

He nods. "There's a reason we still teach it to our recruits. Captain Skye is our best—and quite frankly, only—shot right now at learning about them. They chose her, like she said. And we don't know why. But right now, it's the best chance we've got to avert the next Great War."

General Titan still looks skeptical. "Our mission here from Secretary General Andromeda was to find intel about the Astrals. Something we can use . . ."

"Exactly," Apollo says. "And that's what Captain Skye and her team got us."

General Titan shifts her gaze to me. "I must commend you, Major Apollo. And your team. You're right . . . this is highly actionable—and more—it's the only intel we've got."

She signals to her team and turns to leave. "We need to get to work right away."

I dare to speak up, my heart thudding in my chest.

"General, if I may, what is the plan?"

She gives me a hard look that makes me wither a little. "We've got to get to work in the lab right away to find a reliable way to connect to them . . . one that won't kill you."

"Yes, General," I say, feeling relieved. "You mean, that won't fry my brain?"

She manages a small smile. Just the corner of her lip quirks upward.

But that feels like a big win.

"Captain, you're officially on lockdown . . . is that clear? Major Apollo, no more risky missions. You're too valuable to us alive. You're our only link to the Astrals."

"Yes, General," we both say, while my team takes that in. Then she pops off a salute and marches down the corridor, leaving us alone. Major Apollo exhales loudly.

Then he fixes his gaze on me. "You heard her, right?"

"Yes, sir. No more risky missions."

But I can tell he doesn't fully trust me. Even so, he dismisses us to our barracks. Turmoil still assaults my heart, but hope has cracked it open a little bit. General Titan said she'd get her scientist team working on a safe way for me to communicate with the Astrals.

Before it's too late.

CHAPTER 45

DRAE

"Buckle up," Rho says as Gunner pilots us through Earth's atmosphere. I wasn't expecting to be back in space so soon. But we didn't have a choice. After meeting with Trebond, Xena drove us to the abandoned airfield, where we boarded the Raider ship. Rho and her girlfriend showed us to our sling chairs. I'm not sure, but I felt like Rho was giving Willow a fair amount of side-eye, making me wonder how much she knows.

And now, here we are—stowed away aboard a Raider ship, being smuggled off Earthside on a highly clandestine and dangerous mission to save humanity. But what's new?

The more things change, I think ruefully, *the more they stay the same*.

"Aye, gonna be a rough ride," Gunner adds with that strange Raider accent.

I feel the outline of the drive, carefully slipping it into my pocket before buckling up my harness and tightening the straps. I feel the sling chairs adjust to my weight.

I'm thrilled to be back with Rho and her girlfriend, Gunner. She's the second in charge under Kari's father. Rho has even adopted a Raider uniform and style, though her nano hair and implants still shift with her mood. And right now—

She looks bright pink—*thrilled*.

Meanwhile, Gunner looks the same as the last time I saw her with short, choppy hair and a pirated Space Force uniform. But most importantly, she's the best pilot in Captain Skye's fleet. And she still seems deeply in love with Rho. It's fantastic to see them so happy together.

But one thing is freaking me out. "Are those Mrs. Smee's boosters?" I gulp. "The highly illegal ones? That are untested and . . . prone to exploding?"

"The very ones!" Gunner sounds far too cheerful. "Although, in this case, we have tested them out. As you recall."

"How could I forget?" I mutter, remembering my last jaunt to space.

"Hold on tight," Gunner says. "Warp drives and boosters engaging . . ."

Willow reaches over and grabs my hand. Her palm is cold and clammy.

She looks downright panicked. "Uh, now probably isn't the best time to disclose my intense fear of flying."

"Kind of too late," Rho says from the cockpit. We're buckled into the cabin. "You should've told us *before* we left Earth's atmosphere. The Old Lady says we don't have any time to waste."

Gunner adds, "Sorry, not sorry."

"Where are we going?" Willow asks in a shaky voice. She glances out the window, where the dark expanse spreads out around our ship while Earth tilts under the sun's glare.

"Welcome to sailing on the star-seas," Rho says, sounding like a grizzled pro. "Hold on tight! We're about to go . . . interstellar . . ."

"Interstellar?" Willow gasps, holding on to her harness tighter and looking sick.

Gunner adds, "Technically it's this unnamed super-secret research base where Kari is currently stationed."

Rho giggles. "Yeah, and it has an abandoned Astral settlement. And these fun crystal trees that we mine for our warp tech. We've been lurking in the rings by the planet it orbits . . ."

"Yeah, it's kind of stalker-ish if you ask me," Gunner adds. "But Kari's dad is a little bit overprotective. After all that time he lost with her due to Space Force lies."

"Yeah, but that's a long story," Rho says, elbowing her. "Don't overshare. I know you're neurodivergent, but remember we've been working on that? You're supposed to be a secret agent?"

Gunner looks sheepish.

"I know, but I just don't feel right not telling the poor lass everything."

"NTKB," Rho says. "Need to know basis. That's what the Old Lady said."

Gunner smirks. "Well, I feel like she *needs* to know what she got herself into."

"You're impossible," Rho huffs.

"And you're cute when you're mad."

Then they start kissing. I want to be annoyed at their *bickering to sucking face* relationship, but I can't help but smile.

"So, let me get this straight," Willow cuts in, not sharing my happiness. "You're taking me to an interstellar moon base . . . that doesn't have a name . . . but it does have an alien settlement . . . in the middle of some kind of weird interfamily drama?"

"Yeah, that's the tip of the iceberg," Rho says. "But you catch our drift."

"Sorry, we couldn't tell you before we left orbit," Gunner chimes in. "Old Lady's orders. Part of our security protocols. Especially with zero-G newbies."

"Zero-G newbies?" Willow says.

"That means you, lass," Gunner replies. "Rache here, this ain't his first blast-off. Do you need a puke bag?"

That doesn't help either.

Willow starts to look a bit green. But I stroke her arm and try to calm her down. "Don't worry! Take deep breaths. It's not as bad as they're making it sound."

"Nope!" Rho says. "It's way worse."

I roll my eyes. "Not helping!"

But they both laugh, clearly enjoying the pantomime of being scary Raiders, which couldn't be further from the truth.

However, with all the fake newsfeeds, it's easy to buy into their antics. Most civilians are terrified of the Raiders, believing them to be cruel savages.

Even cannibals.

Just one of the many truths I've had to learn—or maybe unlearn—when this whole adventure first began for me.

Willow leans her head on my shoulder, and while I should feel comforted, guilt churns in my gut like acid. I catch Rho glaring at her, then at me. Her hair and eyes turn vicious red—angry crimson.

And I know why.

But I'm trapped. Literally, strapped into this harness. And she's afraid . . .

Rho mouths to me, *We'll talk later.*

I want to shrivel up and die right there in my sling chair. Or run as far away from here as possible. But I have nowhere to go. I'm stuck between a rock and a hard place. Or rather, between the terrible, deadly vacuum of space and the terrible, deadly wrath of Kari's best friend.

I'm not sure which is scarier.

But it might be Rho with that demonic hair and eye combo staring me down.

Thankfully, there's a distraction as Gunner starts the countdown.

"Three . . . two . . . one . . . *engage!*"

In a great rush of propulsive energy that rattles the cabin and jitters my teeth, we accelerate and leave Earth far behind. The sling chairs adjust to offset the tremendous pressure, but still black spots dance in my vision. My neural implant remains silent and blocked.

That's when the meds kick in, injected directly from our sling chairs—

And everything goes black.

"No, leave me alone . . ."

I wake up from a dream where I'm falling with no end to someone roughly shaking my arm. She's holding a syringe.

I jerk to attention.

"Asteroid fires, what are you doing?"

"Needed to wake your ass up."

"What's in the syringe?"

"Adrenaline. Good stuff."

It looks like we're still in transit somewhere in deep space. The autopilot is on with Gunner snoozing her captain's chair. I glance to my right.

Willow remains sound asleep with her head resting on my arm. A thin ribbon of drool trickles down.

I feel a sudden surge of affection, chased by crippling guilt. Rho sees it.

"Ah, isn't she cute?" she quips in an overly sweet voice. "Don't worry—your adorable little secret agent girlfriend isn't about to wake up anytime soon."

Then she jabs my shoulder . . . hard.

"Ouch!" I yelp. "What was that for?"

Her hair and eyes are back to fire red. "You have a lot of explaining to do."

With that, she drags me to the back of the cabin. I can't help feeling like I'm in trouble. Big trouble. Her red eyes and hair don't help either. She flops down—

And glares at me.

"What?" I say in a scared voice.

"Explain. Now. Please."

Each word is like a dagger. I run my hand through my tangles of long hair.

"Uh, what do you mean?"

She lets out a loud sigh. "Look, I know I left you hanging at Berkeley and ran off with my girlfriend to become a space pirate. So, without me . . . you've gone astray . . . and not in a good way."

"There's a good way to stray?"

She shrugs. "Sometimes. Cheating isn't always bad in my experience."

I frown. "Wait, it's not?"

"Ugh, hetero-normies are challenging. It's like communicating with an alien. Or maybe, I'm the alien, and you're normie."

"*Hetero*-what's?"

I can't keep up. My head is spinning.

"Look, Kari didn't tell me . . . everything exactly," Rho goes on. "She didn't have to. We have best friend ESP. Plus, the whole *the-fate-of-the-world-is-depending-on-us-again* situation, so it's kind of selfish to vent about our love life."

"That's what this is about?"

She glares at me. "Of course that's what this is about! She also told her father a lot. And none of it was good . . ."

I let out a slow groan. "Don't I fucking know it." I let my hand fall into my hands. "I hate it, too."

"You *hate* it?" she shoots back. "You don't look *in hate* with your little friend over there. Maybe *in like* . . . maybe *in love*—"

"Ugh, not love."

"You're sure?" She sounds skeptical.

"Very. Sure."

"So . . . do explain."

"Right, it's super confusing to me, too," I stammer, trying to find the right words. "I love Kari. Not exceptions or asterisks either. Real love. True love."

She raises her eyebrow. "You could've fooled me."

"Yeah, but it's the first time . . . for both of us . . . and we keep messing up," I say, miserably. "The lag time has been killing us. I barely hear from her at all, and when I do, we have so much pressure on us. Space Force intel, secret missions, the Resistance."

"Facts. Okay, I'm softening. But only a little because I have extreme empathy. It's a blessing and a curse. Just ask Gunner."

That gives me courage, something I've been lacking. "Yeah, and proximity . . . is a thing," I admit. "She's just there for me. And seems like she cares. She also understands what it's like being a secret agent while trying to make it through college. Maybe she's the only one."

"Except Kari. And me."

"Yeah, but you left . . . and so did she."

"I'm sorry—but I warned you that if you broke my best friend's heart, I'd kill you. At first, I thought I'd have Gunner do it. But no, it's gonna be me. I want to pull the trigger—"

"Ugh, please don't blast me yet," I say, genuinely sickened. "I admit it. I kissed Willow . . . just once . . ."

"So you didn't just mentally cheat like Kari thinks . . . you really cheated . . ."

"Yes."

The word comes out hollow. My stomach turns sickly.

Rho's hair turns pale yellow-green, exactly how I feel.

"This is bad."

That's all she can muster.

"I know."

That's all I can muster.

The silence hangs heavy over the low thrum of the warp drives propelling us onward relentlessly, toward our destination . . . where Kari awaits.

"So, what are you going to tell her?" Rho asks in a soft voice. All the fire has drained from her, replaced by blue.

Sadness.

"I don't know. And that's the problem. Plus, there's this . . ."

I palm the drive, showing it to her, with the shifter intel. It looks so small but it holds the power to change everything.

"The fate of the world again?"

"Yeah. But her heart is on the line too."

"What a mess," Rho says. "I've been through a lot of breakups and makeups in my time. I've loved and I've lost. I've cheated—I admit it—and been the bad actor, and I've been cheated on . . ."

"You have?" I'm surprised.

She nods. "Gunner changed me. For the better. Plus, if she caught me shagging someone else . . . well . . . let's just say I'm pretty sure that she'd *un-alive* them."

"Good call. I agree."

"But Kari isn't like me—she's different. She doesn't fall in love or trust anyone. And if you break her heart, I have a bad feeling she'll never forgive you."

"I know," I say in a rough voice. My throat feels like sandpaper. And my heart? It drops through my chest . . .

Sinking like a stone.

"Willow . . . doesn't mean anything," I say. "Kari . . . is like the sun and the moon and all the stars . . . she's everything."

"You're right about that," Rho says. "But will that line work on her?"

The second she says that, I feel how much it sounds like a line. Like something I'd say to get a girl back in high school after she caught me being unfaithful. A situation that I'd like to say seldom happened but that's another lie.

"You poor boy," Rho says, patting my leg and then standing up. "Good luck."

Beeping erupts from the cockpit as Gunner stirs, then pops awake. I don't need to hear her announcement to know what it means—we're almost there.

I return to my sling chair to climb into my harness for docking. But that's when I see—Willow is wide awake and waiting for me. How much of that did she hear?

The way she looks at me . . .

Makes me worry.

I love Kari, and I meant what I said. But Willow is also important. The confusion settles into my head and my heart, as I struggle for some clarity.

Kari, I'm coming for you . . .

I hope it's not too late.

CHAPTER 46

KARI

A week goes by with precious little communication.

All the newsfeeds keep repeating the same footage that makes the colleges look more like a battlefield while spewing hardline rhetoric. I have Anton smuggle a secret message to my father to try to get word Earthside and to the Resistance. But I haven't heard anything back.

Even my father seems to have gone dark, making me worry more.

We also haven't heard any updates from General Titan in the lab. We've mostly been confined to our barracks, and I'm growing more and more restless. I hate sitting still.

And doing nothing.

I feel so helpless.

My team tries to cheer me up, and I smile and go through the motions, but the truth is that I'm losing it more each day. Without the Sympathetic Program, I feel like space debris floating aimlessly through the cosmos. I didn't realize how much those weekly communications anchored me and kept me moored. Without them, I'm at the mercy of inertia, and whatever gravitational forces pull me toward their immense mass, worrying about things I can't control.

Why did they choose you?

General Titan asked me that. And I answered honestly. *I don't know.* Maybe it has something to do with the role I played in averting their first secret invasion. Maybe it's my connection to Drae—and the fact that it was both of us together.

But now, we're fractured apart. And in danger of breaking to pieces forever. Whatever tentative love sprouted in our hearts seems to be dying under the distance and time, and the exertion of external forces. Willow and Apollo—our dual temptations. I also keep waking from violent nightmares each night where I see Earthside bombarded by a barrage of explosions, the surface consumed by flames, eradicating anything and everything that lives and dares to breathe.

I know it's . . . *them.*

The Astrals.

Their intention for Earth. They want to eradicate humanity. They want me to feel how angry they are . . . how hurt . . . how they don't trust us to exist as a species.

In these nightmares, I try to plead with them. I tell them that I'm different. That humans can grow, change, and evolve beyond our warlike tendencies, that we're not all like those guardians who killed their civilians. I try to show them good moments that I hoard in my memory. Bea baking me faux chocolate chip cookies. Jumping on my bed. Ma hugging me.

And Drae.

How our love blossomed in this war-torn future. Even if it didn't last.

But they don't listen.

BURN. BURN. BURN.

I wake gasping with a scream on my breath. I don't dare tell anyone about my nightmares, or that I suspect the dreams are real, and that they're now connecting to me directly without me being psychically in their settlement, that whatever they put in my head allows them to access my consciousness when my walls are down and I'm fast asleep.

I'm afraid that nobody will believe me. That I'll be diagnosed with a bad case of space trauma and get kicked out. That General Titan will halt the research into how to open safe lines of communication with them. But the dark circles under my eyes haunt my days, along with the dark feeling spiraling in my head and telling me that I'm on the brink of losing everything.

Or maybe, it's already lost.

And I just don't know it yet.

Finally, something pierces the darkness and some light shines through.

Anton bursts into our barracks. I sit up from bed, where I've been stewing, while Luna hops off her top bunk.

"Your father," he says in a hushed voice, fiddling with his watch.

"Did he respond?"

Anton nods. "He's here . . . in person. He says it's urgent. He has new intel. We have to sneak you off base to meet with him again."

"But General Titan said to stay put," Luna says. "We'll have to be extra careful."

"Extra super-duper careful," Anton agrees. "Also, your father isn't alone . . ."

"Wait, what do you mean?" I ask in surprise. "Who is with him?"

Anton fiddles with his watch again, then finally replies.

"Drae."

Drae is in space. And he's here.

In person.

I can't believe it. My whole body reverberates with the shock of this news. But also relief that he's safe and unharmed. However, if he left college and the Resistance smuggled him off Earthside, then whatever intel they found, it must be serious. Or they wouldn't risk it.

It's too dangerous.

Civilians aren't allowed in space.

All these thoughts tumble through my head as we go through the motions of sneaking off base, using the postal ships as our stealth vessels. My team stays behind, partially to cover for me. I pray General Titan doesn't notice my absence. I do a quick mental calculation from the last time I heard from Drae. The fateful message that triggered me into mistrust and heartbreak.

Anton sneaks me out through the post office and up their elevator shaft that carries the mail bins. The small, sleek postal ship is already powering up. He slips inside the cockpit, while I hide in the jump seat. Then we blast off, leaving our secret base behind in our space dust.

"You ready for this?" Anton asks once we reach orbit.

"No, but I don't have a choice."

"What's the . . . uh . . . status?" he says in a worried voice. "With you and Drae?" He risks a glance my way, while our ship cuts through the expanse of velvety space that unspools outside.

I let out a loud sigh. "No *blasted* idea."

Anton snorts a laugh. "Should I be worried? Do you need emotional support? I'm sorry, but relationships aren't exactly my strong suit. Nadia is better for this—or maybe Genesis."

"No matter what, we have to work together. Too much is at stake."

He nods in a diplomatic way, though he can tell I'm hiding my true emotions, and we finish the journey in heavy silence. My thoughts keep spinning through different gravities.

It's been over a week and a half. Long enough for Drae to warp out here, especially with the Raider ships and their special booster tech. He must have left Earthside right before—or right after—the riots and book burning broke out on campus. My heart lurches. In the aftermath of everything that's happening, I wonder if I'm overreacting to his feelings for Willow.

The whole ride off base, I'm simmering in a tumult of emotions. Relief, yearning, love, wanting to kiss him . . . but also wanting to punch him in the face at the same time. It's a toxic brew. My hatred for him in high school mixing with my recent lust for him, all strung together by fraying tendrils of love sliced through with heartbreak, poisonous but strangely tasty.

How did Rho do it? Go through so many relationships? Only to rebound into another lovefest? However, something about her and Gunner feels different this time. Less superficial.

Deeper and more permanent.

Like she found her *forever* person. That makes me smile. But then, sadness sweeps through me. I thought I found mine too. Are we fixable? Or is it too late for us?

One last, scary thought hits me. It's been almost two weeks since he sent that last exchange, the one that almost broke me to pieces. He hadn't technically done anything.

Yet.

But what's happened since then?

"Prepare for docking," Anton says as we burst through the planet's glittery rings, trailing ribbons of space dust. My father's Raider vessel materializes suddenly from nothing.

We start spinning, making my stomach flip, before we lock on.

Hiss.

Our cabin decompresses as the airlock latches onto his ship. We clamber from our smaller vessel, emerging into my father's domain. To my relief, he greets us right away.

"Kari, we have to hurry," my father says, quickly giving me a tight hug.

"What is it? He's . . . here?"

He catches my drift right away. "This was too important to trust to a message. He came in person . . . and so did she."

"Wait, who?"

Before he can respond, we reach the cabin and burst through the door.

And I see her standing there.

Willow.

I know it's her.

I can't explain it exactly. She's lurking in the corner with her arms crossed. I can feel something in the way she glances at me. Animosity. Resentment. Jealousy.

It hits me right away.

But then Drae rises from his chair. Our eyes lock together—and our thoughts.

I try to put up walls and fight the connection, but it overwhelms me.

I sink down into a sling chair.

Rho and Gunner give me quick hugs, then vanish from the cabin. Only my father stays, along with the two of them.

Drae and Willow.

"Why did you blast off to space?" It comes out more harshly than I intended.

"Kari, it's . . . important," Drae starts as he pulls out what looks like a tiny drive. "The Old Lady insisted we deliver it."

"Plus, our campus is a war zone," Willow says with an affected shrug. "She thought it would be good to lie low in space for a few days. I'm Willow . . ."

She holds out her hand to shake. I want to tell her off. Everything about her reads so fake and calculating to me.

But I fake it for now. Her palm feels cold and clammy to my touch.

"Resistance?" I say to her carefully.

"Yup, and his agent handler on campus," she says, winking at Drae.

In a way that sickens me.

She doesn't know about us. Not fully.

Drae flinches when I think that. So, he can hear my thoughts. Our implants have locked together again. However, I'm trying to shut him out for one reason—I need to stay focused.

I can't lose it right now.

But clearly, I'm failing. And he's already inside me.

"You know who I am?" I ask her.

"Of course. The famous Hikari Skye. Space Force hero. Who doesn't?"

Her quip falls flat.

"Pretty much the whole universe," I shoot back. "Being a secret agent and all that. Kind of comes with the territory."

She blushes—and thankfully, shuts up. I want to hate her, but she does have some admirable spunk. Her purple eyes and hair remind me of Rho's, too. Plus, we're both fighting for the same cause.

I want to hate her, but I see why Drae likes her, and that kills me a little more. Worse, she's the total opposite of me. Chatty and friendly, and quite girly yet tough with her punk-style, flouncy skirt paired with fishnets, and combat boots. The combination is completely alluring.

I'm reserved, and that's on a good day. My hair is clipped into a short cut, per Space Force regulations, but it's not stylish. I don't have civilian clothes anymore, and even when I did, they weren't feminine in any way. More tomboyish and utilitarian, again lacking in style.

I avert my gaze and clear my throat. I can sense Drae trying to get my attention, and how sorry he feels for putting me in this awkward situation in the first place.

"So, what's this new intel?" I say, doing my best to ignore her, but failing.

"Right, it's big . . . and dangerous," Drae says quickly. "It's about the Astrals."

"What did they find?" I ask, tensing in expectation.

"Best that you see it for yourself," he says, handing the drive to my father. He pops it into a slot in a portable tablet, and the grainy surveillance footage starts playing. The footage shows a school bus idling in a parking lot . . . with the Golden Gate Bridge in the background.

Suddenly, a blur of energy rushes by the camera, distorting the screen.

The energy flickers—then resolves into human form.

"Wait . . . what is that?" I ask in confusion.

Drae replies, tapping at the screen. "That's the bus driver who got killed in the attack. Or rather, it's supposed to be. But watch what happens after this."

I watch the screen, riveted by the raw footage. The supposed driver drags a duffel bag from the bus and dumps it into the bay, where it plunges deep below the surface.

"What's in the bag?" I ask, pretty sure I'm not going to like the answer.

"The *real* driver," Drae says darkly.

"He was dead before the attack?" I start. "But then, who's the imposter?"

Suddenly, I remember what I saw down in the settlement.

The light-beings. The way they moved . . . and shifted . . .

And it all clicks in.

"Asteroid fires, they're shifters!"

"Yes, and they can impersonate humans. And, well, anyone they want."

"So, that's how they did it," I say, jumping to my feet and pacing around. "That's how they infiltrated our Earthside defenses to plant the bomb on the bus. That's big. And it's dangerous." My thoughts spiral into a million implications. "If they can do that, then they could have already planted operatives . . . anywhere they want."

"Exactly," my father jumps in. "Now you see why we had to come in person. The invasion might not be coming . . . it might already be happening on Earth."

"And we'd have no idea," I say with a shaky exhale. "They could have infiltrated Space Force. The Earthside Federation. They could be behind all the tension and unrest dividing the government."

"Even the Raiders," my father says quickly. "Don't worry. We're already screening everybody. The one way to get around it—ask them questions that only the real person could know. They can impersonate us, but they can't be us."

"Not completely," Drae says. "Not yet, but they're working on that, too."

"Right. I found something big, too."

Quickly, I brief them on everything that happened in the Astral settlement. The way I could connect to them. How they're all neurally linked somehow.

I finish by saying that they've chosen to communicate with me. And that we're working on a way to open diplomatic channels—and avert the coming war.

When I finish, we're all pretty stunned and overwhelmed. But time is ticking down. Drae sits next to me, taking my hand. I want to pull it away, but I'm too shocked and paralyzed to fight him, too. Willow watches us with a scowl. She sets her lips. The true connection between us must be apparent. She looks bothered—and more than a little annoyed. Just great.

"We have to be careful who we tell," Drae continues. "If this falls into the wrong hands, they could bury it."

"You mean . . . a shifter."

Drae nods. "Exactly. Or a hardliner who wants the war to happen . . ."

He trails off, then adds, "Is there anyone you trust inside Space Force? Besides your team, of course. Ideally, someone higher up, with power."

The words leap from my lips without hesitation. "Major Apollo. My CO. He's different. I trust him completely."

I see Drae recoil slightly when I say that. I wonder if he can sense my true feelings for Apollo through the neural link, how we came so close to kissing. From the hurt in his eyes . . .

I'm guessing so.

My father seems to pick up on this tension. He clears his throat.

"Uh, let's give you two a moment together," he says, shepherding Anton and Willow from the cabin. "But just for a little bit. I wish we had more time . . ."

With that, they vanish from the cabin, leaving me and Drae . . . alone together.

With no buffers, the tension simmers into a raging inferno of emotions. I can't keep my walls up; they come tumbling down. I can't keep fighting our connection, not when he's standing right here in front of me, flesh and blood and beating heart and yearning and wanting, all pent up for the last many weeks.

I don't want to, but I can't help it. I thrust my arms around him, pulling him to me, inhaling his scent of must and sweat and spice. I breathe it in, drink it down. And then we're kissing. Our lips lock together, hungry and desperate, but they mix with the salt of my tears.

That I didn't even know I was crying. My thoughts tumble out at him.
I miss you. I love you. I hate you.
He absorbs it all at once, and I feel his confusion, his guilt, his remorse . . .
I'm sorry. I'm sorry. I'm sorry.
She pales in comparison to you.
You're my red giant.
The sun that I orbit around. Without you, nothing in my existence makes sense.
I am weak. I am a coward.
You don't deserve me.

And now, he's crying too. And we're kissing and crying and miserable and still in love even though our hearts are breaking. Why didn't Rho tell me?

That you can be in love?
And heartbroken?
At the same time?
Show me what you did, I think to him.

And then I see the memory replay. Drae and Willow on a pizza date, then running across campus . . . and kissing.

Before Jude catches them.
But their lips . . . touched.
How could you?

My brain screams at him. He's holding me, and I'm pounding on his chest with my fists, and he's absorbing it all.

But then—
He drops me.
Major Apollo, you and him.

Now, it's his turn to be heartbroken. I watch his face contort as he learns the full extent of my lust for my CO. The flirtatious banter. The wanting to kiss him. The yearning for . . . more than that. And now, he's even more betrayed by the knowledge of my trust in Apollo.

You drove me to him. Part of why I gave in to my feelings is how betrayed I felt.
Drae holds me—and stares into my eyes with tears falling from his own.
Two wrongs don't make a right.
And one thing is clear.
We're both shattered.

My head pounds and my blood pressure threatens to drop out, and at last, we break apart. I don't remember much after that. Everything is a blur, consumed by the pain of the heartbreak times two. The cabin door hisses open, and Anton rushes to my side. He shoots daggers at Drae.

Willow rushes to his side.

And I think that's the moment that I know the truth. She may be a Resistance operative, skilled at deceptions, but she's been operating against me this whole time. And why?

Ambition. It hits me suddenly, then with certainty.

Drae is important to the Resistance, and she wants that power. I double over in pain. It splits my head and my heart, cleaving them in half, then fracturing them into pieces. Parts of me will always be left behind, like shards of shrapnel lodged into his mind and heart.

Anton is dragging me away, telling me we have to get back to base before it gets any worse. But how can it get any worse?

I want to tell him that.

When you've already lost everything, what more is there to lose? But I can't form the words as he keeps pulling me away from Drae. We're almost at the door to the airlock.

I look back and catch his gaze.

I hold it.

Don't trust her . . . can't trust her! I aim and fire that thought at him like I'm blasting him with my weapon, even though it's holstered. He jerks back.

I know he heard me.

I wonder if this is the last moment we'll ever be together. I wonder if anything remains. I'm so devastated, but I also want to protect him from what I realized. Willow can't be trusted. She glares at me when nobody else can see it, while she pats his back and tries to soothe him.

How fast can you go from lovers back to being enemies? I wonder dimly.

But I already know the answer—

In the blink of a kiss.

The last thing I remember is them together with her hand over his shoulders as Anton is dragging me the other way. I think maybe I'm screaming and crying. Then boarding the postal ship. Anton fastening my harness and blasting off, and that's when I lose it completely.

I crumble to nothing.

I fall into the abyss.

My mind fractures and my heart breaks. No, more like . . . shatters.

Darkness consumes me.

And everything goes black.

CHAPTER 47

DRAE

I watch Kari walk away—and realize she might be walking out of my life for the last time. I can't stop thinking about what happened—when our minds locked together. Her betrayal hits me hard. But I know that I'm the reason she strayed. That it's because I did it first.

Willow watches with narrowed eyes until she's gone. Her proximity to me feels almost territorial. Suddenly, I don't want to be anywhere near her anymore. But I'm stuck.

And she's angry. I can see it. Not just angry, she also feels totally betrayed, too.

And everything is my fault.

"Why didn't you tell me?" she says once they're gone. "I mean, I knew she was your Sympathetic and that the connection isn't like anything else. But I didn't realize . . ."

I wince. "That I loved her?"

"Yeah, that. How could you?" Willow has tears in her eyes. "You betrayed her. But you betrayed me, too. I know I'm not innocent either. I blurred the lines . . ."

"Stop—it's my fault," I say in a weak voice. My head pounds fiercely, and my vision doubles. "I guess I liked the fantasy. You were right there, too! While she's millions of warp miles away."

"So that's all I am to you?" she spits at me. "A stand-in? A warm body? Until your true love comes back Earthside?"

"No, it's not like that! Willow, I care about you, too." The second the words leave my mouth, I know they're true.

And I realize I've been hiding from that truth the whole time, not wanting to admit to myself how they've grown, through proximity, but also through her deeper understanding of my situation.

"You care about me—but you love her! I saw it plain as day."

"I loved her. I love her. I will always love her," I admit. "Some part of me belongs to her now. But you were right. I've never been good enough for her."

"I . . . am?" she says, folding her arms over her chest. But she's softening.

"Yes, you were right about how she treats me, too. I couldn't see it before. But maybe we're not meant to be together. Maybe we're like a star that burns too bright, destined to go supernova . . . and destroy everything in our path . . ."

"Is that what just happened?" Willow demands. "Stop with the pity party. You knew what you were doing was wrong. But you were fine dragging both of us down with you."

My head throbs again, dangerously, and my vision darkens. "That might've been the explosion that crushes us into a black hole until there's nothing left."

"Nothing escapes a black hole," Willow says. "Not even light. The darkness is impenetrable, permanent, maybe older than the universe. So, what does that make me?"

"Dawn . . ." I whisper to her, cupping her face in my hand. "Like the softest light that cracks the darkness of night. You're the promise that a new day might come."

"Dawn?" she muses, leaning into my touch. "So, you're saying there's hope?"

I nod sadly, struggling to maintain my thoughts. Her light helps, but it's not the same. I keep seeing the look on Kari's face as Anton dragged her away. Now I know where I've seen it before—

It's the same one from high school. After I tried to kiss her without consent, and she punched me in the face.

So, it's official—

Kari is back to hating me.

And there's nothing I can do about it. This is all my fault. But then, I remember her desirous feelings for her CO. And my blood boils, too. Maybe this was all a terrible mistake. Our Pairing. Our love.

All of it . . .

Why did I think I could change for her? Even that I should change?

Now, look . . . our world is burning . . . about to be destroyed. Just like our fractured minds and broken hearts.

That's when my legs wobble. My vision goes dark. I think I'm falling, fainting. Everything else remains vague in my memory. Willow screaming for help.

Rho and Gunner dragging me onto their ship. I can barely walk. My legs have gone soft and gelatinous, while my head swims with horrible images. Most of all—

Kari crumpling after learning the truth about me and Willow. But also, Kari and her CO together. *Major Apollo.* That's his name. My mind splinters with images of them together.

I know I'm not any better.

Probably worse.

My attraction to Willow even might have pushed her into his arms. That thought stabs me like a thousand knives. The pain of this becomes my existence, and my existence becomes my pain. Dimly, I feel them buckling me into the sling chair. Willow squeezing my hand.

Then sounding panicked—

"Drae, it's going to be okay! Stay with us . . . we're warping you back Earthside. Just hang in there . . . we can't lose you . . . you're too important . . . please stay with me . . ."

"Wh-what's happening to him?" Gunner asks, sounding afraid.

"Something to do with the neural implants and the Sympathetic Pairing," Rho says in a sorrowful voice.

"You mean, heartbreak?" Gunner says in alarm. "It can do that . . ."

"When your minds are connected—and your neural synapses intertwined—I guess this is what it looks like when you suffer a broken heart . . ."

I can't talk; I can't move.

But I hear them talking about me. However, if I could talk, I would tell them that they're right. That my heart is breaking into a million tiny pieces. That I might be dying, too.

"I'm hoping the farther we get him away from her," Rho says, "the more he can recover from this . . ."

"The proximity principle?" Gunner says, thinking it over. "I hope you're right. When they're together, the neural links connect them. We need to get him out of here—and fast."

That's the last thing I remember before Gunner pushes the ship into warp drive with the contraband boosters—and everything blurs and goes black.

And I leave this world for a while.

I'm not sure if I'll ever come back.

Kari wraps her arms around Major Apollo, pulling him in for a passionate kiss. They shimmer and blur, shifting into one being, where I can't tell where he ends and she begins, and I scream—

No, stop! I love her!

But nothing escapes my lips. I'm helpless to do anything but watch.

Willow appears before me, every bit the temptress, with her flirtatious smile, the same one she weaponized against Jude, luring me into her embrace . . . and I can't escape.

Her smell; her taste; her warmth.

And I'm inside her, and she's on top of me, riding all the pleasure out of me.

Until I'm spent.

I don't know if I'm dead or alive, if my soul has been flung out of my body for the ultimate judgment to be rendered, or if this is just what it's like when your mind fractures and your heart shatters.

Time expands and shrinks in the propulsive rush. I stop caring about myself. All I care about is . . . Kari.

I know I'm a hypocrite.

And a coward.

But I just hope she will be okay. I can live with my own dark fate, but I can't stand the idea that I caused her harm.

And then hallucinations start up again, bombarding me with horrible images.

Kari and Apollo.

Until I can't stand it anymore. Until I think I'd rather die than live this way.

Miraculously, I wake up to the stark lighting of the ship's interior cabin.

"You're okay!" Willow gasps. "Drae, we thought we'd lost you . . ."

"Gave us all heart attacks a few times," Gunner says, checking my IV and flicking the bag to keep it draining into my arm. "Sorry, I had to dig in your arm. I'm not a trained medic. Just I've run headfirst into a lot of blasters, so I've learned some tricks."

My mouth feels thick and chalky. My lips are dry and chapped. My throat burns.

And it looks like we've come out of warp. Through the cabin windows, the blue, green, and white swirls of Earth tilt under the ceaseless glare of the sun.

We made it back Earthside. I must have been out for days.

Maybe longer.

I'm shocked to learn that.

"If you're okay, then say something!" Rho hurries over from the cockpit.

"*Something . . .*" I force out from my cracked lips. It comes out hoarse.

"Oh, thank the stars," Rho says. "I was told you could be brain-dead."

"Sure felt like I died a few times," I say in a rough voice. "My brain especially."

Rho crosses her arms. "Well, maybe you deserved that . . ."

"Nearly dying?" I croak out.

"Yeah, a near-death experience sounds about right," she grumbles. "For breaking my best friend's heart, you asshole."

"Ugh, I know . . ." I say remorsefully. "I probably deserve much worse . . ."

"Near-death, sure. Not actually dying," Rho quips back. "Plus, it turns out, we sort of need you alive. Turns out you're still important to saving the universe."

"Don't remind me."

My head still hurts terribly. And I feel nauseous. But I'm alive. That much is true. I hope Kari fared better than me . . .

"Have you heard anything . . ." I ask, shooting a look at Rho.

Willow immediately looks crestfallen, but quickly covers it. She's caught on to Rho's death stares when she touches me.

"Sorry, nothing, mate," Gunner says with zero tact. "Hopefully she's not dead though. That would be a bummer—"

I'm getting the feeling that she lacks any filter. Rho shoots her a look.

"Gunner, really?" she snaps.

"Oh, sorry . . . I'll be in the cabin if you need me . . ." she stammers and rushes off.

Guilt rushes through me. Now, I'm deeply afraid. "Kari . . . I don't know what I'd do if . . . she didn't make it . . ."

"Drae, stop it," Rho says in a soft voice. "I know Kari better than just about anyone on this astral plane. Trust me, she's strong and one heck of a fighter."

"You're right," I agree. "She's the strongest person I know. Not just physically, but mentally . . ."

"Exactly! And it's gonna take more than Draeden Rache reverting to being an asshole to kill her. You got that?"

Worry still plagues me, but she's right. Kari is stronger than me, and if I survived, then she will, too. Before we can talk further, Gunner's voice echoes out from the cabin.

"Breaking newsfeed alert! We just came out of warp, so looks like we missed it while in transit. Hold on, I'll grab it . . . and put it up on the cabin monitors!"

It's another minute before it broadcasts over the cabin for everyone to hear. The monitors come to life with vivid images. The reporter—a blonde perfectly made up with red lipstick in a crisp, navy pantsuit—speaks in front of a smoking podium erected on a stage.

"Secretary-General Andromeda has been assassinated. The explosive device tore through her podium while she was giving an address on the college riots."

She pauses, looking grave, with deep lines cracking through her makeup.

"I repeat—Secretary-General Andromeda has been killed in a terrorist attack while giving a speech. While the investigation is still underway, our sources tell us that the attack was likely perpetrated by our enemies . . ."

She pauses, looking straight at the camera to drive her next words home.

"The Astrals."

Everyone takes that in, looking sick. Nobody knows what to say. Even Gunner, who hasn't lived Earthside in a long time, looks shocked by this revelation.

The reporter continues on the live newsfeed. "Seizing on the California Federation's weakness, the Proxies have declared their separation from the Earth Federation."

She looks down, listening into her ear. "Hold on, I'm getting more breaking news . . ." She listens again, then continues reporting on the new information.

"Sources tell us that in the wake of these breaking developments, a new secretary-general has gained enough support and will be officially named soon . . ."

She listens to her earpiece again, then continues. "Magnus Luther and his hard-line faction will be taking over the California Federation government."

I gasp at that revelation. How is this possible? Jude's father . . . is the next secretary-general?

CHAPTER 48

KARI

I wake in the infirmary from tumultuous nightmares that felt too real. The same ones on repeat. Earth being invaded; Earth burning away to dust.

I scream and watch.

And I'm helpless to avert it.

I keep screaming into the dark void of my dreams. And all I know is—

They want me to watch. They want me to know what it feels like to watch your people die and your world be destroyed.

I blink in the stark lighting. There's a soft beeping in rhythm with my heart, and a drip in my veins, and my friends.

I'm lying in a hospital bed. The sheets are rough and coated in my sweat.

"She's awake!" Luna says, elbowing Nadia, who jerks awake from where she was fast asleep in a hard plastic chair.

"Go, tell the others! They've been worried sick. And fetch her doc."

"Oh, thank the stars," Nadia says, bolting to her feet. Then she rushes out of my room. I watch her leave, confusion rushing through me. My head feels fuzzy.

"Wh-what happened?" I manage in a groggy voice, flopping back on the rough pillow. My head feels like it weighs a million pounds. My throat is dry and scratchy. And my memory is foggy.

"Uh, officially . . . food poisoning," Luna says, lowering her voice. "We sort of all . . . faked a bad case to cover for you."

That's when I notice the bandage from her IV on her elbow. "You did . . . what?"

"It's surprisingly easy," Luna says with a shrug. "You just barf a whole bunch, then act all faint and dehydrated."

"Cover for what . . . ?"

"Well, what do you remember?" Luna says, looking suddenly worried.

I concentrate really hard but keep hitting a wall in my mind.

Finally, a few pieces chip away . . . and I remember.

"*Drae.*"

It comes out in a soft whisper.

"So yeah, you were probably suffering from . . . neural-link-induced heartbreak."

I blink, taking that in.

She pats my hand gently. "Remember how they warned you about you had with Drae? Apparently, it's a real thing. Anton says they left you alone together, and then, well, you sort of . . . freaked out bad."

I lick my dry lips, contemplating that. "How long have I been down bad?"

"You're not going to like this."

"Just tell me already."

"A whole week."

I bolt upright, my head spinning. "How is that possible?"

"Well, we did some research. Apparently, it's your neurons trying to repair themselves after you fried them."

"Why does that keep happening?" I mutter under my breath, remembering the Astrals and that whole shock thing.

"Uh, you're lucky?" she quips. "The good news is . . . you came around. So, that means you're not gonna croak."

"Yet," I say back. "There's still time."

We both share a dark laugh.

"And they bought the food poisoning? You must be incredible actors."

Luna grins. "Food poisoning can also be surprisingly debilitating, even deadly. And yes, we all acted our asses off."

"I wish I could've seen it."

"Well, you're welcome."

We both laugh, despite the situation. I'm not sure if humor is a remedy, but I think it heals me a little more.

Then we turn more serious.

"The shifter intel?" I say, suddenly remembering the drive with the footage.

"Anton has it and made a copy," Luna says right away. "He's keeping it safe until you're stronger and can personally brief Major Apollo. In the meantime, he's alerted the postmasters. Secretly, they're already screening all their workers."

I relax slightly. "Think we can trust Major Apollo?"

"I have a good feeling about him," she says with a firm nod. "He's on our side. He wants to avoid the war, too."

"But I've been wrong before."

I don't say *Drae* but I'm thinking it. However, Luna shakes her head.

"No, you've always been spot on," she disagrees. "When you're up and stronger, you can brief him on the new intel."

I flop back on my pillow. "But I shouldn't have been out of commission. I let you all down . . . and for what? Because I couldn't control my emotions?"

But Luna shakes her head. "You didn't let us down. That's what a team is for."

"Still, I failed you."

"Oh, shut up and stop being a martyr. Plus, your emotions are why you care so much—and fight so hard for what you believe. Without them, you'd be like a dead husk of a person. I'm guessing that's also why the Astrals trust you."

"Ugh, but I hate my emotions. They're so demanding and needy . . ."

She smirks. "And they seem to hate you right now, too. But you're on the mend. You need to rest though."

"And Drae?"

"Rho and Gunner are taking him and the *girl-who-shall-not-be-named* back Earthside. They'll report what you learned back to Trebond and Resistance."

"Ha, thanks for sparing me her name. But how'd you know?"

Luna shrugs. "Well, Anton said you could cut the tension with a knife."

"Ugh, that obvious?"

"Guess your secret agent skills don't apply to romantic entanglements."

"You can say that again."

"But Kari," Luna says, standing up. "Don't change a thing. Stop fighting with yourself. We've got bigger enemies."

"I know," I sigh. "You're right."

She pauses at the door and looks back.

"Also, remember . . . Drae isn't one of them. No matter how you feel right now."

"But how do you know?" I huff, still upset . . . about, well . . . everything.

Even though I'm guilty of errant thoughts and feelings, too. Still, it burns me.

"Because I know you—and you wouldn't fall for someone with a bad heart."

It's another long two days before they discharge me from the infirmary. My friends come to visit, and they joke around and tease me a little but tell me precious little about what's going on.

I can't tell they're stressed about something, but won't cough it up.

They must be under orders. But from . . . who?

Then it dawns on me.

Major Apollo.

"Kari, your job is to get stronger," Luna says, patting my leg. "Your mind is our more important asset right now."

"Yeah, don't ask me why those dumb aliens picked you," Nadia sighs. "Yeah, we need you back and at one hundred percent. If they get the communication working, you're our only hope."

"Also, Major Apollo trusts you," Anton adds. "You have to be the one to tell him."

He slides the drive into my palm.

"Did you show the team?" I ask, keeping my voice low.

He nods. "Yup, they're all up to speed on our little alien friends' . . . abilities."

"Think they've already infiltrated . . . well . . . everything?" I whisper.

Concern flashes over everyone's faces. "I hope not. But our friend Occam . . ."

"He would say . . . *yes*," I finish for him.

The seriousness falls over the room, but then Percy breaks it. "Hey, stop stressing her out already!"

"Yeah, plus there's hope," Genesis adds. "Why else would they talk to her?"

"Uh, more like hijack my mind," I say in a dark voice. "But yeah, I agree. Why try to communicate if there's no hope?"

"That's the spirit," Luna says.

"Yeah, but why her?"

"Right now, they seem intent on torturing them, to be honest," I confess.

Then I tell them about my nightmares.

"You think it's the Astrals? I bet they're testing you," Anton says finally. "To see how you react. This is about . . . empathy for their suffering."

Luna nods to that. "Mirroring."

"What's that?"

"Well, it's psychological stuff," she goes on. "They're showing you a mirror of what happened to them by putting it into the context of your world and people."

"To see if I get it?" I say softly.

"Yes, and how you'll react," she replies. "Do you want retaliation and retribution? Or do you want to find another way to break the cycle?"

I feel the drive in my palm. "Well, that's our only hope. We know they're brilliant and more advanced, and worse . . . they're already way ahead of us."

We joke and banter, and then they leave me to rest. My eyes flutter shut. I succumb to the darkness of my dreams.

This time, Willow stands over my head holding a knife. She stabs it into my heart. I wake with a start, gasping for air, as she twists the blade deeper and deeper—

Until the monitors stop.

And flatline.

Finally, after I don't know how many more days, Major Apollo comes to visit me himself. They just discharged me, and I'm changing into my uniform, buttoning up my shirt and sliding into my boots.

He raps on the door.

"Permission to enter?"

"Do you even need that?" I say, dropping all pretenses now. I don't have the mental ability to force it.

It seems, neither does he.

"You're okay?" he asks, searching my face. "The docs said you're recovered."

"Apparently, but I feel like shit."

He laughs. "You really had us worried, Captain Skye. Even General Titan has been asking for updates. That must have been some case of food poisoning?"

"Apparently, it can be surprisingly debilitating," I quote from Luna.

By the way he looks at me, I can tell he's guessing that there's more to it.

"And General Titan considers me . . . valuable. That's why she cares."

He shrugs. "Probably. But it counts."

I can't help it; I ask the question that my heart is pounding for me to ask. "And you?"

"You already know the answer to that, Captain Skye. Don't make me say it."

And just like that, my heart flips. And everything jolts to attention in my body. He's close to me; I can feel the heat wafting off his skin like electricity.

But then, I jerk away.

And look down.

"Uh, there's something I have to tell you," I say, avoiding his penetrating gaze. "It's important, and we have to be careful. It can't fall into the wrong hands."

His face falls. He snaps to attention. I want to delay reality, too. But it can't wait. "My office?" he asks.

But I shake my head. "It's not safe there. Anyone could be listening . . ."

He looks worried. "Where then?"

"The post office."

He raises his eyebrows. "They really do hold a lot of power, don't they?"

"You have no idea."

"Wow, some fancy digs," Major Apollo says as Anton shows us into his office. He looks around approvingly, appraising the cozy decorations.

"Postal service has its perks," Anton says, shutting the door. "Especially the library. Postmaster Haven curated it himself."

Apollo peruses some of the titles then pauses. "Isn't this one banned?" He holds up a hefty tome, dusty with age.

"Back Earthside," Anton says with a lopsided smile. "But the laws don't say anything about interstellar space."

Apollo shakes his head, resolving it carefully. "Ha, I like your style."

With that, Anton loads up the drive, then leaves us alone. I'm still a bit wobbly and fuzzy-headed from the infirmary and all those days being down bad.

I also get the feeling that they're keeping stuff from me. But I can't put my finger on what it could be. But I push that aside and try to focus as much as I can.

I gesture to the armchairs, and we both sink into the plush cushioning.

"So, what's this about?" Apollo asks. His patience seems to be wearing thin.

"Major, keep an open mind," I caution before launching into everything I know.

"Always," he says with a nod.

"Okay, here goes nothing."

Quickly, I explain the shifter theory to him, how the Astrals aren't just these light-beings, but that they can change their form, even impersonate humans.

"That's pretty far-fetched," he says after I finish. "How can you be sure?"

That's when I hit play. He watches the footage with surprise washing over his face. I replay the shifting part for him.

"Where'd you get this?" he asks.

His voice sounds tight, worried. But that makes sense. This is big intel. With big ramifications. They could already have infiltrated Space Force and Earth.

I trust him, but I can't tell him that.

"I'm special ops for a reason," I say instead. "Isn't that my job description?"

He doesn't press me, but he does look suspicious. "Who else knows?"

"The postmasters," I admit. "They're already testing their workers, secretly."

I expect Apollo to leap into action, but instead, he leans closer to me. We're so close, so very close, and it sparks something inside me . . . and inside him.

"Promise me something," he says softly. "Before . . . everything that's about to happen . . . well, happens . . ."

"What do you mean?" I gasp.

But he holds fast to me like I'm the last thing that can save him in the universe. "That no matter what happens. We stay true to each other . . ." He trails off.

"Why? What's happening?"

That's when—

He kisses me.

Deeply, urgently, like he can't stop. And I kiss him back just as hungrily.

I've never felt this way before. I've never been kissed like this. Like the world is ending and this is all we have left.

All thoughts of Drae melt away.

The kiss goes on and on. Or maybe it just feels that way. I cling to him, climbing into his lap and straddling him in that oversized armchair, feeling the heat of him, the desire building within him.

The hardness pushes against me and makes me breathless with the wanting.

But then, the screen flickers, reaching the end, and starts to reply on a loop.

That jolts me back to reality.

I watch the Astral flicker and take the form of the driver, then dump the body into the bay before driving off . . .

To kill all those kids.

And that stops me.

I pull away from him. And he looks flushed, but also so guilty, too.

"I'm sorry . . . I don't know . . . what came over me . . ." he stammers.

"We can worry about that later," I say, trying to get a grip on myself. I want to blame my heart shattering and everything I've been through. But I know the truth.

I've been wanting to do that since the moment I first met him—when we first laid eyes on each other. I've just been denying myself, trying to keep it boxed up, stuffed down, from destroying me.

And from what just happened between us, I'm guessing he feels the same way.

"Look, we need to get this intel to Secretary-General Andromeda right away. The Earth Federation needs to know."

That's when the bottom falls out. His next words don't seem real. I wonder if they're coming from some alternate dimension, where the world I knew is still intact, and nothing terrible happened.

"I'm so sorry to tell you this," Apollo says. "We thought it best . . . to let you recover first. But the secretary-general has been assassinated."

"Wh-what do you mean?" I stammer, trying to make sense of that.

"Kari, there is no Earth Federation anymore."

CHAPTER 49

DRAE

I'm back on campus, but it's a campus that I barely recognize anymore. I'm still reeling from what happened with Kari, but slowly I'm beginning to heal. Well, heal as much as I can. My heart will undoubtedly carry permanent scars.

I can't say the same thing about my home. I left Earthside, and when I came back it was like everything had changed. Secretary-General Andromeda has been assassinated—and Jude's father took over. I remember the cryptic things he said to me and Willow that night, and suddenly it all makes perfect sense. He used his son and other Ringer kids to agitate on campus with Anti-Astral rallies, propaganda, and book burning.

With that disturbing reminder, I glance over at the library. But it remains a burned-out husk, still boarded up and abandoned. All those precious books burned to soot and ash.

My heart already broke over Kari, but I think it breaks again over that.

Fed Patrols outnumber students as I rush back from class. I'd guess only a quarter of the students were in attendance. Many left school after the riots and returned home. The campus has a dystopian, abandoned feel now.

I shudder and tuck my head down, shocked by how fast things can change, like quicksand eroding under your feet. I get scanned maybe four times before I reach my dorm. There's more—they're armed with blasters now. The beginning of what I know is coming next . . .

Earthside rearmament.

The strict curfews mean that when not at class or meals, we're on lockdown. Students have to be inside their rooms. I reach my building, and then climb the stairs to my dorm room. Theo left school at his parents' insistence. I found out from Willow. For all I knew, he was gone.

I remember seeing him at that rally, gleefully joining in the book burning.

How fast he got radicalized.

It chills me.

And students all over the federation cheering for genocide. This was the plan all along. I have a sinking feeling about it.

Suddenly, there's a sharp rap on my door. I crack it open, then let her in.

Willow looks about as jumpy as I feel. She blushes, looking guilty as she plops my sagging futon that I inherited from Theo. I still can't believe he left campus . . .

"I just got back from . . . seeing *him*."

She says it like a bad word.

I know exactly who she means—

"Jude."

She winces, then nods.

"Sorry, Trebond's orders. I didn't have a choice. We need more intel—and fast. Turns out, you were right. The library attacks were the final phase of his father's plan."

"Brilliant," I say, sinking down next to her and feeling as deflated as the mattress. "He used his son and his friends to agitate on campus and stoke fear."

She nods. "Yup, and then he used that to build support for his hardline faction that wants Earthside rearmament."

"Andromeda's assassination gave him the moment he needed to seize power."

"They're blaming the Astrals," she says. "I have to admit . . . it does look like them. It's similar to the Golden Gate Attack. Do you think he did it?"

I frown, thinking it over.

"I don't know," I says, remembering growing up with his son. "I used to go over to their house all the time as a kid. But that was long ago, and so much has changed. I've changed, so has he."

"Jude . . . and his father?"

"Well, I can't prove it," I say, feeling sick. "But the timing is too perfect."

"All he had to do was copy the Golden Gate Attack and use a similar explosive device. Anyone could do it . . ."

"Yeah, and I just think the Astrals are smart. They're advanced. They wouldn't pull the same thing twice, not when the first attempt didn't succeed . . ."

"I know. That's what I'm thinking," she says. "Plus, Jude seemed different."

I raise my eyebrows. "How so? Did he let anything else slip?"

I try not to think about what she had to do to get that information from him.

She shakes her head. "He just bragged a lot about the book burning. He was pretty sloppy. He's drinking more . . ."

"Really? Celebrating?"

"No, actually he seemed jumpy. Almost afraid . . . he got a call from his father . . . and he made me leave."

"Did you hear the call?"

"No, I had to get out of there. He kind of freaked out on me. Like he was scared his dad would find out about us. That's what I thought at first . . ."

"You and him?"

She frowns. "Anyway, I had to get out of there. Plus, he's an important asset. But something was strange. He seemed scared of his dad. Is that how he normally acts?"

I'm pretty surprised by that. "No way! He loves his dad. They're super close. In fact, his dad's whole plan is for Jude to take over the federation one day."

Willow thinks that over. "Is that why he's doing all this?"

"Yeah, I think so," I say, remembering back. "When we were kids, he used to talk about how we'd be in charge one day. That was his greatest dream. What he was always working so hard for . . ."

"So, then why would he be scared of his father?" she asks with a worried look. "Plus, he's drinking more. The dorm was littered with empty liquor bottles."

"Yeah, and that's saying a lot for him," I say, sliding closer to her. "I don't know. But you're right. That's pretty strange."

Outside, sirens blare in the distance. We turn to watch through the window as another student is being detained. We both watch as they're e-cuffed and led away.

"Soon, if they keep this up, there won't be anyone left on campus," Willow says.

"I know—I think that's the plan."

We both shudder at that. That's when another announcement blares over the loudspeakers on campus. Those are newly installed too. After the riots.

"By order of Secretary-General Luther, all classes and exams are canceled until further notice. Curfews will be strictly enforced. Stay in your dorm rooms . . ."

"They're canceling classes?" I say, feeling even more shocked.

"And exams," she adds. "Then why are we still here? Why not close the college and send us back home?"

"I have a bad feeling we're going to find out . . ."

Despite the strict curfews, Willow and I sneak out of my dorm, using the back alleys that cut behind the buildings. My heart is thumping wildly by the time we reach our destination—the library. Rather, the basement. We slip through the back door I found with Rho.

The whole building is burned out and abandoned, but the basement somehow survived the worst of the damage. That makes it the perfect meeting place. Nobody would look here.

Or so we hope.

We're greeted by a bunch of jittery students from our DTSA group. They look shell-shocked but determined. And more importantly, they showed up for this meeting.

"Everyone, come to order," Willow says, standing on an old chair with a broken back. "Disarm the Stars is officially in session . . ."

Only a handful of kids are left. But we're lucky to have them. "What do we do now?" one petite girl asks.

"Yeah, they canceled classes," a boy asks. "The hardliners took over!"

I step forward and find my voice. "That's why it's more important than ever that we stay strong and fight back."

"But . . . how?" the girl asks again.

The revolution is only "beginning," I say, trying to stay strong for them. "Both in the stars . . . and down on Earthside. If we don't hold out for what we believe, then all hope is lost. We're the future."

"Disarm the Stars!" they chant softly.

I think of Kari then, and it hurts like a punch to the face, but I recover quickly. I don't have a choice.

"We won't be meeting again for a while," I say, glancing at Willow. "It's just too dangerous. Return to your dorm rooms. Obey the rules and curfew."

They look let down, so I add—

"Don't give up hope! Await further instructions from us. Is that clear?"

They murmur their agreement, then we time them, letting each student slip out one at a time to sneak back to their dorm, so they don't get caught together.

Now it's just me and Willow. The acrid tang of fire still clings to the air. My sneakers are blackened with soot. The remains of what was once all the knowledge of humanity collected here.

I pick something out of the soot. It's part of a book cover, but the title is gone.

Burned from the world.

A tear slips down my cheek.

"Oh, Drae . . . why are you crying?"

"It's just . . . so sad . . ."

That's all I can manage, before she's in my arms, and we're kissing each other like it's the only thing keeping us alive.

I know it's wrong; I know I should stop; and I know that if I do, I'll die.

It's like once you start falling, you keep falling, until you hit the bottom.

If there is a bottom . . .

Her soft lips taste like the sweetest nectar. I can't stop drinking them in. I pick her up, her legs straddling me.

She clings to me hard.

I wonder if she did this with Jude earlier, if he tasted her too. That only drives me to go further, to claim her.

She moans softly as I push her up against the wall. She rides against me, only stoking me to want her more.

"Drae, don't stop . . ." she hisses.

She reaches for my pants, unbuckling the zipper, reaching for me . . .

When suddenly—

The back door creaks open. I jump back, and Willow springs into action.

She rushes to protect me.

But then—

"Stand down, it's just your friendly neighborhood bus driver . . ."

Xena steps into the light cast by the moon filtering through the blackened windows, and we both relax slightly. That's when I notice she's hurt. She's limping and has fresh cuts on her face.

"Xena, are you okay?" I gasp.

But she brushes us off. "Just grazed me . . . nothing I can't handle . . ." But then she stumbles.

We both catch her and pull her over to the chair. Willow produces a bottle of water. She drinks thirstily, wiping her mouth on the sleeve of her uniform.

That's when I see it—

Blood dripping from her arm.

"Xena, what happened?" Willow gasps when she sees the blood.

Xena winces, looking older and more grizzled. "Pardon my intrusion," she starts. "But I needed to warn you. Resistance headquarters was raided tonight by Secretary-General Luther."

Shock hits me, followed by anger. Before I can find my words, Xena continues, her voice quaking . . .

"They took . . . her . . ."

She starts to nod out.

"Who . . . you have to tell us!" Willow says, shaking her back to consciousness.

Her eyes pop back open.

"The Old Lady . . . they took Trebond."

"Oh no, this is bad . . ." Willow says, starting to freak out. "Is she alive?"

Xena nods. "She tried to fight her way out, get them to blast her . . . but those filthy bastards know she's worth more to them alive. Luckily, we got that drive off Earthside . . . with the shifter intel . . ."

"Is that what they were looking for?" I ask, trying to put the pieces together.

"Yup. Our contact flipped on us. Under duress, of course . . . they tortured him. Luther seemed especially interested in making sure that intel never got out."

"Thank the stars," I say with relief, but it fades quickly. "What are they doing to do with Trebond?"

Xena shakes her head. "Nothing good, kiddo. Brace yourself . . . the worst is coming. But she's strong. She's trained to resist any of their *persuasion* techniques."

"Torture! You're talking about torture . . . but that was banned by the Peace Treatise . . ." I trail off, realizing it.

"Everything you believe in is being burned to the ground," Xena says, nodding to the remains of the library.

"You mean the revolution?" I say softly. "It's starting . . ."

Xena nods. "And it's not going the way we'd hoped . . . sorry, kiddo."

She starts to nod out again. "I need to get her medical help . . ." Willow says.

"You know someone?"

She nods quickly. "We have contingency plans in place. In case this happened . . ."

"I'll help you," I say quickly. "You can take my transport . . . it's not much, but my father has power, too. He's aligned with Luther . . . so worst case . . ."

"Diplomatic immunity?" she quips.

"Something like that," I say darkly. But I feel it in my heart. Radicalization taking hold. I wasn't sure I was a soldier.

But now—I want to fight.

They took Trebond. We help Xena up to sneak her off campus. She's heavy, but together we manage to help her stagger to the street, where my transport is waiting.

Willow pulls her into the backseat. That's when Xena's eyes pop open again. She grabs my shirt and hisses—

"He's coming . . . to campus."

I start back. "Who's coming?"

"Luther."

"To UC Berkeley? But why?"

She bobs her head weakly. "Coming to give a speech . . . that's why they canceled classes . . . assembly tomorrow . . ."

"What's it about?" I start—

But Willow waves me off. "I need to get her treatment right away. Be careful . . . I don't know why he's coming . . ."

"Me neither," I say, gritting my teeth.

"But it can't be a coincidence," she adds. "And it can't be anything good."

With that, I shut the door and my transport carries them away into the dark night. I hope they patch Xena up. She's a fighter, I remind myself. But a dark feeling haunts me all the way back to my dorm. I dodge the Fed Patrols, ducking into the shadows.

But a part of me wants them to arrest me—and take me in. The nihilism seizes hold of me, and my fractured brain struggles to fight it and find the light.

I remember kissing Willow right before Xena barged in. How far it went, and how much further it might have gone had we not been interrupted like that. Guilt consumes me like a black cloud. I need to be stronger. I can't keep falling and tripping over myself.

Everything is already in motion. And the worst part?

I have no idea what's happening with Kari in the stars. And now, my college is ground zero for every terrible thing that's about to happen back Earthside. The events of tonight run through my head again. Resistance headquarters was raided. Trebond was arrested. And now—

Luther is coming to Berkeley tomorrow.

I just need to be ready for what's coming . . . whatever that may be.

CHAPTER 50

KARI

I stare at Major Apollo in shock. My lips still tingle from our kiss, but a numbness sweeps through my body, blocking everything else out now.

"Tell me everything," I demand in a shaky voice. "They killed Andromeda?"

"Live on the newsfeeds," he goes on. "She was giving an address about the campus riots calling for peace. An explosion ripped through her lectern."

"When did you hear?" My voice sounds accusing, and I can't help it.

"Few days ago," he admits, looking down. "They rushed the comm delivery, but we're so far out in interstellar space."

"You kept it from me?" I hiss. "And my team . . . I knew something was up."

"I wanted to tell you! But we thought it would set your healing back," he says, rushing to hold me, but I push him away.

The betrayal stings. "You said . . . *we*. You conspired with my team to hide it?"

"Trust me." He sounds miserable. "It killed me to keep you in the dark."

"That means . . . you know it wasn't really food poisoning . . ."

He meets my gaze. "Your Sympathetic did this to you." When he says that, anger sizzles his voice. "Luna came to me. They didn't know who else they could trust."

"Yeah, but I'm not innocent." I give him a look that shoots daggers at him. "Or should I saw, *we're* not innocent."

"Kari, you deserve so much better. I've seen your file. After General Titan conducted the Sympathetic intervention, I looked into him, covertly. And the report I got back about his campus activities . . ."

"I know he's Resistance."

I say it bluntly; I can't keep secrets from him anymore, not now that our lips have touched, and it's all out in the open. May as well blow everything else up.

"Not about him being Resistance," he says. "I figured you already knew that. The redacted parts of your file. How you averted the invasion with that intel."

"I told you I had help."

"I remember it well." He gives me a strained smile. "At our first briefing. But I'm talking about the other stuff."

That makes my blood run cold.

"What . . . other stuff?"

He fishes in his pocket, then produces surveillance footage of him with Willow. Laughing over pizza and books. Kissing clandestinely in front of her dorm. Climbing into his transport together.

Bile rises up in my stomach. I can't bear to look at them, or I might puke.

"Does the fed know?"

He shakes his head quickly. "I used my contacts. They're . . . not official."

I raise my eyebrows. "Not official? You're sure he's safe . . . for now?"

"I had my people make certain. They're watching his back for me. He's important to our efforts, too."

"Our efforts?"

"Peace. Diplomacy." The way he says that makes it clear he means it. "Look, I don't want a war either. But those of us trying to stop it . . . we're outnumbered."

I have my walls up, but I let that in. "So . . . you really are on our side?"

"More than you know," he says softly, averting his gaze. "Let's just say, my interest in our secret mission began long before we crossed paths. I'm the reason your orders got switched. I'm why you got deployed all the way out here."

That gives me chills. They rush through my body like a tidal wave. He brought me out here. He has so many secrets. What else is he hiding?

"What about General Titan?"

He smiles. "Well, I had to strategically make the suggestion and let her think it was her idea. That's called leadership."

"More like manipulation?"

"In special ops, what's the difference?" he says with a sad smile. "We'd hit a dead end trying to get into the settlement. Pressure was mounting. She was skeptical at first, but it wasn't exactly a hard sell."

"So, you had me shipped out here to be your little guinea pig? See if I'd get electrocuted like the other guardians?"

He looks hurt. "No, I knew you were different and that they'd let you in. Guess I was right."

I cross my arms and stare him down.

"And how'd you know that?"

"Let's just say, gut instinct."

I roll my eyes. "More like, you got lucky. And I was a low-level grunt. In Space Force that means—expendable."

He flinches. "Kari, you're not expendable! If anyone made you feel that way, ever, in your entire life, then I'm sorry." He pauses, giving me a hard look. "You're the key . . . maybe to everything . . ."

I have no idea what that means, but it sends my emotions into turmoil again, remembering everyone who has discarded and abandoned me—and betrayed me— like Drae and Willow.

I feel sick again. I push that way and try to refocus on the immediate crises at hand. "And the Earth Federation?"

"Fragmented into Proxy factions," he says. "The old divisions already ran deep, but this finally broke it apart again."

"Who killed Andromeda?" I ask, my head still reeling with a million questions. "Do they think it was the Astrals?"

"Yes, sure sounds like it, doesn't it?" he agrees, but then he catches my eye. "Or maybe . . . it looks like somebody wants us to *think* it's them. But that's the thing—I don't think they did this."

"They're being framed? Like the opposite of the GGA? Where they framed the Siberian Fed, but really it was them."

"Exactly. It's kind of brilliant. Plus, it's a type of payback, don't you think?"

"But who's behind it?"

"Well, who benefits from the assassination? The hardline fascists who want Earth rearmament and to wage war and genocide against the Astrals."

"Fine," I concede. "Let's say I buy your theory. How do you know?"

He purses his lips. "Gut feeling."

"Ha, nice try. But we need proof. I'm afraid your *gut feeling* won't exactly fly."

He looks upset, frowning. "I know, that's why your full recovery was so important. Our only hope is to get safe communication with the Astrals working, so they can prove their innocence."

My heart beats faster at that reminder. It's been over a week. I wonder if General Titan has made progress on that front. We need to get an update—and right away.

But one question stops me.

"Who's the new Supreme General of the California Federation?" I ask.

I have a feeling he's been keeping this from me, too. Not wanting to upset me.

"You're not going to like it."

"Just tell me."

He exhales. "Magnus Luther. Hardliner. Very connected at the fed."

My heart drops. "Asteroid fires . . . Jude's dad?"

"That's right. Your file indicates you attended high school with his son."

I'm still shocked. "He took over?"

He nods. "In the wake of the assassination and Earth Federation crumbling, he built support in California by calling for war against the Astrals, who he claims perpetrated the attack."

"That's bad," I mutter. "Like really, really bad. Jude was the worst bully in school—and Drae's best friend. Well, *former* best friend. But that's the problem. He makes a dangerous enemy."

Apollo nods, looking worried. "Well, my contacts say Luther used his son and his son's friends to stoke the campus unrest, then used that as a reason to build support for Earth rearmament."

"So, that was his plan all along?" I say in shock. "That's brilliant—and it'll probably work. That explains why the campuses are ground zero."

"Yes, Luther used the unrest at the colleges to drive up fear and support for his hardline, fascist policies. That's how democracy dies—by popular demand."

"Ugh, it's so sick. After Andromeda got killed, I bet the newsfeeds were practically begging Luther to take over."

A tense silence falls over us. He reaches for my hand and squeezes it, sending heat radiating through my body. I know this isn't the right time for this. But then again, maybe it is the right time . . . because it also might be the only time.

Everything's happening so fast. Everything is falling apart. The world feels like it's burning. The universe.

Everything.

And we're standing in the ash that's falling like rain, trying to salvage something from the wrath of the inferno.

"What do we do now?" I ask softly.

He strokes my cheek. He buries my gaze in the depths of his watery eyes.

He kisses me then.

Not hungrily, but sadly. Like he knows it might be our last kiss. Our goodbye kiss. I hold on to it because it's all I have. Because whatever Draeden and I had, whatever beautiful moments we shared, they're lost to us now, maybe forever.

A tear gathers at the corner of my eyes, and he kisses that away too, savoring the saltiness of my desolation, sharing in it.

We both know what we have to do now, even if it's risky and dangerous.

"How are you feeling?" he asks, stroking my cheek again, cradling it.

"Afraid. But strong, too."

"Kari, you don't have to do it. We can try to find another way—"

But I cut him off.

"No, this is the only way. The Astrals chose me. And we're running out of time. If we don't open those diplomatic channels, then war is coming. And it might be the last war we ever fight."

We both know it.

There's no turning back now. The wheels are turning, the gears clanking together like in the Campanile, our fates set into motion, and we are but actors on a larger stage, cast among the blood and stars, praying for peace in the face of a world that wants to burn.

Suddenly, another breaking newsfeed alert comes through, even though we're behind.

"War Declared on Astrals! Secretary-General Luther to Give Address at University of California, Berkeley." We both scan the newsfeed in our retinal displays.

"Oh no, Berkeley," I say with a rush of fear that threatens to steal my words. "Why would he speak at a college . . . of all places?"

"They're blaming the Astrals for the assassination," he says. "We don't have much time to stop this war. Now, I bet they move up their time frame for invasion."

Helplessness floods through me. I still care about Drae, even if I'm heartbroken. I don't want anything bad to befall him or the people we care about back Earthside. My family may be safe in the stars on my dad's ship, but for how long? With the fracturing of the Earth Federation, this war is destined to infect the stars, too. Nowhere is safe, and nobody will be safe from what's coming.

We both stand. He takes my hand, one last time, stroking my flesh, before dropping it and shifting back into CO mode with his underling at his side. I also stiffen up.

"What do we do now?"

"Hurry, the lab," he says. "We have to find out if General Titan and her team got that communication device working."

"But remember the shifter intel?" I say, following him toward the door. "How do we know we can trust her . . . that she's not a secret agent, or one of them?"

He frowns. "General Titan is a lot of things, but no way she's Astral. I've served with her before this outpost."

"But they could have replaced her. Like the bus driver."

"No way, I'd have noticed. Part of special ops is training not just to spy on your enemies," he says with a wink. "Let's just say, I keep a close eye on everyone. Including you, Captain Skye."

That sinks in. I wonder how much he knows about me sneaking off base to meet with my Raider father and about my connection to the Resistance on Earth.

It all goes unsaid—

But now I'm guessing a lot.

"Besides, what choice do we have?" he says, thrusting the door open. "Everything is happening fast. This is our only shot at stopping the war, right?"

"We'll have to be careful though. We don't know who we can trust anymore."

"You ready?"

Major Apollo waits for my go-ahead. We're standing in front of the wall to the secret lab. My head is spinning from everything that's happening and still a little jumbled from the heartbreak.

But I can't tell him that. Not with war and Earth rearmament imminent, unless we can find a way to prove the Astrals didn't kill Secretary-General Andromeda, but that it was a plot for fascists to take over—all lead by Jude Luther's dad.

The more I think about it, the more certain I am that Luther is behind this. The campus unrest. Using his son and his son's friends like Loki, who got transferred to another school, to stir the pot and stoke pro-genocide sentiment.

It's brilliant, really.

The Ringer kids all promised a future running the federation one day, all granted admission into the elite colleges, the perfect place to set it all into motion.

Then, once the cascades of explosions start with riots and unrest, to scare everyone via the newsfeeds into supporting Earth rearmament under the guise of "protecting our children."

A falsehood, for they won't be protected. Rearming Earth threatens every fragile bit of peace that we've rebuilt since the last Great War. And with the coming Astral invasion—*EARTH! EARTH! EARTH!*—there won't be any bastions of humanity left alive anyway.

But small people who lust for power will use anything they can to get it.

Blast the consequences.

This cascade of thoughts flashes through my mind in high-speed. But another thought breaks through—

KARI, IT'S NOT TOO LATE!

YOU CAN STOP IT.

DON'T LOSE HOPE.

NOW.

I blink hard, shocked by the clarity of the message. Is it them . . . or is my brain that damaged and fractured? Can I even trust my own thoughts anymore?

"Kari, you okay?"

That snaps me back to reality. Major Apollo watches me with great concern.

"No, but I don't have a choice. This is our only chance to avert the invasion."

The wall in front of us looks ordinary. But Apollo stands right in front of us.

"General Titan, let us in," he says. "She's ready . . . it's time."

My heart drops. So, she's been waiting for me to be strong enough for this.

Beep!

The wall starts to unfold like I saw my first day on base. The solid barrier breaks apart, revealing a secret door. We step through, then it reseals behind us.

Inside, it's total chaos, with scientists in white lab coats rushing around, fiddling with their tablets and the electronic machines that pack the austere space.

"What're they doing?" I gasp.

"Trying to get it working, I'm guessing," Apollo says, taking it in. "And with everything happening back Earthside, we're running out of the most precious resource in the universe."

"Time," I realize.

"Exactly. Hurry, we need to find her. I'm not allowed back here usually. This is General Titan's domain. She just gave me strict orders to bring you to her when you were ready to test the device out."

"Why didn't you tell me?"

"Because it was important to me that you made the choice for yourself."

I nod. "Thank you. I mean it."

That's when General Titan appears, less composed than usual. She's a bit breathless, with strands of hair escaping from her tight bun. We snap salutes.

"At ease, Major . . . Captain." She taps at her tablet. "You're just in time."

"Is it working?" I ask nervously. "The communication device."

She blinks—a split-second reaction—but I notice it. Then she recovers.

"We hope so," she says. "We have a prototype that will connect to your neural link. But we need to test it on you first."

She gestures to the corridor and marches off. "Follow me, please."

I start to get a bad feeling as we head deeper into the cavern. Suddenly, crystal light veins appear in the walls, making it clear that this used to belong to them.

The Astrals.

Clearly, this base was built on top of one of their settlements. I feel Major Apollo tense up beside me. He didn't know either. He's just realizing it, too.

We enter a large cavern that's been converted into a laboratory. There's a chamber with a device that looks like it goes over my head to connect to my implant. Wires run out of it, feeding directly into the crystalline veins that run through the walls, pulsing with energy.

"Welcome to my secret weapons research laboratory," General Titan says.

That's when I see something that I will never forget as long as I live.

I stare in shock—

On either side, rooms appear carved into solid rock. Electric force fields have been erected to seal them off. I see bodies behind the barriers—flashes of light—flinging themselves at the barriers.

HELP US! KARI, HELP US!

SAVE US!

PLEASE!

Their thoughts hit me all at once in a chorus of voices, calling for help. They're Astrals being held prisoner . . . and I have a sinking feeling . . . General Titan has been experimenting on them this whole time. Torturing them, from the looks of it.

They fling themselves at the energy barrier, only to be shocked and flung back, where they flicker and shrivel in pain. I can hear their tortured cries.

And the communication device? I'm getting a bad feeling that it's not what I intended—clearly, it's a weapon.

She said it herself.

Weapons research.

"Captain Skye," Titan goes on with a cruel smile. "I can't thank you enough. Without your discoveries, I don't know that my project would've succeeded."

"Wh-what do you mean?" I ask, feeling suddenly sick and backing away.

"Oh yes," General Titan says. "Meet our little friends. They're quite dramatic."

"What are . . . they?" I say, unable to keep my voice even. The voices bombard me, shrieking even louder for my help.

From her calm demeanor, I'm guessing I'm the only one who can hear them.

"Test subjects," General Titan says in a cold voice. "Technically, they're prisoners of war. Pretty neat trick, huh? We used their own tech to imprison them."

"Astrals! You're experimenting on them," I say in an accusing voice.

General Titan gives me a hard look. "We figured out how to hurt them, even kill a few. But they're surprisingly resilient. Their energy recharges . . . we're not sure how. However, thanks to you, we finally found a way to annihilate them."

"Annihilate?" I hiss, feeling my stomach turn. "You mean, genocide?"

She shrugs. "Such a nasty little word. But yes—precisely. Every last one of them. They've been a threat to humanity for too long. They're the plague on the universe. That's why I've dedicated my research to one thing—destroying them."

She gestures to the machine connected to the crystalline light veins in the walls.

"And you're going to help me do it."

My knees buckle.

I can't believe it.

They're using what I discovered about the Astrals not for peace—but to destroy them.

And I'm the one who's going to help them do it.

CHAPTER 51

DRAE

Attendance at Secretary-General Luther's speech is mandatory. It almost looks like a graduation ceremony. White folding chairs are lined up in neat rows on the perfectly manicured lawn. Students shuffle in and take their seats.

A stage has been erected with a press pool in front of it to maximize the photo opportunity. The only signs that anything is amiss are the Fed Patrols roaming the perimeters and scanning everyone, and the graffiti marking the buildings.

Some of it has been removed, but a lot of it remains stubbornly plastered to the old brick-and-mortar facades. Most are Anti-Astral and pro-genocide tags. But I spot one "Disarm the Stars!" still intact.

That gives me hope.

Some of us remain to fight.

Even from the shadows.

"Any idea what this Luther's speech is about?" Willow whispers to me as we make our way to Memorial Glade.

She made it back before dawn, chauffeured by my transport. And with good news. Thankfully, after some touch and go moments when her blood pressure tanked a few times, she's going to pull through. The Resistance has a lot of allies.

One happened to be a trauma surgeon in Berkeley. That just saved her life.

But after the news that Trebond got arrested, I couldn't stand the thought of losing Xena, too. She's second-in-command under the Old Lady and vital to all the Resistance operations. Without both of them, it would be a major blow.

Captain Skye—Kari's father—remains in charge in the stars. But he's far away and has his hands full with the Raiders and our Space Force allies. Who would be left to lead our Earthside efforts?

"The usual war-mongering?" I whisper back. "Annihilate the Astrals."

"Definitely a lot of bluster," she agrees. "According to our contacts in the fed, Earth rearmament is imminent . . ."

"They're already mobilizing?"

She sets her lips. "I think the first platoon is being recalled from space next week. But they won't be the last . . ."

"To secure the colleges?"

"Our sources say that's why he canceled classes—it's unsafe. We need more security. Hence, guardians . . ."

"Soldiers? On campus?"

"Yup, it's a war zone. Literally."

I take all that in. "But the Proxies will follow suit. They won't let California be the only federation with military stationed Earthside. Plus, we'd be violating the Peace Treatise . . ."

"Exactly. That gives them all the green light to do the same. If we break the promise that Secretary-General Trantor made all those years ago after the war."

"Everything Trebond feared is coming true . . ." I say in a dark voice.

Suddenly, a siren blares—

And we skid to a halt. My heart plummets through my chest, even though I should be used to these intrusions.

The Fed Patrol rolls up to us. "Halt for scanning," it barks. Then a laser shoots out to scan our retinas and identify us.

"Proceed," it declares finally.

I wait while Willow goes through the same demeaning procedure. Then we hurry toward the seating area. There's a VIP section cordoned off at the front.

"Look over there. I wonder who that's for . . ." I point the section out to Willow.

But I don't have to wait long for an answer. Suddenly, I hear a familiar voice.

It calls to me across the lawn.

"Draeden!"

I freeze, my heart dropping. Only one person still uses my full moniker.

A deeper voice accompanies it.

"We thought we'd surprise you!"

A woman decked out in Space Force regalia decorated with pins and medals waves to me, while her husband smiles. He's dressed in his usual black suit and shiny black shoes that fed agents wear.

"Oh no, is that your . . ." Willow starts.

"Ugh, it's my parents," I hiss back. "Of course they're here. My dad works with Luther. He probably gave my dad a big promotion for backing the hardliners."

"And your mother, the war hero," she whispers back. "Only . . . it was all a cover-up that framed Kari's father for murder and desertion. I read your file."

"That about sums it up."

I want to avoid them more than I've ever wanted to avoid anything my whole life. But they're smiling and waving.

I don't have a choice.

I put on a big smile and dig deep to play the part of their successful college son. Impulsively, I grab Willow's hand and drag her along. I need a shield if I'm going to pull this little act off. Plus, she's more than proven her thespian chops.

"Uh, what are you doing?" she hisses.

"Just follow my lead and play along," I mutter through my big, fake smile. "I'm improvising, and you're good at that."

I drag her over to the VIP section by the front of the stage, right behind the press pool, where the photographers and newsfeed reporters are standing by.

"Mom . . . Dad . . . what a surprise!" I say, grabbing at my chest to pantomime a heart attack. "You really got me . . ."

"Well, you've been hard to reach lately," Dad says, reminding me how many calls have gone to voicemail.

In my defense, I was warping to interstellar space, and then out of commission. But I can't tell them that.

Trebond arranged for their messages to get intercepted and returned with text replies instead to put them off my case.

"Uh, sorry . . ." I try to sound genuinely remorseful. "It's just been super hectic on campus . . ." I lower my voice. "I've been helping Jude with his little pet project, if you catch my drift . . ."

Their eyes widen. "I told you he's been a busy boy," Dad says, elbowing her.

"Good job, son," Mom says in an approving voice. "I'm glad you're on the right side of history . . ." She trails off, making it clear that they were worried about where my true allegiances lay.

I've known that was the case since last year, when Jude was spying on me, reporting on my friendship with Rho and newly discovered reading habits.

"And who's this?" Mom says.

She narrows her eyes, fixing on Willow. Before I can say anything, she jumps in, blushing and leaning into me.

"Drae, aren't you going to tell them?"

"Uh, right . . ."

"Tell us . . . *what*?" Mom demands.

"Yeah, what's the big secret?" Dad adds. Even he looks suspicious now.

I swallow hard—

And force the words out.

"This is Willow . . . my girlfriend."

I can't believe I just said that. They both look surprised, then they start to grill her. Asking about where she's from, her family, what she's studying here.

Luckily, Willow is a pro. Her cover story gushes out from her lips effortlessly, while her mannerisms are polite, shy, and friendly, everything they're hoping for.

"And tell me more about you," she says, deftly changing the subject. "I know you're a war hero, Sergeant Rache. I just want to thank you for your service and your sacrifice for our great federation."

Willow just spoke the magic words. My mom practically transforms under her praise and fawning. She straightens her shoulders, standing up straighter.

"I'm proud to have done my duty." She trades a glance with my father. "Well, we are simply thrilled to meet you."

"Yeah, I was wondering when he'd shack up with the old ball-and-chain."

Mom rolls her eyes. "Please, they're in college and dating. Don't start planning their wedding already!"

They both laugh.

"Oh, I don't mind," Willow says. "Drae is such a catch. A girl can dream."

"So can a mother," she replies.

"What about the dad?" he adds.

"Looks like the pressure is on," Willow says, batting her eyelashes and pouting.

I chuckle and play along, pulling her closer and kissing her on the forehead.

"There's no pressure when it comes to you! I'm the one who's dreaming . . ."

Everyone laughs. My father leans in and whispers in my ear. "Son, now I know why you've been so busy . . ."

He raises his eyebrows suggestively. I blush, uncomfortable with the lewd comment. But I'm also thankful. Willow really is a great alibi and perfect cover.

But then something makes my stomach flip. I catch sight of Jude sitting in the VIP section with his cronies.

He glares at me. That's when I look down and realize—

I'm still holding Willow's hand.

I drop it cold right then. But it's too late. He's seen the whole charade.

He looks jealous. But I notice something else, too. Dark circles line his eyes. His face looks gaunt and haggard, not clean-shaven. Willow was right . . .

He looks afraid.

But of what?

Before I can worry about it any more, everything gets underway. Patriotic music blares over the loudspeakers. It's our national anthem, swelling to a crescendo.

Willow and I hurry back to our seats with the other students. I'm grateful to be away from my parents. I don't have to play the part of the perfect son anymore.

The music builds in volume, drawing cheers from the crowd. I find myself clapping along, mouthing the words.

Even though I'm disillusioned, the music from the post-war era still makes me feel emotional. It reminds me what I'm fighting for—Secretary-General Trantor would be rolling over in his grave with everything that's happening.

He was the architect behind Earth disarmament and the historic Peace Treatise. He saw the aftermath of the Great War. The death toll and destruction of large swatches of our planet that still remain radioactive and uninhabitable.

He fought for peace.

Just like us.

But he failed to achieve full disarmament. We just exported our militaries to space and kept enlisting kids and shipping them up there to die, far away from Earth, where life continued, blissfully unaware of the loss of life, insulated from the carnage of the forever wars and the damage wrought in space.

Like what happened to the Astral settlement, when that Proxy war broke out over resources, and we slaughtered their civilian population and started the war.

Now, they're coming for us.

And our response?

To match violence for violence, defaulting to a military solution, one that's sure to get us blistered this time. Not just California, but humanity.

All these thoughts cascade through my head in a kinetic rush that thumps my heart and makes blood thrum in my veins. I have to hold fast to what I believe.

Or everything is lost.

We are the front lines—

And we have to keep fighting.

I try to remember that as Secretary-General Luther strides out onto the stage. I reach for Willow's hand, needing some reassurance that I'm not in this alone.

I don't care if Jude notices. And something else—it just feels right. Introducing her to my parents did, too. That makes me feel horribly guilty.

But my mother hates Kari and her family. There's zero chance they would ever accept her as my girlfriend. Even suggesting that would get me disowned.

Don't get me wrong. I don't like my parents—but I still love them. I know that sounds crazy given everything that's happened and the pro-war beliefs.

But I can't help it.

They're my only parents. My mother is flawed, but she has space trauma. Her service turned her into a twisted shell of herself and warped her mind this way.

And my father?

He's a true patriot, through and through. He lives and breathes for the federation—and he would die for it, too. He's committed to my mother. I have to respect them on some level for their beliefs, even as it alienates me from them.

They don't know better. That's part of it. They weren't really given much of a choice. She enlisted, while Dad followed my path to college and then a cushy government job that promised him this.

A place in the leadership.

They didn't have a professor like Trebond to pierce the veil and open their eyes to the dark truth of our world, and show them that there was another way.

Mr. Egbert, my old high school teacher turned professor, climbs the stage.

"Please welcome the dean of the University of California, Berkeley," blares over the loudspeakers, shocking me.

"He's the dean now?" I hiss to Willow.

"Of course—he's a fed stooge," she whispers back. "Luther's puppet."

But this is the moment where I feel everything breaking inside me, and what I thought was a bastion of higher learning that could save me from myself and help me change into a better person, dies.

"Today, I'm thrilled to announce," he speaks into the podium, "Secretary-General Luther has chosen our great institution to make a historic speech about the future of our great federation."

Applause rings out from the audience, as flashbulbs flicker from the press pool.

"Please join me in giving him a proper UC Berkeley welcome," Egbert finishes.

The music starts up again, only more somber this time to signal the tonal shift. More flashes, and then—

Secretary-General Luther steps out of the armored transport, flanked by his security. Only I notice something different. They're wearing Space Force armbands—and they're armed with blasters. The sidearms are clearly visible.

On purpose.

To make a point.

We knew it was coming, but it's still shocking to see weapons being blatantly paraded out Earthside for the cameras.

I give Luther a once-over. His sharp face is framed by blond hair peppered with gray. He looks like an older version of Jude, except for his sizable paunch.

I remember when he came to campus with my father to search Professor Trebond's room after they tried to arrest her, but she got the jump on them and took off before they could catch her.

And now, he finally got her.

Watching him, anger surges through me, despite my history with him as a kid. I glance at Jude, expecting him to be on his feet, cheering . . . but it's the opposite. He almost looks repulsed.

That worries me. What happened between them? What does Jude know?

Luther reaches the podium and beams for the cameras. Unlike Andromeda, he's not camera-friendly. His demeanor is gruff, even stern, and authoritarian.

"The California Federation remains strong in the wake of the horrible assassination of Secretary-General Andromeda," Luther declares, managing to sound bereaved, though it doesn't reach his eyes, which remain sharp.

On the large screen behind him, the California Federation seal morphs into her face—short, gray bob framing her weathered face and piercing blue eyes.

So alive in the picture—

Yet no longer breathing. Obliterated to pieces in that horrible terrorist attack.

I shudder as the screen shifts to show her death, broadcast live on the newsfeeds. It ends with the podium replaced by flames and then smoke.

A deep hush falls over the crowd, then it turns to fiery anger. Just as Luther intended. I notice his lips twitch at it.

Cries come from the crowd—

"Annihilate the Astrals!"

"Death to the Invaders!"

Jude stands and pumps his fist in the air, rallying his minions, who join him.

Luther basks in the insurrection. The Fed Patrols don't try to quell this unrest.

It's state sanctioned.

Willow and I parrot the chants, not wanting to stick out in the crowd . . . for obvious reasons. What happened to Trebond and Xena remains fresh in my mind. I glance at my parents. Despite her disability, my mother is on her feet.

Her face contorts with hatred. I imagine it's the same expression she had when she turned on her own platoon, mistaking them for enemy soldiers. Meanwhile, my father stands and claps politely, ever the dignitary. They make a good team stationed in their VIP seats.

"I'm so proud my son attends this great institution of learning," Luther goes on. "We also commemorate the victims of the Golden Gate Attack. I ask for a moment of silence for everyone we lost."

The silence engulfs the crowd. I bow my head and shut my eyes. But my heart is beating faster in anticipation of what Luther is going to announce today.

After the requisite time elapses, he launches back into his speech. His tone turns noticeably sharper and darker.

"Today marks a new era in our war against the Astrals. I hereby declare martial law and request that guardians immediately be stationed on Earth to protect us from these terrorist attacks."

Even the crowd is shocked by this declaration. This marks the end of the Peace Treatise officially. Even though we knew it was coming, the reality hits different, harder and deeper.

Slowly, the applause trickles back, then builds into a standing ovation.

"We are the California Federation," Luther goes on. "The Proxies are not our allies or equals—they serve us now."

Flashes explode from the press pool, while the crowd keeps cheering him on. I reach over and clasp Willow's hand.

"Asteroid fires . . ." I whisper.

"This is bad," she whispers back.

The press and cheering crowd mean one thing. His nationalism and authoritarianism are being approved and transmitted across the federation.

Without free press, there is nobody to dissent or offer a different opinion. I can still see the ash from all the burned books tarnishing the lawn underneath the stage.

I feel sick, watching this fascist charade. I spot a few other DTSA members in the crowd, but we all act the part. It's too dangerous to give it away.

"I have several other important announcements today," Luther continues. "Henceforth, we are formally suspending the Sympathetic Program. Upon further review, we have found it to be a dangerous initiative that fosters resistance and dissidents. We cannot allow it to continue under our great federation."

I gasp, feeling the blood drain from my face. When he says that, his eyes find me in the crowd—and narrow sharply.

Is he talking about me . . . and Kari?

Before I can react, searing pain cuts through my skull, right at the base of my skull. It takes a moment before I realize what's happening—they're disconnecting my neural implant. I can feel it fizzling.

I sink down into my chair, grabbing at my head. The agony consumes me.

Estrella, I think urgently, *are you there?*

But only the silence of my mind answers. My last remaining link to Kari—

It's gone just like that.

Willow tries to soothe me, but my desolation can't be kept at bay.

While Luther watches from his perch, other students around us do the same thing. All must have been in the program.

I notice the DTSA members all clutching their heads. So they were all in the program like me—all paired with guardians. That's why they wanted to fight for peace. So, Luther is right.

But not fully. The program doesn't create dissidents. It fosters empathy and lets us see what's really happening in the stars, unlike most people Earthside who remain happily oblivious to the lives lost, to the sacrifice of blood and stars.

"I thank you all for your service, but now you are free to return to your lives and pursue your studies," Luther says. "Without the temptation that the program fostered within our vulnerable youth."

The crowd cheers, but this time, it sounds forced. Like they're afraid of him—and afraid to be caught not approving.

His security detail is busy scanning the crowd, looking for anything amiss—

With their blasters at the ready.

That isn't lost on the crowd.

Finally, the searing pain in my head relents, but the emptiness might be worse. Since that day we got paired, I've never been truly alone. I always had Estrella, my neural implant, and it connected me to Kari through our weekly messages.

Now, that's all gone.

And I broke her heart.

What hope is there that we could come back from that? Another terrible thought occurs to me. Was our connection only because of the program? Did we really love each other, or did it manipulate us?

Like Luther claims?

Before I can dwell on it, or process my complicated feelings and grief, something worse happens. Luther signals to his armed security detail. They march over to an armored transport idling by the stage.

They doors pop open—

And they drag Trebond out. She fights, but they force her to the stage. Her eyes lock onto me and Willow—*I'm sorry.*

That's all she mouths.

And then, I feel my knees buckle and like everything I had in this world—my connection to Kari, my professor and mentor and Resistance leader—is being forcefully taken from me in this moment.

And there's nothing I can do.

CHAPTER 52

KARI

"No, I won't help you," I say, backing away from General Titan in horror. "Genocide goes against everything I elite in! Everything Space Force stands for!"

"Oh, you're so naïve," General Titan says, rolling her eyes. "You're green as the fluorescent turf back Earthside. Talk to me after you've experienced real war."

She hikes her pants leg up, exposing the robotic prothesis that replaced her appendage below the knee. She flexes, the joints whirring and working perfectly.

"That's not a justification." I stare her down. "Two wrongs don't make a right."

She scoffs at me, dropping her pants back down to cover it. "This program isn't wrong," she continues. "It's the future. Soon, you'll understand that."

Meanwhile, Major Apollo looks paralyzed, torn between two opposing forces—his underling and secret lover, and his commanding officer.

But the way his face is drained of color tells me that he didn't know either.

And he's equally shocked.

I know I'm supposed to fall into line like a good officer and obey my orders. This is way above my pay grade. But that's where she's wrong—I'm not that green. I've seen real war. It took my father away from me when I was just a kid.

That whole stopping the last invasion thing? Well, we fought our way through that, too. War isn't just visceral carnage, it's psychological, and sometimes that part is more damaging. Those scars are invisible, but they run just as deep, maybe deeper.

I think of Drae's mother on her armchair, dulled by pills and whiskey, watching the newsfeeds nonstop. She has injuries, but also space trauma. And how many other veterans? The collateral damage of our forever wars in the stars.

"That's the thing—you need my help," I say, grasping for any way out of this. "But what if I refuse? Your project won't work. You need me because they chose me. I'm the link to them, right?"

"Well, we can do this the easy way." She shrugs. "Or the hard way. I had hoped you'd see reason. They're our enemies, Captain. Don't get it twisted."

"Only because we attacked them and killed them first! We stared the war!"

"Ah, yes. Unfortunate that you managed to find a record of that. I tried to bury it. Using the Sympathetic Program recordings? That was quite clever."

"So it was you . . . the whole time."

"Guilty as charged," she says. "But too bad I have been granted immunity. This program was sanctioned by the highest level of the Earth Federation."

But that's when I see them.

Strategically placed guardians armed with blasters standing by the door.

It's a subtle shift.

But they move their hands to their weapons, releasing the safety at their touch. I go to reach for my blaster—

But I grip air.

Of course, my sidearm was taken from me when I was rushed to the infirmary. I didn't even realize it. Not that I could fight my way out of the secret lab.

I'm outnumbered and trapped.

I start to hyperventilate, my head swimming. Black edges creep into my vision. *SAVE US, KARI!* The chorus bombards my sensitive neurons.

But I'm helpless, I think in desperation.

Their voices answer in a chorus.

YOU AREN'T ALONE! WE ARE HERE! WE ARE WITH YOU! ALWAYS WITH YOU. YOU ARE NEVER ALONE.

The guardians start to approach with their blasters drawn. They grab my arms and start forcing me toward the machine. But Apollo jumps between us, blocking them. "Stop now! That's an order."

They halt, glancing from him to Titan, unsure of whose orders to follow.

He whips around to face Titan.

"General, what are you doing?" Apollo demands. His fingers twitch at his blaster. But he doesn't draw it . . . yet.

"Don't act so shocked, Major." General Titan frowns. "Remember your place."

But he doesn't back down. "I can't believe we've had POWs locked up down here. And I didn't know about it."

His gaze flicks to the cells, where the light-beings are being imprisoned. They flicker in pain, begging for their freedom.

Apollo flinches at the sight of it.

But Titan remains stone-faced. "Major, this lab necessitates the highest levels of security clearance. Only the secretary general knew. But alas, she's dead . . ."

"So, who's in charge of the program now?" he demands. "Luther?"

She frowns, "He hasn't been briefed yet. The Earth Federation is no more."

"So you answer to . . ."

She flashes a devilish smile.

"Nobody, technically. Now, you're catching on!" She whirls around. "Luther may have coalesced power Earthside, but up here in space, it's a power vacuum."

The pun seems intended from the evil way she smiles just then. "Who's to keep us from seizing control now?" she goes on. "You can be my second-in-command."

Major Apollo looks . . . incensed. Anger wafts off him like heat. But then, he works hard to control his emotions. "So, this was your plan? The whole time?"

General Titan takes a step closer to him. "Alistair, but don't you see?"

I gape at the informal use of his name. She drags her hand across his cheek, making him flinch. But he doesn't fully move away from her. And now I have to wonder the true nature of their relationship. My heart thumps harder.

Jealousy.

It was primed by Drae, but now it roars through me like a torrent.

How could he?

Seduce me?

And they have a history. Why didn't I see it before? Of course he does. Something about him just gets inside your head. He's so intensely sexy. The way he breaks boundaries—and seems to see something inside you that nobody else has ever seen or understood.

He's damn near irresistible.

And not just to me, apparently. His charms travel far and wide through space.

I'm such a fool to fall for it.

Almost like he hears my thought, he grabs her hand and flings it away.

"That was a *long* time ago."

"Oh, so now there's a statute of limitations to love?"

"It wasn't love—it was lust," he spits at her. "And I broke it off."

"Oh, and you requested a transfer. What a shame. But I never stopped thinking about you—and what you did to me when nobody was watching us."

"I've spent every day trying to forget," he says, glaring at her. "That's long over. Dead and buried. It was years ago."

"Ha, sure! Is that what you tell yourself to sleep at night?" She purses her lips. "When I came calling, you were so eager to transfer out here. You practically begged me to add you to my team."

He looks hurt. "It wasn't for you—it was for the mission—to stop the war. I didn't love you, but I believed in your work and what you were doing . . ." He gestures to the cells with the Astrals. "But not like this!" He gives her a pleading look. "Alicia, you've changed! The old you would never commit war crimes . . . in the name of science!"

"Maybe you didn't know me as well as you think!" she scoffs. "But you sure came running as soon as I sent for you."

She goes to touch him again, but he knocks her hand away like it's poisonous.

Now, it's her turn to look incensed. She glares at him.

"Too bad, Alistair," she says in a sorrowful voice. "I thought we had a future together. Regardless, I suggest you pick your side soon. And choose wisely."

He narrows his eyes at her. "What do you mean?"

She gives him a seductive look. "Don't you see? Luther may be seen as Earth's savior right now with his petty warmongering and flimsy charades. But it won't last. The Astrals are coming."

She leans closer, whispering in his ear. "But what if I'm the one who destroys them? Then I'm the savior of humanity."

"No, you're a war criminal."

"Yeah, right—more like war hero!"

"Not from my perspective. You're just like the greatest monsters in history."

"Oh, I don't think so. That all depends on the point of view. The winners write the history lessons. I'll be heralded as the greatest war hero. Celebrated for ages. They'll build statues of me. And nobody—not Luther and certainly not you—will be able to stop me from ascending to the leadership of Earthside and space, too."

Apollo just looks disgusted. "Save it for your speeches. I know you—the *real* you. You don't want to save humanity, you want to gain power. There's a difference. People will see through it."

"Oh, will they? With the newsfeeds in my control? Plus, I'll command Space Force. Earthside is disarmed, weak and defenseless. They can't fight back."

"You wouldn't dare turn Space Force against Earthside," he says, shocked.

"Oh, I hope it doesn't come to that. The Proxies are weak and afraid. Luther is a coward. So, who will dare oppose me?"

Her plan is brilliant and chilling, and I'm caught at the center of it.

Sadness washes off his face. "Alicia, I knew you were ambitious. But I thought you'd use your position for good."

She shrugs. "Shows how well you knew me. Maybe I was faking it too?"

Cruelty tips her words. But then she gets back down to business. "Luther is probably making his speech. Puffing out his chest. I'll let him act the part, until I'm ready to reveal my true power."

She shifts her gaze to me.

"And for the next part, I need you." She flicks her wrist to the guardians.

They drag me over to her.

"How . . . does it work?" I say, stalling for time and intel. Some way to get out of this mess . . . before it's too late to stop her.

"Ha, I thought nobody would think to ask me!" Now she looks positively gleeful. "We did our own tests on these . . . *subjects*," she says with disdain, nodding at the Astrals locked up. "Looking for their weakness. But as you can see for yourself, they weren't very cooperative."

She turns back to me. "So, we were stumped. That part is true. Until you came along, my dear! What a brilliant idea from Alistair, too! He saw something in you that I would've missed. In fact, when you first showed up on base, I thought he made a terrible mistake."

"Wh-what do you mean?" I stammer.

"Asteroid fires, you were so pathetic! Weak and afraid. But then, I saw your Sympathetic scores were off the charts. That was the first sign that he was right."

"Kari, I'm so sorry," Apollo says in a remorseful voice. "That I dragged you into this mess. It's all my fault . . ."

"Oh, do shut up," Titan says with a grimace. "You've grown so tiresome and pathetic with that wounded puppy act."

He flinches like she slapped him. But I can tell he really meant what he said. However, I need to keep her talking, keep her spilling her guts to me. She's so hyped up on her nefarious plan that she wants to brag about it, and Apollo isn't about it.

So, it has to be me.

"And then, I got into the settlement," I chime in. "When everybody else failed."

"Yes, and made a critical discovery," Titan says, flicking at her tablet and pulling up images on the screens. "You were correct in your hypotheses, too."

"The neural connection?"

She nods. "It made sense, too. Your measurements were off the chart. That allowed them to tap into your neural implant somehow . . . and talk to you."

What I don't mention is that they've been talking to me ever since. Even when I'm not on their settlement. I'm sure of it now. Through my dreams turned nightmares, but now in real time.

I hear their voices in my head.

I don't know how they're doing it. But I'm certain. The proof? My gut feeling.

To quote Apollo.

But I can't tell her that. She flicks through the screens, landing on a technical readout of the device.

"You poor, naïve soul," Titan goes on. "It was actually your idea to find a way for you to communicate with them."

My heart sinks at that news.

"But instead, you made a weapon?"

"Not just any weapon—a *psychic* weapon," she confirms. "Basically, it's a mind virus. You said it yourself. They're all linked together through their neural networks, akin to our implants, but much more powerful and with no lag time."

"A mind virus?" I say, realizing that's bad. "What does it do exactly . . ."

"Ah, we use you as the Trojan horse to deliver it right into their neural network. Once inserted, it will spread like a computer virus, infecting all of their minds and shattering them, thus eradicating the Astrals in one fell swoop."

She smiles darkly. "The prototype should be working. We just need to hook you up and test it out." She nods to the prisoners. "We'll try on one of them first."

"And even if I consent to be your Trojan horse, not that you care," I say in a shaky voice. "Wh-what happens to me?"

She shrugs. "You survived your little stay in the infirmary," she says, shocking me. "Oh, I know all about your little rendezvous with your lover boy."

"Wait, you knew about that?"

She nods. "But look at you! Surprisingly resilient, just like them. You survived getting your mind shattered."

"So, I'll survive your little experiment?" I say, feeling sickened.

"I can't promise it won't hurt like hell. But my projections indicate that you should survive Phase One," she goes on. "Which is important, of course. Because I need you alive for Phase Two."

I swallow hard. "And what's that?"

"Annihilation," she says. "Or maybe you prefer your favorite term?"

"Genocide."

"Ah, semantics," she says. "But as for Phase Two? You're not likely to survive that one. I mean, the mind virus will eventually infect you and destroy you."

I start shaking violently when she says that, but the guardians hold me up. Then, something worse happens.

It's Apollo.

"General, I've made up my mind," he says, approaching her. "You're right. I need to choose sides."

"And?" she says, skeptical.

"I choose you," he says, coming closer. "This could end the war. Once and for all. A weapon to destroy the threat forever."

"So, you see reason now?" she says, still hesitant. "You know, it's not the first time a great weapon has been developed to end a war. The atomic bomb, for example. But there are so many more."

"I'm sorry . . . I lost it," he says. "I was just shocked. And betrayed that you'd keep something this big from me."

He lays his hand on her cheek. She softens when he does that. "Alicia, I thought . . . we were different. That we didn't keep secrets from each other." He looks down. "I was hurt."

"And why should I believe you now?" she says, but it's clear she's in his thrall.

"This is why . . ."

With that, he leans in and kisses her deeply, passionately, like it will never end.

Just like he kissed me.

So, he is a traitor. I was wrong to trust him. My heart shrivels and breaks again.

I thought once it broke that it wasn't possible for it to break again. I can't believe how wrong I was . . . so very wrong. It seems the organ has the infinite ability to swell with love, but also to break, over and over again, until it stops beating and you gasp your last breath.

It feels like a million years when he finally pulls back from kissing her.

They're both flushed.

"Alicia, just let me be the one to do it," he whispers. "I want to prove myself."

"Good boy," she says approvingly. "Once we get her into the device, it will disable her ability to resist our orders."

"That's brilliant," he says. "So, she will be like our puppet?"

"Indeed. Now you're getting it."

He turns to me with dead eyes. Like all the light has drained out of them.

I don't even recognize him.

That's when the bottom drops out. He orders the guardians to stand down.

He takes my arms, roughly, and forces me toward the chair. There's nothing I can do about it. I want to fight back, try to escape, but I can't . . . I'm just too broken.

By everything.

I thought Drae was the worst thing that could happen to me, but I was wrong. Apollo is a million times worse.

"*How could you?*" I hiss at him.

"*I'm sorry . . .*" he whispers back.

Something in me dies in that moment, too. Something important. Something that's core to my very being. Even the Astrals' voices fade out when it happens.

He didn't blast me—but he killed me.

Titan doesn't hear us. She's turned away to pick up the helmet contraption that jacks into my neural implant—and will hijack my brain and make me do what I'm told like a good soldier.

I watch helplessly as it's lowered over my head—closer and closer—and the Astral screams break through my brain.

But I'm trapped.

CHAPTER 53

DRAE

The rest of the ceremony is a blur. I don't know if it's because I'm shocked, my brain is too damaged from the heartbreak and neural implant being disconnected, or because my fragile psyche can't handle it. Most likely?

All of the above.

Willow digs her nails into my hand, while my heart drops like a rock. Trebond struggles, but they force her to her knees.

"Lilly Trebond is a dissident and leader of the terrorist Resistance group. I led the investigation to apprehend her for teaching non-federation-approved curriculum, but she became a fugitive."

Hushed whispering cuts through the crowd. Finally, Jude looks excited.

"I made it my mission to track her down and apprehend her . . . personally."

Cheers erupt at that statement. I can't believe it. That means Luther led the raid himself on Resistance headquarters. I have a sick feeling my father was there, too. I can't help but wonder what they found, if it could implicate us.

"I hereby reinstate capital punishment in the California Federation with my powers under martial law . . ." He gives her a hard look. "I order her executed by blaster squad."

Shocked whispers cut through the crowd. A few students faint on the spot.

This is taking it much further than anyone expected. Even my mother looks troubled for a quick moment *just a split second of doubt*—but then she covers it.

But I notice it.

Is it her space trauma at the sight of the blasters? Or finally, she sees the dark side of following these beliefs to their bitter end? However, Jude no longer has any qualms. He cheers boisterously, looking triumphant that his old professor finally got what she deserved.

My head spins, and I feel sick, but I have to do something . . . anything. I lurch to my feet, staggering toward the stage, but a hand clamps down on my arm. And holds me firmly in place.

A voice hisses in my ear—

"Don't . . . you . . . dare . . ."

It's Willow.

I look over with a start. "Look, they're going to . . . blast her . . ." I stammer.

But she doesn't let go. "Drae, you're too important. We need you alive."

The flashbulbs explode rapid-fire, while I try to keep from losing it—or doing something crazy. Trebond is dragged to the grassy lawn and tied to a lamppost.

They blindfold her.

Then the security detail lines up with their blasters and levy them at her.

She doesn't cower. She squares her shoulders . . . like the guardian she was . . .

"Disarm the Stars!" she chants in a clear voice.

Secretary-General Luther looks livid. "What are you idiots waiting for?" he seethes into the microphone, clearly furious that they didn't gag her. "Fire your blasters—kill her!"

Still, they hesitate to shoot.

Trebond seizes on the moment.

"This is wrong! It goes against everything we stand for as a federation! If you're listening—if you hear me—don't let them continue to tarnish our stars with blood!"

Her voice echoes out, loud and clear.

The crowd looks appalled by the display. The flashbulbs explode faster, catching every moment in vivid detail. I'm sure this must be live streaming on all the newsfeeds. So, while they could edit the footage later, her message was broadcast. And it can't be taken back now.

Tears threaten to spill from my eyes.

I blink them back, hoping everyone is focused on her, and not looking in our direction.

"Fight to disarm the stars and for peace before it's too late—"

Luther leans into the microphone, spittle flying out. Feedback explodes in a high-pitched squeal, making everyone cringe, along with his command. "Execute her . . . now!"

Finally, that kicks them into motion.

The blaster squad fires. One first, then the others in quick succession.

The shots explode—

They hit her square in the chest, smoking her fatigues and crumpling her to the ground. She collapses in a heap. The sharp tang of burning fills the lawn. It doesn't smell clean like the books when they burned. I realize—

It's the stench of singed flesh.

Chased by my own fury. Her chest smokes like her beloved books did. I swallow down bile as we stand and cheer. We have no choice. But I notice a shift in the tenor of the applause. It's more perfunctory, less lively. Even Jude looks a little shocked at the live execution.

Most of them have never been around munitions, let alone witnessed somebody dying in front of their eyes. My mother has . . . and that's why her reaction came prior to the actual blasting. She knew what was coming.

They drag Trebond's body away, as if sensing the crowd's unease and that things are about to turn. Her blindfold slips and her dead eyes stare out, glassy and devoid of any life.

Despite her skilled acting abilities, Willow can't hide her sorrow. Tears leak from her eyes. Trebond was like her mother. She raised her after her own mother got killed on a Resistance mission. But she brushes them away, re-forming her expression into a stoic mask. But her eyes give her away; they burn with rage. And they fix on—

Secretary-General Luther.

He signals for silence, leaning into the microphone and trying to salvage the moment that didn't go exactly to plan. "But I'm not here about our past—I'm here for our future."

To his relief, the crowd is listening again. The body is being disposed of, erasing the blood. But I can still see the dark spot seeping into the lawn where the blaster shots hit.

"Reluctantly, I have accepted war powers from my cabinet," he says in a fake voice that tells me that's a lie. "So that I can follow in the footsteps of Secretary-General Yaron Trantor, the founder of the California Federation, who led us to victory triumph in the Great War."

Now the applause returns with no reservations. I make my hands smack together, but my palms sting. That's when I see something strange. Luther flickers—*for a split second*—it's like electricity runs through his visage. I blink and he's normal. Is it only a trick of light and shadow?

The flashes keep firing from the press pool.

They could have been it.

But a darker thought hits me—

Could Luther be a deep fake? A shifter planted at the upper echelons of our government to lead us down the path to our own destruction? My heart beats faster. Could that explain why Jude seems afraid of his father now? And why he's been acting strange?

The Astrals are shifters. They could impersonate anyone, like that bus driver. But nobody knows that. Now, I realize something that Xena said. It's a good thing that we got that intel to space before they raided the Resistance headquarters. Luther was after Trebond.

But what if what he really wanted was to find that evidence and destroy it, so he could prevent anyone from discovering the next phase of the Astral plan? The next phase isn't coming from the skies; it's coming from inside our own ranks. The way they operate, they try to use our own worst instincts against us like some kind of ultimate judgment.

Letting us destroy ourselves.

All to the sound of boisterous applause, thus affirming how warlike and destructive humanity really is . . . and how deserving of genocide and annihilation.

Suddenly, I don't know what to believe anymore.

What's real? What's fake? Who can I trust anymore?

It's deeply unsettling.

Willow senses my unease. She reaches for my hand. Right now, she's the only thing keeping me sane. And grounded. And from losing it completely. Her touch feels like a final betrayal—to Kari.

But it's also the only thing keeping me alive. I wish that it wasn't. I wish I wasn't such a fucking coward. But I can't help it.

My weakness levels me. I'm not good enough for her. But then Willow's words come back to me. About how Kari always put me down and made me feel not good enough. But what if she's wrong?

I also remember the last moment I saw Kari, and what she communicated—

Don't trust her . . . can't trust her!

I heard it through my now defunct neural implant that connected to her. But was that jealousy at seeing me with Willow? The heartbreak and mind-shattering effects of our broken bond? Our dual betrayals tearing us both apart? Or . . . did she see something I missed?

Confusion rushes through me, turning everything I know and believe upside down, while the crowd cheers like crazy. Luther quickly descends the stage and returns to his armored transport, which takes off, flanked by his security detail.

And that's when I notice the school buses. They pull up outside Sather Gate. The crowd cheers for them as the bus drivers each step out and take a bow. The whole thing seems like a tribute to the Golden Gate Attack. Then I see it—Xena standing among them.

That can't be an accident.

Her arm is bandaged in a sling, but she blends in perfectly with the other drivers.

Suddenly, Willow grabs my arm.

"It's time to go. Now."

"Where . . . are you taking me?" I hiss as she leads me through the crowd. I notice the other DTSA members filtering over from their seats and following us toward the bus.

This was all planned.

Willow leans in—and her next words shock me.

"Trebond left orders . . . just in case. UC Berkeley isn't safe anymore. We have to get you off campus . . . and fast. You're too important now to risk anything happening to you."

We reach the bus. Xena rushes us to the bench seats. About twenty other students join us, all from DTSA. They surround me like my own private militia. I notice more—

They're all armed with blasters.

Before I can react—or even protest—Xena guns the gas and the bus pulls out, joining the stream of traffic and blending in with the other yellow buses, the perfect camouflage. The buses are inconspicuous and harmless, hiding in plain sight. And they disappear like ghosts.

Willow slides onto the bench seat next to me. Berkeley disappears in the rearview mirror. I have a feeling I won't see it again for a long time. I lean over and whisper in her ear—

"What do you mean . . . *too important*? Where are you taking me?"

Willow meets my gaze. My heart beats faster in anticipation.

"The Old Lady's final orders. Drae, you're the new leader of the Resistance."

CHAPTER 54

KARI

"No, don't do this," I whisper to Apollo as General Titan lowers the device over my head. "It's not too late . . ."

But he doesn't react. His eyes are cold. His face remains an expressionless mask.

"Shut up, you're pathetic," Titan says with a frown. "This will do the trick."

Apollo steps back, allowing Titan to place the helmet over my head. It's clunky, clearly a prototype, with wires running from it and connecting the walls.

She turns to fire it up, jacking it into my numeral implant, when suddenly—

I hear sounds of struggle. I jerk my head over just in time to see it.

Apollo moves lightning fast, disarming the guardians and knocking them out with a few quick moves. He's faster than should be possible, moving with impossible speed, almost as if teleporting . . . That's when it hits me.

His form ripples with energy, then re-forms into solid flesh. One second he's on one side of the room, and the next—

He's right next to me . . .

Yanking the helmet off and throwing it to the ground. It clatters loudly.

Titan gapes at us.

"Alistair, what are you doing?" She gasps in surprise but it morphs into hate.

I stare at him in shock too.

We both realize what's happening at the same time, but she says it first.

"Wait, you're one of them!"

He looks so human again. But I remember how he moved and changed form back there, disarming the guards.

He's a shifter. He's . . . Astral.

He grins at Titan with such malevolence that it permeates his being, making him flicker in and out of view.

The crystalline veins in the wall flicker in rhythm to his pulsating visage.

"I'm sorry, Alicia," he says softly. "So, you'll understand why I can't let you have her. And go through with this genocide."

He flicks his hand, and bolts of electricity shoot out of the crystal veins in the walls, igniting the laboratory and shorting out all the circuitry. Instantly, the barriers holding the Astrals captive vanish. They rush out like ghosts charged with electricity, flicking and powerful.

"Save yourselves," he says in a calm voice to the flickering beings.

They don't need to be told twice.

One second, they're in the lab with us, and the next, they flicker a few times and vanish from the room as if evaporating into nothing. General Titan reaches for her blaster.

She fires at Major Apollo—

Blast! Blast! Blast!

I scream, "Nooooooo!"

The shots hit him point blank—

But they don't hurt him; he's not injured. Instead, he just absorbs them. His body flickers, then stabilizes. If anything, it seems to make him grow stronger from the energy conversion.

Now, General Titan looks terrified.

"No, Alistair . . . stop . . . are you going to kill me?" she says, cowering away.

The whole lab starts to catch fire, growing hotter. The sprinklers try to come on, but he flicks his wrist again, shortcutting them. The water stops.

He wants it to burn.

He bends down in front of her. Their faces are only inches apart. Sickened still, I remember how he kissed her recently.

"No, I'm not."

"And why not?" she says, shocked.

"Because then I'd be no better than you. And I want to be better . . ."

He straightens up, tucking his glorious, shimmering hair behind his ear. He's never looked more beautiful—

And more terrifying.

"But not all of my . . . comrades do."

That stuns me, but it also makes sense. They really are like us. Some of them want war, while some fight for peace. He stares down at Titan, who squirms away from him pathetically.

"Your fate will be the same as your research," he says in a cold voice.

I'm still sitting in the chair, paralyzed and unsure what to do. I wonder if he's forgotten about me for a second.

But then he's right next to me.

Again, impossibly fast.

"How did you do that?"

He smiles. "Let's just say, you found out more about us than any human ever has. Even her with her evil experiments. But there's still so much you don't know—now is your chance."

I'm intrigued, but fear still grips me. He senses it, but he peers into my eyes.

"It's still me, Kari," he whispers.

"How . . . do I know?"

That's when—he kisses me again. My whole body tingles with this kiss, and I can feel him in my mind, probing it.

So, that wasn't all my imagination.

He really was inside my head.

I WAS . . . BUT YOU FOUGHT ME. YOU DIDN'T MAKE IT EASY.

"Asteroid fires, how did you do that? And how can I trust you? You kissed her."

He looks crestfallen and ashamed. "With her, it was always a deception. I never felt anything. I'm a secret agent. My mission was to infiltrate Space Force and get close to her . . . so I could stop her."

"And me?"

"But you weren't part of the mission. You never were. I never understood *love* that humans talk about . . . until you."

The fire blazes harder. Sparks shoot out as the computers go up. This blaze is unnatural; it burns with blue fire.

He holds out his hand.

Come with me if you want to live.

The light is back in his eyes. His voice sounds different, too. It takes a minute before I realize—it's because I hear it inside my head. He didn't speak aloud.

He's somehow tapped directly into my neural implant. *Wait, you're the reason . . . I could connect to the Astrals . . .*

You're different, Kari, he replies through our connection. *I wanted to see what you would do once you learned the truth about us.*

There's so much I want to say, so much I want to ask . . .

I can't believe I KISSED an alien . . . The thoughts fly through my head at warp speed. He smirks at that last thought.

In that case, I kissed a human.

I hear his thought shaded by a kaleidoscope of emotions. He's more adept at this neural stuff than me. At letting me in and blocking me out.

But he lets me in now . . .

And I'm swept away. He's amused, but also full of lust and want for . . .

Me.

Suddenly, I realize that it's like it was with Drae. Except times a thousand.

No, maybe a million.

I feel his full range of emotions now—and it's like looking through a crystal at a thousand rainbows. It ignites something powerful in my head—and in my heart.

But my implant—it's monitored.

He shakes his head.

I can block them out.

My heart flutters, making me feel weak in places that I didn't think it was possible. I'm lost in the irresistible attraction that pulls me into him like a force greater than any gravity.

Almost like nothing else matters.

I can feel the heat of his desire burning for me.

It burns between us.

What else can you do?

You have to come with me to find out . . .

Suddenly, alarms blare in the base. Not only is the fire getting out of control, though I suspect he could douse it whenever he wanted, but they're coming for us now.

We don't have much time.

His visage flickers with worry, shimmering with electric light like the crystalline veins. Even the unnatural fire seems to dance to his rhythm like he's connected to it, too.

He disabled General Titan and her guardians effortlessly, but can he single-handedly defeat a whole platoon? I suspect not . . . but I don't know the limits to his power.

"Kari, it's now or never," he says. "Will you come with me? Without you, they can't plant the weapon. There's still time to avert the war . . . but I need your consent first."

I hesitate. I think of Drae down on Earthside. But also my friends—the ones I got tangled up in this mess when I got them transferred to my team. But also the Oath of Enlistment that I swore. I know Space Force is crumbling to pieces around us, or more accurately, burning to ash.

But it meant something important to me. It still does . . .

I vowed never to desert my post.

He hears my thought. "Kari, your father wasn't a deserter—he's fighting for what's right—and neither are you."

Still, something paralyzes me, holding me back. Can I trust this shape-shifting Astral? The alarms continue blaring their shrill warning. We only have a few seconds left.

"This isn't the end," he says. "It's only the beginning. I fear if you don't come with me, both of our species will annihilate each other until there's nothing left. Not all the Astrals are like me! You taught me something important about humans. That you aren't all the same either."

"You're like . . . me."

He nods, gently. "That's why I need your help. We have to do this together."

That hits me hard. He's right.

We have to find a way to stop the forever wars.

I make up my mind. In this moment, I tell him the words that will change my future. His future. And that of everyone we know and love. There is only one possible answer.

It leaves my lips as a whisper of promise.

"I'll go with you."

EPILOGUE

KARI

We escape through the post office, avoiding the guardians gunning for us. The fire in the lab is a good distraction. Apollo keeps his head down. We're both in our Space Force uniforms.

So far, we don't draw their attention. But time will run out. As soon as they discover General Titan, she'll send them after us. Even if Apollo can take them down, reinforcements will warp to base. He can't defeat everyone. We have to get out of here. We take off running, whipping around the corridors that I've come to learn by heart. He could leave me in his dust—or *electricity*—but he doesn't. He grips my hand and guides me, gently but firmly.

We burst into the post office.

To my shock, Anton doesn't look surprised to see us. He grins his lopsided smile.

"Ah, what took you so long?"

"Wait, you knew?"

That's when my team steps out of the back to the protest of the bots beeping.

"We all knew," Nadia says as Percy, Genesis, and Luna nod.

Apollo blushes. His human affectations are so . . . *real*. Like he's not just shifting and mimicking our appearance. He feels like a human, too.

"Contingency plan," Apollo says sheepishly. "I learned something important from you."

"Oh, you did?"

"It turns out, you do need a team. And now, we need support more than ever. The postmasters make powerful allies. We need them on our side. Your father and the Raiders, too."

But Anton cuts in.

"Uh, maybe we can talk about this later? When they're not coming to blast us?"

"Yeah, we've got the door," Nadia says, unholstering her weapon.

Luna and the others flank her. They keep out of sight, but they're there just in case somebody tries to follow us out.

"Good point," I say, reaching for Apollo's hand. Where our flesh touches feels like electricity coursing through me.

But I hold on tight.

"To be continued?" I say to my team.

"We'll hold down the fort," Luna says. "We all want the same thing, remember?"

Peace.

And I know in my heart it's true. They can't hear my thoughts like Apollo, but they feel it anyway. I know I can trust them. Apollo is right. We can't do this alone. We need all the help we can get.

"Follow me . . . and hurry," Anton says, leading us through the post office, to the elevator that leads to the docking bay.

We emerge with the alarms still blaring, but everyone is focused on the emergency and the fire burning in the lab. They barely pay us any notice or the postmaster. They just care about their Anti-Astral weapon going up in smoke . . . *literally*. Even though it won't work without me.

He smiles and backs away.

"Goodbye . . ." I start to Anton.

But he shakes his head. "See you later, Kari."

With one last salute, he backs away, leaving us his fastest postal ship.

It's fired up and ready to go. We board, traipsing into the cabin. It's a small ship, designed to carry packages at warp speed. But that means it's . . . fast.

"What happened to the . . . others?"

He smiles in a knowing way. "Right, we have different means of traveling."

"So, why the ship?"

He reaches over and kisses me lightly, gently.

"Because you don't . . . your fragile human body would shred apart."

"Ah, I see . . . this is better."

With that, I engage the thrusters and we blast off, headed into this unknown future. It feels like the world is crumbling around us. We escape just in time.

I know they'll hunt us. I know they're already coming. I know they won't give up, not after what we did to that lab.

Will they believe Titan? The evidence has all but vanished or been destroyed. With any luck, if she survives the fire, they'll think she's got space trauma.

Regardless, I'll be branded a deserter now, the thing I've always feared the most. But suddenly—

It doesn't scare me.

The power that held over me evaporates as if it never existed at all. After all, Apollo is right. That was all built on a lie manufactured to frame my dad—and vindicate Drae's mother.

I'm a deserter, I think again.

Instead, it exhilarates me.

I wonder if this is what my father felt when he joined the Raiders and tasted the freedom of the star-seas for the first time, not bound by oath and service, but only your own code.

We leave the base, soaring into the darkest, deepest depths of space. He starts to engage the warp drives, but then I stop him.

"What do I call you now?"

"You don't like my name?" he says, his eyes twinkling like all the stars. "I thought it had a nice ring to it."

"Alistair?" I tease him. "Guessing that's not your real name."

"Would you believe . . . we don't have names? Not the way you think of them?"

I take that in. "Honestly, there's not much I wouldn't believe after today."

"I don't blame you."

"What happened to the real Major Apollo? Did you . . . kill him? Like that bus driver in the Golden Gate Attack?"

He flickers, upset. "Of course not! We're not all like that recording . . ."

"Then where is he?"

"The real Major Apollo died on the battlefield in a Proxy war. Fighting the Siberian Fed. Made it easy to impersonate him. Just stumble back with some blaster injuries."

I can feel the pulsing of his emotional cadence, the way I used to feel Drae, so I know he's telling the truth. But something else still bothers me. I can't help asking about it.

"He had the relationship with General Titan? And broke it off all those years ago?"

He nods with a pained expression. "Trust me. It surprised me too when I got stationed out here. This wasn't in his file! You can imagine my shock during our first briefing . . ."

He grimaces to let me know what happened.

"So, what did you do?"

"What I could!" he says with a laugh that reaches his eyes. "Trust me . . . it hasn't been easy putting her off either. She has some . . . shall we say . . . major boundary issues."

"You can say that again."

The memory of her trying to force me to commit genocide against the Astrals is still fresh in my mind. We share a knowing smile. Now, I feel foolish for being jealous. *It wasn't him.*

"Sorry I got upset about that."

"Oh, I don't blame you. In your boots, I'd probably have the same reaction."

He laughs, and it sounds sweet and pure. I hear it inside my head, too. I'd grown used to Harold, but he's disabled now . . . and it's this alien inside my head. Life can change in an instant.

"Alistair? You said you liked the name. What does it mean?"

"*Defender of the people.* Happy accident of sorts. But I think it fits my mission."

I nod, absorbing that. My heart ratchets up a notch, beating faster. I remember how fast he moved back in the lab; how fluidly he fought and disarmed those guardians. He's not human, not even superhuman. He's something else. He's *alien* . . . *other* . . . *Astral*. All our words to describe him feel so clumsy now, like they can't do this light-being justice. He matches my intense gaze.

I want to kiss him.

Our eyes remain locked together. The desire floods through both of us.

"Kari, there was only ever you. Alien. Astral. It doesn't matter . . . only you."

And then, he's kissing me again, and I'm lost in that kiss for what feels like forever like time bends and warps around us, the way that light does. When we finally part—

I'm breathless and lost in him.

He types rapidly, entering coordinates into the navigator.

Where are we going? I think to him. The question fires out, demanding an answer, the way my lips demanded that kiss. He reaches for the warp thrusters to engage them.

This time, he replies aloud, as if only for my delicate human sensibilities.

"We're going to my . . . home."

Acknowledgments

This is a book I wasn't sure I'd ever get to write. So, to be finished and writing the end notes feels like a miracle.

A Sacrifice of Blood and Stars—the first book in the series—was a passion project that I wrote on the side while tackling a whole seven-book series (Disney Chills) alongside other projects for Lucasfilm and more. I wrote it in my dark little corner. I didn't know if anyone would take a risk and publish it—let alone want a series. Then my editor Stephanie Beard, whom I began my career with on the Continuum trilogy, stepped in. Thanks to her vision and the incredible and passionate team at Podium, including the fabulous audiobook narrators Cindy Kay and Daryl Mayfield, my series set in the war-torn stars came to life here on our fair Earth. Thanks always to my agent, Deborah Schneider, and managers, David Server and Ray Miller.

When it came to tackling the second book in the trilogy, I knew things would have to get messy! Like really, really messy. At the end of the first book, we left Kari and Drae with a nice *happily ever after* . . . for now. The title *A Sacrifice of Flesh and Fury* accurately represents everything my characters have to give up for the survival of Earth . . . and also love. Both are battlefields in this book—and they both escalate in intensity. I wrote it as I watched our own world falling victim to the same fate. Many of the themes of this book only grow stronger over time.

In the real world, our military policy is officially shifting to focus on space. The *New York Times* ran a front-page article about this major shift in US military policy and called it the new arms race against China and Russia. Meanwhile, I long planned to write about U of Berkeley erupting into protests that would take over the campus with my characters at the center of it. I wrote those chapters while watching that happen at colleges all over the country in real time. I won't say that made it easier to write, but it did make me persevere. Hopefully my characters and this story will speak to some of these ongoing events transpiring in our own world.

The world is messy; the book got messy. It was a roller coaster to write, but I'm proud of how it came out. Second books are notoriously difficult to tackle (especially in trilogies). You have to build out the world and story without fully fulfilling the promise of the series at the same time. They carry a heavy burden. I hope I did the story and my characters justice.

Lastly, thanks to my readers and everyone who read and loved the first book. Special thanks to my mentors and fellow authors, Jonathan Maberry and Scott Sigler, for their kind words.

Book 3 is coming!

Best always,
Jennifer Brody
Joshua Tree, CA

About the Author

Jennifer Brody, also known as Vera Strange, is the award-winning author of the Disney Chills series, the Continuum Trilogy, and Stoker finalist *Spectre Deep 6*, which prompted *Forbes* to call her "a star in the graphic novel world." She is the coauthor of *All Is Found: A Frozen Anthology* and *Star Wars: Stories of Jedi and Sith*, in which she penned the Darth Vader story. A graduate of Harvard University, Brody is also a film/TV producer and writer and a creative writing instructor. She began her career in Hollywood working for A-list directors and movie studios on many films, including the *Lord of the Rings* trilogy, *The Texas Chainsaw Massacre*, and *The Golden Compass*. Brody lives and writes in Joshua Tree, California.

www.ingramcontent.com/pod-product-compliance
Lightning Source LLC
Jackson TN
JSHW022222180425
82910JS00001B/3